# Under Saturn's Sun

## A.V. PARKS

***Under Saturn's Sun***
(The Saturni, book 2)
Copyright © 2025 A.V. Parks
All Rights Reserved

This book or any portion thereof may not be reproduced without the express written permission of the publisher, except for the use of brief quotations in a book review and certain other noncommercial uses permitted by copyright law.

This is a work of fiction. Names, characters, places, and incidents either are products of the author's imagination or are used fictitiously.

First edition 2025

Published in Canton, GA, USA by *thewordverve* (www.thewordverve.com)

eBook ISBN:      978-1-956856-67-5
Paperback ISBN:  978-1-956856-68-2

Library of Congress Control Number: 2025911383

Cover and interior design by Robin Krauss at Linden Design
www.lindendesign.biz
eBook formatting by thewordverve

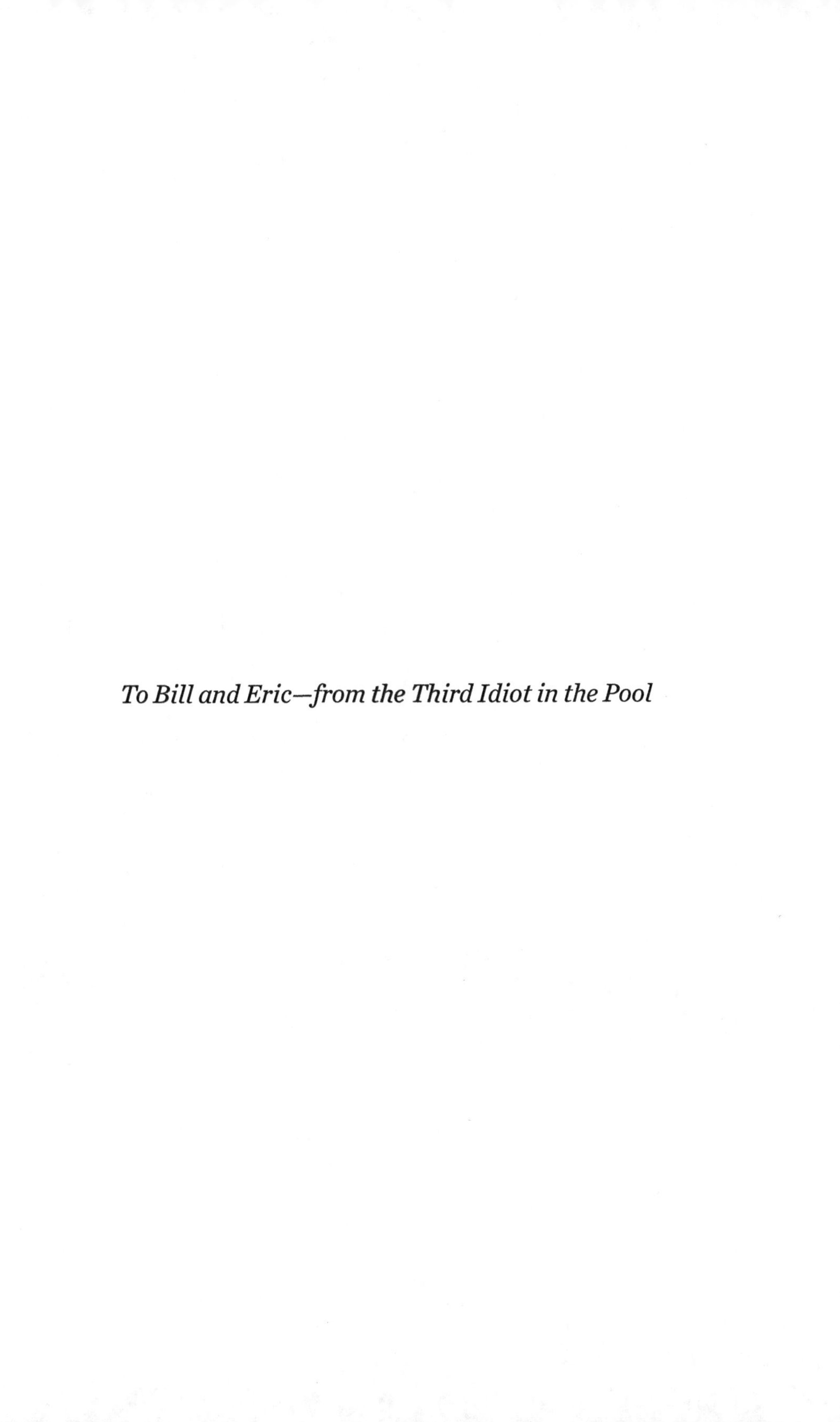

*To Bill and Eric—from the Third Idiot in the Pool*

Excerpt from
*The Science of the Mysteries . . .*

**The *Introim***

Disembodied spirits emanating from the Grand Aeons, sent to Earth to help and enlighten Mankind.

**The Saturni**: Those *Introim* who became embodied and sought to maintain their power and satisfy their appetites by eating every living thing.

**The *Lwas***: The Introim who refused to join the Saturni, exiled to the fringes of society and the enslaved peoples of the world.

**The Skin Eaters**: Creations of the Saturni, human in origin but endowed with supernatural powers and enchained by their addictions.

**The Great Saturni**: The four great powers of wealth, glamor, rationality, and faith, which rule our current world.

**The Four Gifts**: The four great *Lwas* who are said to offset the Great Saturni.

**The *Jumbies***: Those children who, chosen to be Skin Eaters, fail in their initiation.

**The Mounts**: Those children who are said to be uniquely receptive to being possessed by the Lwas and giving them human form.

# Content Advisory

This is a work of dark fantasy and Southern Gothic fiction.
It contains ritualistic violence and morally ambiguous behavior,
and scenes that may be upsetting to some readers.
Reader discretion is advised.

# CHAPTER ONE

Nina Lamb was dreaming.

In the dream, she was walking through a jungle at night, with the small sounds of the tropics all around her—insects chirring, frogs croaking, and small stealthy animals moving in the darkness, with the splash of fish in unseen water nearby. She walked as one so often walks in dreams, weightless, and the humid air felt like a lighter kind of water through which she herself swam, bodiless. The wind raised her hair, and a light shone down, revealing the moon floating on the surface of a deep pool up ahead, its surface as dark as ink and as reflective as a polished mirror. All around the pool were trees, their gnarled roots reaching deep down into the mud, and there were huge dogs standing on the bank of the pool, their bodies big as lions and their gaunt black empty faces dominated by eyes scoured clean like the eyes in skulls. The *horroi*.

She flinched away from them, and with that movement, woke herself up and rolled out of bed. "Ow!" she said, still half asleep, and with the idea that someone had just hit her with a big flat board. Sitting up, she determined no one was attacking her, and all she was attacking was the floor. She could see her room at the Daedalus School in New Orleans: a plain iron bedstead, a plain bureau and desk, a plain chair, and the window open, showing her the garden, softly lit by moonlight. *Wow*, she thought. *I have got to stop dreaming like that.*

She got up and walked over to the window, rubbing her

shoulder, where she'd landed hard. The moss-draped oaks of the school garden soothed her, beautiful and stately and as old as the city itself. Here was peace and quiet, soft elegance, and the only serenity she could remember ever having known, since she had no idea who she was or where she came from. Her past life was a mystery, and she couldn't remember anything before Hurricane Katrina and her coming to live at Daedalus the previous spring.

"Damn," she said, sitting down on the windowsill and breathing deeply. The school cat, Mercy, who sometimes slept with her, came over and rubbed against her calves, and she scratched the big black tom absently. She was dreaming about the jungle at Bois Caiman every night now, the deep forest in Haiti where the revolution had started, and where gods and men had danced together once, and sworn vengeance on those who had enslaved them. She was dreaming about the voodoo priests who had called out in their need to the old, forgotten powers of the world to help them, and how those powers had come to their aid and driven out their oppressors, at what cost: oceans of blood, gallons of suffering, a world cut down and all the great forests, snakes, winds, and the fertile island itself ruined, and a people sent scattering across the trampled earth.

Nina felt a connection with the slaves who had fought for their freedom in Haiti, although she didn't know why. Part of it was that she knew what it was like to feel powerless. Abandoned. Lost. No physical chains bound her to Daedalus, but the real problem was she had no idea where else she would go, if she were given half a chance. She had no memory of other places, since she couldn't remember who she was.

And the people at the Daedalus School had (with a few significant exceptions) been kind. The teachers there might be Skin Eaters, strange undead cannibals who had to survive by eating human flesh, but they had also given her a home.

In fact, some of them had become her best friends. But now they were all away for the summer, and she had been left there pretty much on her own, reading about Haiti under the direction of professor Seneschal, the school's doddering old history teacher. A few other staff members had remained as well, but they were all doing their own things. professor Samson, the Transformation and Animal Dominance teacher, went to the gay bars every night and had just finished up his summer break at the campy Southern Decadence Festival. professor Aspidistrus, who taught Alchemy and was himself half human and half plant, had spent the summer visiting relatives in the lakes and lagoons in City Park. professor Threet, the nervous little Sky Geography professor, had spent most of her nights up in the carriage house plotting the constellations with the school's noctoscope.

And Agatha Danvers, the school's prickly housekeeper, hadn't gone anywhere, preferring to lock herself up in her rooms on the second floor with the air conditioning going full blast, pointedly not responding to any requests for clean linen, fresh coffee, or secretarial services until classes resumed in the second week of September.

This effectively meant Nina had had the school to herself, and for a while that had even been fun. She'd explored all the hidden nooks and crannies of the building, from the spooky chapel to the attic. She wasn't sure why she did it, except that she had the feeling it might come in handy at some point. So that was how she'd spent her summer, until now, when she was waking up in the middle of the night dreaming of dead dogs and ghostly swamps and the terrible, wonderful sense that something beautiful and dangerous was about to happen to her.

She sharpened her gaze. What was that down in the garden? She thought she saw a tall, dark man standing just beneath her window. She squinted. The moonlight made him look like a boy, the light's thin crescent illuminating his slim figure and his plain dark suit, but his inky eyes and stern mouth were those of a being centuries old. A being she knew.

*Oh shit,* she thought, jumping up from the window ledge and grabbing her robe. He'd seen her sitting there in nothing but her T-shirt and panties. Great. She wrapped her robe around herself and though *What should I do now? Pretend I didn't see him? Go back to sleep? Go down there ... W-what ?* What was the protocol with a sexy older man who pretended to despise her, who'd been gone all summer and nobody knew where and who (once, briefly, and almost against his will) had seared her mouth with a kiss?

Nina decided she had to know what this was all about, so she grabbed a pair of shorts and yanked them on and then crept downstairs to let herself out into the cool, fragrant garden. When she got to her midnight visitor, he still hadn't moved.

"I was wondering how long it would take you to realize you had company."

She rolled her eyes. "If you wanted me to sneak out, you should have thrown pebbles up at the window."

"And risk breaking the glass? Agatha would kill me." Agatha was Strickland Danvers's one remaining sister, and Strickland was the assistant headmaster of the Daedalus School. He continued to look up toward her room as his lips twitched. "What were you dreaming about anyway?"

"None of your business." She stared at him. "How long have you been out here?"

"Long enough to hear you scream." He made a slight gesture. "Not out loud, of course. You should know by now that only I can hear your thoughts when you dream, no one else can."

Which was true. She'd had a psychic connection with this man from the first day she'd met him, her first morning at Daedalus. And while it made both of them uncomfortable, it had only grown stronger in the two months they'd spent together the previous spring. That was why Nina hadn't entirely regretted his disappearance at the start of the summer. Claiming he had to have a life "apart from babysitting," he had plunged into traveling, reportedly going as far away as Europe and Africa. Nina had heard about him secondhand from professor Seneschal, when the latter's senile mumblings had actually made sense.

She suspected what Professor Danvers really wanted was a life apart from her, apart from the weird dance of attraction and repulsion, love and hate, that made them both each other's trap and prey. And feeling more than a little pissed off as a result (like professor Creepy-Pants wasn't lucky to have a shot at her) she'd been happy to see him go.

But now he was back, and she had a familiar shivery sensation as though she'd just eaten a raw oyster. How could he do this to her, especially when he was just standing there looking up at the building like he was inspecting the thick mat of creeping vines that grew like a curtain of deeper darkness, across the shadowy facade of the school?

"How was your trip?" she asked, feeling like any words were better than silence. "Where were you? Germany or Malta or the Sudan? I heard different versions."

"You heard right," he said. "I was in all those places, as well as the Isle of Man. Of course, the only person who'd be rude enough to gossip about me in my absence and pander to your insufferable curiosity would have to be our mentally challenged History teacher. Am I right, or am I right?"

He didn't wait for an answer, but turned and seated himself on a wrought-iron bench, motioning her to join him as though they were at a garden party. She sat, feeling the cool night air raise goosebumps on her bare arms and legs.

"And since you have seen fit to pry into my private affairs,

I assume you figured out the reason for my travels? No?" He raised an eyebrow. "Think, Miss Lamb. You're not usually so slow. Don't make me regret coming back. I could have more intriguing conversations in Khartoum around a campfire of camel dung."

She flushed and bit back an angry reply—I'll tell you what you can do with your camel dung—because there was something about those three places, wasn't there? The Sudan . . . Germany . . . Malta . . . of course. All three were places where history had once outrun mankind's memory and left great standing stones as mute witnesses to the past. There were magic circles there, where, it was rumored, the membranes between this world and the unseen world were porous . . . thin . . . not unlike New Orleans.

And there were old legends that said that immortal beings, the *Introim*, had once come

down to earth in places like that, and incarnated in human form to help mankind. And she had even seen—or thought she'd seen—or imagined that she'd seen them once, in a vision that felt an awful lot like a memory. Glowing orbs of light in every color of the rainbow, falling in showers from the sky onto a darkened world like snow.

She said, "You've been looking for the *Introim*, haven't you? The old gods."

"That, Miss Lamb, is a marginally correct answer. As a matter of fact, I know where a number of the old gods are right this very minute. I was there when you freed them, remember?"

Nina did remember, although she was surprised the professor had brought it up. He had, after all, been dying at the time, not to mention being bound hand and foot. The four great *Lwas*, the old voodoo gods of love and wisdom and nature and destruction, had once been housed at the Daedalus School by their enemies, trapped in a safe until somehow (and Nina still only had the roughest idea how) she'd managed to free them. Their appearance had, figuratively at least, allowed all hell to break loose, and in the process, the professor had been healed while his old enemy, General Azazel, had quite literally exploded.

Needless to say, General Azazel's daughter, Dr. Isolde Freeland, one of the most powerful of the evil *Introim*, the Saturni, hadn't been pleased.

"Sir?"

"Yes?"

"If you know where the Great *Lwas* are: Erzuli and Damballa and Grand Bois and Oya, then—"

"Yes?"

She glanced at him, thinking how exhausted he looked. No, worse than that—he looked raw and bruised and damaged in some way, as though the miles he'd traveled hadn't just tired his body, but opened up old wounds half-healed in his mind. What did it mean trying to summon more of their kind? That didn't seem likely. If you could just call down angelic beings whenever you wanted them, then the world would be full of them. Besides, the Introim weren't fluffy pink cherubs you could ask for help. In fact, they were strong enough that nobody would be idiotic enough to want any more of them around.

"But you went to find out what else those places could tell you . . . isn't that right, sir?" And when he raised his eyebrows, as though silently encouraging her to go on, she said, "It's . . . you wanted to find out how to deal with the world now that the old gods have been freed, and now that the Saturni know about it. You wanted to see if those places spoke to you, or if they could help you to remember."

*And, when he still didn't answer*, she thought, *what wouldn't we all give to remember?*

What else had they forgotten?

"And . . . and the headmaster," she said, realizing she'd forgotten the most important person in this whole equation. "You wanted to find out where the headmaster of Daedalus is now. Mr. O'Brien. Isn't that right? You wanted to find out what's happened to him, because you know he's still around, don't you, sir? You know he's not dead, or not, I mean, not like really dead—"

But the professor reacted to her last words with a suddenness that made her gasp. He grabbed her with one hand and placed the fingertips of his other hand over her lips, not really smothering her, but shutting her up with the sudden intimacy of his gesture.

"Shh," he said. "You never know what saying a name aloud will mean, or who might be listening." He hesitated. "Yes, if you must know, I went for all of those reasons. Events are changing, and I hoped by going to the places where they had changed once so irrevocably, I might learn something of use for the future. I hoped to wake up my own mind, with the mental equivalent of a cold shower. But if you must know, you eternally interfering child, I went specifically to find someone else."

*Niobe*, she thought. *His long-lost sister, and his long-lost love.* Nina felt a great sinking weight in her chest, because Goddamn it, it wasn't fair. Why didn't it make any difference that she—Nina— had saved him from certain death, real death, the kind that could claim even the undead beings of his kind? Why didn't it matter that his sister didn't even want to see him anymore? Her last note to Nina had read, "Tell Strickland I still love him, but you can have him with my blessings." She—Niobe—had been hiding out at the Daedalus Home in plain sight as the cook, but no one had known about it except Agatha, and the professor had been openly furious when he realized she'd been so close to him and had escaped him once again.

*Of course*, Nina thought. *He'd go to the ends of the earth to find her, and now he has.*

He seemed to guess a little of her thoughts, because he grimaced and said, "No. Not my sister. Someone I had to hunt for, because she didn't want to be found, unlike my sister, who appears to have developed the annoying habit of playing hide and seek. And now that I have found her, this other person, we have to go and see her tonight. That's actually why I'm here."

Nina became aware once more that she was sitting there half-undressed, and she didn't want to go anywhere, at least not until she'd put on a bra under her T-shirt. She tried to stall him.

"Sir, I—I can't. You know we're not allowed out at night. Those are the school rules. And besides—"

"Goddamn it, who do you think makes the school rules!" He sighed and gave her an impatient wave. "All right. I'll give you five minutes to make yourself 'decent,' however you want to define that. We're going to Bourbon Street, so you won't need white gloves. Oh, and do wear a scarf. Flying messes up your hair."

She only realized two things after she'd left him and hurried back into the building. He'd said flying. And he'd said make yourself decent, which meant he'd noticed she wasn't wearing a bra. Wow. She quickly slipped on underwear and a light sweatshirt to go with her shorts, grabbed a purse, and tied a black and gold Saints scarf around her long dark hair.

When she got back to the garden, he looked her over from head to toe and said, "Wonderful. You look like a co-ed from Daytona. We'll fit right in. Come on, I've got a mirror in the carriage house."

Why do I need a mirror now, she wondered, but he was already striding ahead of her toward the back of the garden, and she could only follow him. Once they were inside the carriage house, he didn't go upstairs to the classroom, but instead ducked into what appeared to be a storage closet, and gestured for her to join him.

"Um, sir . . ." She held back, feeling like the weirdness quotient of the night was ratcheting up to Code Red. He gave an exasperated snort.

"Oh, come on, Miss Lamb, don't be ridiculous. I'm not going to molest you. It's about time you learned that 'flying' for our kind refers to more than just levitating through the air. Yes, of course, we can do that, but I scarcely think we'd go unobserved if we flew down the middle of Bourbon Street on a Saturday night, do you? No, we'll 'fly' using a time-honored method for Skin Eater travel, via Guinee. I'm going to go out on a limb and guess no one at this benighted school has ever bothered to instruct you in this?"

Mutely, she shook her head.

"I'm not surprised. The Saturni like to keep the students ignorant. All right, pay close attention. You can perform this action with any reflective surface, but mirrors are the most exact.

We'll both look into the mirror at the same time and then allow ourselves to be drawn into it."

Nina fought back the desire to smile. It sounded like *Through The Looking-Glass*, really, charming, innocent, although she'd learned enough strangeness in the last several months to learn that life with the Skin Eaters, or "Skinnies," was rarely innocent, and only darkly charming. She said, "Like mirror scrying, right?"

"In substance, yes." Professor Danvers moved to her side. He had taught her mirror scrying the previous spring. "In this case, we will not be ignoring our own reflections in the glass, but instead merging with them." He held up a hand mirror and lowered his head until both their faces were reflected in it, his pale features next to hers. "The effect will be not to fight against the mirror's pull, but to embrace it." His breath tickled against her ear. "We will be drawn into Guinee, a place out of place, roughly perpendicular to our own plane, and then we can pivot and go anywhere we want to go. It's simple, really."

None of that sounded simple to Nina's ears, especially when

Professor Danvers's voice was still murmuring against her hair as his arms tightened around her. "Don't be frightened. Some people find Guinee unnerving in their first experience, but I assure you, it's nothing more than a kind of metaphysical bus terminal. Just close your eyes to its strangeness, and you won't find it bothersome at all."

Which was so not true. She wanted to kick him after it was all over. One second they were standing in the closet, and the next moment the mirror, reflecting back their faces, was shimmering and growing opaque and somehow *thick*—like translucent glue— and then they were being pulled into it by invisible hands, tiny, cool, wet hands that dissolved back into water the moment they touched their skin. It wasn't unpleasant—the small hands drawing them in were gentle—but the sensation was still disorienting, as though dozens of mouths were softly sucking on their flesh. *Tentacles*, Nina thought. *The creatures must have tentacles, whatever they are,* although even as she thought that, the watery touches disappeared completely and her sight was suffused by a soft blue emptiness.

Everywhere around her was water. They were actually under some kind of shimmering sea, although she didn't feel wet, and her breathing was perfectly normal. She didn't even blow bubbles. Shapes began to cohere, and she had a momentary glimpse of beautiful pink and darker red and pale yellow and darkest purple coral—vast structures, towering edifices, soaring cathedrals of feathery branches of living coral, rising up impossibly high over her head. The coral was threaded through and wound around and braided together with a mosaic of round, pale objects: skulls, she realized, human skulls, thousands and thousands of them, used as geometric decorations as in a watery charnel house. It wasn't horrible, exactly—the skulls were clean and the shimmery water washed through them with liquid light—but it was filled with a deeply foreign mystery. She could feel a silent hallelujah of power humming along her spine, making her head spin with simultaneous joy and terror.

Then she was being pulled abruptly forward, like being sucked into a whirlpool, and she felt like she was flying through the watery air, far faster than she liked. She was moving so fast that she could barely register the strange, complex labyrinth of rooms and corridors and archways and basilicas all around her. She tried to see if Professor Danvers was still with her, but all she could feel was the vortex. It was spinning her around, sending her sense of direction reeling and making her unsure if she was standing upright or falling head over heels—and then abruptly, it stopped.

They were standing on a corner in the French Quarter (actually the corner of Bourbon and Bienville Streets, she saw, looking up at a sign) and directly across from them was a garish neon squiggle that read "Mayhem's," and underneath it, in smaller letters, "Exotic Dancers Answer Your Every Prayer, and when we say everything, we mean *everything*!"

Nina looked up at Professor Danvers and pointedly raised her eyebrows. "Excuse me? You're taking me to a strip club?"

The professor shook his head. He looked profoundly uncomfortable. "I assure you, Miss Lamb, if we could have met our required contact in some more suitable location, I would have suggested it, but unfortunately, this is her current location, and she refuses to budge from it. God only knows why. If I didn't know better, I'd say she likes pole dancing for a bunch of horny frat boys!"

Nina tried to make sense of any of that. Okay, so they were going into a strip club to see a stripper. That at least sounded logical. Why Professor Danvers had to see this particular stripper when there were about 200 other strippers within a five-block radius would, she supposed, be explained in the fullness of time.

That just left the completely bizarre and wholly other-worldly manner in which they'd just gotten there. As the professor turned and crossed the street, she said, "Hey, wait a minute. Before we go anywhere, I'd really like to know what this is all about."

Professor Danvers stopped and consulted heaven while standing in the middle of Bourbon Street, no easy feat at that hour. The street was packed from sidewalk to sidewalk with rowdy, drunk, sweaty, and staggering parties. It was approaching midnight, and everyone who'd come to New Orleans to get drunk, get laid, get arrested, or at least try had come out in force. The gutters were awash in beer and daiquiris.

Retracing his steps, he said, "Miss Lamb, you are without a doubt the most infuriating companion any man has brought here tonight, including pick pockets and crack whores. Now, for the last time, will you come on? I told you, we need to speak to this person tonight, and she's here, which gives us a limited number of choices. As to why, would it help if I told you it has to do with the Saturni and the Great *Lwas* and the prophecy that someone will one day destroy the Skin Eaters? Good. Because it does. Now get your sweet little ass over here and come inside with me. They won't let you in on your own, you're still underage."

She walked across the street with the feeling her head was coming loose from her body, and all she could think was, sweet little ass? Did he just actually say that?

She was given no chance to speculate, as the professor grabbed her arm and pulled her through the open neon-lit doorway. A large man in black leather and piercings raised his eyebrows, but made no comment. Clearly men did all sorts of things with barely legal women in here, and her status went unremarked. They hurried through a smallish room where several much larger-than-life photographs of women's private parts were displayed like so many B-list celebrities, and down a short passageway to the bar. Once inside, raucous disco music assaulted their ears, and they approached a gorgeous olive-skinned woman with red hair gyrating around a pole, her body in tasseled pasties and a sequined G-string, a canvas of iridescent flesh.

Professor Danvers bent down again and whispered in Nina's ear. His voice once more tickled her sensitive skin, and she thought she heard in its subtle baritone the barest hint of a smile as he said, "Miss Lamb, I'd like to introduce you to the Cumaean Sybil."

# Chapter Two

The Cumaean Sybil, famed in Rome for her prophecies beyond all others, immortal, sacrosanct, revered and terrible, executed a perfect vertical split, swept her legs up till her bare toes were pointing at the ceiling, and then walked her feet down an imaginary wall to end up standing next to her pole and bowing to thunderous applause. She turned around in all directions, showing off her immortal ass to everyone in the close-pressed audience, and then skipped down from the stage and hugged Professor Danvers and said, "Hi! What kept you?"

She was, Nina could see now that they were standing on the same level, maybe twenty, tops. She had a silicon body Nina could never have hoped to match, and her face was fresh and her lips moist and she swung around hanging onto the professor's neck and fizzed, "Omigod, this is all so much fun! I mean, like, this is way more fun than the Circus Maximus! I could, like, so totally do this all night long!"

"Calm down," Professor Danvers said, peeling her hands off him with difficulty and frowning, although Nina could tell he wasn't really angry. She'd already caught the professor's involuntary gasp as those bouncing double-ds first made contact with his chest. He raised his chin and said, "Amaltheia, please pull yourself together. You're making a ridiculous spectacle of your self. And need I remind you, it ill-becomes a woman of your years?"

"Oh, eat shit, Droopy-Dog, like I care about that?" She turned to Nina and said, "Hi. Call me Amy, by the way. I'm dying for a cigarette," she added, dropping her voice. "You got any? You know they won't even let me smoke in here, isn't that something? I can shake my bootie for the clientele and have guys creaming all over their Dockers, but grab a butt? Shee-it."

Nina shook her head. "Sorry, I don't smoke," and the Sybil pouted. "Oh, right. Nobody smokes anymore. Like all those guys over there sucking up the brewskies don't know they're all going to die of something else anyway?"

She pointed at the first man leaning against the bar and counted them off in turn. "Electrocution, hit-and-run, chicken bone down the throat, suicide, gun-shot wound, weird ass bad reaction to asthma meds, and that little skinny dude at the end's already got a brain tumor the size of a ping pong ball, so why bother? They could all like totally smoke!"

Nina was fascinated. "Can you actually tell what's going to happen to everybody else before it happens?"

"Pretty much. Nobody listens. And no, I'm not going to tell you. That's against the rules. So . . ." She turned back to the professor and put her hands on his shoulders and ground herself against his thigh. "What's shakin', Daddy-O?"

"Amy, please . . ." Professor Danvers put his hands on both girls' arms and forcibly marched them over to a door marked Staff. Once he'd shut the door behind them, they were muffled a little from the disco-thump of the music, which prompted the Sybil to shrug and lead the way down toward her dressing room. Once seated in a plastic chair, she gestured at the other chairs lined up in front of the long mirrors and said, "Sit anywhere. All the other girls are out there turning tricks and giving lap dances. So not my thing. After all, I am a professional. You know, you can get somebody to suck you off in the bathroom here for fifty bucks? I'd call that a steal. If I were into getting sucked off, that is. Which I'm not. I mean, not by most of the skanks around here. You gotta have some standards. But if that's what you want, hey, I'd say go for it. It's got to be among the best deals in town."

She fished in a sequined bag and got out a joint and a lighter. "At least they let us smoke back here," she added, taking a big toke and closing her eyes. "Ummm . . . much mo' better. You want some?" she added, holding out the joint to Nina, who decided the evening was already strange enough without the addition of THC. Professor Danvers, however, much to her not-that-well-hidden surprise, accepted the joint and took a big hit.

"Thanks," he said, handing it back, his voice constrained by his indrawn breath. Nina filed that image away in a mental scrapbook that might have been labeled Bizarro Memories. She glanced back and forth between the darkly handsome professor and the still-naked Sybil, who was now picking at the bright red nail polish on her toenails, and said, "Um . . . do you mind giving me a tiny little hint about what's going on here?"

Professor Danvers released his breath and said, "I'd love to, but I myself don't know that much. Word was, Amaltheia, that you wanted to see us both, Miss Lamb and me, at the same time, hence our visit here tonight. Now if this was just about us getting you cigarettes—"

"Oh, STFU," the Sybil said, taking another toke and then pinching out the joint. She stashed it away for later. "That's shut-the-fuck-up, by the way. You go barging around everywhere in the world trying to find me, moving heaven and earth, and then you get all bent out of shape when I make the simple request that you both come here at the same time? Well, screw you. The reason I wanted to see you both is that this concerns you both, and you'd better listen up, because I'm not writing any of this down for later. The seed of the pelican will return, and the mother will sacrifice herself for her child, but in vain. The horses will be mounted, and the war will begin. The lion will dress himself up as a sheep, and even the lamb will be deceived for a while. Follow the water and the mirrors. That's where your savior lies. Oh, and yeah, I almost forgot. I've also got this for you."

She dug in the sequined bag again and pulled out a small square of cardboard. Nina accepted it and glanced at it, surprised to see an engraving there of a much-younger Professor Danvers, standing in a garden along with his two sisters. They looked like they were all dressed up for a masquerade party in eighteenth-century clothes—lace and full skirts and feathered hats, and the professor in tight knee-breeches—and they were surrounded by flowers and tall philodendron leaves, a lush jungle of vines and palm trees and thick stands of bamboo, with the wide veranda of a plantation house in the background.

They looked alive.

They looked happy.

They looked young.

And if they were—figuring it out—if they were all those things, alive and happy and young—then this engraving had to have been made at least two centuries ago, when the Danvers siblings were still mortal, before they'd become Skin Eaters.

She looked up at the Sybil, who was busy fixing her cherry red lipstick, and asked, "How did you get this?" but Professor Danvers made a dismissive gesture and said, "Oh, for God's sake, put it away. Amaltheia's just messing with you. She likes to do that. Why she feels the need for props is something I don't even want to get into. But I assure you, my family's memorabilia is entirely beside the point. The sybilline prophecies are one thing. Cheap souvenirs on the other hand . . ." He made a gesture. "Let's just say you're being played by a maestro and leave it at that."

Nina put the engraving in her purse, deciding she'd look at it later. She said, "So, um . . . about all that other stuff, the pelican's seed and the wolf in sheep's clothing and all that?"

"The lion," the Sybil corrected her. "Not the wolf." She stood up and bent over almost double to brush out her long red hair, sticking her ass in Professor Danvers's face in the process.

"Amaltheia," he sighed, "you're getting on my last remaining nerve."

"Oops, sorry." She righted herself. "Anyway, it's all in the water, much better than writing things down on leaves. That's what I used to do. Write shit down on leaves and then they all blew away? Kind of the point, actually." She sighed. "I told you. Nobody listens."

She checked herself out in the mirror one last time, and Nina met her eyes, seeing centuries of age there just for an instant, tunnels of time going so far back into the past her own mind reeled at the knowledge. For one brief moment the face opposite hers wasn't fresh and young, but immensely old, the face of a tiny old woman so small she could have been kept in a birdcage, so tired that all she wanted to do was die. Then it was gone, a split-second later, but the Sybil knew what she'd seen.

"Yeah," she sighed, "all right. All that pop-chick shit's just bravado. I'm a lot older than I look. Piss off a god, eat human flesh, make deals with the devil . . . no matter what you do, and we've all done something, it all comes down to the same thing. You slip off the normal universe train and get on the eternity express. Me, I pissed off Apollo and he made me immortal. And lemme tell you, that shit is so overrated. Same old, same old till you're about ready to scream."

She lowered her voice and added, so only Nina could hear, "That's why you've got to do what I did, finally, and make the whole fucking game work for you. Use it to your advantage. You can take all of that shit seriously, and *care*, or you can just let it slide. Water off a duck's back. Just remember, the descent to hell is easy. The door's open all day long. But to go back . . . retrace your steps to the sweet air of heaven?" She pitched her voice even lower and whispered, "That's where the rubber hits the road. And once you care, once you really give a shit? Then they got you by the short and curlies, and God help you, because nobody else can."

She fluffed out her hair, mimed a kiss, and gave her body a little shake, which bounced her tits and sent the tassels spinning in opposite directions. Nina was still wondering how she did that when the Cumaean Sybil sashayed out the door and said, "Now 'scuse me, guys, I gotta go make a living."

And she was gone.

# Chapter Three

Nina and Professor Danvers found their way back out onto Bourbon Street and walked down the crowded sidewalk in silence, dodging drunks and cascading beer cups and big ass beads as they went. Nina was in a daze. They'd almost reached St. Peter Street when she asked, "Where are we going now?"

The professor snapped, "Pat O'Brien's. I need a drink."

He turned into the famed watering hole, and Nina followed him, figuring (rightly) that if she could get into Mayhem, Pat O's should be a breeze. They found a table outside by the fountain, colored lights playing through the shimmering waters, and ordered a beer for her and a double Jameson's for the professor. While they waited, she watched the colors play over his expressionless face: pink, blue, green, and red, shading the harsh lines around his strong nose and mouth so he looked demonic one moment, the next pensive, and the next ever so slightly ill.

"Professor, are you okay?"

"Of course. Contact with the mysteries is always so exhilarating. Do you know how she became a prophetess? Apollo offered her his gifts in return for her love. She demanded immortality as well, and he threw that in. Then, when she had all his goodies, and the god of prophecy was effectively groveling at her feet, she spurned him. She left him in the lurch." Professor Danvers brooded. "Women so often find bargains onerous once their demands have been met. So he let her live forever, but he didn't give her eternal youth. She aged and aged and could never be released. Although, apparently, she's figured out a way around that after thirty-some-odd centuries."

Their drinks came, and he downed half of his in a single swallow. "Oh, never mind. I should never have taken you there. What was I thinking? A young girl of your innocence? Even if I'm a lost soul already, I still ought to be shot."

Nina didn't know how to take this. Was Professor Danvers actually apologizing to her?

She sipped her beer, feeling flustered, feeling shy, and feeling a blush creep over her face.

Feeling the need to say something, she asked, "So what does this new prophecy mean, do you think? The seed of the pelican will return, and the mother will sacrifice herself for her child, and horses will be mounted, and we're supposed to follow the water and the mirrors? Does that mean . . ." She frowned. Reflections. "Does that mean we're supposed to go back to Guinee?"

"We are going back to Guinee tonight, so I can deposit you back in your room without having Agatha accuse me of kidnapping you. Oh, it's all nonsense. I don't know why I hoped an undying airhead like the Sybil would have anything useful to tell us. I guess you get what you pay for and given the fact that she's currently living on what can be stuck in her ass, she seems to have found her proper level." He shook his head. "Apollo was definitely over-charged."

Nina kept silent. She knew he was being mean and unpleasant because he was unsettled, too, regardless of his denial. The line between his eyebrows looked like a badly-healed scar. He finished his whiskey and said, "Come on, pour your drink in a go-cup and let's get out of here. I have a splitting headache."

He got up from the table without even looking to see if she was following him, and Nina chugged her beer and burped softly as she hurried after him, deciding that whatever else he was, as a date, Professor Danvers majorly sucked.

They had barely gotten back out onto the street when Nina felt someone bump against her and say, "'Scuse me," just as a knot of tourists passed. They were being led by a dwarf (Little Person, she reminded herself, was now the proper term) dressed in a flamboyant vampire's outfit: top hat, opera cape, the whole thing. There were at least twenty people following him, hanging on his every word as he marched them down the sidewalk talking about haunted houses. They forced Nina and Professor Danvers to back up against the side of Preservation Hall, and it took her a moment to realize what had just happened.

"Hey! Mini-Dracula there just stole my purse!"

The professor lunged after her to keep her from plunging into the middle of the crowd, but he caught empty air. She pushed past the startled tourists and grabbed the dwarf's shoulder and yelled, "Hey! Asshole! Nice purse! Too bad it's mine!" and tried to wrestle it from his grasp. He turned and snarled at her, "Get out of here, girlie, you have no idea what you're doing," and punched her hard in the stomach. She let go of the bag—his punch, landing in her mid-section, had momentarily winded her—and he took off, executing a broken-field run through the drunken masses.

Nina didn't even stop to think, but peeled off after him, even though a part of her thought, this is ridiculous, I'm going to get trampled by a bunch of LSU jocks before I get twenty feet. And even if I grab him, what am I going to do? Kick some teeny-weeny ass? Still, she elbowed her way through the yielding crowd (which did seem to have gotten the idea that a robbery had taken place) and tackled the small caped figure, who immediately flipped over on his back and shrieked, "Don't hurt me! Don't hurt me! I've got rights! Little people have lawyers too! I'll sue your whole family from here to Paducah, just see if I won't!"

"Oh, shut up and just give me my purse back. I don't want to hurt you. Here." She lifted her hands away from him, but still kept her thighs locked around his waist, just in case.

"Like hell, you don't want to hurt me! Help! Help!" He writhed under her like a snake, until it really did look like they were miming a sex act in public. Then he grabbed her and pulled her face down to him, so for one weird moment she thought he was going to kiss her.

"Listen, baby-cakes, for your own good, don't get involved with Strickland Danvers and his gang. Now c'mon, kid, just gimme the bag. I ain't got all night. Those Anne Rice assholes still wanna go see where the vampire Lestat took a leak, and I still gotta show 'em."

"No way." She tightened her hand on the bag. They were so close she could see a small crescent-shaped scar on his forehead. "I'm yelling for the police in about two seconds. Who are you, and how do you know about the professor?"

"Ow, you're breaking my wrist!" He held onto the purse and growled, "Okay, kid, you asked for it. I'm Janus, and I'm your worst nightmare. Now shove off. You want to go follow a bunch of cannibal freaks down to hell, what can I say? You ain't gonna like the climate."

He let go of the bag so suddenly she rocked back on her heels, losing her grip on his midsection, and he was up and away a split second later, moving with surprising agility on his short, stumpy legs, disappearing into the crowd. She was left sitting flat on her butt in the middle of the filthy street, holding her bag, and feeling like a complete fool. Especially when Professor Danvers strolled over and asked in his most insufferable voice, "Resting, Miss Lamb?"

She scrambled to her feet, holding her bag tightly in both hands. She was flushed and furious and she tried to cover it up with bravado. "That little douche-bag there tried to rob me!"

"And so you should have let him, Miss Lamb, rather than risk him attacking you." His voice sounded fed up, casual, bored. "You had no idea whether he was armed or not. He might have had a gun. He might have had anything. You may not care about your safety, but I do have a responsibility to protect all my students. Even the stupidly heroic ones."

He turned away, and she thought how hard it was to know what he was thinking, since his default mode was always being a dick. She raised her chin and said, "Still, I got my purse back," and he sighed and said, "Yes, you did. Now do you mind if I take you home before any other adventures befall you?"

He took her arm and steered her back down Bourbon Street the way they had come. His pace was as brisk as it could be given the crowd. "You always were a magnet for trouble," he grumbled, "from the first moment we met, and you certainly don't seem to have changed over the summer."

His voice sounded strange, almost muffled, as though he were speaking against his will. She wondered where he was going with this. "I'm sorry," he said finally, stopping and turning toward her. "I had hoped we might be approaching a way to be finished with one another, for both our sakes. Yours, even more so than mine. However, apparently that's not to be."

He looked down at her, his face an inscrutable mask once more, and she raised her gaze to his, letting him see that whatever else she was, she wasn't afraid to look him in the eye. His eyes were the ones that slid away, scanning the crowd, and then came back to her, trapped. They might still be standing in the midst of a hundred total strangers, but there are different kinds of intimacy, and they might also have been alone, for all the notice anyone took of them.

"I don't want to hurt you, Nina."

It was one of the rare times when he'd addressed her by her given name. She searched his face for some accompanying tenderness, but there was none, only the iron-dark gaze of a man who seemed absolutely determined to keep every line of distance between them. There was the distance in their true natures (living and dead), the distance in their rank (teacher and student), and most of all, the real distance in their ages (yes, she reminded herself, he might look young, but he was really over 200 years old—a fact for which she had ample concrete evidence in her purse).

Was that why the dwarf had tried to rob her?

And as she continued to try to read his expression, he said, "Come on," taking her arm again and escorting her down a side street away from all the neon and noise. They walked in silence for a couple of blocks, until they got to a quiet neighborhood of closed antique shops and darkened furniture stores.

"In here." He drew her into a doorway, where on either side of them loomed large, barely lit display windows showcasing rooms fit for royalty: enormous, canopied beds and marble-topped dressers, dining room sets for twenty, velvet upholstered armchairs, and lavish sideboards backed with gloomy, silver-streaked mirrors.

"Here. This one will do." He turned her to face one of the mirrors, his fingers brushing against her cheek again for a moment. Looking straight into the glass, she saw his drawn face reflected back once more next to hers, a worn, ghostly image next to her own. She could feel the cold emanating from his body, the deep, bone-aching chill of his non-life, and while it was not unwelcome on such a hot night—kind of like air conditioning—it still made her shiver.

"Professor?"

"Yes?"

"Are we, um . . . going back to Guinee now?"

"Yes." His voice was tight, as cold as his skin. His face, angular and taut, didn't look away from their reflected images. He might have been made of stone, for all the reassurance he gave her.

"You . . . you don't think any of that stuff the Sibyl said, about, like, the war beginning . . . and all that other stuff . . . lions dressing up as sheep . . . you don't think that's going to happen right now, do you?"

"God knows." He sighed. "I don't know that much more about any of this than you do."

"Okay." She took another quick breath. She could do honesty. If he was actually willing to be honest, it would be a nice change from snark. "Okay, so, just one more thing. Um, professor . . . I don't think you need to worry about hurting me. I'm tougher than I look."

"I wouldn't be too sure of that." His lips twitched in what, in another parallel universe, might have been a smile. She decided that was the best she was going to get, and smiled back at him, which made him sigh and say, "Miss Lamb, I give you my word that I will try very, very hard not to eat you. Beyond that, I can't say anything. Now hold still. The return trip through Guinee is usually quicker, although there's always the risk of detours. This time, as we fall into the mirror, picture the garden at Daedalus, and I will do likewise. With any luck, we'll be back there before you take a dozen breaths."

With any luck? What did that mean? Nina didn't have time to ask him, because the mirror's age-splotched depths were thickening almost at once, curdling and becoming opaque. The milky blue waves were reaching out again to touch them, and those little sucker fingers were once more caressing them and drawing them back under the waters. She could see again the same towering citadels of coral and skulls, rising up higher than her sight could reach, all knitted together with long strands of seaweed, and the same endless vistas of corridors, chancels, naves, and rooms all opening out into other rooms, all spreading out before her, their vaults fretted with thigh and finger-bones, traceries of knuckles, delicate scapulas, and teeth. She became aware this time that there were other people traveling throughout this twilit world: some rushing forward with great purpose and energy, their clothes flowing and flapping behind them, while others floated as if in a trance.

Some of the people she saw moving beside them were clearly asleep, their faces calm and relaxed, while some were wasted with disease. Some were beautiful and severe and expressionless, with features that might have been painted on like masks, while others were fire-blackened and water-logged, maggot-rotted and liquifying, and some were mere skulls themselves, their eye sockets home to fish.

She turned and looked down a long corridor of vaulted rooms that stretched far away from her to her left, seemingly to infinity, and saw a silhouette partway along it, a woman in a long black dress with long black hair, a woman she thought she knew. Niobe Danvers, in her guise as the powerful sorceress, Sister Aquilina. She started and moved involuntarily toward her, feeling the watery atmosphere ripple in silvery waves as she pushed away from her previous course. She thought she heard the professor's voice calling to her in the far, far distance, but she couldn't be sure, and besides, she really wanted to see if the woman drifting away from her now was who she thought it was, or a stranger. She moved toward her, feeling excited and troubled in equal measure to see her in this strange place. Niobe wasn't walking so much as floating up ahead of her, her pace unhurried but steady, her long skirts drifting behind her across the watery floor, and Nina pushed and struggled to try and catch up. What had been easy before, when she'd traveled with the professor, suddenly became difficult now. An unseen current appeared to be holding her back.

She reached out her arms and tried to kick with her legs, a modified breaststroke that lifted her feet and propelled her forward at a sudden angle, up and around a corner. She caught at the upright of a passing doorway to stop her careening spin, and her hands slid off the smooth bones there, making her turn over and over in bizarre slow somersaults, the motion oddly making her travel even faster. The water became her conduit again: it sluiced her down a side corridor at considerable speed, making the skulls blend together into a gray-white blur. Finally, it spat her out into a cul-de-sac, bones all around her, no other exit but the entrance in which she stood. She realized she was in a room lined with skulls floor to ceiling and wall to wall, all of which were strangely decorated: there were names written across many of their foreheads, and voodoo drawings and cabalistic signs painted on some.

Sister Aquilina was nowhere to be seen, but there was something else there, a large, amorphous mass in one corner like a blue-black jellyfish, vestigial hands and feet sticking out of its sludgy substance and bulging black eyes regarding her, while a mouth opened in its belly, bisected it from one side to the other like a hinge. Inside were revealed dozens and dozens of sharp black points, hundreds of them, blinking at her like other eyes while light glinted from their razored tips. She recoiled and tried to scream—and a hand grasped her upper arm and a voice snapped, "Now, Miss Lamb! Picture the garden, now!" and then they were flying upward, through water so fast-moving and roiling and bubbling she couldn't breath, traveling so quickly she couldn't see anything at all, and she wondered idly if they were going to get the bends.

Of course, as soon as it had begun, it stopped, and she could feel cool air on her arms and legs again. She pulled away from Professor Danvers and promptly threw up on the grass.

"I'm sorry," she said, when she had caught her breath. "I know you told me about the detours. I'm sorry, but I saw her, and I had to follow her. It was your sister. Niobe. It was her."

"I know." He sat back down on the bench again, and she had the idea he might be about to be sick too. "I saw her too. And you saw the Nadir. I'm truly sorry about that. He's ridiculous, but there you are. The concentration of people's fears about death might be anything, black emptiness or an angel with a flaming sword, but instead, it's that nebulous lump of goo, like animated snot. Makes you despair about the human imagination." He rubbed his hand over his face. "If you've recovered, you should probably go back to your room now. I scarcely think either of us is fit right now to carry on a decent conversation."

He looked so bleak, so haunted and hollowed out, that she couldn't just abruptly leave him like that. She went to him and knelt down between his knees, and if the position struck him as ludicrous or erotic, for once he was too polite to say so.

"Why was she there?" she asked.

"I don't know." He shook his head. "Maybe she was just traveling, like we were."

"Some of those people were asleep, and some of them were dead."

"Yes." He sat up a little straighter. "As you may have guessed, another name for Guinee is the Land of the Dead. It's not exactly Hades. It's a lot more complicated. People go there when they die, or when they dream, or when they disintegrate . . . some people are remarkably resilient and have to literally dissolve before they relinquish their hold on consciousness. And some people go there . . ." He shook his head. "Never mind, I've said too much already, and I'm tired. Go to bed, Nina. And if you know what's good for you, bolt the door." He touched her cheek. "You never do know what's good for you, though, do you? God, what am I going to do with you?"

Abruptly he stood up and walked away. "Get out of my sight," he threw back over his shoulder, the way another man—and the thought struck her keenly—might have said, "Good night, sleep tight. Don't let the bedbugs bite."

She remained on her knees a moment longer, muttering a few choice rude words under her breath and then got up and went back inside. When she got to her room, she hesitated and did lock the door. It felt almost as good as slamming it, and had the added benefit of not waking up the rest of the school in the process.

# Chapter Four

But sleep was out of the question. She stripped off her hoodie and shook her hair loose from its scarf, rubbing her fingernails vigorously against her scalp as though that could reset her brain.

What in God's name had just happened? The Sybil . . . the weird dwarf, Janus . . . Guinee? What did they all mean? The strange prophecy of the Sybil's (like she hadn't heard enough prophetic riddles in six months with the Skinnies) was particularly disturbing. "The lion will dress himself up as a sheep, and even the lamb will be deceived." That had to mean her, right? She wasn't an expert in divination, but Nina Lamb was her name (at least the only name she knew).

And what else had the Sybil said? "You can take all that shit seriously, or you can just let it slide. Water off a duck's back." She, the Sybil, had decided to spend her eternal life pole dancing. Nina could do the same thing (although she doubted she could ever learn that tassel trick) or she could *care*.

At which point "they" would have her by the short and curlies. Whoever "they" were.

She slumped back down on the bed, feeling both exhausted and wired. Mercy padded up her body from where he'd been asleep on the foot of the bed and lay down on her chest, but his soft kneading of her shoulder wasn't that relaxing. A breeze blew in through her open window, and her rinkydink wind-up alarm clock (no one was allowed to have any electronic devices at Daedalus) told her it was just after three a.m. Time to get some sleep indeed, but her mind was whirling, and after a moment she got up and turned on the lamp on her bedside table. There was one thing she could do besides lying there in the dark, and it didn't involve remembering skulls or Professor Danvers or Bourbon Street or strange glob-monsters with teeth that symbolized mankind's deepest fears of death.

She picked up her purse and dug out the engraving the Sybil had given her, and then held it up to the light to study it. Which was when she noticed the strangest thing. There were two other people in the picture now, neither of whom she'd noticed before.

There were the three Danvers siblings, all looking young and equally beautiful. Now, however, there were clearly two other people standing there with them, an older man standing off to one side, and a child standing between Niobe and Strickland. The little boy (or girl) was maybe four or five years old, standing with Strickland's hand on one shoulder, a small, blurry figure in an old-fashioned white pinafore and stockings, so he (or she) looked like a fluffy doll.

The older man, by contrast, was perfectly clear, and had a face Nina knew. Mr. O'Brien. The headmaster of the Daedalus School.

She could recognize his keen gaze and his lined, craggy features, his long, flowing white hair and close-cropped beard. She remembered the one time she had met him before, and how intimidated she'd been by those ice-blue eyes, which made her think of a stern grandfather. He was dressed much as he'd been at their only meeting, in a perfectly ordinary suit—in contrast to the Danvers's eighteenth-century garb—and looked not so much happy to be there, as distantly polite. She slowly put the engraving down on the table, wondering how she could have missed seeing him before.

It was only for a moment, she told herself, and I was distracted by the Sybil sticking her butt in Professor Danvers's face, but still, the headmaster was such a strange, mysterious presence in her life, she felt unsettled to have missed him. She thought back to the one time she'd spoken to him, when everyone else had assured her he was dead. Gone away. Vanished. Her friend Bella had even told her he was terrible, a kind of sadistic child molester who'd once showed him the futility of existence. Nina knew she had every reason to be afraid of him, but she also yearned for the headmaster to be real, because he seemed like the one person who might be able to explain everything to her.

She lay back down on her bed, thinking how this concrete evidence of the headmaster's existence, even though it wasn't very concrete, made her feel strange and excited and shivery all at the same time. What were the implications? That the headmaster had been around when the three Danvers siblings were alive? But he was dressed in modern-day clothes, so the whole setup seemed wrong. She picked up the engraving and studied it again. Who was the child? The face was so small she couldn't make out its features at all. Its hair could have been any color; its body was almost invisible in that stupid pinafore. She sighed and lay back down again, feeling the night's activities come crashing down on her, and a moment later, she was asleep.

She dreamed of corridors and rooms, not just of bones, but of rich furnishings and cold emptiness: rooms that were stuffed with silks and tufted black pillows and long black draperies and smooth onyx surfaces, and rooms that were bare and stripped, like the walls and floors of a house after it had been scoured. She read words written on the walls: We must all change, but we 'die' only because we think we must, and not so long ago, the dead spoke to the living, and they still speak now. She looked at strange paintings: artificial flowers with the words flower and sweet woven into their petals, and beautiful smiling men and women like ads for cosmetics with the words written under them: buy their teeth, buy their eyes, buy their skin.

She fought to escape the dreams, and finally awoke, sweating, panting, desperate, in the watery light of morning, and the first thing she did was pick up the engraving and stare at it again.

But there were no answers to be found in the picture. The three Danvers siblings stood there as before, in the middle of an overgrown garden full of lush flowers and tropical plants. And that's all there was. No older man stood with them, and no child, no slight presence caught in mid-motion, and Professor Danvers's hand hung loose at his side. A bright sun beat down on their heads, and even the shadows it threw across the lawn were unsparing. Nothing but grass and trees.

The two other people had disappeared as if they had never existed.

# Chapter Five

A week later, the rest of the students of the Daedalus School came back from their summer vacations, and Nina was reunited with her two best friends.

Alastaire Roget came bounding up the stairs and burst into Nina's room, grabbing her and crushing her in a big bear hug. When she could breathe again, Nina said, "Wow, you've . . . grown. A lot. Since last spring. And also, um . . . you're a boy now."

"Yeah, kinda." Alastaire flung himself/herself on the bed and shrugged out of his jacket. "I've still got tits. See? It's weird." He showed off his breasts, which still made a substantial rise in his T-shirt, despite otherwise washboard abs. He snickered. "Guys and girls were hitting on me indiscriminately. The French are definitely strange."

Alastaire and his adoptive family had been vacationing in Europe, where the Skinnies' ability to shift sexes had apparently not gone unappreciated. Nina thought that all in all, Alastaire made a pretty fine-looking boy. His face was still delicate and heart-shaped, but now his raw-boned awkwardness promised a tall strength once he grew into it, and his cupid's bow mouth looked good surrounded by a little close-cropped stubble.

By contrast, Bellocq Chopin, who came in a moment later and also hugged Nina, had definitely gone female over the summer. Nina wondered how his family had taken it. His father, Ly Than Chopin, was a powerful Skinny who set great store on his only son being, well, his only son. The fact that Bella had always liked guys and been somewhat effeminate had created a lot of tension, especially since the slender Vietnamese youth was brilliant and possessed of a savage wit.

But now, Bella had been transformed into a beauty, with a pale sculpted face set off by long jet black hair that fell almost to her waist. She still seemed a little shy about it, as though she were still in drag.

"I'm still learning about make-up," she said, making a little what-you-see-is-what-you-get gesture at her eyes and lips. Nina thought she looked wonderful, and told her so.

"You really like it? I was kind of wondering about the whole eyeshadow thing." She went to Nina's mirror and checked herself out. Alastaire, who was at the same time checking Bella out, pretended he wasn't. The previous spring, they'd spent almost the entire time pretending they hated each other, and Nina, who was amused at the change, decided not to say anything for fear of making them self-conscious.

"So, what have you been up to?" Alastaire asked, scooting over on the bed until he was out of the late-afternoon sunlight. Mercy came up in his lap and he picked him up and cuddled him, and then remembered guys weren't supposed to cuddle soft furry animals and put him back down again.

"Not much." Nina sat at her desk. "I've been working with professor Seneschal and reading about Haiti. I figured we need to know more about the great Haitian gods . . . the *Lwas* . . . for anything that was coming."

"God, you've been *studying*." Alastaire's sympathy was heartfelt.

"You would say that," Bella said, tossing her long hair back in a very credible flounce. She came and sat on the bed as well, as far away from Alastaire as possible. She turned to Nina and asked, "So what have you found out? I did some rooting around in the

Library of Congress while I was up in Washington, but the Saturni have all the old texts under wraps, so it's hard to find anything worthwhile. It's all 'Voodoo Drums and Satanic Rituals' and about how all these backward ex-slaves stick pins in dolls and have orgies." She rolled her eyes. "So Post-Colonial. Where's Che Guevara when you need him?"

Nina nodded. "A lot of the books professor Seneschal has are pretty racist, too, but I guess that's kind of the point. It's the religion of the people who lost. I did score one major find, however."

She held up a small book, and when Bella and Alastaire both raised their eyebrows, she explained, "It's called *The Science of the Mysteries*. Professor Danvers had it, and well . . . I kind of swiped it from his office. I figured since he wasn't here . . ." She shrugged. "Anyway, it's written by Anonymous, but it's inscribed by somebody whose initials were C.B. And it's all about 'The Sacrament of Crossing' and what it really means to be a Skin Eater, but it's also got a lot about Haiti and lots of other stuff.

"Listen to this." She opened the book and read, "'It is not my intention, whether through excessive generation of fear, or through its opposite, the incitement of macabre and prurient interest, to in any way celebrate the Saturni. Their horror needs no chronicler to exaggerate its menace, nor do they lack for followers. In fact, more and more people today seem to flock to their banner, all unknowing of the fearful bargain they undertake in allying themselves with such perfect fiends.'"

"Whoa . . ." Alastaire raked his hands through his hair until it was standing on end, a not-bad look. "This guy said that?"

"Um-hmm. There's more. 'My guide in my exploration of the island was a native woman named Anais. She said, "Someday the *Lwa* will find their perfect mounts and be embodied again, and then there will be a great fight between the *Lwas* and the Saturni, and many will die."'"

"No wonder he didn't want to let anybody know who he was," Bella said, picking up the book and studying its spine. "What's the S. C. Press?"

"I don't know. South Carolina? The book doesn't have a regular copyright listing, it just lists the title. And the thing is, I think this guy's still alive. One of the books Seneschal gave me is called Voodoo: Fact or Fiction?, and it pretty much says all voodoo's full of shit, but it does say the author of The Science of the Mysteries is one of the leading authorities on tribal belief systems. And that reference was written in 2004."

"Huh." Bella paged through the book. "He must be a Skinny, then, if he's been alive for that long. I wonder why I never heard of him."

"Do you know every Skinny who's ever published a book?"

"No, Mr. Snide, but I do keep track. And this should be part of the curriculum. But as far as I know, no one here has ever mentioned it."

Nina decided she'd had enough discussions of books, and besides, she was bursting to ask her friends for their opinion on her recent "date" with Professor Danvers. Taking a deep breath, she asked, "So, um . . . like what do either of you guys know about the Cumaean Sybil?"

Alastaire predictably said, "Beats me. Who's the Cumaean Sybil?" While Bella (equally predictably) said, "The Cumaean Sybil was one of the four great prophets of ancient Rome, and she advised Virgil and Tarquinius Superbus. Her books were burned by General Flavius Stilicho, who was a Christian, and five years later, Rome was overrun by the Visigoths. Why do you ask?"

"Oh, just curious." Nina grinned. "Actually, I met her. The other night. She was pole-dancing over at a club on Bourbon Street."

If she'd expected to surprise her friends with this, she was disappointed. Alastaire merely said, "Cool!" and Bella nodded and said, "So that's what it was. My father got invited to a so-called 'Boys Night Out' the day after we got back from DC. Jack Benway wanted them all to go down to some club in the Quarter and catch someone—the Sybil presumably—and get her to prophesy for them. But when they got there, apparently it was all just regular strippers. So they stayed anyway and got home at three o'clock in the morning minus a couple grand and drunk as skunks. My mother was majorly pissed."

Nina, who had met Bella's beautiful and scary mother, Nhi Trung, decided she didn't want to even think about what Nhi Trung Chopin was like when she got mad.

She said, "Well, yeah, the Cumaean Sybil was there. And she told me all this bizarre stuff. And then Professor Danvers took me for a beer at Pat O'Brien's, and I got robbed by a dwarf, and we went to Guinee and . . . okay, maybe I'd better start at the beginning."

She gave them a rundown of the night's events, and was rewarded this time with twin stares. Bella recovered first and said, "Okay, take it from the top and tell me exactly what the Sybil said and exactly what you saw in the engraving."

Nina obliged, even showing Bella the picture itself, which now of course showed just the three Danvers siblings again. Alastaire was more interested in Guinee.

"So let me get this straight," he said. "You go through a mirror and you end up in an underwater palace full of skulls? Why has nobody ever told me about this shit?!"

"Because it's very advanced, and the Saturni decided we didn't need to learn it," Bella said, taking the engraving over to the window so she could look at it in the fading light. She stood in the shadows, out of the direct rays of the setting sun, and held the picture at arm's length, squinting and shading her eyes.

"You can light the lamp if you want," Nina said. She knew both her friends hated the sun, and besides, the light there wasn't that great, but Bella shook her head.

"I'm checking it for any optical filters that might have been put on it. Sometimes you can see them shimmer in sunlight. That could explain why you saw something here once but not again. However, this looks clean." She handed the engraving back and sat back down on the bed again. "And anyway, it's flat-out impossible. William Lincoln didn't invent a machine for showing animated drawings till 1867 and Louis Lumiere didn't invent the Cinematograph till 1895."

"I'm glad you're back," Alastaire said, lying down and covering his eyes. "I was getting a little bored not knowing the history of every single fucking thing on the planet."

"Wait a minute," Nina said. "Let me get this straight. Both of you guys travel with your parents, don't you? So why doesn't Alastaire know anything about Guinee?"

"Because like I told you, it's advanced." Bella sighed. "Kids are kind of zoned out before anyone puts them through it. It's like our parents put us in a light trance. Some of us, of course, have read about it, how you allow the mirror's pull to draw you in until you merge with your reflection, but we're not allowed to experience it directly." She smirked. "Then again, some of us probably wouldn't notice anything unusual if they were transported up Jacob's ladder and got a peek at God's junk and the heavenly host."

"Stop it, you two," Nina said almost automatically. She put the engraving under the blotter on her desk and put *The Science of the Mysteries* on top of it, so she wouldn't be tempted to look at the picture five hundred more times than she had already. "The main thing," she continued, turning back to her friends, "is that the Sybil said a war is going to begin. That can only mean the fight between Sister Aquilina and the Saturni is going to heat up, big-time. I wish I'd been able to talk to Sister Aquilina while I was in

Guinee," she added. "I should have kept a better eye on things, instead of getting all turned around and freaked out by that creepy Nadir thing. I could have followed her if I'd been more careful, seen where she went. God, I wish I could go back!"

"Well . . ." Alastaire raised his eyebrows. "Why can't you? You've got a mirror, don't you? Just go 'mirror mirror on the wall' and see what happens."

"I can't." Nina sighed. "I tried. The next day after I went there, I tried so hard I practically went blind staring into a hand mirror all afternoon and trying to make it melt. And then I tried with the water in the fountain out in the garden, and practically passed out and fell in. It's no good. I guess you have to do it with somebody who knows how. Bella, you said it was advanced. Is there somebody here I could ask? I mean, besides Professor Danvers?"

Bella frowned. "Professor Hermes might know, but I really doubt he's going to tell you, he's such a stickler for the rules. And I'm not sure whether anyone else would have the skills to show you the required technique. See, Guinee is like a totally adult Skinny thing. Professor Danvers was amazingly out of line taking you there."

She shook her head, looking shocked that a school official would do such a thing, and Nina, who was well aware that Professor Danvers's attitude toward "the rules" was sketchy, said, "Yeah, well, he did. So what's the big deal? He told me Guinee was like the Land of the Dead, and people go there when they die, or when they dream, or when they discorporate . . . when they finally lose their last hold on consciousness. He said some people are remarkably resilient and have to literally dissolve before they let go of life. And he said there were other ways people went there, but then he caught himself and said he'd already told me too much. So what is Guinee *really*?"

Bella hesitated and bit her lip.

"Oh, come on," Nina added. "How bad can it be? I went there, remember. It was spooky and kind of bizarre, but it wasn't like . . . hell. Right? I mean . . . all right, tell me. Is it like hell? I mean *really hell*?"

"No." Bella looked down at her hands, which were still strong and boyish. How strange that someone could be so feminine and masculine at the same time. "Guinee isn't hell. Guinee is the place where the *Introim* came from."

"Wait a minute." Nina shook her head. "I thought the *Introim* came down from the sky in globes of light? That's what everybody says. Now you're telling me the old gods came up out of the sea, like . . . I don't know what. Like *mer*people?"

But Bella, as a boy or a girl, was nothing if not pedantic. "No, not anything like *mer*people. You're still thinking about Guinee as though it were a real place, a physical sea, like the Atlantic Ocean. But Guinee's on another plane altogether, a plane perpendicular to our own." She held up her two hands, palms flat, making a cross. "It's not 'up' or 'down' or 'left' or 'right' from us. It's *other*. It's on the other side of a membrane from where we are."

Nina could just barely picture that, like trying to think in more than three dimensions.

"And that's where the *Introim* lived before they fell down into our plane?"

"Yes. At least that's what the legends say." Bella looked nervously over her shoulder, because like everyone at Daedalus, she knew it was an infraction of the rules to talk or even think about magic. "The legends say the *Introim* were once pure forces in Ville au Camps, which is something like the capital city of Guinee. You understand I'm talking about things that don't have any real counterpart in everyday life, right? It's not like there's an actual city you can go to inside of Guinee, where the *Lwas* and the Saturni once lived before they split up into two rival groups.

At least I don't think there is . . ." Bella lifted one shoulder. "It's more like a metaphor. Ville au Camps is like . . . like concentrated Guinee. If Guinee is at right angles to us, then Ville au Camps is at right angles to it, and . . . oh, it's hopeless."

Bella flung herself back down on the bed, and added, "Suffice it to say, Guinee is like the most important place in the whole universe for us. Professor Danvers might as well have taken you to the Church of the Holy Sepulchre or inside the Qa'aba. It's like . . . I don't know. It's actually kind of blasphemous."

Nina had never heard Bella speak about anything before with that kind of reverence, and for some reason, it unsettled her. She wasn't sure she liked having been to the Skin Eaters' "holiest of holies," whatever that meant. She said, "Well, anyway, you're telling me I can't go there again, so we're going to have to find some other way of tracking Sister Aquilina down. If this war is going to start, she needs to know that. The Sybil may have escaped your father and the Saturni for now, but she may be in danger too. I wish Professor Danvers had told me what was actually going on the night we went to meet her! As it is, I feel like I was worrying about all the wrong things. Like having my purse stolen and whether or not he liked me."

And when both Bella and Alastaire stared at her, she said, "Oh, come on, you two both know I've got the world's biggest crush on him, and it's all utterly hopeless and pathetic, and if you didn't guess it last spring, you just weren't paying attention! Now let's go downstairs and get some dinner, I'm starving," she added, to put an end to this discussion, and as they trooped downstairs Alastaire whispered to Bella, "I had no idea!" and Bella sighed and said, "That's because you're about as observant as a blind man wearing sunglasses. I knew it all along."

Meals at Daedalus were served in the Commons, where there were new tables and chairs, Nina noticed, to replace the beat-up ones they'd been using all summer. A new hardwood floor had also been laid over the water-warped boards that had been there the previous spring. Generally, they seemed to have spruced things up for the return of the student body; still, it was strange having the room full of people again, and yet having so many empty spaces. The whole section of the room where the *jumbies* had sat was empty. Nina was glad they were gone—it had been horrible sitting in the same classes with them, and knowing they were just destined to be food for the adult Skinnies—but now it made the room feel colder than ever.

The teachers were all sitting at the long table at the front of the room. Professor Danvers was playing with his food as usual, since he never had any appetite, and preferred to take his grisly nourishment in the form of a blood-and-whiskey cocktail. Professor Samson was there, in bush jacket and eyeshadow; pale professor Hermes; green professor Aspidistrus, burly professor Mwindo and skinny professor Threet and gorgeous professor Ariadne and . . .

"Nina," Bella said. "I thought you said you were studying with professor Seneschal all summer. Where is he?"

The aged history professor came in just as they were speaking, looking even more disheveled than usual, his hair uncombed and his suit buttoned up the wrong way. But what was most noticeable about him was how scared he looked. His eyes, normally hazy, looked focused and alert, and Nina was just going to remark that something had woken him up, when a sharp voice sang out in fake-boredom from a nearby table, "Good Lord, I thought we stopped admitting charity cases last spring."

And Nina turned around to see her worst enemy in the whole world. Simone Freeland.

# Chapter Six

The fact that Simone was looking gorgeous as usual didn't help. The black girl had dyed her hair platinum, and wore it plaited into tight cornrows close to her perfect skull and cascading in dozens of braids down her back. Her soft cheeks actually glowed. She looked like the embodiment of a perfect Creole princess, except for the hateful look on her face.

"Nice to see you too," Nina snapped. "What'd you do, get caught in a shower of bleach?"

"Pathetic. Just pathetic. I had hoped some of us might have matured over the summer."

"Guess it's just your tough luck I'm still a smart-ass who's unimpressed with your Beyonce butt."

It was a lame response, and Nina knew it. Agatha Danvers, who was sitting up at the front table, tapped her spoon against her water glass and said pointedly, "Children, please take your seats and eat your dinner and shut up. I don't have time for this."

She looked like she had a colossal headache. Since she'd gone back to cooking for the school, this was the first full meal she'd had to prepare, and the results were predictably depressing. For their start of term "feast" they had what looked like Spam with fried eggs on top.

The eggs were as hard as rubber, and the Spam was ice cold.

"I've got some eclairs back in my room," Alastaire whispered as they sat down and picked up their knives and forks. "I brought them back from Paris. They're a little stale, but they still taste way better than this."

Nina simply nodded, not wanting to get Agatha any madder than she was by not eating. Trying to do something so she could choke down the God-awful food, she grabbed a ketchup bottle and shook some onto her Spam. Unfortunately, she shook too hard, and the next thing she knew, her whole plate was swimming in red glop.

"Shit," she muttered, grabbing a couple of napkins, and a little blonde girl sitting opposite her said, "I could use some of that. Here, let me help."

Her voice was so soft Nina could barely hear her. She was maybe five feet tall, and she was so pale and wispy she might have been an albino butterfly. But she stretched across the table and bent down so her face was inches above Nina's plate and then sucked noisily and drew a thin stream of ketchup up into her mouth like a waterspout. Positioning her mouth above her own plate, she released the condiment in a graceful swirl, dabbing a last portion onto her fried egg. The whole process was delicate and dainty and absolutely disgusting at the same time, and Nina had to resist a simultaneous impulse to applaud and gag.

"That's . . . quite a talent," she said, glancing at Bella and Alastaire, who were sitting on either side of her and looking at the little blonde girl with identical stunned expressions.

"Whoa . . ." Alastaire finally said. "Girlfriend, that was fucking awesome!"

"Among other things," Bella said. She was obviously trying to be nice, but she pushed her own untouched plate away as though it was the very last thing she wanted to see just then.

"Where did you learn your, um . . . unusual eating habits? If you don't mind my asking."

"Oh, that?" The pale girl shrugged. "I've always been able to do things like that. Exert a gravitational field. Make things come to me wherever I need them. You know . . . food to my mouth. A Kleenex when I need to blow my nose. I can amplify sounds to my ears. Oh, and I can summon change to my fingers when I want to take the streetcar. You know, silly stuff like that."

"You can summon money?" Alastaire was wistful. "Boy, I wish I could do that."

"It doesn't work with big things. My stepmother says it's just a quirk, like being double-jointed."

The pale girl ate an experimental bite of her dinner, and then said, "Actually, even the ketchup doesn't help. I'm Phoebe, by the way." She held out her hand. "Phoebe Passerine."

Nina wasn't always fond of shaking hands at Daedalus. Most of the student body was too cold, being already somewhat/kinda dead. She didn't want to be rude, however, so she extended her still-warm hand and just brushed Phoebe's outstretched fingers. Cold as ice. Whatever else Phoebe was, she was already well on the way to becoming a Skinny.

"Where are you from?" she asked her.

"Oh . . . around." Phoebe drank some sweet tea and reached for a slice of bread. "Actually, the bread's not bad. You could try putting some ketchup on that."

"So I told that striving bitch she could just kiss my fine black ass. My God, what a bore. She actually asked what we did at Tyche dances. Like I'm going to tell her! Bougie, please."

"That's our resident snob," Bella explained, indicating Simone and her rich friends.

"Tyche's the female version of the Fortuna Club, very high-level Skin Eater cachet, New Orleans-style. They have everybody from rich mortals to Saturni trying to get in, so the men can play poker and the women can all go to luncheons and hear lectures about fine art . . . but perhaps you already know about that?"

"Um . . . no," Phoebe said vaguely. She had her head cocked to one side, and as the three friends watched, she seemed to be forming words with her lips, although no sounds came out.

"Um . . . earth to Phoebe," Alastaire said after a minute. "Are you okay?"

"Oh yes," she said, giving her head a little shake. "I can also summon thoughts. Sometimes. Just then, I was trying to find out what they actually do at Tyche dances, but you're right, it's all just silly deb stuff." She finished her sweet tea and pushed back from the table.

"Well, I'd better go unpack my things. I want to get a good night's sleep before classes start. Don't want to be a slow-poke. Alastaire . . . Bella . . . Nina . . . it was very nice to meet you all."

And with a wave she walked away.

The three friends decided she was the strangest person they'd met at Daedalus in a long time, which was indeed saying something. But they were more interested in getting out of there and getting to Alastaire's stale eclairs. A few moments later, they pushed back their chairs along with everyone else and made a bee-line for the stairs and a feast of chocolate fondant and pastry.

It was only when they were on their third eclairs that it occurred to any of them how Phoebe had known all their names.

# Chapter Seven

Over the next several days, they ran into Phoebe Passerine here and there—she was in Nina's Advanced Alchemy class with professor Aspidistrus and in Transformation and Animal Dominance, where her preferred animal form, matching her ethereal appearance, was a pale green lunar moth. She was remarkably well-read, being able to recite huge chunks of the Aeneid and the Odyssey from memory, much to the delight of the literature teacher, professor Mwindo.

And she was unbelievable in Sky Geography. The first time professor Threet assigned them an open-book quiz to plot the moons of Saturn, she was able to fill in all sixty-two moons in record time, from monstrous Titan to the tiniest little moonlets. She laughed and said it was because Phoebe was the name of one of Saturn's most distant moons, a retrograde orbiting mystery that might, scientists thought, be captured Dark Matter.

Alastaire groaned. "Just what this school needs, two female geeks who know everything."

And then he glanced at Nina and added, "All right, three! Three female geeks! I feel like I should just sit back on a couch and drink beer. You all make me feel retarded."

"Well," Bella said, "at least you've got a solid grip on reality. That's something anyway."

Phoebe sometimes ate with them, but she often sat by herself, just staring off dreamily into space, and so, predictably, she became a target for all the free-floating malice that always circulates in any school. One day at lunch, Nina was sitting reading *The Midnight Times* (she'd started subscribing to the reactionary newspaper because it was a mouth-piece for the Saturni, figuring Know Thine Enemy) when she saw Sharon La Croix, one of Simone's acolytes, walk by Phoebe's table and accidentally/on purpose knock whatever unspeakable thing was on her plate (it looked like meatloaf) onto her lap.

"Oops, sorry," Sharon drawled, clearly not. "I tripped."

"'S okay." Phoebe started wiping the offending mystery meat off her skirt and seemed honestly unconcerned. *Maybe she can just siphon it up through her nose*, Nina thought, with a rude impulse to giggle. Sharon, however, wasn't finished with her yet.

"You're pretty mellow. Are you high?"

"No." Phoebe didn't quite meet her eyes, her body language shy, but she still seemed more oblivious than scared. Nina, who had a bad feeling where this might be heading, put her newspaper aside and watched more closely.

"I think you're tripping hard, girlfriend." Sharon made a circular movement around her head and mugged to Simone and the two other girls who always sat with her. "Stoned to the dome." She kicked Phoebe's chair so it bumped several inches across the floor. "C'mon, hippie chick, let's see if you can walk a straight line. I bet you can't. I'll bet you ten bucks you fall flat on your face."

"Doesn't that stuff get old?" Nina asked with polite interest, raising her voice so all the girls could hear her. "I mean, just asking. After like second grade, don't you guys want to move on to something more fulfilling, like carjacking or setting small fires?"

"Nina, when will you ever learn? When we want you all up in our business, we'll ask you." Simone sounded as caring as a boa constrictor. "Right now, I'd suggest you butt out before I start getting creative with my name-calling."

"Ooh, I'm shakin', Goldilocks." Nina got up and approached Phoebe's table. "C'mon." She held out her hand. "Let's go get some junk food and teeth-rotting sodas instead of this cafeteria crap. We can hit the gas station down on Magazine Street. I'm buying."

She reached out to touch Phoebe's arm, but just then a sharp jolt of electricity jumped between the smaller girl's skin and hers, and all the utensils on the table—the salt and pepper shakers, plates, cups and glasses, and a big bowl of mashed potatoes—all leapt in the air and crashed back down again, potato-goo spattering everywhere. Nina jumped back and said, "Holy shit!" even while she thought, something like that happened once before, didn't it? The previous spring, when she had touched a plate of sweetbreads being held by Simone's powerful stepmother, the sweetbreads had danced around like Mexican jumping beans in response to the same kind of powerful spark.

*But that can't be right,* Nina thought. *Simone's mother is a Saturnus. Phoebe's just a kid, and she's nice. A little weird, maybe, but aren't we all?*

She looked at the little girl, who still seemed bemused, as though she were trying to remember a telephone number. Meanwhile, all the utensils on the table continued their wild jittering, and Sharon La Croix retreated to Simone's side, her eyes cutting sideways at Phoebe like a frightened dog.

"Are you okay?" Nina ventured, feeling like that was probably the stupidest question on earth, but not knowing what else to say. Phoebe looked up and said, "Oh, sure, I'm fine. I was just trying to understand what—" She frowned, and a salt shaker went whizzing across the room and smashed through a window. "What Sharon meant by saying all those mean things. That is your name, right?" she asked her tormentor, who swallowed and nodded.

"Sometimes, you know, when I get curious and, I don't know . . . a little upset . . . things start to happen." Phoebe looked down at the mess on the table, where things were quieting down, and said, "Wow. Did I do all that?"

"Um, yes. You did all that." Nina knew she didn't want to continue this conversation in front of Simone and her posse, and oddly enough, Simone seemed to feel the same way. She got up and said, "C'mon, ladies, let's bounce," and led the way out of the Commons without looking back. When the bitch quartet had left, Nina glanced around at the remaining students and asked Phoebe, "Do... do you have to be somewhere right away?"

"No." Phoebe was idly scraping the pieces of food and broken plates together in a single pile by running her hands over them, but she stood up, still looking calm. "I don't have to be in Calculation Science till 2:30. Where do you want to go?"

"Anywhere but here." Nina saw Agatha emerging from the kitchen, and knew when she saw the debris, she'd pitch a fit. "Do you . . . are you allergic to sunlight like most of the other students here? I don't mean to get personal, but you did mention you rode the streetcar, so I thought maybe that meant you *can* go outside during the day."

"Oh yes, that's fine. I quite enjoy sunlight." Phoebe followed Nina out a side corridor, and when they got to the heavy oak door at the end of it, the taller girl pushed it open and they entered the garden. A few magnolia leaves were blowing across the grass, but as always, the garden looked lush, an empty tropical oasis in the warm September air.

Nina led the way to the same wrought-iron bench where she'd sat with Professor Danvers (stop thinking about him, she reminded herself) and after they'd sat down, she said, "I just wanted to talk to you alone, because frankly, you're going to get killed here at Daedalus if you keep doing stuff like that. This isn't a place that takes kindly to people who are, well, let's just say 'unusual.'"

And then she rethought that, and added, "I mean, aside from

the whole dead-and-immortal thing. Which I'm guessing you already know about. And yes, when I said you were going to get 'killed' here at Daedalus, of course you are going to get killed at Daedalus, but . . . well, that's not what I meant."

"Of course not." Phoebe was gazing around the garden with real pleasure, and then she inhaled deeply and a large spray of oleander blossoms wafted over to press against her face.

Putting the flowers in her lap, she said, "They're poisonous, you know."

"Yeah . . . I'd heard that."

"So many things are two things at once. Don't you find that? Life and death. Hot and cold. Good and evil." She looked at Nina. "You have a spider crawling in your hair."

"Ugh," Nina said, brushing her hands over her head to get rid of it. "Where? Is it gone? Where is it?"

"It's right here," Phoebe said. She reached out one finger and the spider looped a gossamer thread over to it and crept up her hand. "They're good luck, you know. Don't kill it."

"I . . . um, thanks. I guess it's a lucky thing you stopped me." Nina watched Phoebe commune with the spider and thought, *why am I even bothering?* Phoebe had her own quiet way of dealing with things, and for all she knew, it might serve her fine in the closed community of Daedalus. The thing was, it didn't feel like that community was going to stay closed very much longer. If a war was coming with the Saturni . . . if Sister Aquilina and her doomed orphaned children were really going up against the most powerful and evil beings in the universe . . . and if the Cumaean Sybil had seen fit to rope her—Nina Lamb—into this train wreck . . . then she knew where her alliances had to be. She'd seen too much of the Saturni to reconcile herself to their complete triumph. No, she would fight, and she had the awful feeling Bella and Alastaire would fight alongside her, because they were both pig-headed stubborn romantics who would willingly throw themselves off a cliff to be on the right moral side. Even though Alastaire would have denied any such impulse to his dying breath, and Bella would have sneered that she would never involve herself in anything so illogical and profoundly silly.

So Nina's first impulse to protect Phoebe had in it about 50 percent compassion, and 50 percent the impulse to throw her a life preserver while she was still around to do it. *When I'm a lost soul wandering around in Guinee because the Saturni have whooped my ass*, she thought, *I'm not going to be of much use to anybody.*

She tried again. "It's just that . . . um, people here tend to take sides. There's the Simone clique with all of her friends. And there are a lot of other kids who aren't in her social set, but who would desperately like to be. This is New Orleans, remember. Everybody wants to be in the right clubs. Then there are the brainiacs who just want to study and get into Holmgard or Princeton . . . a lot of Skinnies go there, even though it's technically a mortal school . . . and the idiots who just want to goof off and party, and the people who just want to fast-track into the Saturni banks and politics, and the jocks who are all just really into Animal Dominance and Transformation."

*And how are we unlike any other high school?* she thought. She shook her head, trying to find the right words. "It's just that . . . things may get a little tense in the next several months . . ." (*or years*, she thought) "and I wouldn't want you to get hurt. Even if it was, you know . . . just emotional damage. Like people singling you out and hurting your feelings."

"Oh, I'll be fine." Phoebe smiled as a bird landed in her lap and laid an egg. "How do you know the dwarf, Janus?"

Nina was so surprised she practically laid an egg herself. She stammered, "I-I only met him once, when he was trying to mug me! How do you . . . who the hell *are* you, Phoebe?"

The younger girl didn't seem to mind being asked such a rude question. She caressed the bird and said, "I'm a student here, just like you. Well, not like you, Nina. Let's just say I'm a normal person who has a few . . . quirks, that's all. Like being able to communicate with things. And looking at things in the bigger picture. It's amazing how many things are unimportant when you put a little distance between yourself and them. Like people being unpleasant to you or mean . . . or even people being pleasant. Loving and hating are both just sides of a much more multi-sided coin, when you learn to think in more than four dimensions.

"And as for who I am exactly, well, I'm one of the last members of a very old family that's, unfortunately, kind of run out of steam by now." She bent her head to stroke the bird, and the sunlight illuminated her forehead, where Nina noticed a crescent-shaped scar. "What's left are mostly crazy old aunts and uncles, and a few cousins. Oh, I mean my natural family," she added. "My adoptive family, the Passerines, are apparently very nice, although I've never actually met them. They live in Europe . . . or somewhere . . . but the Benway Foundation sends my letters to them and I get letters back, and they seem fine. It's my natural family that's kind of weird, and I guess inbred. They live in a place called the Bayou Road Guest House. It's a B & B over on Esplanade. "And the reason I know Janus is because he's my brother."

# Chapter Eight

The mystery of Phoebe Passerine was just one of the many things that crowded into Nina's mind as the school year got fully underway. And very soon she and her friends had far worse things to worry about, as the Saturni descended on Daedalus.

They didn't come all at once. Two of the most prominent arrivals were Simone's parents, Archer and Isolde Freeland, who showed up a week after term began and moved into one of the best guest suites on the second floor. John Benway, the powerful head of the Saturni, arrived a day later, along with Father Ignatius Ragoczy, head of the Vatican's Curis Dei. They were followed by Sabien Belu, a liver-spotted old banker, his skin ill-fitting, as though it had once been stretched over a much larger man's frame, and Oswald Babb, a media consultant, all baby-faced vitriol in Armani and Gucci. Toshiro Nagoichi, a Japanese businessman, showed up with his Yakuza bodyguard in the middle of the night. And then there was Cecily Namath, the movie star, so cooly lovely she didn't look real, who drove up in a stretch limo followed by six SUVs full of paparazzi, who had heard she was shooting somewhere in the Garden District.

They were all given lavish accommodations, but that's where any level of comfort ended. Because everyone was walking around on eggshells, and any pretense of this being a normal school year vanished.

"What do they want?" Bella fretted. "Why are they here now?

Why couldn't they have gone someplace else? Anyplace else! It's like they're breathing down all our necks."

Nina told her friend to calm down.

"It's kind of good in a way," she reasoned. "This way we can find out what they've got planned. Although why I'm still alive is a good question." She shrugged. "Maybe the fact that I blew up their commanding general last spring isn't that big a deal. I mean what do you figure? Things like that probably happen every day."

She tried to make light of it, but the fact that the Saturni were there continued to scare her. The whole school was seething with resentment. All the teachers viewed their "guests" as a colossal intrusion on their sacrosanct class schedules, but their bitching was ecumenical: us versus them. Nina was just one of many students and was in no way singled out.

"Yes," professor Mwindo said, sighing loudly, "I know our current guests are fascinating, but there's no need to spend all day gawking at them like a school of hypnotized fish."

He was driven to this pronouncement by everyone in his classroom—boys and girls alike—staring through the window at Cecily Namath, clad only in a thong, doing her yoga practice.

Professor Mwindo pulled the window shade down and said, "Open your books, please, to The Missing Prince by Meister Eckhart, in which he speaks of the Skin Eater tradition of a lost or awaited savior. Mr. Archeron, would you please read lines one through eight and give us your interpretation?"

A straggle-haired young man in the first row rose and read, in an unfortunately nasal voice:

> "*My soul awaits the one most high,*
> *Lost and regained he was once dead*
> *And lives again, and will not die*
> *Till Cerberus its many heads*
> *Reveal. Oh sweet prince, come again*

*To judge the living dead, and give*
*Help to the ones who trust in vain,*
*And teach us once again to live.'*

"…and, um, I'm afraid I don't have any idea what it means, sir. I know you assigned it, and I did read it, but—" he ducked his head "—I had an awful lot of homework to do for professor Ariadne, and I'm afraid I spent all night researching soap tinctures, and … well, I don't know. Sir."

He sat back down again amid laughter and some ironic hand-clapping, and professor Mwindo sighed and said, "All right, let's throw it open to the floor. Anyone else here have any idea what Meister Eckhart is talking about?"

He ignored Bella, who was waving her hand from the front row. Nina reflected that he must get as sick as Alastaire did of Bella always having all the answers. She raised her hand and said, "Um, is he waiting for someone who will specifically redeem the Skin Eaters and help them to 'live' again? I mean, er, metaphorically, I guess? Of—of course you guys can't really 'live' again, I mean like come back to mortal life. Not … not that you'd even want to," she added quickly, seeing professor Mwindo frown. "I guess he means like, 'come back to a full appreciation of life' or some kind of a 'be all that you can be' idea."

"Oh, brother," she heard Bella mutter. And when the professor gave in and made a little oh, get on with it gesture, Bella said in a rush, "Meister Eckhart was one of the foremost apologists for the Skin Eaters, so of course he never wanted to suggest that any of them wanted to come back to mortal life. He's talking about the belief that through advanced calculation, mankind could communicate directly with the so-called mind of 'God,' what came to be referred to as the Heresy of the Free Spirit. In it, the seeds of what we've come to call Calculation Science were used to transcend the limitations and strictures set up by the Church, in the same way gnosticism claimed to be able to achieve perfect union with the divine intellect, and . . ."

Bella finally faltered, and added a little uncertainly, "And anyway, they all ended up burning everybody at the stake . . . the Church, I mean. This was all back in the fourteenth century. Meister Eckhart is, well, he's kind of a study of mine."

"You really are the world's biggest wonk," Nina said afterward, hugging Bella after they left the class. Since switching her sex, Bella was a lot more approachable physically (Nina wouldn't have dreamed of touching Bella when he was a boy). But she was also more vulnerable, and now her lower lip quivered.

"Yes. I really made a fool of myself, didn't I?"

"What are you saying? You knew the answer! You knew the answer better than old Wind-bag Mwindo did! I'll bet he's writing down what you said right now, just so he can incorporate it into the lesson plan for his next class."

"You really think so?" Bella brightened. "Because it really is fascinating. There's this whole tradition of a Lost Prince in Skin Eater mythology, kind of analogous to the legends of

Hiram Abiff and the building of Solomon's Temple . . ."

Nina stopped listening as they descended the big main staircase of the school, carpeted in such thick red plush it felt like she was walking on blood-soaked moss. She was thinking about how it might be nice to go out in the sunlight again, now that her classes were done for the day. Perhaps sit in the garden and do her homework. It was, after all, an even better guarantee of solitude than the library could offer. Even the Saturni didn't go outside if they could help it.

She thought, *I'll just grab an apple from the kitchen and tell Bella where I'm going, so she doesn't think I'm ditching her.* But her heart sank as she rounded the last landing and heard voices raised in tumultuous argument, and realized they'd just walked into the middle of a knock-down drag-out fight between the Danvers family and the Saturni.

"If you had bothered to inquire into recent events before summoning every single member of the Corpus Saturnum to *move in here*, you might have realized your enemies aren't even in New Orleans anymore!" Professor Danvers's voice was controlled, but it was also loud enough for him to be heard out on St. Charles Avenue. "Instead, you disrupt the *entire place* with your paranoia and your ridiculous insistence that they're going to return to the 'scene of the crime,' as you put it. And in the meantime, we have to put up with your entourages and your underlings and your secretaries and your massage therapists and now this! Your toadies! How many other people do you want to jam in here? It's like fucking Mardi Gras!"

"Strickland, stop frothing at the mouth." Dr. Isolde Freeland, Simone's ice queen mother, brushed imaginary dust from her white silk blouse. "It's just six extra people, and they're only here for one night. Surely Agatha can cope. Perhaps you could just send out for some Popeye's fried chicken."

"We can certainly feed your guests," Agatha Danvers said, her voice like acid. She was shaking with rage, and her face was as white as her brother's. "We can feed them and host them and do anything else you like, but Strickland's right, we're trying to run a school here. The whole faculty's up in arms, everyone's at sixes and sevens—"

"Aggie, be reasonable." Father Ignatius's voice was, as usual, feather-light. "Without us, you'd have no school. You'd have nothing. We hold your very livelihoods in the palms of our hands, so do you really want us to drop them? We can, you know."

"You can also go to hell." Strickland's voice was no longer shouting at anyone, but it was firm. He walked over toward the front door, his hands behind his back, his pace deliberate.

"Without us you'd have no future, so it's a stalemate. No Skin Eater children means no future armies for you to mobilize, no future semi-immortal cannon fodder. No, Goddamn it, don't look around and pout like a Vatican drag queen! Do me the courtesy of looking me in the eye, if nothing else. You can be supercilious with everybody else, but not with me!"

*He knows I'm here,* Nina thought, standing frozen in the half-shadows on the stairs, with Bella pressed against the wall behind her. *That's why he's walking over toward the door, to distract them.* She tried very hard not to move or even breathe. With the strange connection she and the assistant headmaster shared at such odd and inconvenient moments, she heard his voice inside her head, *"You really have the world's worst timing, Miss Lamb."* Her heart racing, she thought back, *Should I leave?* and heard him say, *"No. Stay still. I may need you."*

"Our bonds with the Saturni are, let's just say 'complicated,' and leave it at that." The assistant headmaster had switched, as if unconsciously, into lecturing mode. "Daedalus isn't, strictly speaking, vital to your schemes, but it is convenient. Without us, your activities would be a lot more visible, if nothing else. We Skin Eaters may be your lapdogs, but like the *horroi* you once had and lost, we can still bite."

The *horroi,* she thought. The terrible ghost dogs that lived with Sister Aquilina. She had seen them in her dreams, and at the house on Pauline Street, where Sister Aquilina had once lived. So the *horroi* had once belonged to the Saturni? Was that their grief, their howling sorrow, that they had once belonged to evil so palpable their very eyes were scoured clean by the sight?

She shuddered, although she was trying to keep still.

"Fuck this," John Benway snapped. The powerful head of the Benway Corporation looked fed up as always. "One thing I hate is going over old ground. Danvers, the last time we saw your sister, she was here. Now you're telling us she's left the state and we should believe you, why? You two are just the latest in a long, long line of people who've thought it would be a good idea to lie to us." His gaze went from the professor to Agatha and back again. "A long, long line. And it's always ended badly."

"Is that a threat?"

"Of course it's a Goddamn threat! What do you think I'm doing here, playing with myself? I don't like being here any more than you like having us!"

But there was something unconvincing about his disgust, and Nina wondered, why did the Saturni bring everybody there? Was there something about Daedalus that was more than just 'convenient'?

She stood there trying not to breathe, feeling her heart beat like a noisy, hammering traitor in her chest. She desperately wanted to sneak back up the stairs, but Professor Danvers's telepathic instructions kept her rooted in place.

"Frankly," Benway said, "I was going to ask you if you'd received any word from your sister, but since you brought it up, I've got to tell you I don't believe you either way. You and Agatha are far too eager to throw us out. What did the Cumaean Sybil say?"

"I-I beg your pardon?"

"Oh, I doubt she said that." Isolde laughed. "She's much too in your face for polite evasions. We know you went there, Strickland. And with her."

Professor Danvers's voice was tight. "Riddles, Isolde?"

"The little bitch. The sacrificial 'Lamb'." Isolde's husband, Archer Freeland, laughed. "We know what's going on. We know you've still got her hidden away here, for all your blank looks and buttoned-up denials. Where have you got her, anyway?" His laughter was lewd. "In your room? C'mon, you can tell us. Are you fucking her?"

Nina felt Professor Danvers's distaste, although his voice merely feigned disinterest.

"You really have no manners at all, do you? You don't care what you say, even in front of my remaining sister, and your wife. Ah well. No, Archer, I am not in your indelicate phrase 'fucking' her. I told you, Miss Lamb has left. She went with Niobe."

*So that's why they haven't made a big deal about my being here,* Nina thought. Professor Danvers had somehow convinced them that she'd gone. But how? They had to have seen her! She'd been in Commons every night having dinner. She'd been in all her classes. Then how . . .

And in the next moment, she heard Professor Danvers's voice in her head saying, *"All in good time. Right now, Miss Lamb, why don't you try coming downstairs and joining us?"*

And even though there was absolutely *no way* she was going to do that, she felt her feet move against her will, and her knees bent and she was walking down the stairs, even though she was trying with every ounce of her strength to resist it. Even Bella's panicked grip on her arm wasn't enough to stop her.

She walked down the stairs.

And they didn't see her.

She had the idea that they must be seeing something—maybe a faint ripple of air, maybe an anonymous shadow—but she certainly didn't draw anyone's attention as she moved forward, still seemingly by remote control. She heard Professor Danvers's voice in her head murmuring, "That's it, you're doing fine. Just head for the big mirror over on the wall."

*What the f—??*

*"Just do it."*

*They'll see me! They'll see it's me!*

*"Will they? Don't be too sure about that."*

*What are you doing?* she hissed telepathically. *Are* you *making me do this?*

"Partly. *You were wondering about this too, weren't you? Why they hadn't gone after you? Why they didn't recognize you? Well, this may explain it."*

She wanted to tell him he could explain his way right into a broken nose, but she was afraid to stop walking. She kept moving, wondering if he was also the one who had made her invisible.

"*No,* he answered. *The protection you have is far beyond my skills. I just needed to make sure you had it, so I decided to test it—"*

*You decided to test it? With me?*

"*Yes. For God's sake, calm down. Now go to the mirror and go through it. Now. Please. You'll be safe in Guinee. Go."*

She didn't like the idea of going to creepy Guinee without him, even though she'd been trying to get there for days. But she liked the idea of hanging around there with the Saturni even less. She looked into the mirror and saw herself transformed into someone completely featureless … someone so anonymous she truly didn't register … someone you couldn't see, even when you were looking right at her, and she thought, *okay, that's weird, but it's also a really, really useful trick. I wonder who's doing it?*

She narrowed her eyes, trying to see if there was any trace of her left in the completely featureless being reflected back at her, but the illusion was so perfect it unsettled her. *I feel like I'm not even here,* she thought. She could already feel the pull of the invisible fish-like hands on her, and then the mirror shimmered in front of her and got all thick and gooey again, and she felt herself being dragged toward it.

And was there a split second when the Saturni noticed? She saw Isolde Freeland whip around and stare at her, and she thought she heard her say sharply, "Strickland, what is that?"

But in the next instant it didn't matter. She was being pulled forward by the same small, cool, wet hands, and the same beautiful and awful coral city was forming and towering over her. She told herself she needed to be very careful this time, and look around and take note of everything and not to take any more detours or walk into any more Sludge Monsters or anything else that could eat her or kill her or frighten her. *Right. Like that would be really easy.* She took a deep breath, willing herself to be calm despite her still jangling nerves. Professor Danvers had said she'd be *safe* here. So. One step, and then another, although it was as always more like swimming. Or flying. She told herself she could do this. Carefully, with as little movement as possible, she looked around her to see who else was there.

And as before, the strange high halls and twisting corridors of Guinee were full of the movement of other people, some passing through, some bemused, some sightless, and some clearly dead or caught between one type of existence and the next. She marveled at it all. So many people. So many strange, odd shapes. Some of them looked human, while others were clearly different—some had wings, some feathers, some fins. Some were a tracery of fire burning like oil in water, a smoky orange flame. Some were charred husks, the life burned out. Some were encased in skin, smooth embryos, unborn. A woman passed her, an arm's reach away, her watery flesh a petrie dish of decomposition, maggots squirming into new life. A boy drifted past her at waist height, his cock grasped in his fist, his face convulsed. There were the damned and the angelic and the merely accidental here, the innocent and the adept combined, and she felt again the thrum of holiness echoing from the skull-clad walls.

And something else. Weeping. A deeply mortal, frightened, human keening of breathelessness and loss, the sound of someone drowning in their own tears, their breath ragged. Nina felt a deep, visceral pull to go to this person—if indeed it was a person, and not a corpse or a ghost—and comfort it in its heartbreak. *But be careful,* she thought. *There could be tricks here.* She remembered to move very slowly, putting one foot down in front of the other as she walked down a long arcade of overarching ribs, their coffered interstices ornamented with tiny rosettes of vertebrae. Here at the end, there was a crossroad, running left and right, and directly in front of her, a door. The handle was cool against her hand. She turned it, its metal grip moving easily, and was about to pull it open when a sharp blow pushed her to one side, making her turn around and say, "Ow! What the hell's going on?"

Facing her was Simone Freeland, but Simone as she'd never seen her before—her long blonde braids waving around her face like snakes and her dark skin accentuating the whites of her eyes. Those eyes were wide and furious and terrified all at once, and she spat out as if it were the worst insult in the world, "What the hell are you doing here? Are you absolutely crazy? If you open that door, you'll get us all killed! The worst thing in the world is in there, so knowing you, you probably want to let it out!"

# Chapter Nine

Nina's first comment was, "You recognized me."

"No shit. Why wouldn't I recognize you? I see you every day."

"No, that's not what I meant. I—I meant you recognized me all along, you didn't think I was invisible, or, I don't know, some sort of bewitched non-being or something. So why didn't you tell your parents I was still at Daedalus? Why didn't you rat me out?"

And her next thought was, *What are you doing here? Are they just giving away free tours to Guinee and you won one?*

Simone's beautiful face creased with something Nina had never thought she'd see-indecision. She bit her lip and then said, "Come on, it's too dangerous here. Let's go someplace quieter."

Nina wasn't sure she trusted Simone not to drag her off into some watery skull-cave and kill her, but she was also too curious to resist. Anything that scared Simone this badly had to be seriously messed up. She put up her chin and said, "Okay, you say where," and Simone glanced around and then said, "Anywhere but here. That crying is really creeping me out."

She led them down a narrow blue-green passageway between high blank walls, until they emerged into something like an enclosed square, maybe fifty feet across, with dark buildings on every side. There were impressive skull altars arranged all around the square, each with a glass-fronted case containing various mummified artifacts. There was a hand, an ear (which made

Nina giggle, it looked so silly) and a tiny thing that looked like a dried-up piece of chocolate.

"What are all these things supposed to be?" she asked, hating to admit her ignorance.

"Relics." Simone shrugged. "We don't know whose they are, in some cases. The ear?

That's Van Gogh's."

"*The* Vincent Van Gogh?"

"I'm so regretting bringing you here. Yes, 'the' Vincent Van Gogh. Starry Night. The whole thing. That little dried-up piece of shit there is the heart of Heinrich von Kleist." She pointed at what Nina had taken for a piece of chocolate. "He wrote that machines are infinitely smarter and more graceful than people, because they're not self-conscious."

"Do you believe that?"

"I don't know." Simone tossed her hair back, her own grace impeccable, even underwater. She hoisted herself up onto an altar behind which a huge, towering statue of an avenging angel stood. Its sword was held high, and its wings were made of thigh bones spread out like a fan. Nina steeled herself and hopped up onto the altar next to her.

"So . . . um, what are you doing here? I mean . . ." Nina struggled with how to put this. "Do you come here often?"

Simone, to her credit, laughed. "No. It's hard to get into Guinee on your own." She narrowed her eyes and said, "Presumably someone gave you access, too, and I can even guess who. In my case . . ." Her eyes slid away to scan the room. "My mother sent me."

Nina's mind flashed back to the time last spring, when she'd seen Simone's mother twist her arm behind her back and tell her not to screw things up. Now, however, Simone didn't look like she was hiding any bruises. Instead, Nina realized that Dr. Freeland might have pushed her daughter into Guinee for the same reason Professor Danvers had sent her there. To protect her.

"Did she . . .?" Nina made her voice sound as matter-of-fact as possible. "Did she send you here for safety?"

Simone's lovely shoulders rose and fell. She still wasn't looking at Nina, which might, Nina decided, be a good thing. Whenever their gazes met, they seemed to tear each other apart just on general principles. Maybe a little less eye contact would make it easier for them to have an actual conversation.

"My mom's . . . subtle. She'd never say something that obvious, but yes, I think she did."

Nina figured she'd be polite. "She must really love you."

"Ha!" Simone's laughter was sharp. "'Love' isn't a word in the Freeland vocabulary."

The black girl examined her perfectly manicured nails, and Nina had the idea if she hadn't been so cool, she might have nibbled on one of them. Not knowing how to respond, she finally settled on, "So why did she send you through here to Waterworld? Is she afraid someone's going to hit on her perfect daughter before she gets to marry you off?"

"Yes. Actually. In a way." Simone's lip curled. "The guy's named Sir Keith Wolf, and he's a total dick."

Nina thought she recognized him. "Isn't he the guy who owns Wolf News, and all those radio stations?"

"Yeah." Simone crossed her legs. "He's like seriously trying to worm his way into the Saturni's inner circle, even though he's a mortal. Can you believe it? He's not even a Skin Eater." She did that hair flip again. "Not a fucking prayer, but Benway thinks it's funny to humor him. And yes, he's got a big appetite for brown sugar. A lot of those racists do." She looked at Nina appraisingly. "So watch yourself."

Nina digested this in silence. She knew she was of mixed race, but that was all. Like everything else about her past before the hurricane, any knowledge about her parents had been washed away. Now sitting there in the strange, wavy blue light of Guinee, listening to the faint hiss-hiss of the invisible waves breaking and retreating through caverns of death and breathing in the watery atmosphere that still felt like air, she thought this might, in a way, be an olive branch.

There might almost have been a truce between them.

"So why can you see me when your parents can't?"

"I have no idea." Simone waved her hand. "Maybe because they're pure-blooded Saturni? I mean, think about it. They've never been human in any way, they're pure self-willed forces, so they don't know about people's insides. I don't mean like their spleens or anything, but their interior thoughts and feelings, the private bits of people that can't be disguised."

Simone rolled her eyes and laughed even at herself. "Their souls."

"You think we have souls?"

"I think it's easier to believe that here where we're snorting sea-water and sitting around with people's ears than it is upstairs."

Nina laughed as well. "Well, thanks for the warning. I've got enough drama in my life without having some Eurotrash fascist lusting after my bod."

"You never know. You could get your own talk show."

"Nah. The douche factor would still be way too high."

The other girl's mouth twitched. "You know, you're funny when you're not being a total grandfather-killing bitch."

Nina tried her own shoulder-lift. It wasn't quite as graceful as Simone's, but it was close.

"Yeah, well, I'm sorry about that. He was trying to kill the assistant headmaster."

"Whom you have on speed-dial for your own personal booty call."

Nina flinched. She said, a little too quickly, "That's ridiculous. He's like two hundred years old, and besides, even if he only looks thirty, he's still thirty."

"And that makes him inappropriate, how?"

Nina took a minute to process this. She said finally, much more slowly than she wanted to, "So . . . let me get this straight. By your saying Professor Danvers is a legitimate lust magnet, am I safe in assuming you like him too?"

Simone hesitated longer than she had before. When she spoke again, she looked away across the square, to where a trio of mummified corpses stood propped up in their own glass case. They wore frilly bonnets, delicate white dresses, and flowers in their hair, and looked like they were ready to go on a really, really disgusting picnic.

"I did like him once. Professor Danvers has some major issues, as I guess you're finding out. We did a crossing. He put some of his death into me and took a little of my life. And bottom line? It was ghastly." She shut her eyes. "Something went terribly wrong."

Clearly Simone was trying to pretend it was no big deal, but Nina saw her shiver and wrap her arms around herself. She didn't want to hear anymore, and at the same time, she desperately did.

"What happened?"

"I imagine he did it partly to get in tight with my parents. Which was okay. I mean I understand ambition. I wasn't even bothered by that. And he was okay, I mean he didn't rape me or anything. It wasn't even my first crossing. But still . . . it was like being torn to pieces. I can't tell you how much it hurt."

The rich girl swallowed. "Like knives slicing through me. Afterward, all I wanted to do was get out of there and go off by myself. And he looked like it was rough for him, too, although I don't know . . . some men seem to like that. Some guys think it's a real turn-on when a woman screams." She continued to look at the trio of embalmed girls, and Nina saw a muscle tighten in her jaw. "So, does he like it when you scream? Or haven't you crossed with him yet?"

Simone's eyes moved to her and regarded her speculatively. And then they widened with shock, and Nina thought, *Oh God, I wish I had a poker face. Or maybe just a poker. Then I could bash Simone's head in. Or maybe my own.*

"Well, well, well . . ." the rich girl said, and all her cruelty was back by a factor of ten.

"Haven't you crossed with anyone yet? Shit, you're not telling me the big bad kick-ass Buffy of Daedalus is really a Skin Eater virgin?"

Nina felt the heat index of her face accelerate to the point where she thought the water around her might boil. She said, trying to sound calm, "N-no. I mean, *no*, I haven't crossed with anyone yet. *Some* of us aren't major league ho's who'll put out for anybody with an immortal hard-on."

Which didn't help. Simone was laughing, really laughing, and after a moment Nina muttered, "Yeah, okay, maybe not the best choice of words . . ." and she felt her own laughter bubbling up, despite the wholly creepy idea that Professor Danvers might like girls who scream.

And just for a moment, it felt like they were almost friends, giggling about the same cute boy.

Which was bizarre enough, but the next minute Nina felt like she was being sucked up through the ceiling in a long, invisible straw, and between her hair whipping around her face and the sensation that she was being stretched out like an elongated strand of spaghetti, she abandoned all thoughts of a kumbaya moment and instead focused on not panicking and flailing around like an idiot.

*Wait— wait—* she thought, as Simone disappeared, even though the feeling that she was becoming thinner and thinner made it impossible to breathe, and she felt like if she was stretched any further, she'd break apart like an over-stretched piece of Silly Putty. She dearly hoped it was Professor Danvers doing the pulling, and not Simone's mother, but there was no time to question her destination in any case, because the lack of oxygen was starting to make her dizzy and she could feel her head spinning, black spots dancing in front of her eyes.

Just before she passed out, she felt herself collapse onto a very nice oriental rug, and she enjoyed feeling her regular size again, and spent a few seconds getting well acquainted with the weave and pattern of the carpet. Meanwhile, she tried very, very hard not to puke.

"Shall I give you some Tums next time?" came the murmured comment from up above her, which was followed a moment later by Professor Danvers's hands cupping her shoulders with surprising gentleness. "Traveling to Guinee seems to play havoc with your digestion."

His voice was soft, and he was stroking her back and her shoulders in little comforting circles. With considerable effort, she stopped her dry heaving and said, "It's . . . just a little unusual, that's all. I'm sure after a while I'll get used to being smothered and drowned and pulled apart and squashed into two dimensions. I guess I'm just a slow learner."

She heard a chuckle, low in his throat, which was so beguiling she lost the last of her nausea and became very still, concentrating on the feeling of his hands on her back. His slow stroking of her muscles. His kindness. How could someone like that enjoy causing somebody else pain? And not a little pain either. Simone had said it felt like knives. This was such a puzzle she shifted and sat up and looked at him, and he immediately stopped stroking her and went and sat back down behind his desk, as though she'd caught him off-guard. Which she supposed in a way she had.

"Sir?"

"Yes?"

"What was that all about? What just happened? One minute I was coming downstairs and the next minute you had me testing out whether I was protected by a . . . a spell or something." She shook her head. "I mean, I know you guys don't believe in magic, but I'm sorry, I don't know what other word to use. You wanted to find out if someone . . . or something . . . was making me invisible to those people. And there was. Which is okay. Great! And then the next thing I knew you were sending me to Guinee." The truth of what had actually happened washed over her. "Why, for God's sake? You can't just jerk me around. What does it all mean?"

He sighed. "Miss Lamb, of course I can jerk you around. I'm the assistant headmaster here, and you're a student. That means I hold effective veto power over every action of your life, waking or otherwise, whether you like it or not, and regardless of whether it's fair or not. The fact that I did it to protect you, as I said, should at least keep you from biting my head off. Would you have preferred if I'd left you there to chat pleasantly with Jack Benway until even his blind pride and colossal ignorance allowed him to smell a rat?"

"N-no," she admitted, feeling like she'd lost the edge of her argument without even quite knowing what her argument was. She realized she was still sitting on the floor, and scrambled to her feet, but her legs were wobbly and she lurched forward and reached for the edge of his desk to steady herself. "But . . . sir, you don't understand. The next minute I was in Guinee, and there was someone crying, and Simone Freeland was there and she said it was incredibly dangerous, and . . ."

"Simone was there?" he interrupted her. His surprise was evident.

"Yes. She said her mom had sent her through to get her away from some old geezer who was trying to hit on her, someone named Wolf . . . Keith Wolf, I think it was?"

Professor Danvers's eyebrows shot up. "The media mogul? My God, will wonders never cease. Well, go on. There's clearly more you want to tell me."

"No, sir," she said, clamping her mind down on the memory of Simone's confession of crossing with Professor Danvers, and how much it had hurt. *I do* not *need him seeing that in my mind.* She shook her head. "We just talked for a while, and actually it was kind of nice . . . it's like when you're in Guinee some of the day-to-day crap gets washed away and you can start over again. Then I felt this whole pull-y thing, and I guess that's when you yanked me away. I don't know if she's still there or not. She was . . . well . . . it was strange." Nina hesitated. "It didn't sound like her mom likes her that much, to tell you the honest truth. I mean I always thought she was Little Miss Creole Princess. But this time she just sounded . . . sad. And scared. I . . . I actually felt kind of sorry for her."

"Miss Freeland is many things, but I scarcely think 'pitiful' is the first adjective that springs to mind." Professor Danvers paused and then added drily, "In fact, if Sir Keith Wolf is enamored of her, all I can say is I'm sorry for the unfortunate press-lord."

Nina wanted to laugh, but she wasn't sure if that was appropriate. She said, sticking to her point, "Well anyway, whatever was behind that locked door really freaked her out, and I didn't think anything short of another hurricane could do that. She said it was the worst thing in the world, and it could kill us all. Professor, do you have any idea what she was talking about?"

But Professor Danvers was frowning suddenly, and her attempt at drawing him out had, as usual, fallen flat. He just said, "Hmm. Things are changing faster than I'd expected," which was exactly the sort of thing people always said when they wanted to drive you crazy.

He waved his hand. "Nina, if you're feeling better, please leave me. I have a ridiculous amount of work to do, and our guests certainly aren't helping. I should tell you, Sir Keith and a number of other mortal humans will be joining us for dinner tonight, and as you can well imagine, Agatha's already ready to bite the plaster off the walls. Simone will have to put in an appearance; however, I wouldn't waste any sympathy on her. She's quite capable of looking out for herself."

There was the ghost of a smile around his lips, just the barest hint that they were sharing a joke. *And that's what's so infuriating,* she thought, *he brushes me off and then he flirts with me.* She got out of his office before she could say or do anything else, and walking back upstairs to her room, she still found herself shaking and had to hang onto the banister. *Shit, shit, shit.* At least the Saturni were no longer around. Maybe they were all back in their rooms resting up for tonight's big feast. Nina spared a moment to wonder if they were going to eat human flesh, and what they were going to use now that all the mortal kids in the school had been spirited away. She pictured them going out on the street and finding some old drunk and butchering him, and would his flesh already be marinated? She thought she might be going insane.

Letting herself into her room, she lay down on the bed and stared up at the ceiling, finding its bare plaster oddly comforting after the grand, Gothic caverns and spires of Guinee. Slow, deep breaths. She told herself to think of nothing, to think of blank water, to think of moonlight, to think of empty space. Gradually, her heartbeat slowed and she saw a clear expanse of water, flat and silvery under a night sky. A pond? A lake? She didn't know. She felt like she was floating, and the moon was shining down on her upturned face. She felt a deep longing she knew she'd felt before, and she thought, *Where are you? Where have you gone? I miss you so.*

And then the dream or whatever it was changed, and she thought she saw a familiar woman in a long black dress, and she heard the words in her head, *"I'm still here."* And then, *"Look at the engraving."*

And because there was a logic to dreams that made perfect sense even though in waking life they made no sense at all, Nina got up and lifted her copy of The Science of the Mysteries off her desk and picked up the engraving of the three Danvers siblings and looked at it.

And then she stopped, narrowed her eyes, and looked again. Because the headmaster of the Daedalus School was back, Mr. O'Brien, standing this time in the center of the engraving, and his hand was on the shoulder of the little child, who was now revealed quite clearly to be a little boy.

# CHAPTER TEN

"So who is it?"

"That's what I'm trying to tell you. I don't know who it is. Aren't you two even listening to me? Stop stuffing your faces for a second and concentrate."

Nina pulled the plate of watery scrambled eggs away from under Alastaire's nose, and Bella shoved her own untouched plate away and said, "Of course we're listening, Nina, but how are we supposed to guess who this child is? We haven't even seen him."

Which was perfectly true. Nina had spent the entire evening the day before studying the engraving, even skipping dinner, which in itself had been no hardship. She'd been able to hear the sounds of drunken partying going on downstairs, and at one point someone had even started to sing a verse of "Sit on my face" in a slurry tenor followed by a resounding crash. She could just picture the Saturni whooping it up in the school's private dining room, and she didn't want to go anywhere near them.

But the engraving itself had offered her an equally troubling vision, because now it kept changing. Sometimes the little boy stood next to Professor Danvers, sometimes he was holding Niobe's hand, and once he had been sitting at a little table off to the side while Agatha fed him something out of a cup. Sometimes the headmaster was sitting in a chair reading a book, and once he and Strickland had had their heads together playing chess.

It became a weird kind of game: she'd go off and do something else for a minute (look out the window, take off her school uniform, brush her teeth) and when she looked back, the picture would have changed again. She never saw it move. There didn't seem to be a pattern to the changes, nor was there anything in particular going on: just a collection of people spending an afternoon in fancy dress in a garden. She had the feeling she might be missing some things (what was that round object the headmaster was holding up in one version of the picture, that looked halfway between a small globe and a baseball?) but she couldn't be sure.

Finally, she had fallen asleep exhausted with her cheek on the engraving itself, and only barely missed drooling all over it. She was consequently a little impatient the next morning, especially since the engraving had now stopped changing and was looking exactly the same as it had before.

Alastaire tried to get her to see the bright side. "At least you know it's a boy now, and not a little girl. I mean, there's no chance it's you, is there? And when Nina stared at him, and Bella just looked uncomfortable and stared at the floor, he added, "I mean, you were thinking that, right? That you might be Sister Aquilina's kid?"

Nina had in fact been thinking exactly that, from the first time she'd seen the child in the engraving. But she'd also been telling herself it was impossible. If the picture was 200 years old, surely she hadn't been alive all that time without remembering it? There were limits to even the strongest amnesia. Weren't there? How could you forget centuries?

Besides, if she was Niobe's daughter, what did that make Professor Danvers?

Her relative?

Her uncle?

Her father?

Ugh.

She retreated behind logic. The Skinnies couldn't have any biological children. That's why they adopted them. That's why they abducted children to raise as their own. If the child in the engraving was Niobe's . . . that meant he had to have been born before she became a Skin Eater.

Nina shrugged and said, "Look, I don't know anything. I always come back to wondering who I am, but let's just drop it, okay? There are too many mysteries here as it is. The headmaster, for one thing. I mean he's supposed to be dead, but we know he's not dead, and he's there sometimes, and sometimes he's not, and I just get the feeling he's trying to tell me something . . . but I'm too stupid to see it."

She drank her coffee, which tasted suspiciously like instant. In New Orleans, of all places. Agatha couldn't even make a good cup of coffee. The Commons was full of students who were busy eating the awful breakfast as quickly as possible so they could go out and enjoy their free Sunday. Nina had a feeling the first place they'd head would be Magazine Street, where they could get a decent brunch.

Bella, who had been tactfully keeping silent during the whole discussion of Nina's parentage, chimed in now, "So what does the headmaster do whenever you see him? And what objects has he been holding?"

"Well . . ." Nina frowned. She ticked them off on her fingers. "Sometimes he's holding a small ball, about five or six inches across." She showed them. "It's blue sometimes and white others, and sometimes it's dark gray. Sometimes he's got his hands up like this." She held her arms up in a posture of surrender, palms out. "Sometimes they're down at his sides, but he's still got his palms out. In those cases, he's not holding anything. And other times he's just hanging out, you know. Reading and stuff."

"Could you see the title of the book he's reading?"

"No," Nina admitted, embarrassed that she hadn't thought of that. "It's a big book, like a picture book. Bright yellow. It looks kind of like a kid's book, but did they have things like Dr. Seuss back in those days?"

Bella shrugged. "You realize, of course, that the engraving might not be that old?"

"I thought of that. People dress up here in New Orleans all the time, or wherever it is. It looks tropical. But even so, why would three adults be reading a children's book? It looks—I don't know. Silly."

"Hmm." Bella had gotten out her polynomial engine and was typing some letters and numbers into it. Since Alastaire had given Nina her PE the previous spring (and Nina had promptly put it away in a drawer and forgotten all about it) both she and Nina craned over Bella's shoulders to see what she was doing.

"What's 'X = arcanum/3 + (2 x 4)y'?" Alastaire asked, and Nina added, "Um, yeah . . . what he said."

"It's a past-tense algorithm," Bella said, scrolling down a list of possible topics and punching in: date, location, children's book (possibly), and cloaked. "This should give us some indication of whether the engraving is really old or not, and might address some of your other questions as well."

She put the tips of her fingers on the little metal plates on either side of the small clockwork box and shut her eyes in concentration. After a few moments she said, "Hmm, the engraving appears to be genuine, as far as I can tell. It shows a house in Haiti before the revolution, but there are some strange anomalies."

She punched in some more numbers and letters, and Nina reflected that maybe she ought to get out her polynomial engine and practice. She felt frustrated she hadn't thought of doing this herself. Why can't I be smart and logical like Bella, she wondered, or brave and calm like Alastaire (who, true to form, was slurping up the rest of his eggs, having clearly decided that a lousy breakfast was better than nothing). She felt very dissatisfied with herself, and said, "Well, maybe I should just give the engraving to one of you to hang onto for a while, and maybe you'll have better luck with it. I don't seem to be able to figure out anything."

"No, that won't work," Bella said, putting down her PE and rubbing her temples. "It's a Mezzotint conundrum."

"A whosit?"

"A Mezzotint conundrum. It's a device intended to convey a message in code, like a rebus. You know how a rebus is like a picture of an eye and a heart and the letter U, and it means 'I Love You?' Well, this is like that, but it's only intended to be seen by one person, in this case you. I mean, Y-O-U, not the letter . . . well, okay, yes, you understand. Anyway, a Mezzotint conundrum's incredibly difficult to make, and they're almost impossible to fake, which means the engraving's definitely trying to tell you something."

Bella frowned and touched her polynomial engine, as though she were checking to make sure she'd gotten every last piece of information out of it. Nina thought it almost looked like she was afraid she might receive a shock from it. She felt impatient and stood up.

"Wonderful. Let's go for a walk. I feel claustrophobic . . . Guinee's really depressing. I feel like everything around me's pressing in and making me want to do something, and I don't even know what. Yeah, yeah, I know, you guys don't like sunlight, but can't you just wear a hat? Carry an umbrella? Jeez, it's like I'm living with a couple of albinos. I've gotta get out of here."

She grabbed a baseball cap from a coat rack in the hallway and stuffed it onto Alastaire's head as Bella grabbed an umbrella, and they followed her outside. The students were streaming out through the front gate, most of them wrapped up in scarves and jackets to protect them from the sun. One girl was actually wearing a bedsheet. *God, this really is a weird place*, Nina thought. How strange that in the course of six months, she'd gone from viewing Daedalus as a prison to thinking of it as her home. Now she thought claustrophobia wasn't really the right word for how she felt. She didn't feel hemmed in so much as pressured, like she was being sucked up through a different kind of straw. Things were changing, faster than even Professor Danvers knew, and she almost wished she could go back to feeling terrified again. It would be better, in a way, than feeling nostalgic.

*I don't want to miss this place when I go*, she thought. *I don't want to miss these people*, and she had the feeling she might be going (somewhere? anywhere?) sooner than she expected.

Still, the day was fine, and the Garden District was hazy with the diffused light of autumn in the deep South, a season so warm it made the dry leaves and acorns on the sidewalks seem like leftovers from somebody else's fall. They walked down Chestnut Street, not really with any destination in mind, just looking at the different houses—Greek revival, classical Georgian, Queen Anne, and the occasional modern ranch house all set down next to one another in a companionable jumble so it felt like a small town. As always, Nina marveled that a busy city, rebuilding and coming back since the storm, lay just a few streets away. Here, everything felt timeless. Slippery Annie, a toothless old black woman who wandered the streets wearing a bathrobe and Mardi Gras beads, shuffled past them talking to herself, and barely glanced in their direction.

"Look, there's a little snake," Nina said, pointing to a small, bright green snake, barely six inches long, which lay in awkward kinks on the sidewalk. "Is it hurt? It looks like it's hurt."

Alastaire squatted down next to it and touched it. "It's in some kind of spasm," he said, picking it up and stroking its smooth skin. "Look. When I try and straighten it out, it wants to knot right back up again into a . . . almost like it's trying to make a spiral."

It was true. As they watched, the snake curled tightly around itself, making a ball, and Bella said, "Put it down! For God's sake, Alastaire, put it down this minute!"

"What, are you afraid of snakes?" Alastaire waved it at her, grinning. "I thought you were the science wonk. Are you going all girlie on us?"

His smile was teasing, but he lowered the snake again when he saw how frightened Bella was. The Vietnamese girl backed away from them, her ivory face so pale it was almost green.

"It's a sign," she whispered. "Snakes do that when a terrible storm is coming. Something worse than a hurricane, something like the end of . . . of . . . shit, I really don't want to say this, but the end of the world."

Alastaire, to give him credit, stepped away from the snake so fast it might have been a cottonmouth. It slithered away into the grass and disappeared. He said, after taking a moment to catch his breath, "Okay, so you've officially made me wish I was wearing Depends. Now, you want to explain that?"

Bella looked away, down the street, to where a dog was barking someplace. She kicked a stray piece of asphalt (*God,* Nina thought, *the streets really are falling apart since the storm*) and said, "Well, I've been reading things. Quite a lot, actually."

"Uh . . . gee. What a quote-unquote surprise." Alastaire dropped the snark and actually took Bella's hand, giving it a quick, embarrassed squeeze. "I'm sorry. What have you been reading? Something seriously weird, I'm guessing?"

"Yes." The slender girl took a slow breath. Nina remembered

him as a boy: sensitive and thin-skinned. He/she looked even more fragile now.

"It's about the Skin Eater Lost Prince. You remember we studied about him in class?" Alastaire looked blank, so Bella wasted a moment to do her requisite sigh and explained, "He's like a savior, or a . . . I don't know, a destroyer. It's ambiguous, he could be both. For a while, yes, I thought it might be Nina, but I don't think so. The pronoun is universally male. But the thing is, there are various signs and omens that are supposed to happen when the Lost Prince is due to make his appearance. Snakes will send signals. Masks will drop. I don't know what that means exactly, but I'm guessing it means people will reveal their true selves. Mirror-images will show up. I don't know. I don't know anything."

She smiled a little reluctantly. "Yeah, I know what you're thinking. You want me to put that in writing. I will if you want. It's just that . . . I think Guinee's a part of it, too, and the prophecy the Sybil told Nina."

She quoted, "'Follow the water and the mirrors. That's where your savior lies.' See, it all fits. It all means the Lost Prince is out there somewhere already, and wherever he is, it's already happening. Whatever terrible or wonderful thing is coming, his return is already in the works. And whatever we're supposed to do, well . . . we're a part of it too." She shook her head. "Whether we want to be or not. We're already in this thing up to our teeth."

She swallowed and added in a lower voice, "I've been thinking about Sister Aquilina too. Or Niobe Danvers, whatever you want to call her. I think her disappearing may have just made things worse. The Saturni are all stirred up, and they don't care about any of us, you know. That's the real truth. If there really is some kind of war coming, and they can't use us as bait or as pawns . . . well, we may just be excess baggage. That's what I'm most afraid of. And if Niobe's really planning on fighting back . . . I mean Sister Aquilina . . ."

She broke off and looked across the street, and they saw her eyes go wide. They were standing in front of a tall, ramshackle house that was a maze of gables and turrets and stained-glass windows, all painted every color of the rainbow, and almost all of it obscured by leaves. There was a big live oak tree out front, dripping with vines, a fig tree heavy with figs, a loquat tree with bright yellow fruit, and another tree whose fruit was bright orange. The wrought-iron fence was peeling and hadn't been painted in decades, and high tufts of grass were growing up between the posts. The house itself looked hidden in plain sight, a massive structure you might not even notice until you were right on top of it, but that wasn't what had caught her attention.

What she had noticed, what they all noticed at the same time, and what made Alastaire say, "Wait a minute—" and Nina say, "WTF—" was the name on the mailbox.

The script was written in curlicues of black ink, so it stood out against the tarnished brass.

And the name written there was Captain Bowman.

# Chapter Eleven

"Huh."

Nina looked at Alastaire and said, "Huh? Is that all you can say? We just find ourselves standing in front of a house that belongs to somebody named Bowman, and Bowman was the name Niobe used when she hid out at the school last spring, and all you can say is 'Huh'? What are you, a moron?"

"Hey, don't call me names!" Alastaire looked angry. "What do you want me to say? It's a coincidence, Neens. What's the big whoop? Lots of people are named Bowman."

"You don't think it makes a difference, even though Bella just said masks would drop and snakes would send signals and mirror-images would show up, and we could be faced with the death of the Skin Eaters and everything we know, and all that's not a big deal?"

"Actually, it's the existential question," said a man, standing on the other side of the fence, regarding them pleasantly. "What do we do when all the rule books get thrown out the window? Nietzsche celebrated the death of God, but then Nietzsche died raving. How do you do?" he added. "I'm Captain Bowman. I just came out to get my mail."

He lifted the lid of the mailbox, and said, "Alas, no one writes to the general. Or me, apparently, but I heard you talking, and I just decided to butt in, which is actually quite a habit of mine. I did want to point out, though, that coincidences are often a feature of life, and nothing to be afraid of. For instance, Bowman is indeed a common name. You find it all over the place."

The tall man standing there looked to be in his mid-sixties, with a trim gray beard and thick eyebrows. He added, "So since you already know who I am, may I ask you who you are?"

The fact that they were all dressed in Daedalus School uniforms (which were heavy on black and red satin) made Nina think it must be pretty obvious what they were. Oddly enough, though, the captain looked honestly curious.

"Um, we're all students from . . ." She dropped her voice and muttered, "the Daedalus School," and Captain Bowman said, "Um-hmm. Actually, I meant your names."

"Oh . . . oh, okay, yeah. I'm Nina Lamb, and this is Alastaire Roget and Bella . . . um . . . or is it still Bellocq?" She looked at Bella, who shrugged. "Bella Chopin. He's . . . I mean she's . . . she's still going through some identity issues."

"Aren't we all?"

Captain Bowman, whose eyes were pale blue, gave her a keen look, which made her feel unnerved for some reason. She said, "I . . . I know you just said it was a common name, but you're . . . you're not related to Sally Bowman, are you?"

"I don't think so." He frowned. "No, almost certainly not. And here I was thinking you were fans of my book. Perhaps you've read it? *The Science of the Mysteries.*"

Nina blinked. "You wrote that book?"

"Yes, indeed." There was a twinkle in Captain Bowman's eyes. "Go ahead and ask me whatever else you want."

"Well, give me a minute. I'm still processing."

"Take all the time you want. Perhaps you'd like a persimmon?"

He reached over to a small tree and picked a smooth orange-skinned fruit. "Persimmons are really fascinating." He put the fruit in her hand. "They're beautiful, like habanero peppers, but not everything that looks luscious is without risk. Habaneros will burn your mouth they're so hot. Persimmons are the same way. Some are sweet. Some, though, like the kind from this tree, are incredibly sour. They have tannins in them like tea. So to really experience them, you have to wait for them to ripen until they almost rot, and then the flesh gets all soft and pulpy, and it's delicious. Like custard."

Nina looked at the beautiful fruit, which looked like something you'd want to taste right that second and frowned. *So it's all a trick,* she thought. Like so many things in life, it was a lie. Even something as simple as eating was filled with danger, when human meat was on the menu. Better to starve. She handed the fruit back to him.

Captain Bowman took a big bite out of the persimmon and chewed with gusto as the juice ran down his chin. She couldn't help herself. She laughed.

"You got me!"

"Yes. That's also something to bear in mind. Warnings aren't always prohibitions. And actually, all hungers are natural. Fruit, flowers, even galaxies all have their own presiding spirits, and their rules are good simply because they are their rules. And they're honest. By the way, would you like to come inside?" he added, gesturing toward the house. "I have some other food there that's less tricky. Sweet tea, and I believe I have some marzipan cake which I'm told is quite good. We could discuss the *Mysteries* some more. I'm sure you have many questions."

The idea of having tea and cake with this bizarre stranger didn't entirely make her feel all warm and fuzzy, but picking his brains did sound like a good idea. She tossed her head and said, "Sure," and opened the gate, and then looked back over her shoulder and asked her friends, "You guys want to join me, or should I meet you later on back at the school?"

Bella looked like she expected the captain to expose himself, and Alastaire didn't look much happier, but they both said, "Um

. . . sure, we're coming," and followed her up the path. As they did so, the sound of barking came to them again, and a moment later two large dogs came racing around the side of the house, a German shepherd and a black lab, eager to throw themselves on the new arrivals and make their (very slobbery) acquaintance.

"Mind the dogs," the captain murmured, and Nina repressed a laugh. With their paws on everyone's shoulders, they were hard to ignore, much less "mind." She said, "Wow, they're really friendly. What are their names?"

"Leopold and Loeb? Sacco and Vanzetti? I don't know, it depends on what kind of a mood I'm in. So many things have so many names."

He opened the door and added, "Come on inside. I'm afraid things are a bit of a mess right now, but then that's very often the case."

Actually "a bit of a mess" turned out to be a gigantic understatement. They could barely get in the front door, what with the hallway being jammed full of overflowing cartons of paper, tall stacks of newspapers, enormous, tottering piles of books, and, in a far corner, what looked like a huge flag pinned up so it covered one whole wall. It was finely embroidered with sequins and pieces of cloth and paintings and tiny glass beads, and showed a colossal woman, her skin and face and arms and legs all made out of smaller images so she looked like a mosaic of tiny pictures, or a strange, unsettling (but actually kind of beautiful) Frankenstein monster.

"La Manman Gaye," the captain said, nodding his head toward her in a completely unselfconscious gesture of worship. "She was embroidered by a dear friend of mine ages ago. I imagine she could be translated as 'Mama Gaia,' if you wanted to get all New Agey about her. She represents the union of all the *Lwas*, or spirits in voodoo. The whole pantheon. Of course it's a somewhat radical idea. Good and evil so rarely cohabit in our Manichean world. In that image, they're portrayed as one and the same."

He sidled between two piles of what looked like encyclopedias piled up nearly to the ceiling, and said, "I think we can probably find more room in the music room than anywhere else." He pointed to his right. "I'll just work my way back to the kitchen if you don't mind, and see what refreshments I can find . . . please, make yourselves at home . . ."

He disappeared into the dimness at the back of the hall, and Nina, Alastaire, and Bella made their way into what they guessed was the music room, which did indeed have a large upright piano backed up against one wall, but which also held a small printing press, stacks of newsprint, a collection of antique rifles piled up in one corner, and boxes labeled with the word "Ammo" in various languages.

Alastaire looked around and said, "Okay, so tell me again why we're here? This guy's like a loony survivalist! He probably has gold bullion buried under the floor, and enough canned goods to survive for six months if terrorists take out the Superdome. Let's bail."

"No," Nina said. "I mean, okay, he's a little weird . . . but I've got a feeling about him. I think he can tell us stuff. And we need to know what's going on. This shit's getting too strange otherwise. I mean this guy literally wrote the book on mysteries, and he's supposed to be a world expert on tribal religions, and he certainly knows a lot about voodoo. So grab hold of your man marbles and let's at least hear to what he has to say."

Captain Bowman caught her last words as he came back in, carrying a tray with a pitcher of iced tea, four glasses, and a plate piled with several thick slices of cake. He smiled as he looked around for a place to put it and finally settled on the top of the printing press.

Nina said, "Um . . . sorry if that sounded rude."

"No need to apologize. That was very well spoken. I forget you young people today are somewhat impatient. However, there's still time for civilized practices, like the taking of tea and refreshment." He handed around the glasses, and Alastaire took a large bite of cake and seemed resigned to the idea of sticking around, at least for a little while.

"Now. Miss Lamb." Captain Bowman sat down and regarded her. "I'm going to be blunt, not merely because of the need for haste, but because you remind me of someone I once loved very dearly. Someone I was unfortunately unable to protect, however much I wanted to. I was too young, perhaps, and too selfish . . ."

"The woman Anais?" Nina asked. "Your guide in Haiti?"

He raised his eyebrows and said, "Why yes, I suppose you're right about that, too, although I was thinking about somebody else. So often I've been weak, or impetuous, or distracted." He shook his head. "Anyway, you realize that you're in terrible danger."

"Yeah," Nina muttered. "I kind of got that idea. Actually, I was hoping you might give us some idea of how to fight them. The Saturni, I mean."

"Why, of course. That's what I'm here for."

"Really?" Nina thought that was a little too convenient, but she plunged ahead anyway. "For one thing, do you have any idea why they can't see me? I mean, they can see that I'm somebody, they can see somebody's there, but they can't recognize it's me. It's like I'm hiding in plain sight."

Captain Bowman nodded and said, "That sounds like a *miroir d'intent*. It's a reflection of what people expect you to be, or literally what they project your intent should look like. It's quite a complicated enchantment, but it means that if someone expects you to be a very different person than who you are, they can't see you. In effect, you are hiding in plain sight, because they're not really looking for you, they're only looking for who they think you are."

"And does it always work? I mean, am I invisible to them indefinitely?" This sounded pretty good, but unfortunately the captain shook his head.

"No. It's usually quite site specific. I imagine it only works at the school. It's hard to make everyone mistake what they're seeing and think apple, when what they're really seeing is an orange. For example, I can see you quite clearly."

"Yeah, I guess so." Nina abandoned her plan to become Invisibility Girl and avoid the upcoming fight altogether. Instead she asked, "So you've been fighting the Saturni for quite a while?"

"Yes, ever since I became aware of their menace." Captain Bowman frowned. "I was ignorant of the scope of their malice for far too long. But since I've realized what it entails, I've devoted my life to its annihilation."

"Which involves stockpiling weapons and hoarding old newspapers?"

Bella had recovered enough of her poise to start asking questions, and the captain turned and beamed at her. "Yes! You really are an extraordinarily bright young woman. No longer the ugly duckling, I see. Bella the Swan."

Alastaire made a stifled *yuk-yuk* noise, and when their host raised his eyebrows, he said apologetically, "Er . . . never mind."

"No, that's all right. I don't mind at all. Actually, birds are such wonderful metaphors. Now you, young man, I'd consider you a peacock."

"Really?" Alastaire looked pleased, although a little dubious. In his black jacket and trousers, he was nobody's idea of colorful. "What makes you say that?"

"Your manner. Your sparkle. You have passion and style, and a little theatricality, hmm? Yes, a peacock. Definitely a peacock."

Alastaire squared his shoulders and looked extraordinarily pleased at what Nina wasn't sure was a compliment, but she didn't want to burst his bubble. She said, gesturing at the newspapers and guns, "So all this stuff is weapons?"

Captain Bowman nodded and said, "Yes. Although of course it wouldn't harm them. The Saturni are incorporeal in their purest essence. Bullets and ballots are equally meaningless in their sight. That's why certain people I'm involved with have to fight so hard, simply to stay abreast of them. I'm speaking of course about the Santa Compagna."

"The Santa who?"

"The holy company. That's the organization with which I'm allied. We have several branches throughout the world. The name, of course, is very old, I believe dating back to the fifteenth century or possibly earlier—"

He broke off, because Bella had made a choking sound and was now rising and backing away from him in horror. A slight frown knit the older man's bushy gray eyebrows, but he didn't say anything. Bella breathed, "I knew it. I knew you were involved with something bad! Why did I let myself be seduced by cake and tea and you—" She spat at Alastaire. "You're such a fool to drag us both in here! Just because you'd go to hell and back if Nina asked you to, just because you're crazy in love with her and . . . and . . ."

"I'm not," Alastaire blurted out. "I mean, sure, I like Nina, I like her a lot, but she's more like a sister to me, and besides, I like you too, and—"

"It doesn't matter." Bella was shaking, and tears were running down her beautiful face. "It doesn't matter why we're here. He's a monster! Don't you realize that? The Santa Compagna are a group of human beings who are committed to destroying every last Skin Eater on earth! They were founded by Savonarola in 1496 during his fight with Alexander Borgia, and they took their motto from him, 'God alone is powerful, because God alone is good . . .'"

*Poor Bella*, Nina thought, *she's a wonk even when she's flipping out.* But her first thought was to comfort her friend. She said, "Bell—" and at the same time Captain Bowman said, "I assure you—" but Bella cut him off.

"Tell them the truth! Tell them about the Silo de Carlomagna in the chapel of Sancti Spiritus!"

The captain's face fell, and he heaved a heavy sigh. When no one else said anything for a moment, he said, "All right. I admit it. There were times when the Compagna went too far. In Roncesvalles, in Spain, they lured some two dozen Skin Eaters to a tower called the Silo de Carlomagna and locked them in for sport. This was during the Napoleonic wars, and the Campagna may have felt that a ritual blood-letting was necessary. But I'm making excuses, when they're really aren't any. Perhaps it's just better to say they all went mad.

"In any event, the Skin Eaters were locked into the Silo without any food, either human meat or blood or anything else. Of course it was only a matter of time before they began to feed on each other, and the Compagna . . . took wagers. They bet on who would eat who first. Goya drew some of the slaughter for his Disasters of War, and it's . . . harrowing. Yes. You have a right to be angry. But that's not who they are now. Not who they've been for centuries."

"Bullshit."

Bella's very delicacy made the obscenity sound that much worse. She wasn't crying anymore, but her strained face was furious. "You still hate us."

"No."

"You still want to destroy us."

"No. We want to destroy your makers. You're as much victims of the Saturni as anyone else. Would you honestly say you would have accepted the lives you lead now—or since I'm guessing you're still changing, perhaps I should say the lives you will one day lead—had you known the costs? Can you honestly say you had a choice?"

*No,* Nina thought. Of course none of them had any choice, whether it was the students at Daedalus, or the teachers. They'd all been seduced by promises of power and perpetuity, the glitter of wealth and importance, the allure of being the cool kids in the class. Only when they'd been torn from their natural families and orphaned from every connection with the natural world had they realized their mistake.

Captain Bowman was still looking at Bella with kindness and something approaching pity, as the slender girl considered his words and turned her hands over and over and stared at them, as though the solution to her dilemma might be written across her palms. Finally, she sighed.

"Yes, I suppose it comes to the same thing, doesn't it?" she said quietly. "Who knows what would happen to the Skin Eaters in a world where there were no more Saturni? And yet some of us are committed to destroying them too. At least *we* are. As ridiculous as that sounds. I know we're just kids, but . . ."

"Sometimes young people hold the hope of the world," the captain said. "Because they're too optimistic to think they might actually lose."

He pinched the bridge of his nose and added, "When you get to be my age, you have far too many failures to remember, despite whatever successes you might have achieved. Too many lost visions. I can stare the future in the face with equanimity because I've had nearly everything thrown at me that the world can throw, but you?"

He gazed at them all in turn, his eyes level. "You ain't seen nothing yet. You could remake the cosmos. You could break the power of the Saturni for good. You could set the Skin Eaters free, you and the others, the *Lwas* and the Danverses. I tried. God knows I tried, but they wouldn't trust me. So now I'm hoping I can place my trust in you."

Nina decided this was all well and good, and way better than finding out he was a serial killer, but she still wanted to bring things to earth. "Is that why you snuck your book into Daedalus?" she asked him. "Is that why you've been pulling all these strings?"

"You overestimate my influence, Miss Lamb. Really, things very often take their own course. I told you, I'm a Johnny-Come-Lately, all I've done is pull together what knowledge I have now. The forces that shaped your destiny, and shaped your school, are far more subtle. Your headmaster, for example, is a fairly slippery character."

"You mean because some people think he's alive and some people think he's dead?" Nina frowned. "Or because some people think he's nice and some people think he's a vicious prick?"

"Actually," the captain said, "I do think occasionally your headmaster can be a vicious prick. But he's definitely alive. As far as that goes."

Nina felt more confused than ever. The captain looked at his watch and said, "Well, I'm enjoying this immensely, but shouldn't you kids be getting back to school? It's after five o'clock. Isn't dinner at six?"

"It is if Agatha Danvers gets around to cooking it," Alastaire said, although Nina thought, *How does he know when dinner is?*

Bella stood up at once and said, "Yes, we should be getting back. Look, I'm sorry if I was rude, you seem like a nice person. But . . ." She swallowed. "You know I'm going to have to check out everything you've said and see if it makes any sense in terms of whatever else I can find out. It's not like I'm calling you a liar, or anything like that. It's just this is a big leap of faith for me. So I've got to take it slow."

"I quite understand." The captain's eyes shone, and the admiration there was even stronger than it had been before. "I would expect no less. Question authority, as we used to say in the '60s. And Mr. Roget." He turned to Alastaire. "Thank you also for coming. Your bravery is as clear as your intelligence, for all your attempts to hide it. I think Miss Lamb is lucky to have both of you as her friends. And now, Miss Lamb . . ."

He turned to her and then hesitated. "I don't know if this will do you any good, but should you have any questions, I'd be more than happy to answer them. You may not be able to come and visit me. I may not be here forever . . . one can never say one has moved for the last time short of the grave. But if you write to this address . . ." He handed her a card. "I'll always be happy to respond.

"And now," he added, "I think you'd better all run along back, for fear of being missed. It's been delightful to make your acquaintance. You've been even more fascinating than I imagined you would be. Now, if you'll just follow me, I'll show you the way out."

He led them back through the maze of cardboard boxes, books, chairs, firearms, carvings, flags, and paintings, until they finally reached the front door, and the dogs romped around them again as if they'd been gone for months. And then the captain escorted them down the brick path between the overgrown hedges and let them out again into the street.

They walked a full block in silence before anyone spoke.

"Well, that was interesting," Bella said. "I feel like I've just met Adolf Hitler dressed up as Santa Claus."

"Oh, come on, he wasn't that bad." Alastaire shrugged. "Good cake."

"Come on, were you even listening?" Bella shivered. "'I'm glad you liked my book. I'm a member of the Santa Compagna.' This guy was just playing us! It's like he's some weird kind of chess player, just like the headmaster. They're both pricks."

Bella walked on with her head down and her hands fisted in the pockets of her skirt, and Nina reached out and put her arm around her.

"Hey," she said. "It's all right. You don't ever have to see him again."

"Yeah, but you will. I can see it in your eyes. Hey, I know, I know . . ." Bella shrugged. "I'm just being a pussy."

"Yeah," Alastaire said, falling into step next to her. "And I like it. You're a great piece of ass."

"Oh, shut up."

They walked on a little further, and then Bella asked, "What's on the card he gave you?"

"Oh, just some address on Egania Street." Nina shrugged. "I should probably just throw it away."

"No, let me see it."

Bella looked at the card, and Nina watched her frown. "That's in the Lower Ninth Ward," she said finally. "There's nothing down there now. It's just a ghost town."

"See, that's what I mean. It's all crap."

"No, but . . ." Bella shook her head again. "Maybe that's the point. Maybe a ghost town is where ghosts go. See, there are these two beautiful houses down there. At least there were once, before the storm. They were built by a Skin Eater a hundred years ago to look like steamboats, but that's not the point. It's what the two houses were called."

Nina knew at that moment that she didn't want to know what the two houses were called, but she still felt compelled to ask, "What? 'The Twin Houses of the Rising Sun?'"

"No," Bella said. She handed the card back to Nina. "You see, they used to keep children there in one of them. They called that house the Orphanage. It was like a low-rent version of Daedalus. And the other house was called the Convent. It was where a bunch of voodoo priestesses lived. They all took names like nuns, you know, Sister Tonnere and Sister La Croix, Sister Tom-Tom and Sister Serpentia. So, don't you think that's another kind of a coincidence?"

Bella took a deep breath and said what they all were thinking. "Don't you think that's exactly where you'd go, if your name was Sister Aquilina?"

# Chapter Twelve

The fall term of the Daedalus School was one long exercise in frustration. For one thing, there were Saturni everywhere: more and more of them every day, until it finally felt like Daedalus was a weird version of Camp David with Spanish moss.

There were also more and more mortals showing up who wanted to work with the Saturni and curry favor. Rich businessmen like Keith Wolf and the heads of banks and the holders of major oil leases rubbed elbows in the hallways with exasperated teachers and awkward students, and when they were all forced to dine together in the Commons, the result was predictably chaos. Agatha Danvers flatly refused to serve that many people, so they had to hire a catering service, which at least provided better food. Jack Benway and Father Ignatius and the Freelands kept to themselves for the most part, but the lesser Saturni had to fall back on congregating in the lounge and playing cards with the students, and when Alastaire caught Oswald Babb cheating, he punched him in the nose, and only afterward realized he might have signed his own death warrant.

Fortunately, the baby-faced Saturnus found it exciting to be beaten by a strapping young teenager (he was seriously into rough trade) and after that, Babb sent Alastaire little notes at odd hours, sometimes written in what looked like blood. Bella told him he should follow up on it.

"You could make your fortune."

"I am *not* listening to this."

"Just beat him with a riding crop. Let him grope you."

"Jee-zus, Bella, did you really have to put that image in my head?"

"Maybe you could wear cute little leather pants while you did it." The Vietnamese girl giggled, and Nina figured she must be feeling better.

"You could use a ball-gag on him. That way you wouldn't have to listen to him talk."

"I'm going to use a ball-gag on you in about five seconds if you don't shut up."

Nina let them argue among themselves and leaned back against the crumbling stone wall of the carriage house. There in the sunlight where they were sitting it was warm, but the weather had turned cold with Christmas a week away, and Bella and Alastaire, in the shade, were both wearing sweaters.

She thought about how strange it was that even here at Daedalus, she was the only student without Christmas plans. None of the Skinnies were in any way religious, but they all got into the spirit of the holidays and partied like everyone else, from réveillon dinners to big spending sprees at the mall. Everywhere in the Garden District, the great mansions were lit with huge Christmas trees and lavish garlands, while the more modest houses boasted plastic snowmen, tinsel, and inflatable reindeer.

Nina couldn't say she had any real memories of Christmas, but it was hard not to feel like she was missing out. She wondered if they'd get any special food on Christmas morning.

Knowing Agatha, they'd probably get cold oatmeal and be lucky to have that.

She sighed and squinted her eyes to study the Sybil's engraving one more time. It had been changing more and more often lately and showing her different things. Sometimes the headmaster was holding up a book with the text pointed right at her. She couldn't make out the words, but she could see colorful illustrations: fish and foxes and alligators and birds.

At other times, the garden in the engraving was empty, as though everyone had gone away. Leaves littered the grass, and the furniture looked old and dilapidated. The shrubs and flowers had grown wild, and it seemed like a long time had passed. One time she saw a man curled up on the garden bench sleeping, and he looked like a derelict.

The engraving had taken to changing so much, she now kept it in her pocket to check on it frequently throughout the day. Looking at it now, she saw snow falling. She looked up and said, "You sure you guys don't want to take a look at this? Because—"

And then she looked back at the engraving, and stopped.

Standing there in the middle of the garden, where several inches of sparkling snow now covering the palm trees and the lush foliage, was an impossible figure in puffed pantaloons, long stockings, high curly-toed boots, and a lacey white shirt, who looked like an overdressed extra in a really cheesy Shakespeare play. He was holding up a large banner which read, "Coming Soon! For One Night Only! The Lucky Thirteenth Night Ball at The Fortuna Club! Tell Your Friends! You'll Be Amazed at The Results!"

"Um, Alastaire . . . Bella . . . I really *really* wish you could see this . . ."

"What?" Alastaire took the engraving away from her and looked at it and then handed it back. "What are we supposed to see? It's just a Danvers family snapshot like it always is."

"All right, all right. I'll describe it." She took a deep breath. And when she had finished,

Alastaire was staring at her, and Bella was biting her lip. "No, and before you say anything, I'm not making this up!" she shouted. "And I'm not going nuts either! Bizarro Elizabethan dude was definitely there, and he was all like 'Check it out, come to the circus! One night only at the Fortuna Club! Come one, come all!'"

"No, it's not that," Bella said finally, with a nervous little laugh. "It's definitely not 'come one, come all. They'd have a fit if it was like that."

"Who's 'they' and why would they have a fit?"

"The Fortunati. The Fortunate Ones. The fortunate sons, in fact, because they don't let women in the club. Not even their wives or girlfriends, except for once a year. It's the Fortuna Club, down on Canal Street. I told you, my father's a member. And yes, they do have an annual Thirteenth Night Ball. It's the day after Twelfth Night."

Alastaire confirmed this. "My old man would give everything he owns and everything he could ever steal to get into the Fortuna Club, but it's strictly high-stakes players. Krewe of Lycidas. That's a Mardi Gras Krewe that doesn't even parade anymore, they're too exclusive. Anyway, it's all multi-billionaires, and it's Skin Eaters and Saturni and humans all together, only it helps if you're 'in the know.' Some of their entertainments can get pretty bloody. At least that's what I've heard. Bella, you'd know more about it than I do."

"I know enough to know I wouldn't willingly join the Fortuna Club, *ever*, if they issued me an engraved invitation," Bella said shaking her head. "And at least now . . ." She gestured at her anatomy. "I guess my father won't make me."

Nina felt as if her earlier irritation had been multiplied tenfold, at the way they were both just tippy toeing around things. She said, "So the Thirteenth Night Ball is pretty awful?"

"It's the biggest deal of the year, so yes, on a scale of one-to-ten, the 'awful' quotient is usually fairly high." Bella looked away and picked at some blades of grass. "See, Twelfth Night starts carnival season, but Twelfth Night is also the Feast of the Epiphany, the day the three wise men are supposed to have found Jesus. So the Saturni celebrate Thirteenth Night as a reverse Epiphany, where they find Jesus and eat him. It, um, always involves a blood sacrifice."

Nina swallowed, and suddenly she wasn't irritated at all. "A blood sacrifice like Aztec people cutting out people's hearts and people being skewered on stakes, kind of sacrifice?"

"Um-hmm. Oh, it's all very elegant." Bella looked down. "They pick someone who's a big deal in the community, like a city councilman or an important businessman. More power, right? They usually pass him a special favor, a golden apple. That's how he knows he's been chosen. They anoint him and crown him as their king, and there's like this big tableau. And then at the end . . . they, um, well, they kill him. And eat him."

Bella said that last part very quickly and looked down.

Nina said, "You're kidding, right? Why would anybody join a club like that, where they could be killed?"

"Because nobody ever thinks it's going to happen to them. It's like, I'll never get sick, I'll never lose all my money and be homeless, I'll never have to be on welfare. Nobody ever thinks that kind of stuff will happen to them. It's always the other guy."

"Still, if there was even a chance . . ."

"I'm telling you, it involves an insane amount of power. Although to be fair, when they do realize it's them, whoever it is usually does pitch a fit. They scream and yell and beg for mercy, and everybody else cheers them on. It's called having a 'lively' king. It's supposed to bring good luck."

Nina didn't say anything for a long moment. She could tell Alastaire was listening closely, although he'd flung one arm up over his eyes as though shielding his face from the sun.

Nina saw his chest move and wondered how much he'd known about the place his father was so crazy to join. She said after a discreet pause, "Well, okay, so we're not talking about your average Sunday School pageant here. I get it. So the question now is, why does clown-boy in the picture want me to know about it? And why did he want me to tell my friends, i.e. you?"

Bella let out a long sigh. "I don't know. Maybe he … or whoever's really behind the conundrum … just wants you to know it exists. Maybe it's a warning. Like look out. Stay away from the Fortuna Club. It could be that."

"Or it could be because he wants us to go there?" Alastaire snapped, still not looking at either of them. "My God, you guys are so blind sometimes it's amazing you can find your own butts. The Mezzo-whatever-it-is wants us to go to the Fortuna Club's Thirteenth Night Ball, and it wants it enough, and it's important enough, that it's doing something completely ridiculous and noticeable and obvious just to get our attention. Shee-it, I'm supposed to be the dummy and even I get it!"

No one said anything for several seconds, and then Bella muttered, "You're not a dummy, Alastaire. Although yes, I did suspect that might be a possibility. However, it's not absolute. There are lots of other perfectly good explanations for why the Mezzotint might want Nina to know about this."

"Oh, suck my toes, Bella. The picture's talking loud and clear. We just have to figure out how we want to answer it. Although, um, thanks for the compliment."

Alastaire's ears had gotten a little pink. To cover the moment, he added, "So Nina, what do you think? You're the one this whole magic show is speaking to. What do you think we should do?"

"Run like hell in the opposite direction?" Nina acknowledged her joke was feeble. The terrible rite Bella had described, with its bound king and its blasphemous, mocking overtones, made her sick. Yet at the same time, she had to admit the meaning of the engraving seemed pretty clear. It was giving them instructions as plainly as a billboard.

For the first time, Nina thought, *Can I really trust this thing, this Mezzo-whatever it is?* Had the Sybil given her, rather than a gift, a concealed weapon? She said quietly, "Janus wanted to steal it."

"Who's he again?" Alastaire asked.

"The dwarf. Phoebe Passerine's brother. You remember, the guy dressed up as Count Chocula? He tried to steal my purse the night I first got the engraving, and then he said if I wanted to go following a bunch of cannibal freaks down to hell, he couldn't stop me. I figured he was just mad because he couldn't get the engraving for himself, but what if I was wrong? What if . . ." Nina gave a shrug that she tried to keep from becoming a wince. "What if he knew it was dangerous and he was, I don't know, trying to protect me?"

Alastaire shook his head firmly. "If he's Phoebe Passerine's brother, he's from the planet Your-Anus, whatever else he is, so God knows what he might have meant. I'd say ask her, but you'd probably get a half-hour demonstration of her eating dirt or siphoning chicken soup into her ears. You're better off sticking with Sir Puffy Pants."

Nina turned away and looked across the lawn, where the shadows were deeper now, the trees holding darkness netted in their softly swaying leaves. As always, the sheer loveliness of the Daedalus School made her wistful. Why couldn't she just stay here and have a life with the other Skinnies? They were terrible, and they were damned, but they were also brave and smart and some of them, at least, were good. Some of them, she thought, even loved her—that knowledge piercing her like a needle in her throat.

And as she thought that, realized what she was actually looking at. Strickland Danvers and Jack Benway were standing in front of the big mullion-paned window in the second floor teachers' lounge, and with the lights on inside and darkness falling outside, she could see them as clearly as if they were on a stage. And they were having yet another argument.

She didn't even hesitate but got up and crossed the lawn to stand staring up at the window. *Now,* she thought, *I'm looking up at him. Does he know it? Can he feel my mind?*

"Dammit, I wish I knew what they were saying."

She only realized she'd spoken aloud when Bella and Alastaire appeared at her elbow and Bella said, "I could try and see if I can hear anything." A moment later, the Vietnamese girl had shed her clothes and changed into her usual transformational form, a small brown fruit bat, and gone sailing off into the darkness. Watching her fluttering up by the window, Nina asked Alastaire, "Do you think that's really safe?"

"Well, Bella's pretty good at keeping the whole 'animal behavior thing' going," Alastaire admitted. "I always forget to lift my leg."

Nina stifled a laugh, since Alastaire's transformation animal was a borzoi. But a moment later, she jumped and dragged Alastaire back into the shadows, as Professor Danvers slammed the left panel of the window open, nearly catching Bella in the process and making her wheel and dip precariously to regain her balance.

"God almighty! I swear I need to let some fresh air in, just to let myself think! Given the amount of horseshit you're spewing, Jack, we'll need to wash this place out with Clorox!"

*Okay, so he knows I'm here,* Nina thought. *He wants to let me hear better.* She crept back with Alastaire, as v Danvers whirled to face the head of the Saturni again, almost as if he expected to be attacked when his back was turned.

"Or are you planning on snuffing me out like just one more inconvenient candle? I remember last spring. You were willing to sacrifice me just to keep Isolde entertained."

"Oh, stop it." Benway sounded bored, or at least like he was pretending to be bored.

"Are you still pissed off because of that business with General Azazel? I didn't want to kill you. I was very glad when you took out Isolde's old man, as a matter of fact, he was a pain in the ass. I didn't want to kill you then and I don't want to kill you now! I just want to know if we're on the same side."

"Of course we're not on the same side." Professor Danvers retreated into the room, leaving the window open. Bella flitted around by the sill, not quite going inside where she could be seen, but beating her wings as quietly as possible so she could hear. Nina certainly hoped she had a bat's senses when she was transformed like this. All she and Alastaire could hear was a low murmur of voices and the words, "Fun," spoken by Benway at one point, and Professor Danvers's derisive snort.

"What do you think they're talking about?" Alastaire whispered.

"Beats me. What do the Saturni consider fun? World domination and mutilating kittens?" Nina shook her head. "I wish he wouldn't do that," she added. "Laugh at them. Egg them on. It's like he's always got to have the last word. Someday they really will kill him."

Alastaire glanced at her, and Nina was about to add, "Not like I care," when she heard the words "fucking Fortuna Club!" and then she was all ears.

"I refuse! I absolutely refuse to do it! If you want to play your ridiculous little games—"

"It isn't a game, Strickland. As I don't have to remind you." Benway's voice was ground-glass dangerous. "We've waited here for two solid months, but nothing has happened. No sign of your sister, no sign of the brat. It's getting goddamn annoying! You persist in pretending there's no timetable, but the Alignment isn't going to wait around for us while we jerk off! Even I have people I have to answer to. Well, sometimes, anyway. This isn't something that can wait. If you refuse to deliver the goods, okay, at least tell us where your sister is, and let's talk about it. See if we can't work something out. Or at least tell us where the brat is. You really think she'll survive it, if the Void comes down? You're a lot of things, buddy, but I never thought you were stupid."

Nina's thoughts skittered around inside her head like loose marbles. What was Benway talking about? What Alignment? What Void? She wanted to go into the professor's mind and have him answer all her questions, but she felt a resistance there that was almost physical, barring her entrance. The thought occurred to her that he was working as hard as possible to keep her out, to keep Benway from knowing she was anywhere in the vicinity.

"I have no idea what you're talking about," the professor drawled.

"Give up your Goddamn sister!" There was the sound of Benway hitting something: a table, the arm of a chair? Professor Danvers? "She can't be that good! You want women, I'll give you Skin Eaters, mortals, depraved virgins, you name it! What's so great about Niobe?"

But Professor Danvers didn't even bother to be rude. "Absolutely not, Jack. Just give it a rest. What else did you want to suggest? You said there was something else."

"There is." Their voices dimmed again, and Nina dug her fingers into Alastaire's arm until the latter said, "Ow. Quit it. You're giving me bruises."

"Sorry. It's just so frustrating. I hope Bella's taking little batnotes."

"You know she's got a memory like Horton the Elephant. Chill."

They gazed upward, as if sight could offer sound, and watched the figures in the lighted room turn and pivot. They still seemed to be arguing, and at one point, Professor Danvers sat down in a chair and put his head in his hands.

"That can't be good."

"Shh." Alastaire put his arm around Nina without even thinking about it. "It's going to be okay."

Finally, Benway turned and left the room, and a moment later the professor appeared at the window again and stared down into the garden. His face was sharply shadowed; no part of his expression could be read. Then he turned and left as well, and in another moment, Bella was standing next to them, stretching her arms up over her head and shaking the cramps out of them.

"Whew, that was a long time trying to stay stationary. And God, the mosquitos all smelled so delicious. I could barely stand it! Oh well." She shrugged into her T-shirt and jeans again. "C'mon, let's go someplace more private and we can debrief."

Nina cast one last look at the now-empty window and felt something inside her like a physical pull. She wanted so much to stay here. She wanted to call out to the professor, wherever he'd gone, and tell him to come down into the garden. She'd press her hands to his temples and ask him what was wrong, and initially he'd be reluctant, but finally he'd tell her ... *yeah, right,* she thought. What he'd tell her was to go straight to hell, or Guinee, and he'd be all like "Why do you persist in plaguing me, you stupid little girl?" And she'd just end up feeling like shit. She huffed out her breath.

"Let's go back to the carriage house. We can go inside and have the place to ourselves."

When they got there, Bella sat down cross-legged on the floor and said, "Okay, so here's the deal. I don't know how much you guys heard, but they want Professor Danvers to go to the Fortuna Club on Thirteenth Night."

"Crap." Nina sat down opposite Bella, and Alastaire flopped down next to her. "I kind of figured it might be something like that. What do they want him to do, bring Sister Aquilina?"

"No. They want him to bring you."

# Chapter Thirteen

I took Nina a moment to even process that. When she did, she said, "What?"

"Don't yell, I can hear you. I know, I'm not so thrilled about it either. But come on, it makes sense. The Saturni still can't see you, and it's clearly driving them crazy." Bella frowned. "I still don't know why they're all here, actually. I mean why they're massing here. It can't just be about you, but I think a lot of it is. You're their worst nightmare. Even worse than Sister Aquilina. I mean, they know what Sister Aquilina can do. They have no idea what you can do, because you don't have any idea what you can do, either."

*Oh God, I'm so screwed*, Nina thought. "What did they say?"

Bella hesitated, and Nina and Alastaire watched her prodigious memory replay the whole conversation. When she spoke, they knew they were hearing an exact transcript.

"Jack Benway said Professor Danvers knew what he could do, and what he had raised once at his request. I think he meant at Professor Danvers's request. At least that's what it sounded like. He said he could let it loose again, whatever it was, and the professor knew where it would go and what it would want. I think that's when Professor Danvers sat down and hid his face in his hands. Benway said the professor would always be his man, whatever else he was, and that he could always pluck the strings of his creation and wherever he was on earth, he'd come running. He also said he knew the professor's hungers. By which, er, I'm guessing he meant more than just the hunger all adult Skinnies have for human flesh? Right? Although, I don't really know." Bella was suddenly bright red with embarrassment. "Maybe I was just imagining things. I was really starting to get hungry for those mosquitos."

Nina sighed and said, "No, it's okay, I get it. All right, so Benway can still majorly push Professor Danvers's buttons. I guess we already knew that. What else was he talking about? What's the Alignment? And what's the Void?"

Bella shut her eyes and mumbled something.

"What? Speak up. It sounded like they were both really important."

Bella opened her eyes and snapped, "I don't know! All right? I don't *know* what they are."

"Hold on a second." Alastaire stared at her. "This is one time when it would be really handy if you knew something, and you don't?" He blinked. "Then what the hell good are you?"

Bella heaved a handful of straw at him, and Nina quickly intervened.

"You mean you don't know what they are at all, or you don't know every little detail, but you know something?"

"I know a little." Bella's voice was thick. She wouldn't look at Alastaire. "I know the terms. They refer to two very old legends of Guinee. You remember how I said the *Introim* first lived in Guinee, and then they came through into our dimension? Well, it had to happen through some kind of a break. My guess is the Alignment refers to some sort of event or metaphysical moment when the walls of Guinee can be breached, and material from their dimension can break through into ours. It can't happen all the time, otherwise Guinee itself would collapse and for all we know, our world would too. The Void is, well, I don't know. I guess it might be all the rest of creation that isn't in our universe and isn't in Guinee either. You know, like Dark Matter."

Nina and Alastaire both looked blank, and Bella said, "Okay, basic physics. Dark Matter is supposed to account for a large part of the total mass of the universe. It neither emits nor absorbs light, which is why you can't see it. It's like . . . I don't know, concentrated nothingness."

Nina thought of the Nadir, the quintessence of mankind's fear of death. Wasn't that kind of the same thing? Was the Void some kind of a Nadir the size of the world?

"Terrific," Alastaire said, still brushing straw off his clothes. "So this Alignment thing is coming soon, and this Void thing is going to get in and make us all into concentrated nothingness, and meanwhile the Saturni are getting ready to do something really awful, and given their track record, that's saying something. And meanwhile, Nina has to go to this Thirteenth Night Ball and watch people get served up for dinner? I'm sorry, but I just won't accept that."

"Accept it or not. It's going to happen."

"Maybe not." Nina appealed to Bella. "Didn't Professor Danvers refuse? Didn't he say he wouldn't take me to the Fortuna Club? Or did he hedge?"

"He hedged." Bella looked miserable. "I'm sorry, but once Benway started his whole 'I know your hungers' spiel, he just kind of shut down. I don't know whether he was afraid or being careful, or . . ."

"Or what?" Nina asked, feeling like she was going to hate the answer.

"Or whether he really is Benway's man. I mean, we don't know, do we?" Bella swallowed, and there were actual tears in her eyes. "I mean . . . I really hate to tell you this, Nina, but he and Agatha may have defied the Saturni just to save their sister. They may support them in everything else. I know you think he's a hero, but you know all the mixed-up signals you keep getting from this guy?

Well, it could simply mean he's not entirely trustworthy. He may just be looking out for himself."

Nina looked down and thought, *no, I'm not going to get all weepy-girly in front of Bella, just because she knows how much I like the professor. She's right. I don't know which side he's on. He may have taken me to see the Sybil just to set me up* (she remembered him telling her he didn't want her to get hurt, but that could just have been bullshit). She remembered him kissing her (and boy had that gone nowhere in the weeks and months afterward) and she drew a deep breath and tried to wrap her mind around the fact that Professor Danvers might well be willing to turn her over to the Saturni, if the price were right.

She asked, "Was there anything else you heard?"

"Just that Benway wants his answer by the end of the week. He's going away someplace, he didn't say where. Professor Danvers is supposed to tell him what he's willing to do before he goes, and then he said he'll see him at the Club on the night of the party. Nina, um, are you sure you even want to stay here? I mean, at the school?"

"No," Nina said, feeling numb. "No, I'm not sure of anything. You guys got any suggestions?"

"Well, you could go to that house on Egania Street," Alastaire said, and then when they both stared at him, he added, "What? I mean yeah, you've got major sanitation issues there, it is still the Lower Ninth Ward, but it's got to be better than being handed over to the King Creep of Cannibal Land."

Nina blinked, and then said after a moment, "Uh, actually, you know, that's a seriously great idea. I'm just like . . ."

"Surprised I thought of it?" Alastaire frowned. "Right, I'm just the comic sidekick who gets killed halfway through the story. Don't keep reminding me."

"Actually," Bella said, "in this instance, you're a lot smarter than I am. I forgot all about that place."

Nina could tell Bella had decided to forgive Alastaire, and she loved the way Alastaire blushed at the compliment. Bella blushed too, and immediately got back to business. "And it really is a great idea. We could go over there next Sunday on our free day and check it out. And then . . . then if there's anything to it . . . I mean if she's there . . . I mean if Sister Aquilina is . . . well, you know . . . you could just . . . stay there. I guess."

Bella faltered to a stop, and Nina felt a pang at the thought of what all this really meant. She'd have to leave her friends. She'd have to leave Daedalus. She'd have to leave . . . him. She said slowly, "Yeah, I guess so. I mean, I'll miss you guys too. I know, I know, it's better than being turned into a Saturni snack, but God, I hate the idea of running away . . ."

And just then, she heard a voice in her head as clearly as if it had spoken aloud, *"Miss Lamb, if you* don't *mind, I don't have all night to wait for you. I know you're around here someplace with your little friends."* He made it sound like they were midgets. *"Please come to my office* now. *We need to talk."*

"Um . . . I gotta go," Nina gulped, getting to her feet. She looked down into Bella and Alastaire's astonished faces, and added, "Uh . . . bathroom break. I mean, I really gotta go. Let's talk tomorrow, okay? We'll figure out when we're going over to the Ninth Ward, and, er, everything else."

She ran out of the carriage house and was halfway across the lawn when the implication of what she was doing struck her. Just because Professor Danvers summoned her (with his sharp, sardonic, seductive internal voice) she ran to him as obediently as a dog. God, she was pathetic. She was running to the side of a man who might be willing to betray her. She was going to a man who might be willing to kill her. She should at least tell him to stay the hell out of her head, whatever else she did. She looked up at the dark, forbidding facade of Daedalus, and wondered why she had ever thought of it as home. This wasn't her home. She might be an orphan and a stray the world over, but the people here were on nobody's side but their own.

And yet. She found herself walking up the stairs to the second floor, where the familiar heavy oak door faced her with the words "Headmaster's Office" on a brass plaque, and underneath it, scribbled on a white card Scotch-taped to the wood, "Professor Strickland Danvers, Acting Headmaster." She laid her hand on the wood and heard his voice in her head, *"Come in."*

The room was in near darkness, with just the light from the hallway and the wash of starlight through the gaps in the plywood. *Not good,* she told her thumping heart as she advanced toward the dark figure standing there with his back turned to her, squinting down into the street.

"Um . . . sir? You wanted to see me?"

"Yes." He turned to her and she was shocked at the exhaustion in his face. For a moment, he looked very young, almost boyish, with his tie loosened. There was a dusting of stubble on his cheeks, and his eyes looked bloodshot. He passed his hand over his forehead and said, "Miss Lamb, please sit down."

She sat, feeling as though her legs had turned to cooked spaghetti. Professor Danvers sat, too, and looked at her.

"You know what they want," he said quietly.

For the first time, it occurred to her to wonder exactly how much of her mind was an open book to him. Could he read every thought in her head? Surely not that much. Please God, not that much. At least let her have some privacy.

"Yes." She nodded. "Bella was listening, and she filled Alastaire and me in on the main points. They want you to bring me to the

Fortuna Club so they can . . ." *Destroy me,* she thought, and saw him shut his eyes. *Yes. Not a lot of privacy in here, at least not at short distances. Oh hell. Oh hell, hell, hell.*

"Miss Lamb . . . Nina..." He looked down and swallowed, and then looked up at her directly and said in a flat, expressionless voice, "Do you trust me?"

*No!* her rational mind screamed, even as her stupid, treacherous, suicidal mouth said, "Yes. I think so."

She saw a slight relaxing of the tight muscles around the corners of his own lips, as he said after a pause, "Thank you. As I told you, things are changing, and my hope to keep you out of the thick of things may have been a pipe dream. Now, I have to decide how deeply I want to enmesh you, and you deserve to have at least some say in the matter."

*He's offering me a vote,* she thought. He trusted her enough toask her how much she was willing to risk. He respected her— or no, maybe it was just a trap? A trick to make her let down her guard enough for him to offer her up to the Saturni, quite literally on a platter? She shut her eyes and let her stomach and her head spin in different directions, almost as if she'd been snatched right back out of Guinee again.

"Sir," she said finally, trying to choose her words with care, "I don't want to die. I also don't want to be a fool, and I . . . I have a feeling I could easily be a fool right now. I don't know how much you can see into my mind, and if you can see everything, well . . . at least I hope you can see how much I do want to trust you. I didn't have to come here, after all. I could have just run away."

She felt him stir, although she wasn't about to open her eyes now and look at him. This was hard enough as it was. "I . . . I'm not sure if that would have helped, though. It seems like everything's been pushing me toward doing, um, whatever it is that's going to happen, and I can't fight it anymore. I just want you to know . . ."

*Oh God*, she thought, *how do I even put this?*

"I just want you to know I don't blame you, if you, um ... if you think this is all your fault. I don't really think it is. Sir. I mean, I think whatever's going on, I would have been pulled into it anyway, whatever it is. I just ..." She opened her eyes and risked a smile. "I just don't want to get eaten alive in the process."

"Actually, I don't want you to get eaten alive either." He risked a slight smile in return. "And I see your point. We may not any of us have as much free will right now as we think." He looked down. "The Sybil was right about one thing. Even given all the forewarning in the world, we still do manage to step in shit. Despite all her useless pictures."

"Actually," Nina said without thinking, "It's not that useless. It's told me quite a lot. For instance, the headmaster ..."

She noticed the narrowing of his gaze and went forward carefully, watching her words. "Sometimes he's there, and sometimes he isn't. Sometimes he's holding things, a book, a round ball. And sometimes there's somebody else there too. A little boy."

Professor Danvers's intake of breath was so slight she might not even have heard it, if she hadn't been listening closely. As it was, she made herself go on, knowing she had his riveted, if concealed, attention.

"He looks like he's about four or five years old. Blonde, I think, although it's hard to tell in an engraving. He's dressed in a pinafore with white stockings, like, I don't know, like some kind of little rich boy. And sometimes he's there, and sometimes he's not. You can't always see him clearly."

"Henri," Professor Danvers whispered, and there was such an expression of mingled awe and revulsion on his face that Nina wished she'd never brought the kid up in the first place.

When he didn't go on, she said, "You—you know him?"

"I ... might. It might be someone ... I knew once. I don't know.

That's something I didn't anticipate." His lips curved mirthlessly as he added, "The number of things I didn't anticipate is clearly legion."

Nina took a deep breath, and finally asked, "So . . . what do you want me to do? Sir? What was it you brought me up here to ask me?"

He looked at her. And then, as if deciding bluntness was the best policy, he said, "I want you to go with me to the Fortuna Club and attend their blasted party."

He watched her shudder, although it was very slight. She put her head up, and he added, "I assume you want to know why?"

"Actually, sir, I think I do know why. It's because Mr. Benway is impatient, isn't it? And this Alignment thing is coming, and you need to, um . . . well, I guess, to throw him a bone?"

She felt her face flush, and in answer, she saw him swallow. She heard in her head the words, *You're not a bone, you're the most important piece in this entire puzzle . . .* and then he shook himself and closed his mind to her even more firmly. He looked aside.

"You are, in large measure, correct, Miss Lamb. An Alignment is coming, and I need to find out more of what that will actually mean." He waved his hand. "Don't worry. That doesn't concern you at the moment. And I assure you, I am not going to throw any more bones to Jack Benway than I have to." He stood up. "But I do need to placate him. And moreover, I need to find out who he fears . . . and *what* he fears. I need to know what strings can make him jump."

Nina remembered something she'd forgotten. "That's right, he said even he had people he had to answer to. Well, at least sometimes." She thought, *who could be more powerful than the most powerful Saturnus?* It was an intriguing idea.

"Sir?"

"Yes?"

"I . . . well, okay," she said, in a voice that only shook a little. "I guess I—I agree. I mean . . . we don't have an awful lot of other choices, do we? Either I hide from the Saturni and they go after you, or else we go there and find out for certain what they want. And I . . . I want that too. I mean, I want to find out what they want. So, okay, sir. I'm in. I'm your date."

The professor let out a breath and momentarily shut his eyes. When he opened them again, he seemed in perfect control.

"Very well," he said. "I'll make all the necessary arrangements. You'll need a gown. White, I think. And we'll have to find some way to revoke the enchantment that keeps you invisible."

"I . . . think I know about that, sir. I, uh, I read about it some-place." For some reason, she didn't want to mention captain Bowman to him. *Play some things close,* she thought, *and you'll have a few weapons left in reserve in case things really get tough.* "It's called a *miroir d'intent.* Someone set it up so, at the school, I'm all blurry, because they think I'm something I'm not. But it . . . those kinds of things are usually site specific. They don't work just anywhere."

Professor Danvers raised his eyebrows and then said after a moment, "Indeed. A *miroir d'intent* would, I suppose, be one explanation. Very well, we'll take that as a provisional theory. Then you should be fine revealing yourself at the party."

"Fine" sounded like the world's worst possible word choice, but in a way, Nina hoped it was true. Sneaking around, hiding, waiting for the Saturni to make the first move was getting intolerable. Now that she'd committed herself to doing this thing, a strong feeling of impatience was coursing through her veins, and she thought, *Let's just get it over with, all right? Let's go over there tonight.*

She reminded herself she still had to wait almost three weeks till the seventh of January, and the same thought seemed to have occurred to Professor Danvers. He tilted his head and said,

"Miss Lamb, do you have any plans for the holidays?"

"Uh . . . no." She tried not to make it sound like that was the dumbest question on earth. What kind of plans would she have? Maybe jetting off to Rome with Father Ignatius for a little sightseeing?

She caught a glimpse of something that almost looked like a furtive smile on his face, which was gone before she could even begin to decipher it. When he spoke again, his voice was its usual bland purr.

"In that case, perhaps you'd care to join me for Christmas dinner in the school's private dining room?" He held up his hand. "No, my sister will not be catering the event, nor will she be attending. And no, we won't be eating anything vile. I intend to have the meal delivered from Commander's Palace restaurant, and I intend to enjoy every bite. I merely thought, since we're to appear socially together, it might be useful to practice being on equal terms with one another. But if that's not to your liking . . . ?"

Nina swallowed what felt like a basketball-sized mouthful of air, and wheezed out, "Oh . . . okay." She turned to leave, but he added then, almost as an afterthought, "By the way, you don't have to always call me 'sir,' at least when we're alone. My given name is Strickland, and I'd appreciate it if you'd use it."

# Chapter Fourteen

Three weeks later, Nina prepared for her debut at the Fortuna Club.

She began the evening of January 7th with a bubble bath, luxuriating in the hot water and grateful to be the only student in the girls' bathroom. It might not be a sensual oasis, but it did allow her to wash her hair and comb it into a cascade of curls. Afterward, she dressed in the gown Professor Danvers had chosen for her, a beautiful white sheath of soft silk that left her arms bare, and a pair of strappy white sandals that impressed her with his knowledge of shoes. A long shawl of silvery-white lace was the final addition, and as she looked at herself in the mirror, she felt a shock.

*I'm beautiful,* she thought, smiling involuntarily, before she got self-conscious and made a face. She knew it was ridiculous, but she thought that right now, she looked good enough to eat.

*Oops,* she thought, *bad word-choice.* She tried to discipline her emotions, but it was impossible. She was feeling too giddy. She walked down the stairs and saw Professor Danvers waiting for her at the bottom, and in that moment, she felt one of those swoony, syrupy, ridiculous moments when her stomach felt like she was on a roller-coaster and had just hit the drop.

He wore white tie, the overall black of his clothes accentuating his pallor. His hair shone like a crow's wing in the amber light. As he looked up at her, she saw his eyes dilate and focus as though he wanted to imprint her on his mind like a photograph.

"Miss Lamb," he said, stretching out his hand as she descended the last few steps and took his icy fingers in her own. "You look . . . quite presentable. The arms, though." He frowned and then held out a thin platinum bracelet set with emeralds. As he clasped it around her wrist, he murmured, "There. That's the perfect touch. A lovely woman should always look like she's chained. Well, shall we get on with it?"

They went outside and got into a stretch limo waiting at the curb. Apparently, Professor Danvers (*Strickland,* she thought, *I've got to remember to call him Strickland*) didn't share some of the Skin Eaters' claustrophobia about riding in cars.

And as if he read her mind (*Of course,* she told herself, *he* can *read my mind*) he said, "No, I'm not uncomfortable riding in a closed conveyance, since contrary to rumors, I'm not a vampire. Champagne?" he added. He opened the mini bar, revealing an array of bottles. "Or would you prefer something stronger?"

"Um . . ." she said, completely thrown off balance. "Sure. Champagne. Why not?"

He handed her a glass and poured the pale golden liquid up to the brim. She had to resist an impulse to giggle. What was he doing, pretending he was taking her to the prom? She said, trying to bring herself back to earth, "So . . . when you were first in New Orleans, I guess you traveled by carriage, right?"

"Horseback, usually." He sipped. "I preferred to go fast. You can whip a horse into a gallop in an instant, if the beast's well-bred and your seat is firm. In a carriage . . ." He made a gesture. 'There's always the problem of other people. I used to be . . . rather impatient."

*Used to be?* she thought, her mind sliding away from an image of him in riding clothes holding a whip. Strickland Danvers's "seat" wasn't any of her business. She asked, "So, did you have a favorite horse?"

"Actually, yes. His name was Mercury. He had a blaze I convinced myself looked a bit like a caduceus, Mercury's staff, and . . ." He slid his eyes at her and added, "Is this kind of a girl, horsey thing? Because if it is, please count me out."

"I actually don't like horses," she said, demurely drinking her wine. "They're too big. I never learned to feel comfortable at the idea of having one between my legs."

She let him take that for whatever he thought it was worth. She saw his lips twitch and then compress themselves into a deliberately straight line, and two spots of color appeared on his cheeks.

The drive was the most luxurious she'd ever enjoyed, in a car so comfortable even the city's notorious potholes could barely be felt. She watched the lights of the Central Business District approach behind the tinted glass, thinking how there were more lights now, more life, more movement. The city was coming back, a year-plus after the storm, and she thought how wonderful, and then, how fragile it all was. One good hurricane, one good attack by the Saturni, and all this progress could be lost.

A building facing Lee Circle had a beautiful display of lights all down one side, showing a pastel Christmas tree that continually changed colors, sequencing between pale greens and reds and back again. She craned her neck to look at it as they swung around toward Carondelet Street, and she thought, *So pretty. So frivolous and beautiful and perfectly New Orleans, to make a building dance.* She looked at Professor Danvers, and realized they were both looking at the same thing, and she wondered what he was thinking.

All too soon, they reached Canal Street, and the nondescript four-story townhouse that hid the Fortuna Club. Sandwiched in between a Foot Locker and a 24-hour store that sold voodoo dolls and pint bottles of liquor, the graceful building was a throwback to a bygone era, when Canal Street had been a glamorous thoroughfare. Now the elegant streetcars were all in storage, and the whole street looked scruffy. The club, by contrast, looked quiet and prosperous, and absolutely unremarkable, its white marble facade discreetly columned and nothing but a small brass numberplate attached to the door.

The only sign of anything unusual was a beefy New Orleans cop on duty by the curb. As the limo pulled up, he opened the door and helped them both out.

"Do they always have police protection for these things?" she whispered as they were being shown inside.

"I suppose they can't be too careful." Professor Danvers's face was studiously blank. "If one of the Saturni got mugged, all hell might literally break loose."

She swallowed and tried to take in her surroundings as they entered the lush foyer of the building. The walls were polished mahogany hung with burgundy velvet, and there was a deep maroon carpet underfoot, so she felt like a brooch on display in a jewel box. There was a dusky aroma somewhere, a cross between old cigars, incense, and a darker musk like charred wood.

The entrance hall was big on shadows—shadows in the corners, and shadows shrouding the high ceiling where a chandelier flickered with fat wax tapers. A black man in a tuxedo came forward and said softly, "Ah, Professor Danvers, welcome. The members are all upstairs. You can go right on up."

If he even registered the fact that the professor was there with a very young girl, he didn't react to it. Then again, he probably hadn't noticed. His eyes, Nina realized a split-second too late to turn away, were sewn shut like the eyes in a shrunken head, big stitches lacing his cheeks. The skin was thick with scar tissue. He must have had some kind of telepathic sense, however, because he took the professor's coat and her wrap without hesitation, and drifted back into the recesses of some unseen, mysterious cloakroom.

*"Ready?"* she heard inside her head, and she thought back, *As I'll ever be.* They walked down a short hallway, also done up in dark red velvet and thick greasy candles, and up a flight of stairs. Then he opened a door, and together they entered the ballroom.

The first thing that hit her were the lights. After the darkness of the stairs, the ballroom was ablaze with light: candles, gaslight, torches, plus two roaring fires in two huge fireplaces at either end of the room. The place was as bright as noon, and as hot as Hades. As a consequence, at least half the people there had already taken off most of their clothes. I'm overdressed, Nina thought, as she looked at the bare backs and plunging necklines of the women who had even bothered to wear ball gowns. Some of the bolder ones just wore G-strings and jewels and nothing more. Some of the men had already taken off their tailcoats and their starched white shirts, so they wore dress pants and nothing but suspenders above the waist. There was an atmosphere of greedy anticipation in the room, as of children eager to plunge their hands into a waiting treat.

Food was arranged all around the walls—tables full of human ribs, arms and legs arranged on silver platters, severed heads set up at carving stations, and hearts and lungs and entrails all simmering in copper chafing dishes. It was a shrine, a showroom to human slaughter. A full orchestra was playing an old-time-y waltz, and a number of the guests were dancing, their bodies flagrantly touching. Nina watched as a woman jerked off her partner in time to the music, and she felt her gorge rising.

"Don't even think about vomiting," Professor Danvers whispered through tight lips. "Just breathe through your nose till you get used to the smell."

She looked at his face and saw disgust there as well, but also shame. The feast spread out in the room wouldn't be nauseating to him, she realized. To him it would smell delicious. A woman walked by chewing on a whole human leg, the raw meat drizzling blood down her bare neck and mingling over her breasts with the rubies she was wearing, and it took her a moment to recognize her as Bella's mother, Nhi Trung Chopin.

"Hell fucking shit," she said softly, and Professor Danvers's voice whispered in her head. *"Yes. And you still haven't seen anything yet."* And then he paused and added, *"God forgive me."*

She turned to look at him, but he had already severed the link. He was looking across the room and his eyes had caught Jack Benway's, and then suddenly everything went very still.

Strangely enough, she felt anchored by the silence. Suddenly, everything seemed to have snapped into focus. It's show time, she thought, and stood up straighter, letting the smooth folds of her gown cling to her curves like water, knowing she could put at least 90 percent of the old bitches there to shame, even if they were all dressed up like the cast of Cirque du Soleil. Raising her chin, she looked Jack Benway straight in the eye and thought, *Okay, you bastard, see me. I'm right here.*

Benway's gaze narrowed, and it was as if she were able to see him for the first time as well. He still looked like an unmade bed, with his rumpled clothes and his five o'clock shadow. But he also looked puffed up, and worlds were moving beneath his skin, planets and satellites shifting for balance beneath the thin covering of his pallid cheeks. Nina watched in horrified fascination as the chief Saturnus struggled to keep himself together, to keep himself intact, while for a split-second she could see him as he truly was—a colossus, a spiral nebula, a huge, amorphous, animated intestine, lumpy and spasming and squishy and monstrously hungry.

Then Benway smiled and became human again, although his

voice as he spoke was awful, a boom like thunder, for all it still issued from a human throat.

"Come here."

An order as impossible to refuse as a gun to the small of her back. She walked slowly toward him across that immensely long ballroom, and didn't stop until she was standing right in front of him. She felt like Alice in Wonderland facing Humpty-Dumpty.

"So there you are." His voice was sheathed, a rumble.

"I guess so." She decided to cop an attitude. "If I'm not, then at least one of us is hallucinating. And it ain't me."

No response. Apparently, a sense of humor was one of the things the guests left at the door. Nina felt Professor Danvers's presence in her mind as he moved smoothly to her side. *"Stop showing off,"* he told her, and she decided it wouldn't be a good idea to look at him just then.

"Miss Lamb." Benway's hands flexed, and she wondered if he was about to make a grab for her. His eyes looked bright. Celebratory. Covetous. "You've certainly led us a merry chase."

"I'm sorry, sir. That wasn't my intention." Which was actually true, even if it was a little disingenuous. Whoever had arranged for her to be protected by a *miroir d'intent*, it certainly hadn't been her. She wouldn't have known how to cast a *miroir d'intent* even if her life had depended on it. Which she supposed in a way it had.

"Dear, dear Miss Lamb. I'm so extraordinarily glad to see you. We have so many things to discuss. Please, come sit here by me." He gestured to two chairs behind him. Two thrones, in fact, raised up on a little platform. Mentally rolling her eyes, she stepped up next to him and allowed him to take her hand and help her to sit down.

"Miss Lamb, I'm afraid we got off on the wrong foot the last time we met." His voice was like curdled cream.

"You mean when you tried to kill the professor, and I killed the general? Yeah, I guess you could call that the mother of all wrong feet."

"I truly don't wish you harm. Au contraire, I wanted you here tonight to celebrate you. To get to know you better. Because of course, the puzzle is, what are we going to do with you?"

She couldn't think of anything to say except, "Uh . . . leave me alone? That would certainly work for me."

"No, Miss Lamb. Unfortunately, that wouldn't work for us *at all*. At one time that might have been our fondest wish. But now the one thing we can't do is leave you alone."

His eyes darkened, and she saw lightning crackle there for a second. She felt a throb of coldness billow out toward her, like an icy wind in that hot room. The guests at the party, even the most oblivious ones, who'd been happily chowing down on whole rib roasts and entire cakes a few minutes before, had now stopped stuffing their faces and paused to listen. Meanwhile, those closest to Benway, who were clearly loitering around hoping to win his favor, were standing so still it looked like they'd stopped breathing.

Glancing around, she asked, "Where are your pals?" meaning Father Ragoczy and the Freelands. "I thought you guys always traveled in packs, like animals."

"Father Ragoczy is in Rome," Benway said after a moment, "and Dr. Freeland was called away on a medical emergency." His eyes grew opaque and slid away from her like oysters on a plate. She thought, *Well, whatever else you are, you are one lousy liar.*

"Archer Freeland, however, is right here." He turned to the handsome man advancing toward them now with two heavy cups in his hands, cups that reminded her of the big ugly chalice in the chapel at Daedalus. Clearly, these were no ordinary goblets. Simone's ridiculously handsome father, who looked more than ever like a preening male model, was decked out in a white tailcoat and white trousers with a white shirt and a cream-colored bowtie and matching shoes. He smiled his fluoride-bright smile and handed her a cup, before handing the other one to Benway.

"You see," the head of the Saturni went on, "you're inexplicably important, Miss Lamb. That's why we wanted you to preside over our revels. Each year, we choose a queen to reign over our Thirteenth Night Ball, and this year, the queen is you. For know this . . ." He raised his voice so that everybody could hear. "You are the most important person on this earth to us."

Next to her, Professor Danvers coughed out a word that sounded remarkably like bullshit.

Nina agreed, but she didn't want Benway to know it. She pretended to take a sip from her cup and said, "That's nice. I had the idea you guys hated me. I can't think why."

Benway kept his temper, and around her there was polite applause, along with a few murmured comments. Nina hoped they were saying how awesome she looked and what great shoes she had on.

Benway continued, "This is a solemn night for us. At this time and in this place, we reaffirm our natural and unnatural bonds with one another. *De rerum non natura* should be our motto, the way of that which is not natural. Therefore, let us celebrate our self-willed eminence, and dance on the bones of those who would restrain us!"

He flung his hands wide and added, "Let the riot commence!" and the applause this time was much more enthusiastic, like the rousing, whoop-it-up rooting of spectators at the Colosseum. Turning to Nina, he asked, "Shall we dance?"

His voice was more menacing than anything she'd ever heard before. It had a sound like the churning of an enormous garbage disposal. Taking a big gulp of the wine that was in her cup (because all right, getting hammered might not be the best idea in the world, but doing this cold sober was impossible) she said, "Sure, why not? Let's get this party started."

"Ca commence," Benway said, waving his hand, and that was the signal for the orchestra to swing into a demented tune, faster and louder than anything Nina had ever imagined. The guests at the ball all dropped the food they were holding at the same instant (quite literally letting it fall at their feet in a mess of arms and legs and entrails) and locked onto each other's arms to begin spinning madly around the room. Benway led her down to the dance floor and took her hand in his cold, flabby grasp, and she allowed him to put his other arm around her waist. She didn't dare look in the professor's direction. Nothing he could do or think could help her now.

They danced out onto a floor that was already covered with blood, and her main thought was to keep her balance. Slipping and skidding on a muck of churned up offal, she heard Benway say, "Isn't this beautiful?"

Nina had no idea whether he was joking or not. "It's . . . very impressive," she said, as the key changed and the dancers all reversed, stumbling in multi-colored filth. She tried to pick up the hem of her dress to keep it from getting spattered, although she suspected getting down and dirty was all part of the point.

"It's rare for us to be able to celebrate this freely," Benway admitted, and she wondered why? If they were all-powerful, couldn't they just do whatever they liked?

He went on. "Plans, preparations, and procedures must always be worked out. You need to create a time out of time, even for those of us who are timeless."

He cocked his head at her, and she realized that even though they were dancing, he saw this as an opportunity to speak to her privately. "You wouldn't know about that, would you, Miss Lamb? You still don't have any idea who you are, do you?"

*Oh shit,* she thought, *we're back to that again.* Trying to pretend she wasn't completely clueless, she said, "Oh, I don't know . . . I kind of see what you mean. Do the Saturni have to give themselves arbitrary time-outs just so they won't go mad?"

He looked at her curiously, and oddly enough, he didn't seem angry at what she supposed was a really insulting answer. He said, "You would know. Your father's the most arbitrary son of a bitch of them all."

That brought her up short. She stopped dancing and simply looked at him. And then she said, "I'd like to sit down now. I don't want to dance anymore."

He led her back to their chairs, and observed, "You seem upset. You shouldn't be. You could have so many things. What do you truly want?"

*I want you not to exist,* she thought. *I want the people I care about to be safe. I want to get the hell out of here.* However none of those things could be said aloud, so she said after a moment, "I—I'm not sure."

"Oh, come now, everyone has dreams. Hopes. Fantasies." The orchestra had switched to a mazurka, and the dancers, who were either stunt people or else scared to death to stop moving, all whipped around the disgusting dance floor even faster, sweat streaming down their faces and their teeth set in rictus-like grins.

Benway smiled. "You could have all this and more, a hundred times over. Be not merely Queen but Empress of the World. It could be arranged, you know. Want to marry a prince? There are several. Want eternal youth? We could make you lovelier than Venus. Or perhaps just money . . . enough to put every billionaire in the world to shame. You could do a lot if you never had to worry about satisfying your every whim. You could even do good if you wanted to. I mean, it's not my idea of fun, but *chacun a son gout.*"

*Is he actually trying to bribe me?* she wondered. Should she ask for some crown jewels, just to see if they magically appeared. "Um . . . actually, that's all a little beyond me." She sipped her wine. "I'm really more of a glass slipper and pumpkins kind of a girl."

He frowned, but only briefly.

"Or I could give you power. Power over particular people." He leaned toward her and leered—there was really no other word for it—as he jerked his thumb at Professor Danvers, who was still standing just a few feet away. "Like this guy. I could have him crawling on all fours if you wanted him to. Or crawling wherever else you wanted. He'd probably like it. You could have him jumping through more hoops than a trained poodle. What do you think? I think it'd be rather sweet."

Nina didn't dare look over at the professor now, as she mutely shook her head. She tried very hard to keep her mind closed to any comments he might make, and fortunately, he didn't do more than mentally sigh.

"I . . . I think I prefer Professor Danvers just the way he is," she said, "rude and hateful and utterly and completely bored with me." She went on quickly before she lost her nerve. "And actually, the whole idea of power doesn't really appeal to me. It's . . . I don't know . . . kind of tacky."

She saw the shifting clouds behind Benway's eyes shoot more lightning bolts for an instant, but his voice remained pleasant. "What about safety, then?"

He looked around the room, where the opulent orgy had reached a peak of frenzy. Dancers were gasping and falling to their knees to roll frantically in the rich filth on the floor, while the orchestra was still shrilling out an impossible tune so fast no one could have kept up with it. The partygoers, humans and Skin Eaters and Saturni alike, were scooping up handfuls of the unbelievably dirty food to stuff into their mouths, and some of them, she realized, were actually taking bites out of each other—not just marking each other, but chewing off bits of each other's skin and flesh. Nina wanted to scream.

"You mean using protection?" she gasped, taking another big gulp of her wine, although she could feel her head spinning. "I think if you're handing out condoms, you really have sunk to a new low. You're not trying to tempt me, you're just trying to promote safe sex."

"I'm talking about protecting those you love," he said, his voice reverberating like cannon-fire. He raised his forefinger, and one of the dancers in front of him collapsed onto the floor, vomiting blood in huge gouts from a swelling throat. She watched in horror as the man's throat continued to expand and expand like some kind of obscene frog's, until finally it popped, spewing flesh-shards everywhere and pitching him forward to die gargling through a gaping wound.

His partner, barely missing a beat, stepped over him and grabbed the next available man in the dance, her eyes mad with fear.

"I could do that to this entire room," he growled, and the point was obvious. He could probably do it to the entire city of New Orleans, and he might actually try it if she made him mad enough.

"A-all right," she said. "I'm impressed. That was majorly nasty. But you know, if you do blow us all up, think of the mess. I mean, even you guys would have to pay a cover charge."

He smiled, and she had to remind herself he only had a normal number of teeth.

"Or I could do *this* . . ."

He snatched at the air in front of him, and an image appeared, wavey and indistinct. She saw Bella and Alastaire writhing on the floor, clutching their throats as their faces turned dark blue. She saw Phoebe Passerine, her eyes rolling up in her head as she started to shake and twitch. She even saw Simone Freeland, her beautiful mouth open in a shriek. She saw all the students of Daedalus, falling and dying and wailing and begging for mercy, and she asked, "What's going on? What's the matter with them?"

"*Ego devorare*," Benway said, "literally 'self-devourment.' It's an interesting condition. In certain cases, a Skin Eater's own immortality can be turned against him and will then feed on the being's own flesh and blood until it's consumed by its own hungers. Depending on the depths of appetite, it can sometimes take weeks..."

The images vanished, and Nina drew a shaky breath of relief. She reached out with her mind to the professor and asked, *Can he do that?* and he snapped back, *"Not on your life. Tell the old fart to shove his parlor tricks up his ass."*

And she was so unnerved, she actually said it. "Mr. Benway, you can just shove your parlor tricks up your ass. I'm not impressed with visions from the holodeck."

All right, maybe she shouldn't have gone that far. Benway snatched at the air again, and another image appeared, this one blurrier than the last, but still visible. It hovered there like a phantom in black and darker black, but she recognized it instantly for what it was. Sister Aquilina.

"Yes. It's time we got down to brass tacks, isn't it?" His voice was flat, and with the dancers still writhing and flailing around on the floor in front of him, and the orchestra still playing its hellish tune, it was clear no one else was listening. "You think you can play both sides in this game, but your abilities are pitiful. I will get what I want, and I will destroy those foolish enough to challenge me. This one." He raised his chin, and she saw the image of Sister

Aquilina turn and flinch as a sharp wind blew against her, making her shiver and clutch at her own body through her flowing dark robes. "This one will be destroyed by the thing she loves best. The heart is always the sharpest knife, don't you find? What's your heart's whetstone, Miss Lamb? What sharpens your love till it can be turned against you and strike home?"

She shivered and fell silent. Professor Danvers. That was what he was talking about, wasn't it? All the others, Sister Aquilina, Bella, Alastaire, all of them were knives that could pierce her heart, but his pain would be the sharpest stab of all. How stupid she'd been to go into a den of lions with the smell of love still on her, how foolish she'd been to allow them to get that scent. She saw blood bursting from all their throats. She saw their bodies eating themselves. She closed her eyes. *No, no, no,* she thought, *I don't love anyone, don't care about anyone,* although she knew if she couldn't even convince herself of that, she wasn't going to convince anybody else.

She opened her eyes and saw with a faint feeling of "This can't be good" that all the demented dancers had stopped. They were looking at Benway expectantly, and he was looking at her, as if he were waiting patiently for her to come to what should have been an obvious conclusion.

"No," she breathed finally.

"No?"

"No. You can't hurt him. You need him. If you're going to defeat Sister Aquilina, you said you needed 'the thing she loves best.' Well, that's him, isn't it? Her brother?"

"Don't be too sure, Miss Lamb. As I said, your abilities are pitiful. As is your knowledge of our world."

He raised his hand again and another blur appeared above it, hovering, a shiny object spinning around on its axis. As it slowed, she could see it for what it was. A golden apple.

Two burly Skinnies came forward and grabbed the professor by both arms, ripping his shirt open and exposing his chest. He looked absolutely furious. Benway reached toward him and tucked the golden apple into the professor's pocket, and she remembered Bella saying, "They anoint him and crown him their King and Savior, and then they kill him. And eat him."

*This is insane*, she thought, as Benway held up his other hand and a knife appeared in it, jeweled and glittering in the light. He looked like a statue of an ancient god, if a god had ever been carved in a white tie, with his shirt gaping open above his too-tight pants.

She realized the room had gone dead quiet, silent except for the *drip, drip, drip* of the blood and meat and melted ice cream that had been flung up all over the walls, and the sizzle of wax from the fat tapers. She looked at Benway and felt her mind click painfully into gear again.

"No," she said. "I don't believe you. You already threatened him once. You can't cry wolf a second time. It won't work."

"Really?"

Professor Danvers snapped, "She's right, Jack. Again? Last time you wanted to let General Azazel bite my head off. Now you want to sacrifice me? Aside from everything else, I doubt I'd taste very good."

Nina wanted to applaud his courage, but she didn't dare look anywhere else except at Benway's face. She said, "Look, I'm not going to play games with you. You know I, um, I care what happens to Professor Danvers—" She hoped he missed the little hitch in her voice. "But if you're determined to do this, well . . ." She shrugged. "I guess I can't stop you. *Bon appetit.*"

Benway settled for a sneer that would have done the professor proud. "You're very brave, Miss Lamb. What if I make you deliver the killing blow?"

Abruptly, she wished she hadn't drunk so much wine. Her head was swimming, and she felt a burning along her arm as though she'd spent too much time in the sun. The burning increased until it forced her hand up sharply against her will, like a Nazi salute, and it carried her to her feet until she was standing there with her arm raised (please, sir, may I go to the bathroom?) and then, even though she was fighting it with every ounce of her strength, she felt her arm lower . . . and she saw she was reaching toward Benway and the knife.

*Oh no you don't,* she thought, even as she heard Benway's voice in her head, *"You should have thought of that before you drank from my cup and took my hand."* Stumbling away, she reeled out onto the dance floor and did the only thing she could think of. She put two fingers down her throat and made herself vomit everything up, wine, heat, pain, and some kind of disgusting phlegm-y thing that only resolved itself when it was lying on the floor and she could see what it really was—a semi-transparent hand.

Oh shit, she told herself, don't start freaking out now, girl-friend, because you might never stop. She looked at Benway and said, "You put that thing inside of me? Really? I thought you guys can't do magic, all you can do is manipulate people like sock puppets. So you want me to be your tool? Well, screw that." She steadied herself and then lifted her foot and brought it down on the still-twitching hand with a resolute stomp. She felt her high heel skewer it, and squirt out some liquid she didn't want to even look at. "That is so fucking lame," she added, kicking her shoe to send the hand skittering away across the floor. "You guys don't have any better tricks than slipping a girl some rufies in a bar."

Benway held onto his fury, but just barely. She watched as his skin moved, as waves of power and hostility swept through him. He looked like a container of flesh animated by bolts of uncontrollable electricity, so his face twitched and jumped with ugly ripples.

"You don't seem to realize, little girl, we always get what we want!" His voice shot down an octave, and the thunder in his words made the room shake. Everyone was dead still now. Even the candles had stopped dripping.

"Trying to defy us is *insane*! We own everything, so you can't even *live* unless we let you! You are our cattle! Your presidents and your emperors are our toilets! Your God is something we made up! *Now* do you understand?"

He was assuming his true shape again, huge and spiraling and pulsing, and she thought of a snake that had swallowed a whole animal and was trying to digest it and, yet again, a distended bowel. He was becoming inhuman, larger than even the room that contained him, even though he still had hands and arms and legs and some kind of a face. And Archer Freeland was reaching for the knife to deliver the blow himself . . . she could see him raising it to slash the professor's throat . . . and then things started to happen very quickly.

She felt a sharp shove in her mind, along with Professor Danvers's voice telling her, *"Move! Now!"* She didn't want to leave him alone, but he added, I'll be fine, just go, and then, as Benway made a grab for her, she didn't need to think twice. There was a huge mirror along the side of the room behind the bar, and she raced for it, sliding in the muck on the floor but pushing the amazed former dancers out of her way with ruthless speed. She caught a glimpse of Sir Keith Wolf, naked except for a jeweled jock strap, but she didn't stop.

She vaulted up onto the bar, scattering bottles left and right, and made a jump for the mirror. And then the waters of Guinee wrapped around her like cool, soft fingers, and drew her down, and she knew nothing more as they sucked her into their depths.

# Chapter Fifteen

She was walking or swimming down a long, blue tunnel of shimmering bones, and the current raised her hair and sent it floating lazily around her head. She was still wearing her white dress, she realized, although she'd lost her shoes (dammit). All noise had vanished, and she reveled in the quiet whoosh of the water against her ears. *If I never hear another dance number again*, she thought, *I'm going to be one really happy camper.*

Guinee lay quiet. Did netherworlds sleep, she wondered? There was a light shining up ahead, and as she approached it, she saw a deep pool with the moon floating on its surface. How could water have water in it, she wondered? The pool was as reflective as a polished mirror, and all around it were trees, their gnarled roots reaching down into the mud while their twisted limbs rose to touch the vaulted ceiling.

And standing all around the pool were dogs, their bodies as big as lions and their gaunt black empty faces dominated by eyes scoured clean like the eyes in skulls. The *horroi*.

*So*, she thought. *There you are.* Oddly enough, she felt no fear. After what she'd just been through, dogs were the least of her worries. Besides, the *horroi* were quiet, patient, like animals waiting for their master. She reached out one tentative hand, pushing against the cool, soft atmosphere which surrounded them all, and tried to touch them.

Abruptly she felt a sharp current wash over her, and she heard a terrible cry, part whine, part roar. Something was approaching her so fast she could barely see what it was, just a vague impression of blackness: black sludge with vestigial hands and feet, and black eyes bulging over a mouth paved lip to lip with teeth. The Nadir. She kicked off like a diver away from a shark: anywhere was better than this. The water acted once more as a trampoline, sending her bouncing against walls and careening off them like a pinball. Down, down, into a black chasm with glassy sides so smooth she couldn't scrabble on them for a handhold, and then up, pushed by a shoal of translucent beings like miniature babies—tiny fetuses, their eyes glued shot, their fingers webbed and their stilled hearts visible through their transparent chests.

She flinched away, trying not to hurt them, although she realized they were either dead or not yet born. The momentum carried her out of the crevasse and across a long, flat plane of what looked like empty sand . . . coral escarpments and rocks stood up here and there, but mostly there was just the flat earth of the ocean's bottom . . . nothing.

And then suddenly there was something. A barricade of stones rising up in front of her. A barricade that had clearly been built.

The stones were square blocks and stood on top of one another as high as she could crane her head up to look. They stretched off into infinity in either direction. Their surfaces were covered with slime and tiny barnacles, and looked ancient. Carefully kicking off from the bottom, Nina swam slowly upward, letting her hands trail over the stones in front of her, which seemed to hum with a faint energy. They felt slightly warm to the touch.

Up, up, and up she drifted, and as she did so, the barricade subtly changed. Now the stones looked smoother, newer. Their edges were sharply defined. As she rose farther still, there was mortar holding the building blocks in place: dusky pink, the crimson of faded sunsets. And plant life bloomed: small flowers the size of pin heads carpeting the stones in a mosaic of color. She could hear the faint sound of waves breaking somewhere, and now light was filtering down into her watery world. Unbelievably, sunlight shone.

She breeched the surface for just a second—Guinee was greedy and wouldn't release her willingly—but such beauty met her eyes that it made her gasp at the vision. Towers and parapets and domes of light, bright shining roofs of gold and silver, a castle of air more window-paned than walled, and above it all, a sky as red as wine. All that she saw, and more. There were orbs of many colors here, some hovering, some rising and falling in a complex dance with gravity, some fading into obscurity while others burned like fire. And the sun! A diffuse, immense star shone in the sky, bigger than any sun she'd ever seen on earth, cooler and more benign than the hot sun of New Orleans, but big enough that it seemed ready to blot out the heavens. It was big enough that it made her feel like an ant by comparison. A tiny fish. One of the unborn babies. Its light warmed her, drying the droplets of water on her cheeks, but she wanted to hide her head in fear.

Because in the center of this sun burned a cool, steady iris, and in the center of that, there was a red pupil. It was an eye. An unblinking, enormous eye. For one impossible moment it stared at her and she stared back at it, her mouth hanging open, lost between awe and terror.

Then, movement. The waves remembered their mission and rose up, submerging her and pulling her back down again, and she went, half-willingly, happy to sink back into the merely strange after this brief encounter with the inconceivable. The current was robust. She was drawn away in a swirl of bubbles, away from the wall (*not a wall*, she thought, *but a foundation. The foundations of the city!*) so quickly she lost all sense of direction. Gone was the empty sea-bed and the abyss of glass. Here again were the chapels of bone and the skeleton cathedrals, all the skull-paths and altar-pieces of Guinee. They moved past her in a sudden blur, as she felt some intention drawing her on. Obviously, someone had hold of her. Someone was pulling her back out, back to the world, back to the simplicity of horror. She fought against it, using every bit of strength she had. If the professor had her, he'd have to give her some sign. She wasn't going back to the Fortuna Club if she could help it. She wrestled with the unseen force that held her, arms, legs and waist, in its invisible grip, and resorted to threats, curses, begging . . . whatever she could think of . . . although she knew it was all useless. She was being sucked up through a water tube again, and she could feel the familiar thought, *I'm going to puke, I'm going to die,* rushing through her head and chest and bowels .. . and just before she screamed, she felt it all stop.

She found herself lying on warm grass, and the sky above her was its usual light blue, dotted with white clouds like a really cheap greeting card. She was dry, unhurt, and still dressed in the rags of her white dress. And bending over her was a figure out of a nightmare, who was at the same time the one person she wanted to see in the whole world.

Sister Aquilina.

# Chapter Sixteen

"You're still an amazing cook."

"You're just prejudiced." Sister Aquilina helped her to another heaping portion of scrambled eggs and put another blueberry muffin on her plate. The muffin was bursting with fresh blueberries and the eggs were perfect, mixed with leftover jambalaya and accompanied by fresh strips of bacon. Nina ate like a horse.

"You've been eating Skin Eater food too long," Sister Aquilina added. "I don't know why none of us ever learn how to cook properly. It must be psychological. 'I have to eat terrible things, so I can't really enjoy eating.' Don't you find that gets old after a while?"

"You're talking about Strickland," Nina said, and then bit her lip. "Sorry. I mean, um . . . your brother. But . . . well, self-hatred and angst is kind of his stock-in-trade, isn't it?"

"You can say that again." Sister Aquilina sat down at the table and poured herself a cup of coffee. She topped off Nina's cup as well. Sitting in the comfortable kitchen, they could look out at the grass on the lawn at the back of the house on Egania Street. Thick and lush, it gave no testimony to the flood waters that had rushed in there more than a year ago. The kitchen itself was pristine: no mold, no water damage. Upstairs, wide galleries gave broad views out to the levee where Nina had reappeared, and the brown, calm river beyond it. The neighborhood was still barely populated—a number of the houses had been swept away, and what remained were weeds and concrete slabs—but the two houses, the Orphanage and the Convent, were beautiful. "So, how long have you been here?" Nina asked. Sister Aquilina made a face.

"Since right after I left Daedalus. I know, I know, it was terrible I didn't get in touch with you right away, but I truly thought you might be better off where you were. Here . . ." She looked around. "We're pretty much living hand to mouth, and we are wanted by some of the most powerful beings in the universe. I didn't know then that those beings wanted you even more than they wanted me. I guess I kind of overestimated my own importance." She looked at Nina. "Is that also a family trait?"

Nina felt the most confusing sensation, sitting there talking to a woman who was, in some sense, her rival (was that even the right word for it?) and was in another sense her best friend. The woman who had once been Niobe Danvers was looking at her with a small smile, as though entirely aware of her discomfort. Nina couldn't forget Professor Danvers's anguish when he'd learned that his beloved sister had been there, living right there at the Daedalus School for the entire last spring, and he'd been too blind to recognize her. At the same time, Nina also couldn't forget Sister Aquilina's kindness. *Actually,* she thought, *she's always been a lot nicer to me than Strickland's ever been.*

"No," she admitted, "I don't think you're overestimating your own importance. If the Saturni hate me, you pretty much make their heads explode. Not that that would be a bad thing," she added. "I kind of wish they'd all explode after last night."

She had told Sister Aquilina the basics of the evening, and Aquilina's only comment had been, "I wouldn't worry about Strickland too much. He's devious, and I'm not sure what he's up to right now, but he can work his way around Benway. I doubt they'll actually kill him."

Are you sure, Nina wanted to ask, but that would have made it sound too much like she cared. Instead she said, "So, tell me about this place."

"Well, your information is basically correct. These two houses were built by a man named Jubal Obatala and they were a place for Skin Eater children to be kept safe. In those days, we were already established uptown at Daedalus, but the adoption system was a lot less sophisticated. We got children when their prospective parents brought them in, but other kids kind of fell through the cracks. Skin Eaters crossed with kids on their own, and then just left them to fend for themselves. So Jubal got the idea of creating a safe house where those children could learn what had happened to them, and acquire the skills to survive."

As she spoke, she led the way upstairs to the second floor and handed Nina some sheets. No plywood or curtains blocked the windows. With the Ninth Ward still so empty, the windows were left open to the soft January sun. Nina watched as Aquilina swiftly made up a bed in an empty room and the light fell full on her face. She seemed to enjoy its warmth.

Nina had to ask. "So the sun doesn't hurt you?"

"Nope. I think I just got used to the whole darkness thing at Daedalus. We hid too much. When you thought I was human, you didn't question my ability to bear sunlight. We're not monsters, you know, having to hide ourselves away from the world and crawl off into holes. I think it's taken me two centuries to fully accept that. We were tricked by evil beings into giving up the best part of ourselves, our humanity, and then we just went on and on, making more of our kind, tricking more children, creating more victims."

She sighed. With the bed made up, Aquilina walked out onto the gallery, where there was a crisp breeze blowing. She sat down in a wicker chair with her long gown fluttering around her and the wind lifting her hair, looking like an eagle at rest, or a very dark angel. Nina sat down beside her.

"It's disgusting," the older woman continued, "and I'm not saying we aren't all as guilty as hell, but we didn't start it. I think that's the point I'm trying to make here. We were robbed of something very important first and foremost, and after that, we were just too damaged to stop." She shook her head. "Of course, that still doesn't excuse anything. I'm afraid I'm not explaining myself properly."

"I think you're doing a pretty good job." Nina was reminded of the terrible sadness that had always seemed to permeate the Daedalus School, beyond all the student rifts and rivalries. Daedalus was a place of loss, where children yearned for love and the teachers yearned for it, too, and it all ended up being the most obscenely inappropriate mess. Sister Aquilina was looking out over the water-ravaged landscape, and even though she looked young, her eyes held centuries.

Nina asked, "So how did you break free?"

"Crux," the older woman whispered, and then shrugged slightly. "You've met him. What can I say? Saviors aren't always so dreamy, but he certainly was. He came to the Daedalus School during the Second World War, and both Strickland and I fell for him like a couple of tons of bricks. He fell for us, too, I think. He was even more fluid sexually than we were. We became lovers, all three of us, and I think even Agatha was a little jealous, although Aggie's always kind of a hard one to read.

"And, well . . ." She shut her eyes. "We tried to defy them. The Saturni. It was hopeless, of course, and their revenge was everything you can imagine." She held up her hand, and Nina saw once again the thick, ropy scar that circled her wrist. "They sicced the *horroi* on me, but as it turned out, that backfired. I was able to bring them with me when I fled. I think dogs know evil and instinctively shun it, even if they're dead-and-reanimated-monster-dogs. At any rate, they've stayed with me ever since." She smiled ruefully. "Sometimes they've been my only companions."

"You sent them to find me, didn't you?" Nina asked, remembering the dogs by the pool.

"Not in so many words, but yes. Crux knew you were in Guinee. He has a special connection there."

"Because he's a *Lwa*."

"Um-hmm."

"So you faked your own death?"

"Yes. Strickland eventually figured it out, but he was still afraid to go after me, for both our sakes. He was afraid I might kill him, and who knows, maybe I might have, then. Once I became . . . what I am now . . . .it took me a while to control my powers."

Nina gave her a chance, but she clearly wasn't about to say it, so she asked, "Okay, so what are you now?"

"I'm not entirely sure." Sister Aquilina laughed. "Beast or bird? I'm still a Skin Eater, but I don't have to feed very much. Crux helps me with that. Occasionally he'll bring me a little meat, but I think it's from someone who's already died, presumably by natural causes. It tastes . . . dry, somehow." She bit her lip. "Not very good, actually. I much prefer a nice trout meuniere."

"And he's here? Crux, I mean?"

"Oh yes. He comes and goes. The *Lwas* are all like that. You can't pin them down."

"What about the four great *Lwas*? Erzuli and Damballa and Grand Bois and Oya?"

She had the idea they must have joined Sister Aquilina in her exile once they'd been released from their prison at Daedalus, and the older woman nodded. "Yes. They're here too. I must admit, it's been strange sharing our living quarters with four major elementals. Kind of like hosting a herd of invisible mammoths. You can't necessarily keep track of them, but it's hard to just pretend they aren't there.

"They're a shadowy presence, though," she added, looking out toward the river. "Their great powers don't really exist comfortably in the day-to-day world, so they prefer to keep to themselves. Sometimes in the dead of night I can hear them moving, and sometimes you can catch snatches of their conversation. They know something's coming."

Nina shivered. "So tell me more," she said. "Tell me everything else. What happened to the *jumbies*?"

Sister Aquilina smiled, and her smile was grim.

"They're here. Nobody's going to eat them now at any rate. They live next door with the other children, the ones I saved right after the storm. They all get along pretty well, even though their destinies are so different. The *jumbies* have the greatest gift of all, in a way, that they are, and will remain, human and nothing more. No spirits will ever enter them, whether divine or demonic, and no death will claim them until their proper time. I actually quite envy them."

"So explain to me again what the plan is?"

"Well, I think you already know a lot of it. With the four great *Lwas* free, things are changing far faster than the Saturni would like. The lesser *Lwas* now have a chance of coming back as well, not just temporarily, during a voodoo ceremony, but permanently. In bodies."

"The kids you rescued, right?" Nina asked, and Sister Aquilina nodded.

"I took what I could get, but like does call to like, and they came to me. By ones and twos.

Broken. Angry. Lost. But they came. When the time comes,

they'll be able to welcome the *Lwas* into their bodies and hopefully retain their own souls as well. They're brave kids. All of them."

"So how are you hiding them from the Saturni?"

Sister Aquilina smiled. "How have you been doing it?"

"A *miroir d'intent*?" Nina felt a shiver take hold of her, even though the January breeze wasn't that cold. Sister Aquilina merely said, "Yup."

"What . . . you can do that? I thought that was incredibly hard. I mean . . . I mean I didn't mean you couldn't do it, but um . . . are you the one who set up that spell for me?"

"Not exactly." Sister Aquilina stood up so smoothly, it almost didn't look like she was evading the question. "The children were unhappy to leave the house on Pauline Street, I think they'd actually begun to view it as their home, but they were delighted once we came here. They've even been able to establish a garden, and they have animals. Goats. Chickens. It's a regular menagerie. Would you like to see it?"

"In a minute. Sally . . . I mean, Sister . . ." Nina shook her head, torn between Niobe's various aliases. "I mean . . . damn! What am I supposed to call you now?"

"I think you could still call me Sally. Or Niobe. Nobody uses that name anymore."

# Chapter Seventeen

Nina quickly fell in with the routines at the Orphanage and the Convent. She slept at the Convent where Niobe lived along with Crux (when he was there) and three other women whom she immediately named (to herself) the Three Weird Sisters. Their names were Rhea, Thetis, and Mimas, and while Rhea was huge, at least six feet tall, Thetis was normal height, and Mimas was tiny. They were strange looking, their foreheads covered with ritual scars, and they never spoke a word, but they worked harder than any ten men put together. Rhea hoed the garden and planted and raked and moved debris off the adjoining lots and even built a chicken coop with her bare hands, while Thetis repaired the plaster ceilings and fixed furniture, and Mimas sewed clothes and made beautiful beaded flags for all the rooms. Nina recognized the flags as the same kind of flags as Captain Bowman had had. They were brilliant works of art made out of sequins and small pictures and little seed beads all worked into intricate designs. Niobe called them *drapeaux.*

"They honor the *Lwas*," she said, helping Nina tack up a beautiful one that showed a mermaid. "We want to make the place as familiar to them as we can before they get here."

Privately, Nina thought the *Lwas* were getting a pretty sweet deal. All the children were working their butts off preparing for their arrival, both the *jumbies* and the other kids. The *jumbies* were repainting everything in sight, and they also harvested the vegetables and ran errands and helped Rhea and Thetis and Mimas do their work. A *jumbie* named Roticus, whom Nina remembered as a pathetic, terrified waif from Daedalus, was now one of the head gardeners. Meanwhile, the other kids were training for their new jobs as hosts of the *Lwas*. Daneel, who a year ago had been a scared little boy, had grown at least a foot and was working out now with weights in preparation for being mounted by Shango, the God of Lightning. Tish, the violent redhead who still bore the scars of cigarette burns on her arms and legs, sparred with him. She was always accompanied by the strange thin creature they'd nicknamed Flyboy (no one knew his real name) who communicated by buzzing and clicking. It made sense, Nina supposed, since Tish was preparing to be mounted by Dantor, a fierce warrior goddess, while Flyboy would take Guede, the Lord of Death.

The two twins, Emma and Ella, stayed by themselves and communicated in their own private language, already communing with two twin *Lwas*. The albino girl Sibelle and the gay boy Santangelo both worked in the kitchen. Their gods were the *Lwas* of the hearth and root work, and they had found their own way of readying themselves, brewing potions and tinctures. Billie, the rich white runaway, cared for the other children: her goddess would be Yemaya, the mother of the sea.

And then there was a Goth kid who'd host the Lord of the Cemetery; a wounded Iraqi vet who'd host the god of disease; Joe Trunza, who would become the Bull; and Sharazz, who had more piercings than any human being Nina had ever set eyes on before, and who spent his days carefully tattooing himself with symbols of guns and machetes, in preparation for being mounted by the god of war.

The Orphanage was always busy, but it was also strangely fun. For one thing, it was infinitely rowdier than the Convent. There was always music playing, kids running up and down the stairs, bags of junk food everywhere, and constant drama. Joe Trunza was always all up in Sharazz's face about all his piercings ("You gotta thing for needles, man? Ain't nobody gonna stick all those things in me!") and Tish and Billie were mortal enemies in their mutual pursuit of Santangelo, who liked boys and couldn't have cared less. Nina enjoyed them all.

"So, are you guys really okay with this?" she asked Daneel one day, when they were sitting out in the backyard and he was working out with hand weights. He stopped doing reps and wiped his face and asked, "Sure. Why not?"

"I don't know." Nina looked away. "It still seems to me like Niobe just kidnapped you and talked you all into this."

"Actually, it's more complicated than that." He sat down and chugged some Gatorade and then smiled. "Sistah A . . . I'm sorry, you call her Niobe . . . she's like the best thing that ever happened to any of us. Yeah, we were scared at first. The flood washed everything away, and most of us weren't doing so great even before that. Even Billie. Sure, she had all those big Uptown bucks, but her old man was a major perv. So we all needed some TLC, and Sistah A. gave us that. She trusted us to make the right decisions, and when the time came, we did."

"So she did give you a choice?"

"Of course she did."

Nina frowned. She felt like she hadn't been given much choice about a lot of things. She picked some grass and said, "Nobody pressured you? Or, um, told you half-truths and left you to figure it out?"

Daneel picked up one of the hand weights again and started doing arm curls while he thought. Finally, he said, "All right, sometimes Mr. O'Brien was a little weird."

"Mr. O'Brien?" Nina stared at him, feeling her head spin. "How do you know him? The headmaster of the Daedalus School? You've seen him?? He's been here?"

"Yeah, he used to come by a lot. Not recently, though. I don't know about any of that headmaster stuff. He's just a friend of Sistah A's."

"Amazing." Nina threw her grass blades away, watching them flutter in the wind. Chalk up another half-truth. "Okay, so tell me what you mean. You said he was weird."

"Not 'weird' weird, just . . . strange, I guess. He seemed so powerful. And kind of tough. Like if you got on his bad side he'd whup your ass six ways to Sunday."

"But he hasn't been around lately?"

"Nope." Daneel switched to his other arm, his bicep popping with each swing of the thirty-pound weight. He seemed remarkably unconcerned about the headmaster's absence, and Nina left him alone to finish his exercises.

"Yes, of course I know him," Niobe said, when Nina questioned her about it later on. "I knew the headmaster from Daedalus, and he occasionally visited me in our first safe house. I haven't seen him in months, though."

"But he's alive."

"As far as I know."

Niobe lifted a heavy cleaver and brought it down on the cutting board in the kitchen. She was butchering one of the goats. That should have been awful, but they'd had a ceremony first, and it actually hadn't been too bad. Rhea had skinned and cleaned the animal, and now Niobe was cutting up the meat into big chunks preparatory to making a stew. The goat's head was sitting in a pot on the stove regarding them steadily, and that was the only part of the process that kind of freaked Nina out.

"You want me to slice up some onions and garlic?" she asked, to keep from meeting the goat's eyes.

"Sure, if you don't mind. And some habanero peppers." Niobe indicated a pile on the counter. "I forgot what a help you are in the kitchen."

"I wasn't a help. I just tried not to get in the way."

"Very important. Lao Tse based most of Taoism on that principle."

Nina sliced the onions and then started mincing the garlic. The habaneros would have to wait until she put on some rubber gloves, or the tips of her fingers would become radioactive with the heat.

Thinking how the pretty orange peppers looked so innocent when they were in fact so fiery, she remembered the persimmon tree in Captain Bowman's garden. She said idly, "Have you ever read a book called *The Science of the Mysteries*?"

"Why yes—" Niobe's hand slipped in the blood on the cutting board, and she almost sliced herself, before recovering and repositioning her fingers. "It's a fascinating study. He really knows his subject."

"I met him."

"That's right, he used to live in the Garden District. God, he must be a hundred and ten years old by now."

"Actually, I think he's kind of immortal, like you guys."

Niobe stopped cutting up the meat and shut her eyes for a second, and Nina had the idea she might have actually grown even paler than she already was. Then, when she'd recovered, she said, "Really? How fascinating."

Nina wasn't a master of disguise or a powerful magician, but she did know bullshit. And Niobe appeared to recognize that fact.

"Oh, all right," the older woman sighed. "I'll come clean. I knew he was immortal. We knew him in the early '70s, when things came to a head with the Saturni and I left. He offered to help our cause, Strickland's and mine, but . . . we didn't dare. Relations between the Skin Eaters and the Santa Compagna have always been rocky, even when they weren't trying to kill us."

"I heard about that," Nina said, not wanting to meet Niobe's eyes now either. She tipped the minced garlic into a bowl with the onions. "Did they . . . did they actually do, well . . . that stuff at the Silo de Carlomagna?"

"Lock up a bunch of Skin Eaters and take bets on who'd be lunch? No shit. Don't look so surprised, they were monsters. I don't know how the headmaster lives with himself."

"But he . . . come on, he didn't do it! Did he?" Nina wondered how much she knew about him, either. She said softly, "I thought he was nice."

"He is nice." Niobe had finished cutting up the meat and went to rinse off her hands. Whatever uncertainty had struck her for a moment was gone now, and she looked as relaxed as ever. "And he's charming. And he even swore he was on our side. But . . ." She shook her head as she reached into a drawer and handed Nina a pair of rubber gloves. "He's just too slippery. You can't ever pin him down."

Nina reflected that that seemed to be the story of her whole life. Paths leading to nowhere. She asked, "Does he . . . does he know where you guys are now?"

"I guess so. Oh, I might as well tell you all of it. I trusted him once with a very important secret, and he betrayed that trust. No, I'm not going to tell you what the secret was, because it's all water under the bridge now, and even the bridges are gone. At one point I made a really stupid mistake, all right? Strickland and I . . . well, we thought we could do something. Something awful. And it had consequences."

She sat down at the bloody table, and looked up at Nina and asked, "You really want to hear it? We tried to raise the dead. It worked, and it was terrible, and then it didn't work, and we had to hide what we had done. Okay? End of story."

Nina felt her knees tremble as she sat down slowly on the opposite side of the table, and she thought, *Damn it, that goat's head is really getting on my last nerve.*

"You . . . raised the dead?" Somehow they'd moved into a different world, even though they were still sitting in the kitchen with light streaming through the window, and the mockingbirds mimicking the clucking sound of the chickens outside. Everything was perfectly normal, except she was sitting there next to a butchered goat with an undead woman who'd already rescued her from Guinee, so she said, "You mean somebody who wasn't a Skin Eater."

"Right. Somebody human."

"Did you . . . did you go back to Guinee to get them?"

"Hardly." Niobe's laugh was short. "I told you, we had no idea what we were doing. You see, there are rules, even when you're talking about breaking all the natural rules of existence. Yes, Skin Eaters are no longer alive in a technical sense, but they're changed gradually, so they can accept their death. If someone dies abruptly . . . simply, irrevocably . . . well, it's finite. At least it's something that should be finite.

"But we tried it. And the results were ghastly. We reversed a death, at least for a little while, but of course you can't really bring them back." She took a deep breath. "All you can bring back is an abomination."

*All right*, Nina thought, *let's stop this right now.* Feeling like she had to get some air, she stood up and moved to the doorway, breathing in the warm, muddy, grassy scent of the backyard. *I'm here in Louisiana,* she thought. *I'm standing in the middle of the*

*Lower Ninth Ward, with people and livestock and normal stuff going on all around me. I'm not going crazy. I'm not.* She focused on the sound of the wind blowing through the tall grass, and a hoot from the river as a boat went by, unseen behind the levee. Someone a few houses away was using a power saw. She could smell the scent of a tea olive tree blooming somewhere, and the stubborn weeds were growing up, taller than the few remaining houses. Life went on here. *Life.* No matter how much death had gone down in this city, oil and benzine and sewage dumped into the earth and misery and devastation enough to paralyze the heart, the grass still grew. And she realized with an ache how tired she was of death.

Niobe came and stood in the doorway beside her, and Nina turned to look at her. "What did you do in the end?" she asked her. She said it more loudly than she'd intended, because part of her was furious with the older woman for even bringing this up. "How did you get rid of . . . I don't know . . . whatever it was. The 'abomination.' Whatever it was you two had made?"

"We banished it," Niobe whispered. "Not necessarily the cleanest process, but it worked. We banished it to Guinee, somewhere where it could be kept safe, somewhere where it wouldn't be bothered. That's what I told Captain Bowman anyway, and he, unfortunately, spilled the beans."

She pushed her hair back from her forehead, wincing despite her alleged fondness for the sun, and for an instant the tiredness was etched in every line of her face. Nina realized that, while Strickland so often looked young, barely thirty, Niobe in that moment looked ancient.

And as quickly as it had flared up in her, all her anger died out, and all she wanted to do was comfort the older woman, who was so clearly beyond comfort. She said, "I'm sorry," and Niobe shrugged.

"It's no big deal."

"Yes, it is. You're unhappy."

"Unhappiness is a common state. Like hunger and thirst and ... well, certain other things. I'm afraid it comes with the territory."

"Being human?" Nina wasn't sure if this was the right thing to say, but it turned out it was exactly right. Niobe managed a brief smile, and Nina said after a moment, "Um, there is just one other thing."

"What?"

"I was wondering . . ." She stopped. Was she really rude for asking this? "How did you go on after something like that? I mean . . ." She struggled for words. "I feel like I'm just pinging around right now from one nightmare to the next, just banging from one terrible thing to another. How did you . . . you fought the Saturni, and you did this terrible thing, and then you lost your brother and you had to leave your home and all this time you've been on the run and still . . . you seem so centered."

"You mean why didn't I lose my mind? After losing everything else?"

"How could you bear it?" Nina asked, meaning so many different things.

Niobe made a little face, and said, "You know, growing up's not the worst possible outcome. Consider the alternative. I think I managed to survive by not thinking about it too much. If you dwell in possibility, you quickly lose whatever hope you have and start chewing on the furniture. I lived. I still live, and you'll find out you can do it too." Then she turned and went back into the kitchen, going to the pot on the stove, and said, "Come on, you still have to help me get ready. I'm making a feast for tonight, because we're going to have some visitors."

# Chapter Eighteen

Nina only gradually realized what that meant. When Crux showed up, she knew something important was happening. Not that he looked any different. His dreadlocks were still in place, and his coat still looked old and scruffy, and he was wearing sneakers that had seen better days. But none of that diminished his unearthly beauty. He hugged Niobe, and then Nina.

"Took you long enough," he said, walking to the fridge. "You want a beer?"

"No, I—" Nina blinked. "Were you expecting me?"

"Ages ago. We had a pool about when you were going to show up. I'm afraid I lost, I said before Christmas."

"Yes, well . . ." Nina felt a little shy, now that she realized Crux and Niobe were a "couple." At least, she assumed they were. They didn't behave toward one another in a particularly romantic way. They were more like old friends who were so close they could finish each other's sentences. Crux added, "Cost me ten bucks."

"Like you couldn't afford it." Niobe was making corn fritters to go with the goat stew, and she concentrated on mixing the canned corn into the batter while hiding a smile.

"I'm a poor traveler. Living hand to mouth."

"With all the money you make panhandling? You're a con artist. The Artful Dodger."

"You're a cruel woman."

"Yes, I know. Here, set the table." She tossed him a bag of plastic knives and forks.

"No point in being fancy. Things are going to get kind of messy."

Crux opened the bag and started laying out the plastic utensils in piles. Nina wanted to ask them why "messy" was the tone of this particular evening (usually they ate on china plates with real silverware and glassware) but Niobe gave her another bag of paper napkins and she followed Crux's example in laying them out.

"What's the Big Boss Man say?" Crux asked, going back to the stove and sticking his finger in the goat stew, which was simmering and smelled wonderful. He licked the sauce from his finger and added, "Is he even going to show up?"

"Who knows? I'm not his keeper."

"Who's the Big Boss Man?" Nina had barely formed that question when Billie and the Goth boy, Stephen, came in arguing.

"No, you can't just talk about 'collateral' damage like that, like it's no big deal!" The blonde girl looked like she was close to tears. "Everyone's important, everyone's worth saving!"

"Honey, it's all bones eventually." He flicked a silver earring at her, shaped like a human bone. It matched his platinum hair. "You've got to embrace the Reaper, baby. That's key."

"Stevie, you're so full of shit," Tish snapped, coming into the kitchen and setting down a heavy pair of dumbbells on the table. She'd been practicing and had worked up a sweat.

"Nobody's 'reaping' this girlfriend without I take out a whole bunch of Saturni fucks first."

"Toys off the table," Niobe reminded her, and she mumbled, "Sorry," and put the dumbbells down on the floor. Flyboy, her shadow, helped her. He buzzed and ducked his head at Nina, which made her feel oddly flattered that he'd noticed her. Then a whole group of kids came in together, Daneel and Sibelle and Santangelo and Joe Trunza and Sharazz and Bacalou and the twins. The whole family was there.

"I hope you're hungry," Niobe said. "However, first, before we eat, I have a surprise for you. At least it may come as a surprise to some of you. I know you've all been looking forward to this. We have guests."

There was the barest flutter of movement at the corners of the room, and a sigh like the wind, although no wind could have held such a scent of fresh leaves and sea water, ripe fruit and earth and burned hair and candle wax as this wind carried. Nine felt the hair on her arms lift as she recognized the smell from her dreams of Bois Caiman. The jungle. Heat. The stealthy whisper of power grew around her, and she suspected the four Great *Lwas* might have entered the kitchen. Then their breaths were magnified a hundred fold by the untrustworthy breeze, until it seemed an entire world had just joined them in that single room.

Gradually, they appeared. A man with a crown of feathers on his head. A warrior king. Two soft, transparent figures with their arms laced around one another. The twins. A woman with frayed palms fronds over her face, and a terrible woman with her face slashed with knife cuts, and a man with a guitar, and a man with a hammer and tongs from the forge. A man in a suit, top hat and sunglasses, one lens missing. And a leper, and a bull, and a mermaid, her skin blue and silvery cool with scales.

They all appeared. The *Lwas*. Drawn by food and focus and the almighty need and loneliness of their kind. They weren't really visible. They looked like the flickering images of a digital TV breaking up. They came and filled the empty air, and a figure detached itself from their number and approached Flyboy and touched him on the forehead with a single, bony finger.

"Yesssss," the spectre sighed, and Flyboy sighed too. This *Lwa* was little more than a bony hand attached to a dark smudge of nothingness, a formless, oily black column that rose up like greasy smoke, and Nina had a sudden, terrifying memory of the Nadir.

*No*, she thought. *Don't touch him, don't go into that boy, he'll die,* but even as she thought that, Flyboy smiled, the first real smile she'd ever seen on his face. He opened his arms, and the figure of bones and darkness dissolving into him with a soft cry of completion no louder than a lover might make, or a person stepping into a hot bath.

And a moment later there was just Flyboy again, standing there with his head cocked a little to one side. He seemed to be getting used to the new sensation of sharing his body with a god.

"Yes," he said finally, and his voice sounded completely different. He was Guede, the Lord of the Dead, and his voice was like the boom of surf and the rattle of the sea over small shells. The entirety of Guinee reverberated within the small confines of the kitchen. "Yes. This is right. This is where I belong. My brothers and sisters, join me. At last, we've come home."

He turned to the other children and added courteously, "If you'll have us," and they all nodded. There were expressions of fierceness on some of their faces, and fear on others—Sibelle was shivering, and Billie was weeping what might have been tears of either grief or joy—but no one refused. Nina held her breath.

Crux advanced toward the Lord of the Dead and clasped him in his arms, and there was a bubble of laughter in his voice as he said, "My brother. It's been a long time since I could embrace you like this."

And the Lord of the Dead looked at him levelly and said, "You actually missed me?" "Yes," Crux said. "Are you kidding? I've missed all of you. What can I tell you? We've been waiting for you for centuries."

---

Yes, it was messy, and it was long, and eventually they ate all the goat stew and the corn fritters and everything else in the house.

They drank all the rum, and the beer, and then Baron Samedi made a liquor run and came back with six bottles of tequila and limes and they all did shots. At one point Nina asked Niobe, "Do you have any aspirin?"

"No, why?"

"You're going to need some. These *Lwas* are going to have the mother of all hangovers."

By three a.m. Shango and Ogoun had already beaten each other up and were hanging on each other's necks, singing boozy songs. Azaka, The Potions God in Santangelo's body, accompanied them on the guitar. The twins were fast asleep on the sofa, Babalu was rolling joints for everybody, Ayizan and Guede were making out in the guest room, and Yemaya and the Bull were crying on each other's shoulders, for no reason anyone could recall. Most of the *jumbies* had passed out, but the *Lwas* were still going strong. Dantor, the fierce warrior goddess, staggered over to Nina and slurred, "Grea' party!"

"Uh, thanks."

"You want a hit?" She held out a roach.

"No, thanks. Somebody's got to stay sober enough to clean up after you guys."

"Fuck it! This is a celebration! A reunion! You have no motherfucking idea how long we've been waiting for this!" She put her fingers over her lips. "Oops. Sorry, sorry. I forgot you're kind of a goody two-shoes. I didn't mean to oh-fend."

"I'm not a goody two-shoes," Nina snapped, although she thought, *I don't know, maybe I am.* She just felt nervous and exposed in the house, with all the lights on, with everybody drunk and stoned out of their minds and the Saturni waiting somewhere outside in the dark.

"It's just . . . it seems so . . . dangerous," she said, and Dantor just looked at her. "Come on, hot cheeks, you're supposed to know about history. You want to know what we did at Bois Caiman, the last time we did this? We danced. We fucked each other's brains out, and any animals we could get our hands on! Well, God save the mariner! We bathed in their blood and cooked their meat and gnawed on their bones. We ate and puked and swam in life up to our armpits, because we knew exactly what was coming afterward, and don't think we don't know that now. You think you can put off celebrating until the end of a war, when everything's all neat and tidy? Bull. Shit. You have to celebrate right at the beginning, while there's still time."

Nina shook her head and said, "That's not what I meant. I didn't mean you all shouldn't be happy to be back inside bodies, it's just—"

"It's just you're still thinking like a mortal? God almighty, Nina, what the fuck! You think you were ever like them?" She waved her arm at the windows of the kitchen, to indicate the whole world outside, pitch dark now save for the occasional working streetlight, and the even more occasional occupied house. The Ninth Ward lay slumbering like an open field, a land scoured clean of trees and sidewalks and now reclaimed by nature.

Dantor's eyes glowed red as she stared deeply at Nina, and despite the reek of rum on her breath, Nina found she couldn't look away.

"You're one of us, don't you forget it. You got nothing remotely human about you. You think I can't tell? I'm not sure what you are, but I can smell a fake a mile off. You're 'passing,' girl. You're a spirit or a *Lwa* or a god or a devil or something. Don't kid yourself."

"Stop it," a calm voice said. Crux moved gracefully between them, and put his hand on Dantor's arm. At that moment, the distinction between the angry voodoo spirit and the body she was inhabiting couldn't have been clearer. Tish, the skinny redhead, weighed barely a hundred pounds, and Crux could have broken her arm like a twig. Dantor, on the other hand, pulled away and spat, "Hands off, Legba. No touchy-feelies."

"As you wish. But please remember, you're not supposed to terrify her." The male *Lwa* was still smiling, but his tone suggested a reprimand. Dantor made a face and said, "Oooh, I'm shakin'."

"Stop it. She's not like us in one respect at least. She can break. You push her too hard and you'll ruin everything."

"Leggie, you're a fucking pussy."

"So I've been told."

"Oh, all right, all right…" Dantor abruptly got bored and waved the whole issue away, although she was so drunk the gesture made her stumble against the kitchen table. "Fine. No skin off my ass. Go cuddle with her. You always did love the weak ones."

"Pay no attention," Crux said under his breath, as he led Nina away toward the front door. Outside, the air was cool and damp, refreshing after the indoor heat. They walked down the steps and across the street and up toward the levee, dark and quiet in the pale moonlight.

When they'd climbed the bank and stood looking out at the water, the river was like ink, rippling.

"She's just jealous," Crux chuckled. "She wants you for yourself. She's always liked girls better than boys."

"You mean you have preferences?"

"Of course. Why not? We live in bodies to experience them fully, otherwise why mount them at all? Surely you've realized we're not exactly squeamish."

"Yeah, I kind of got that idea after watching Guede and Ayizan go spelunking for each other's tonsils."

Crux smiled. "You've changed a lot since last spring."

"Actually, I'm exactly the same person, just more scared."

"No, you're not. You were willing to hide in Daedalus before. It was a big deal for you to even go out to the Saturn bar. Would you have gone all the way to Guinee?"

"It's not like I had much choice."

"Sure you did. God, I sound like such a cliche. But it's true, you could always have bailed on this whole thing, and nobody would have blamed you."

"You really think so?"

"Well, maybe Strickland would have blamed you. But he's kind of an asshole sometimes."

Nina allowed herself to laugh, and they sat down on the grass together, enjoying the quiet and the river's soft stirrings. "Crux?" she asked after a few minutes.

"Yes?"

"Is he okay?"

"You mean Professor Danvers?"

"Um-hmm. Yes, I know, I know, we agreed. 'Asshole.' Right. Still . . ."

"He's not dead, if that's what you mean. The Saturni didn't eat him on Thirteenth Night. I think a lot of that was theater for your benefit. But he's still . . ."

What Nina wanted to ask. Alive? Undead? Collaborating with them? Stringing them along? She said, "Um, okay. Cool. So I guess everything's all right then."

"Well, 'all right' might be stretching things." Crux hesitated. "He's left the school."

"What? Left Daedalus?"

"Yes. Agatha's holding things together as best she can. It seems he's been seen around town in some less than savory neighborhoods, trying to . . . well, to tell you the truth I'm not sure what he's trying to do. Get himself arrested? Get himself beaten to a pulp? He's certainly been threatened, when people caught him . . . well, indulging himself."

Nina swallowed. The idea of Strickland on a Skin Eater binge wasn't something she even wanted to consider. But she had to ask. "Is he celebrating or . . .?"

"Oh come on, Nina, who are we kidding? The man is a world-class expert at self-punishment. Of course he feels guilty. You vanished. He took you to the Fortuna Club and you were assaulted. He has to have known—"

He stopped, and Nina wanted more than anything for him to complete that sentence, but Crux just shook his head and said, "I'm sorry, I shouldn't have mentioned it."

"No. It's all right. It's what you said. I've changed. I can take it. It's just . . . what I can't stand is always being tricked."

She fell silent again, and now there were tears fighting to escape from her eyes, and she forced herself to look at the dark river and watch its current and think of Guinee and the Nadir and bones and shrines and Vincent Van Gogh's ear, and anything else she could think of, so she wouldn't cry. She felt Crux sitting very quietly beside her, and she knew she wasn't fooling him for a second.

"There are far worse things than lies, Nina," he said finally.

"Oh yeah?" She sniffed. "Like what?"

"Oh God, you're so young. All of you. You. Strickland. Even Niobe. You're all so finite . . . and infinity is so infinitely crueler in some ways."

She longed to know what he meant, and this time she said, "Please, explain that to me. Use words of one syllable. I'm too dumb. Why is infinity cruel? Does it hate us? Is there no truth? Does infinity view us as, I don't know, maybe trespassers, or parasites? Like fleas?"

Crux smiled and said, "I don't think quite like fleas. For one thing, I don't think infinity really notices us." He hesitated. "I'm not sure. If it does . . ." He licked his lips. "Then the question of intent comes into play. If I squash one of those fleas you mentioned, do I do it maliciously, or just by accident? Certainly accidental cruelty is far more forgivable. If I *do* do it deliberately . . . if that's my idea of fun . . . then is it because I'm just bored, or it is a trend? What you might call a character trait?"

He stopped and looked out at the black, black water of the river, and his next words made Nina feel as if an icicle had slipped down her back.

"There's something in the world even worse than the Saturni, darker than the void of space and the abyss of time. There's active, unrepentant, deliberate evil. I'm talking about an evil that has no cause but its own delight, no excuse for its cruelty, and no pretext of ever needing one. Even the Saturni hunger. They long. They're so wedded to their desires that they wake up at night screaming for fear they'll ever be denied. But the evil I'm talking about . . ."

He shut his eyes, and Nina wanted to shut hers, too, and stick her fingers in her ears and go back to the house and get hammered, anything to avoid hearing what came next. But of course she couldn't.

"The evil I'm talking about is at the core of the world. It was here before there was anything, and it made everything. And its name is—"

He stopped, and then said, "Of course I can't tell you."

That was it. Nina threw back her head and screamed, her rage so complete for a moment that she literally saw red. She scrambled to her feet, ready to kick him, punch him, do whatever she could to just make him tell her the truth, and she actually raised one hand to hit him, although it occurred to her at the last minute that it was a really, really bad idea to bitch-slap a god.

Crux for his part simply looked up at her, his luminous eyes truly sad for the first time in their acquaintance, and she realized he felt sorry for not being able to tell her. Whatever held his tongue wasn't a scruple but a proscription, like not being able to go past a force-field. He got up and said, "Come on. Let's go back to the party."

# Chapter Nineteen

Inside, things had deteriorated to the end-stages of revelry. Two *Lwas* were getting sick in the bathroom, several more were passed out on the floor, and there were glasses and bottles and dirty plates and overflowing ashtrays everywhere. Baron Samedi was fast asleep, face down in a bowl of Zapp's potato chips, and Niobe was doing the dishes.

"Shit," she said, wiping her hair back from her face. "I'm getting too old for this."

"You asked for it," Crux said, picking up a towel and starting to dry the serving plates.

Nina helped stack them back in the cabinets.

"I know, I know. And it's for a good cause. Still." She looked around at her trashed house and rolled her eyes. "Teenagers."

Rhea and Thetis were wrestling the furniture back into place (at one point the *Lwas* had pushed everything into the corners so they could dance) and Mimas was tucking the two twins into bed on the couch. Crux chuckled.

"Of course you're right, they are children. That's what will give them power."

"If you say so." Niobe sat down at the kitchen table and poured herself a shot of tequila.

"Here's to it! Brave new world! You want one?"

"Please." Crux poured one for himself, and one for Nina as well. Even though she wasn't sure if they might not want to be alone now (was she one of the despised teenagers?) Nina sat down as well and sipped. The tequila shot right down into her stomach.

"Best way to end a party," Crux said, rolling his glass back and forth between his hands while he shut his eyes and savored the taste. "At Bois Caiman we drank cane liquor. Now *that* stuff'll kill you."

"I keep forgetting you were there," Niobe said. "So long ago. And a world away."

"Well, we weren't acquainted then. Back in San Domingue."

"No." Niobe closed her eyes, remembering the island that was now Haiti. "I can still remember the house. There was a wide gallery running all around the outside, to shade us from the sun. And beyond that were the cane fields and the trees. The island was so lush then. The jewel of the Caribbean. And there was a limestone wall at the foot of the garden, and on the other side a sheer cliff dropped straight down, two hundred feet into the sea."

"And you owned slaves."

"Yes, of course. Well, here too. After we ran away from your revolution and moved here to New Orleans, we still owned people. We were still vile."

"No, never that." He put his hand over hers and gently squeezed. "You were human beings, that's all. Even Skin Eaters are human. And humans make mistakes."

"Yeah, well, we certainly did that." Niobe shut her eyes and knocked back her tequila like a sailor. "We certainly made some doozies."

"I love human slang."

"You know what I'm talking about."

"Yes, I know exactly what you're talking about. And I told you, that's something I can't heal. Much though I've enjoyed trying." He still held his hand over hers, slowly tracing his fingers over her skin, and Nina was starting to feel pretty uncomfortable. "I did everything I could to make you happy, Niobe. Everything I could think of. I just couldn't do that."

*Maybe I should just go,* Nina thought. Things seemed to be getting pretty personal, and while she was still curious to learn anything she could, she didn't want to intrude. She was just about to get up when Niobe shut her eyes and whispered, "God, I still miss him."

*Great,* Nina thought. *That's the very last thing I need to hear right now. I'm getting the hell out of here.*

"Of course you do." Crux's whisper was almost inaudible.

"It's foolish, I know. Beyond foolish . . ."

"The heart has its own timetable, and sometimes even centuries aren't enough."

"And even after how it ended—"

"Shh. I know. I know."

"I want him back!" Niobe's cry wasn't loud, but there seemed to be more sadness in her voice than any woman's throat could bear. A universe of loss. "I want Henri *back*!"

*Henri?* Nina thought, coming to a complete stop. *So who the hell is he?*

Moving as quietly as she could, she cautiously sat back down again in her chair. Crux knew she was there, even though he didn't look up. Something about his voice changed, becoming marginally more guarded. "Niobe? Can you hear me? You know you can't have that. We all agreed. It's too dangerous."

"I know."

"It's dangerous even to speak his name. Not after what the Saturni did with him."

"He was mine. I named him."

"I know. And you know there's too much at stake . . ." Crux

abandoned his pretense that Nina wasn't listening and shook Niobe by the shoulder. "Please, darling. Please come back. You can't go there. Not when somebody else can hear you."

Niobe was fumbling in her pocket for something, and that was Nina's first clue that she was drunk, too drunk and exhausted and pushed beyond even her endurance by everything she'd done. Nina saw a flash of light, and she tried to imagine what the older woman might have been hiding. A flashlight? A cigarette lighter? An instant later she realized what it was. A tiny mirror.

Crux moved like lightning to knock it out of her hand, and the mirror smashed on the tile floor. "Ah . . ." Niobe's voice faded as she looked down at the broken glass, and then she crumpled and put her forehead against Crux's shoulder and whispered, "You're right. Of course. Always are. Always will be. I just thought . . . *tonight of all nights . . .*"

"Shh," the *Lwa* said, rubbing her back, while his other hand held her pressed against him.

He looked up at Nina, and she realized his strange, unearthly eyes were silver with tears.

"Perhaps you'll excuse us for a moment? Let me just get her to bed."

He scooped up the woman who was Sister Aquilina as easily as if she had been a doll, and holding her carefully, walked up the stairs with her. Nina sat there at the table and contemplated drinking the rest of her tequila, but she didn't think it would help. Her head was already reeling, and her heart felt like it might simultaneously jump right out of her chest and break.

Who was Henri? Who was the being whose name Crux wouldn't tell her? Were they one and the same? Were they different? What the hell was going *on*?

She looked up at the ceiling, realizing she was the only person in the whole house who was now awake besides Crux. All the *Lwas* and their human hosts were snoring. Baron Samedi was snuffling into his potato chips. What time was it? She looked at her watch and was surprised to see it was almost five o'clock in the morning. The night outside was still black, but as she listened, she heard a bird sing, just one mockingbird, testing the air and then falling silent. A single exploratory note before the dawn.

Crux finally came down the stairs and found her standing in the back doorway, staring out once more into the garden. "I'm sorry, he said simply. "She gets like that sometimes. She can bear everything for a while, and then . . . I don't know, it all gets to be too much."

"Who's Henri?"

"I'm sorry, I can't—"

"Bullshit. Don't give me that 'my lips are sealed' crap. You guys are better at keeping secrets than the Mob. Did you swear a whole *Omertà* thing?"

Crux's smile was wan, but it was genuine. "Something like that. Really, Nina. There are oaths and promises, and I'm sorry, I can't break them. Please believe me, if I could, you'd be the first to know."

"I know." She sighed. "Is Niobe all right?"

"She'll be fine." He paused. "She has her reasons. It's been harder for her than it has for anyone else."

"So I gather. Crux . . . ?"

"Yes?"

"What did you mean, that you tried everything you could to make her happy? You said you enjoyed it, but you just couldn't do 'that.' Was it, um . . . something personal?" Nina really didn't want to know if there was some sex act Crux had refused to perform, and fortunately he laughed and said, "No, not in the way you think. I told you, we're not squeamish."

"Oh. Good. I mean, um, well . . . good. I was just wondering."

"I tried to make something up to her, but I wasn't able to do it. The *Lwas* just aren't built for that. You may be more fortunate, someday. I hope you will. And I hope you find your path. Because you know your place really isn't here. Especially now that the *Lwas* are back."

His words were like lead weights falling onto her heart, but she couldn't really pretend they came as a surprise. *You knew this was only temporary,* she thought. The training of the kids there at the orphanage was complete. They'd been reunited with their spirits, and they would now be turning their thoughts toward war. What could she do but be in the way? She was no mount for the gods. *I still don't even know who I am,* she thought, and despite what Dantor had said, she knew she wasn't a *Lwa*.

She said quietly, "Crux, I'm scared. What am I supposed to do? Go forward or go back? I don't even have anywhere to live besides here."

He smiled then, his luminous, warm, uncanny smile, and said, "Oh, Nina, you already know the answer to that. Sometimes the only way you can go forward is to go back. You've been our honored guest here, and I hope you've enjoyed yourself, but you knew it had to end. Now's the time, and now you need to move on. You need to go back to Daedalus."

# Chapter Twenty

Nina knew it was true. When Crux dropped her off at the front gate an hour later, she had a weird feeling of déjà vu. Here she was again, standing in front of the ominous facade of the Daedalus School, looking past the heavy wrought-iron gates to the huge, spooky house with its big front door and the two stone angels weeping on either side of it. Here she was again, not knowing what would happen next. She felt like she'd been gone for a year. It was still so early, the light was pinkish gray, just warming into morning. Pushing open the gate, she walked up the path, hearing the fountain splashing and the wind through the trees, and silence.

Where was everybody? She kind of hoped she didn't meet anybody until she got back to her room, but it was odd nobody was up yet. She spared a stray thought to wonder if she still had a room. Had they just written her off as a dropout? Maybe she'd have to go back to sleeping up in the attic, if they even let her do that. Opening the front door, she felt the strange silence press against her ears. Daedalus was often quiet, but this felt different. This felt fearful.

Looming above her head, the high ceiling of the great central hall was fretted with coffered shadows. Dimly, she could see the big stained-glass window in front of her, showing the five birds in flight: a crow, a pelican, a swan, a peacock, and what she now knew was a phoenix. Her footsteps made no sound as she walked up the stairs, her feet sinking into the thick, red plush. How odd to be back, almost like she was a ghost.

She hesitated before the closed door of the headmaster's office. He's not there, she told herself sternly. He's off chewing on somebody's face in some dive bar, but just as she turned to go upstairs, she realized there were voices coming from inside the room. They didn't sound any too happy to be there. In fact, they sounded hurried and whispering. Without giving herself time to wonder if this was a good idea or not, she stopped to listen.

"No," she heard someone say quickly—*Agatha*, she thought. "I haven't said anything to the Freelands yet. Are you insane? Do you think I'm just going to go up to them and say, 'Whoops, sorry, it seems your daughter has disappeared, but don't worry, I'm sure she'll turn up somewhere?'" She snorted. "I value my spleen and my liver too much to let Isolde Freeland make a meal out of them."

Someone else—she couldn't recognize who it was—said quietly, "You know where she is, don't you?"

"I do not! I refuse to even listen to you when you're like this! I prefer you dotty."

"So do I, but you summoned me." The other person sighed. "You want my advice? Ask Strickland."

"I'd rather shoot myself. No, no, come on, don't go away yet. Here, have some more hellebore . . ."

"I hate that stuff." There was the sound of somebody sipping. "Ugh. All right, so listen up. The headmaster's behind all of this, as you well know. As at so many other times, we're just pawns in his games of life and death and . . . eternity. Believe me, I know what I'm talking about. Now before I slip off into la-la land again . . . and no, I'm not drinking any more hellebore! . . . please listen. He sent the Sybil. He started this whole ball rolling. Strickland knew what the stakes were, but he went to see the Sybil anyway, and he took the girl there as well. That's why I'm saying talk to Strickland if you want to know who benefits and who doesn't. And don't listen to him without taking whatever he says with a huge grain of salt."

Nina heard someone getting up, and she scooted away from the door, even though Agatha's voice came from inside, saying, "Wait a minute, you don't understand—"

"Of course I don't understand, Aggie." Whoever the man was, his voice sounded old and tired and a little cranky. "I only get to be awake for five or ten minutes a day, when I'm dosed so full of hellebore my ears are ringing. Now if you're holding something back—"

"No, no . . . I mean nothing important . . ."

"What?"

"It's the girl. Nina. She's, well . . ." Agatha muttered something too low for Nina to hear.

"I'm sorry, you have to speak up. Ringing in the ears, remember?"

"Strickland's got a 'thing' for her, all right? You know him! He never really grew up, he's still got the hormones of a randy teenager. And Miss Lamb is . . ." She muttered something else, and this time the other person in the room laughed.

"Yes, I agree, if I were half my age, I'd look twice myself. Still, you can't mean he'd risk doing something so dangerous . . . something so dangerous for the girl as well . . ."

"He'd do anything, I tell you. He's bound and determined to atone for his past sins, and besides, if Miss Lamb really is who he thinks she is . . . which I doubt to the depths of my soul . . . he says she can save us all. Yes, that's exactly what I'm saying! Strickland thinks she's HIS child. I know, I know, it sounds crazy, you don't even have to tell me. For what it's worth, I always thought Simone—"

And then Agatha broke off and said sharply, "What's that? There's someone outside, I'm sure of it."

Nina just barely had time to duck into the next room down from the professor's office, before the door was yanked open and Agatha peered out. Watching through the crack in the door behind which she'd just retreated, Nina had to repress a completely inappropriate desire to laugh. Agatha looked like someone who was "it" who'd just missed catching somebody else at hide and seek.

"I doubt anyone's around at this hour," said the man inside the room. "Not with the school in lock-down. Father Ignatius has put the literal fear of God in everyone."

*So that's why it's so quiet*, Nina thought. And then, *Shit, I really hope I don't run into* him.

Agatha was shaking her head ruefully as she came out into the corridor. Nina heard her say under her breath, "That creepy old cross-dresser makes my skin crawl," which made it even harder not to laugh. At the same time, Nina was so afraid of making any noise she literally tried not to blink. The room she was hiding in was dark, and she had no idea whether it was a classroom or an office or a closet, but at the moment all that mattered was that it was empty, and Agatha was looking in the other direction. The older woman closed and locked the door to the headmaster's office, and Nina got her first good look at the man she'd been speaking to, and realized who it was.

Professor Seneschal.

But a professor Seneschal who looked like he'd just drunk about sixteen Red Bulls. He was alert and seemed to have single every one of his marbles, even though he looked tired, and there were deep lines next to his eyes as though he were in pain.

"Are you going to be all right getting upstairs?" Agatha asked.

"I'd better be, hadn't I? What are you going to do, tuck me in? Get me some milk and cookies? I've got to teach later. Besides, I've been dealing with this for ages."

"I know." She put his hand on his shoulder, and for a moment Nina was surprised to see actual sympathy on her face. Who knew? Agatha could be a softie.

"It just seems so unfair. I wish there was something more we could do."

"Take me to the Wizard of Oz? Get me some brains?" Professor Seneschal smiled. "No thanks, I previously saw the old wizard, and look where it got me."

He didn't say anything else, but turned and went up the stairs, and Agatha, after checking to make sure he didn't stumble, turned and walked down to the first floor. Nina, watching from behind her door, cautiously allowed herself to exhale.

*Close one*, she thought, resisting yet again the nervous desire to giggle. She waited a few minutes more until she was sure the coast was clear and then opened the door of her hiding place and was about to step outside.

She had no idea what made her hesitate. Maybe it was the light spilling in from the hallway, or the bright yellow cover of the book that caught her attention. White, red, blue, and purple flowers were drawn all over it, and in ornate lettering it said, *Gabby Gator's Big Book of Fun*. A smiling alligator was pictured lying among the flowers, and there were other equally cute forest animals around him: a bear, a pelican, a bright red fox, and a fish.

And there was something else. The minute Nina saw it, she recognized it from the Mezzotint engraving. It was the book the headmaster had been holding.

She snatched it up without even thinking twice, and then pelted up the stairs.

# Chapter Twenty-One

"So . . . you're back." Alastaire slouched in the armchair in Nina's room, his hands stuffed in his pockets. Bella sat on the bed and wouldn't look at her either. For the fifth time that day, Nina tried to explain to her friends that she hadn't done any of this on purpose.

"I told you. It was the only way I could escape from that party. It was completely awful."

"And of course you had to go to that awful party in the first place," Alastaire snapped. "I mean, I thought we agreed—"

"I didn't agree to anything. We talked about my running away, but I decided against it. And besides, what would have been the difference? I still would have ended up at the Convent."

"Without pissing off the entire Saturnic high court and disappearing for a solid month!"

"All right, I'm sorry about that. And I'm sorry I went missing for so long. But once I was there, there was no way for me to get in touch with you—"

"What, you couldn't use a phone? They wouldn't give you a stamp?"

"They don't have telephones at Daedalus!" Nina struggled to hold on to the remains of her temper. "And how the hell was I going to write to you, care of the Saturni?"

"Well, you could have done something."

"WHAT??"

"I don't know! Something besides going off to a dance with

professor Fuck Face and then going rogue! We were worried about you, Neens! Is that so hard to believe?"

Nina was actually quite touched, but she didn't want to give her friends the satisfaction. She tried to pet Mercy, but the black cat jumped up on the bed next to Bella and turned away from her. *Great,* Nina thought. *Everybody's mad at me.*

"For the last time, I only did this to find out about the Void and the Alignment and what the Saturni were planning and—"

"And the reason Sister Aquilina has been establishing her army of children, and what the *Lwas* want. Yes, Nina, we get all that." Bella shook her head. "What you don't seem to get is friends keep friends in the loop. I thought we were a team. And you're still not telling us everything, are you? What else happened at the Convent? You said the *Lwas* got drunk and had a big orgy, but you look like something else seriously messed you up, and all we're asking is *what*?"

"Not like we care," Alastaire added, folding a stick of gum in his mouth and looking out the window.

"Look, I'm sorry, okay?" Nina swallowed her pride. "I messed up. I got distracted. Now, do you forgive me?"

"Hmmph." Bella just looked down at the bedspread.

Nina decided this was the best she was going to get. "Well, anyway, I got back this morning, and you won't believe what happened as I was coming up the stairs. For one thing, I heard Agatha talking to professor Seneschal, and he sounded . . . well, fine. I mean like a normal human being. She said she gave him something that woke him up . . . 'hell' something-or-other . . ."

"Hellebore," Bella said. "It's a mental stimulant. It would be the obvious choice to administer to someone who'd been, well, damaged in the way Captain Bowman told us professor Seneschal had been." The Vietnamese girl decided to sacrifice a little of her resentment to her curiosity and added, "So . . . what did you hear them say?"

"Well." Nina sat down on the bed and gestured to Alastaire to join them. "For one thing, they said Simone Freeland is missing."

"You're kidding." Bella smiled. "Bet that made Agatha's morning."

"True that. Professor Seneschal asked her if she'd told Simone's parents yet, and Agatha said she wasn't that big of an idiot. But they have to learn about it soon, right? I mean, they're right here. They'll expect to be able to see her."

"I don't know." Bella shrugged. "Actually, I think the Saturni have been so wrapped up lately, they may not notice her absence for quite a while. Circling the wagons, if you ask me. When the *Lwas* came down into those kids in the Lower Ninth Ward, the Saturni definitely felt it. You could have heard them cursing as far as Lee Circle."

"I can imagine." Nina shivered. "So you think Dr. and Mr. Freeland may not even care?"

"No," Bella amended. "I think they'll care like hell once they find out Simone's gone.

Unless they're the ones who sent her away."

"Huh." Nina thought about that and then shook her head. "No, Agatha said she was afraid to tell them. Although that could just mean Agatha doesn't know what they did."

She frowned as she thought of something else. "Actually, professor Seneschal said Agatha did know where Simone was, but she denied it. He also told her to ask her brother about it. I know! I know!" she added, since Alastaire had opened his mouth to say something rude.

"I'm not saying Professor Danvers is trustworthy or anything like that, I'm just saying. Professor Seneschal said Agatha should talk to her brother and take everything he said with a huge grain of salt. He also said . . ." She hesitated. "He said the headmaster was the one who was really behind all this. He said we were all just pawns, in his game of life and death and . . . and eternity."

And as she said that, she remembered Crux's words, "Infinity is infinitely cruel." Right now the idea of eternity struck her as one of the cruelest things on the planet. For a moment, she didn't want to tell her friends anything more, not about anyone's thoughts of who she was or whose daughter she might be. Finally she said, "Oh yeah, I forgot. I also found this. Look."

She pulled out the copy of *Gabby Gator's Big Book of Fun*, which she'd hidden under her pillow. She held it out, waiting for them to be impressed.

It took a moment, and then Alastaire said politely, "Um, cute," and Bella said, "Aren't you a little old to be reading at that grade level?"

Nina realized they had no idea what the book meant. She explained, "It's the book the headmaster was holding in the picture. In the Mezzotint. Don't you remember? The one I told you about. See? It's been here at the school the whole time."

Bella took the book and examined it, while Alastaire grudgingly moved over to the bed and sat looking over her shoulder. Here was Gabby Gator playing with his friends, Mr. Bear, Mr. Pelican, Mr. Fox, and Miss Fish. Here they were, sailing in a small, flat-bottomed boat. Here they were, going to church. Here they were at the public library.

And here they were having what looked like a birthday party, with cake and balloons. The drawings were lovely, beautiful watercolors. Still, after a few minutes, Bella said, "I don't know, I guess I was expecting something a little bit more . . . portentous."

"I know what you mean," Nina said. "But still, I'm sure it's the same book. What do you think it means?"

"I don't know." Bella riffled through the pages. "It could mean anything. Or nothing. I don't even know where to start . . ."

"It's obvious." They all looked up to see Phoebe Passerine standing in the doorway, looking at them with a sunny, helpful expression. When nobody said anything for a full half-minute, she came in and sat down in Nina's desk chair and said, "Is this your room? It's nice."

"Uh . . . sure, come on in," Nina said, after she'd already sat down. She looked at the strange girl and said after a moment, "How did you even know what we were talking about?"

"I saw the book. We used to read that when we were little. All of us. May I?" She reached for the book and flipped through it. "Yes, it's just like I remember it. It's a history of the planet Saturn."

"*Excuse* me?"

"Of course." She pointed at the first picture in the book, which showed Gabby Gator and his friends all lined up and waving. "See, here's Saturn and Venus and Mars lined up with the planet Earth. This is from the First Age, when Saturn was still a star. A dwarf star, like our sun. See, that's the Bear. Saturn was a brown dwarf. And the Gator is Venus, and the red Fox is Mars, and we're Earth. See? The fish means we're a water planet. Originally, Saturn was a star lined up in a polar configuration with Earth's celestial north, and Mars and Venus were lined up with it. The result was what looked like a gigantic eye, with an iris and a pupil. See? An eye."

She pointed to a bunch of smiling daisies, one of which did, in fact, have a colorful eye painted in its center. The eye burned with a cool, steady green iris, and at the center there was a red pupil. Nina looked at it and felt a little sick. "No," she said. "No, that's not possible."

"Of course it is. Then after that there was the Great Deluge . . ."

She turned the page, where Gabby and his friends had now

been joined by Mr. Pelican and they were all shown in a boat. Gabby's long gator tail was hanging down into the water, and Mr. Fox was amusing himself by throwing rocks at the riverbank.

"Our present sun arrived," Phoebe went on, pointing to it up in the sky, "and Saturn retreated. Venus became a comet. See how long a tail Gabby's got? That's what wiped out the dinosaurs by the way. At least people think so. And Mars rained asteroids down upon the earth. The pelican, of course, is the Skin Eaters, because the pelican is supposed to use its own blood to feed its young. That means that by the time the new sun appeared in the sky, the Saturni were already here on Earth, and they had already created their slaves. Then . . ."

She turned the next page, where Gabby and his friends were seen going to church, and then shopping at a market.

"Then the Saturni created the idea of priesthoods and the invention of commerce. Everybody was too worrying about what to believe, and making money, to pay any attention to anything else. The Saturni seduced people with stories of alchemy and war. But the truth was still hidden." She pointed to the next picture, where the five animal friends were lying out under the stars, looking up at the night sky. Over in the far corner, the planet Saturn could be seen, circled by its familiar rings. "The old sun was still there. Or the truth, if you prefer to call it that. Still present."

Bella made a strangled noise like she was throwing up.

"That's the biggest pile of horse shit I ever heard!" she exploded. "A planet can't be a planet and a star at the same time! There is no such thing as a polar configuration! And your Sesame Street version of cosmology is just ridiculous! Venus isn't an alligator! The Earth isn't a fish! And the planet Neptune isn't a cocker spaniel either! It's just stupid!"

"Do the Saturni really believe this?" Nina asked Phoebe,

instead of confronting the idea directly, and the younger girl shrugged.

"I don't know. It's true, though. Although some people think it means something else. They think the five friends are really like the five birds in the old Skin Eater prophecy, representing the five alchemical elements: a crow for lead, a swan for thought, a peacock for passion, a pelican for sacrifice, and a phoenix for rebirth. I don't know. I guess they could be that too."

Nina felt like her head was about to explode, and Bella's angry protests weren't helping it. She held up her hand and said, "Okay, time out, Nostradamus. If all this is true, what does it have to do with anything that's happening now? You don't, um . . ." She decided to go out on a limb. "You don't happen to know anything about Sister Aquilina, do you?"

"Oh, yes, I know everything." Phoebe held up her hand and ticked things off. "I know Sister Aquilina is the one you call Niobe now. And I know she's the one who brought the *Lwas* back into human form, and the Saturni are majorly pissed off about it. That's why Father Ignatius keeps trying to keep us all in our rooms and walks around swearing at everybody. And I know the Freelands are fighting with Sabien Belu, and I know Oswald Babb made a pass at Toshiro Nagoichi, and I know Simone Freeland is missing, and . . ."

"Wait a minute, you know about that?" Alastaire said. "We only found out about that this morning!"

"She disappeared last night." Phoebe twiddled her fingers, and the cat Mercy jumped up on her lap to play with them. "I know because I was going downstairs to get a snack . . . dinner was awful as usual . . . and I heard the Freelands talking to Simone and her mother said Simone had to do something, and Simone didn't sound like she wanted to do it very much. And then Dr. Freeland hit her, and said she'd do as she was told, and she said she would, and then I hid because they all came out into the front hall and her mother said do it now and she walked into the big mirror there and disappeared. I guess she went to Guinee."

No one said anything for a moment, and the Phoebe said, "What? Did I say something wrong?"

# Chapter Twenty-Two

Nina and Alastaire and Bella spent the rest of the day lying around in her room and eventually went down to dinner, although with all these new mysteries, nobody had much of an appetite. Father Ignatius watched everybody as they descended the stairs and seemed to be taking attendance. He didn't react to her any more than any of the other Saturni had, and she supposed she should be grateful her *miroir d'intent* was still holding. She sat eating canned ham and canned peas and what tasted like canned bread, and wondered if things could get any worse.

It wasn't until she was plowing her way through her canned peaches that she noticed everyone around her was whispering the names *Phoebe* and *Passerine*. Leaning across the table, she asked a girl sitting there, "What's up with Phoebe? We were just talking to her."

The girl shrugged and said, "Apparently, she's gone."

"Gone? As in 'gone away'? What do you mean, she left the school?"

"Gone as in dropped off the face of the earth, as far as I hear. Kathy Hareton went to her room just before dinner to borrow her Sky Geography notes, but she was AWOL."

With every single particle of her mind and heart, Nina wished she could discuss this with Alastaire and Bella, but with Father Ignatius glaring at them from the teachers' table, she didn't dare. As they were trooping back upstairs, however, she hissed, "So?"

"I don't know," Bella said. "I grant you it's suspicious."

"Girls, no unnecessary chit-chat," Father Ignatius said, coming up behind them and swatting Bella on the backside with a ruler. Nina turned to stare at him, and he had the good grace to look away, embarrassed.

Bella slipped into her own room, and Nina moved to catch up with Alastaire.

"Alastaire, wait, talk to me for a second, what do you think—?"

"I think we better shut up before Father Kink there gets any more creative with that ruler. I'll catch you later."

Alastaire ducked inside his room, and Nina swallowed a scream of frustration and walked on down the hallway to her own door. She went inside and threw herself down on the bed and Mercy jumped up next to her and meowed loudly to get her attention.

"Yeah, yeah, all right . . . you're still here . . . at least everybody's not disappearing . . ."

She reached for the cat and tried to pet him, but he was having none of it. He jumped down onto the floor and then back up onto her desk in one fluid cat-motion and then turned around like he wanted her to applaud. When she didn't, he meowed again, this time putting some serious spin on it.

"What? You're hungry? I know you've got kibbles . . ."

Meowwww. Me*owww*!

"What? You want to go outside? Right, there's the window."

*Meowwwww!*

"What?"

He was bumping his head against a pile of books on her desk, knocking first one of them onto the floor and then another, and finally scraping his claws across the one he liked best. She could practically hear him shredding the binding. "Somebody ought to declaw you," she groused, getting up to toss him back down on the floor, but then she stopped and realized which book he'd been attacking.

*The Science of the Mysteries* by Captain Bowman.

She picked it up (at least to keep the cat from destroying it) and saw the Sybil's engraving underneath it.

And then she sat back down at her desk and stared at it for a long, long time.

No, it couldn't be.

No, she told herself, things didn't work like that.

She lived in a world of shadows and mirrors and riddles. A world where there were no rules, no maps, and no easy answers.

Certainly nothing so simple as a direction.

Still, there the words were, written on a big piece of paper being held up in the engraving by Professor Danvers on one side, and Niobe Danvers on the other. They were standing posed on either side of the garden, staring directly into the camera, and they seemed to be staring directly at her, smirking at her, as if she were the biggest fool in the world.

ASK HIM, the banner said in big bold letters.

Ask who?

*Ask Captain Bowman,* Nina thought. *Ask the man who had said, "Should you have any questions, I'd be more than happy to answer them."*

Nina sat there and wondered if she should do it.

Niobe had said he was slippery and unreliable and he had once betrayed her. He worked for an organization which at one time had tortured the Skin Eaters for sport. But even given all that, right now, wasn't he her best option?

No, she told herself, he's my only option. No one else there was even able to talk to her. And the Sybil's engraving was certainly doing the two-dimensional equivalent of hitting her upside the head. She took a deep breath and stood up.

*I'll have to figure out a way to sneak out of the school,* she thought, but the *miroir d'intent* would probably help her there.

And she'd have to decide how much to tell him. If what Niobe said was true, he couldn't really be trusted.

When should she do it? She could go now (the night and darkness hiding her) or she could wait for daylight. One course offered more safety, but the other offered immediate gratification. *I want to go NOW*, she thought, not spend the night here tossing and turning, wondering about everything. And Mercy seemed to agree with her. He'd crossed to the door and stood rubbing his cheek against it, and that decided it for her. If this pushy cat thought it was a good idea, then who was she to say no?

She scooped him up, whispering, "Okay, kitty, let's go prowling," and quietly let herself out of her room.

Walking down the hallway, she tested each footfall, thankful for the thick carpet that muffled her steps. She could hear voices from the far end of the hall, and as she hesitated, she heard the words, "Goddamn it! Don't any of you shit-for-brains have any new ideas, or am I just surrounded by pinheads! *Think*!"

Jack Benway was clearly throwing a tantrum. Stifling a smile, she put Mercy down to keep him from squirming, although she whispered, "Keep it quiet, okay? One good meow right now and we might literally get our heads bitten off."

Softly, they crept down the stairs, hesitating when they got two steps from the bottom. There was a light on in the lounge, although it didn't look bright. Something flickering, like a candle. Weighing her curiosity against the obvious need for caution, Nina stepped forward to see who it was. She came to a stop when she heard Isolde Freeland's voice murmuring something indistinguishable, and then another woman's voice. The movie star, Cecily Namath.

"Oh, yes." Cecily was clearly into vocalizing. She heard sucking and lapping. "Yes, right there . . . ooooo, yes, *Yes*! Eat me . . . *eat me* . . ."

*Way too much information!* Nina thought, retreating before she even thought to find out what part of the movie star's body was being consumed. She let herself out of the front door, shivering in the cold night air.

February in New Orleans was chancy. By day it might be spring-like, but at night the damp air from the river could cut to the bone. Wrapping her arms around her thin black school uniform, Nina said, "Okay, c'mon, Mercy, it's only three blocks. Let's go."

They walked quickly through the darkened streets. How odd to the see the Garden District like this, mysterious and silent. The houses were all asleep. No cars drove by. A private security van turned the corner, and she hid in the shadows. Who knew who they worked for? The streetlights were still half-off. *It's a year and a half since the storm,* she thought. *Can't they fix anything in this city?* What light remained only puddled in pools that accented the surrounding night. She heard Mercy pattering along next to her, and was glad of the company.

Finally, they got to the house on the corner of Fourth Street, where she was glad to see a light shining through a diamond-shaped window on the second floor. She screwed up her courage and rang the bell.

*If he doesn't answer the door,* she thought, *I'll just run back to the school and sneak back in. But if he's busy and won't let me in, I'll beg him. I'll plead. I'll make a scene. Maybe wake up the dogs. The dogs!* She remembered them at the last minute, and scooped Mercy back up in her arms just as she saw another light go on downstairs, and the door opened. Two large bounding shapes raced down the walkway and started throwing themselves against the gate, and then Captain Bowman whistled and they came back to heel, wagging their tails and grinning in the spill of light from the doorway.

Captain Bowman walked down to the gate and said in a conversational voice, "Ah, Nina. How delightful. I was wondering when you'd come back."

He made no reference to the hour, but led her up the steps and inside. Once they'd wedged their way into the crowded foyer, he said, "Don't worry about the dogs, they love cats. Can I get you something? Some tea, perhaps? A sandwich?"

"Actually, some tea would be great," she said, rubbing her hands together and luxuriating in the house's warmth. She added, "I'm sorry to disturb you, only I had to see you, and I couldn't get away earlier. The school's being really strict."

"Yes, I imagine the Saturni are watching you all like hawks, since the return of the *Lwas*."

He waved her toward the music room and puttered away in the direction of the kitchen. Nina squeezed past the towering piles of books and newspapers and the printing press and the rifles and ammo and took a seat on the sofa. She wasn't entirely surprised he knew all about current events (after all that was kind of his style) but she hoped it also meant he knew more.

She looked around her, thinking how the very chaos of the room felt oddly comforting. At least it was somewhere she knew. Mercy seemed to think it was just fine too. He curled up on the sofa and fell asleep. As she listened to him snore, she thought, *you might at least stay awake and pay attention, after bringing me here.*

"Here we go," the captain said, coming back into the room with a pot of tea and some cups and a pint of what looked like Jack Daniels. In fact, it was Jack Daniels. He tipped some into a cup and filled it the rest of the way with tea, and handed it to her, saying, "I think you could use this. You'll excuse me for saying so, Miss Lamb, but you look like grim death."

"Well . . . I've been . . . kind of busy." She laughed, holding her hands around the warm cup, which felt wonderful. She tipped back the contents and only realized she'd been shaking uncontrollably when she felt her tremors diminish a little. "Um . . . you don't suppose I could have a little more of that, do you?"

"Chug-a-lug." He poured straight whiskey into her cup, without even bothering with the tea. She sipped and felt about a thousand times better than she had since returning from the Convent.

"So tell me ... how much do you know?" she then asked.

He quirked a smile at her. "I'm not the Amazing Randi, Miss Lamb. Why don't you give me a recap?"

"Okay." She took a deep breath and gave him a quick run-down of everything that had happened since they'd last met. He sighed when he heard about the events at the Fortuna Club.

"I'm sorry you had to go through that. It seems rather cruel to have brought you there."

"Yeah, well, I'm still working on that one. So then I escaped into Guinee, and then Niobe Danvers pulled me out and brought me to, um, where she's staying now, and then she brought back the *Lwas* and they had this really major throw-down, and Crux told me there was something infinitely worse than the Saturni but he wouldn't tell me what, and then Niobe had a melt-down and cried about how she wanted someone named Henri back. Captain Bowman, do you know who Henri is?"

"Hmm? Yes. Maybe. I don't know. Let me think about that for a minute." The captain sipped his tea, and Nina waited for him. He finally said, "This terrible being Crux mentioned. Can you tell me Crux's exact words about him?"

"Well, I can try." Nina tried to remember. "He said we were all finite, all of us, even the Skin Eaters, and infinity was something much worse. He said it barely takes notice of us, and if it did, it was a question of intent. He said if you hurt someone by accident, it's better than hurting them deliberately, which means it's kind of a character trait. And he said . . ."

She cast her mind back and found herself shivering again. "He said there was an evil out there in the world that had no cause but its own delight, no excuse for its cruelty, and no pretext of ever needing one. He said even the Saturni hunger. They *long*, that was the exact word he used, and he said they're so wedded to their own desires that they wake up in the dark screaming for fear they'll lose them. But he said the evil he was talking about is at the core of the world . . . and it was here before there was anything . . . and it made the world. And he was about to tell me its name, only—"

"Can't you guess?"

Captain Bowman's voice was light, almost teasing, although there was an undercurrent of sadness in his tone. She thought, *is it Henri? Is that who it is?* Although she had a feeling she might be missing something.

"I'm sorry, I really have no . . ."

"Oh, that's all right. I hardly expected you to know the answer. Here, have some more whiskey." He refilled her cup. "Well, it seems to me you're pretty much drowning in your own 'mysteries' right now. Let's see if we can't sort some of them out."

He rummaged around for a piece of paper and a pencil and wrote out a list for her:

Engraving?

Henri?

Great Evil?

Phoebe and Simone?

Lost Prince?

"I've left out the various speculations regarding you, Miss Lamb, because I'd say that's your overall mystery, and once you find that out, then a great deal that's dark should become light. However, let's see what we can make of these." He let her study the list for a moment.

"Do you see a pattern?"

"Um, no. I'm sorry. I guess I'm just dumb." She felt not merely dumb, but angry with herself, although Captain Bowman continued to smile.

"Nonsense. Sometimes the clearest things can be obscure because of our own preconceptions. For instance, we don't necessarily assume all these things are together for a reason, although of course, they are. They're a list, aren't they? Now let's see . . ." He took the paper from her and pointed to it. "What do these five things all have in common?"

"Well, they're all . . . they all refer to someone." Nina frowned. "Some person. And at least four of them are about somebody I don't know."

"Don't you?"

"No." She shook her head. "I don't know the identity of the Lost Prince. I don't know who Henri is. And I don't know who the Great Evil is. I don't know . . ." She looked up at him. "Are they all related? Are they the same person?"

"Possibly." The captain looked at the list again. "How do you think you'd find out?"

Nina frowned. That question was much harder. Obviously not in a book or a library, not on the Internet, or by asking people at random. She said, "I was kind of hoping you'd tell me."

"I'm flattered, but I'm not that omniscient. Although in fact I suspect the answer's right there in front of you. Where have you gotten your information so far?"

"From Guinee?" Nina shook her head. "But that doesn't make sense either. The engraving doesn't show me Guinee, it just shows me a garden, where real people are standing. Sometimes they're there, and sometimes they're not, but they're not underwater and they're not dead . . . I mean, not *dead* dead."

"And where do they go when they're not in the engraving?"

Nina opened her mouth and then shut it again. She realized she had no idea.

"I think you just need to think about what the engraving actually is. Not what it tells you. A Mezzotint conundrum is by its very nature a riddle, a puzzle . . . but the thing itself . . . it's a flat surface . . . reflecting reality . . ."

Nina gasped. "Are you saying the engraving's a mirror? An actual portal?"

She tried to remember what the Cumaean Sybil had told her. "The seed of the pelican will return, and the mother will sacrifice herself for her child, but in vain. The horses will be mounted, and the war will begin. The lion will dress himself up as a sheep, and even the lamb will be deceived for a while. Follow the water and the mirrors. That's where your savior lies."

And then she'd given her the engraving.

"You were being played by a maestro," Captain Bowman said. "The Sybil's been known to confound even the best of us. Let's think about what she said. 'The horses will be mounted.' Well, that's obvious, the *Lwas* will mount the children, their human hosts. 'The lion will dress himself up as a sheep, and even the lamb will be deceived.' You've been deceived, haven't you, Miss Lamb? I'd say for quite a while you've been given only half-answers and half-truths."

Nina sat and thought about that, and she felt her heart beat faster as she realized how true it was. For all the care and love of her friends, no one had been entirely up front with her.

"Aha," Captain Bowman said.

"Aha? What kind of comment is that? Are you like Sherlock Holmes all of a sudden? 'It's elementary, my dear Nina?'"

"I'm sorry . . ." Captain Bowman laughed so hard he had to set down his teacup. "It's just it's been a long time since anyone's called me out for my pomposity. It's very refreshing. All right, I'll speak plainly. You realize now how easy it is for people to use you for their own ends. And you realize now how you have to decide where to go next."

Nina thought about that. If what he was saying was true, then the engraving was a portal to Guinee. So when people disappeared from it, they returned to Guinee, at least temporarily. The headmaster and the little boy were at least part-time residents of the shadowy world beneath the waters.

And the child, who was somehow related to Niobe, must be the child she still mourned and missed.

"Captain Bowman, Henri's the little boy in the engraving, isn't he?"

"Yes," he said. "I think he is."

"And he's there, somewhere? In Guinee?"

"Yes."

"And is he the Lost Prince?"

"Perhaps. Those sorts of things are complicated. I can't say for sure."

"And he's Niobe's son? Whom she misses? And whom she raised from the dead?"

Captain Bowman sighed and said, "Oh, Nina, Nina, I can't tell you how sorry I am about that. I truly didn't mean to betray her. I knew she'd had a child who had died, back when she was still mortal, so when she told me what she and Strickland had done, it was easy enough to fill in the blanks. I didn't mean to cause her any harm. My attempt was rather to heal. I thought if there was some way to restore her child, and at the same time make peace between her and the Saturni . . ."

"So what happened?" Nina felt her voice go up at least an octave. The captain was shaking his head and seemed to be revisiting a memory of profound guilt. He spilled the beans, she remembered Niobe saying, and she whispered, "You told them where the child was, didn't you?"

"Yes." Captain Bowman let his breath out. "Sometimes you have to weigh various goods, and in the end, saving Strickland and Niobe from an open rift with the Saturni seemed more important than pushing ahead with the Saturni's eventual destruction. I knew their power could bring Niobe's child back, and I thought that might be enough for her. I thought if she had to choose between Henri and Crux…she'd choose Henri…and let them have Crux . . . I know, I know, it sounds cold-blooded, but sometimes in a war you have to make choices, and this seemed like the best idea at the time. Only . . ."

"Only what?"

"Only Jack Benway wasn't remotely interested in reconciling with anybody. I told him where Henri was, and he laughed. I told him he could have Niobe Danvers and her brother as his staunchest allies—at least for a while—and he said he didn't want them, didn't need them, and hoped they'd rot in whatever hell they chose." Captain Bowman got out a handkerchief and wiped his eyes and un-self-consciously blew his nose. "And then he sealed Henri up in Guinee at the end of a long, long hallway of bones, where he weeps, and weeps unceasingly. And he'll stay there forever, apparently. It's really terrible. Benway preferred making everyone unhappy to securing even an important hostage and an important ally. And that's when I realized once and for all how truly evil he was."

Nina balled up her fists and thought, *That can't be all there is to it, is there? There must be something more. Think*, she told herself.

The captain had ratted out Niobe and given Henri to the Saturni. And the Saturni had imprisoned him in Guinee. But why? Just for spite?

*No*, she thought, They had to have imprisoned him there because they knew eventually Niobe would go in there after him.

But she hadn't gone.

Which had to mean, Nina realized, that she still didn't know where he was.

*But I know*, Nina thought. *At the end of a long hallway of bones, behind a locked door.*

So did that mean she should go there and save him? Freeing Niobe's child sounded wonderful, but foolhardy. She said, "I feel terrible, but what I can do?"

"Well, there are many versions of being trapped, you know." Captain Bowman poured a finger more of Jack into each of their cups, and held his up in a mock salute. "There's being trapped by sense, or fear. There's being trapped by duty, or honor. Sometimes they conflict. You could spend several lifetimes worrying yourself in and out of the impulse to be a hero, but finally only you can decide what you're capable of. No one else can or should be expected to decide that for you."

*Thanks*, Nina thought. *Free will's a bitch.* She looked at the captain, and for a split second, she saw something in his expression that made her pause. A kind of waiting. He seemed to be watching with intense concentration to see what effect his words would have on her, and she thought, *What does he care? What's his part in all this? Which side is he on?*

She had only a moment to think about that, and then the impression was gone. He was merely a nice old man again, sipping his tea as he said, "You do have to think about it."

"What?"

"The degree to which other people may be depending on you.

Oh, I don't mean strangers. I mean the actual people you know and love. You may be one of those rare people who knows how to resolve impossibilities, and that's always a talent worth nurturing. However, in the meantime . . ."

He smiled. "Perhaps you'd better be getting back to Daedalus. Who knows what may have been going on in your absence?"

# Chapter Twenty-Three

Nina wondered, not for the first time, exactly what Captain Bowman knew and how he knew it, when she arrived back at the Daedalus School to discover all hell was breaking loose.

She realized something was up when she was still a block away, and saw light spilling out from around every piece of plywood blocking the windows. There was a bustle of activity out on the street, and she could hear shouts and doors slamming and people running back and forth. She shivered when she heard the eerie baying of the wolves. They must have gotten out of the school pack to search for whoever it was . . . and she had a feeling she knew who that might be. Creeping into the shadows by the big front gate, she watched as professor Samson ran by, wearing a pair of bright purple pajamas, whistling and trying to get the wolves in line. Even though she had an affinity with animals, Nina had the feeling if she didn't get back inside soon, she'd be wolf-meat.

She tried not to breathe as Isolde Freeland stalked by not five feet away from her, with Cecily Namath in tow. The movie star appeared to be crying. "Oh, shut up," the Saturni woman snapped. "I can't be bothered with you right now. This is serious." Peeking through the gate, she saw Father Ignatius being chewed out by Jack Benway in language ripe enough to make a sailor cringe, but even that momentary pleasure didn't explain much.

She felt Mercy twining around her legs, but she couldn't even move to lift him up, as she was too scared of drawing anyone's attention. And then she looked toward the front steps and saw him.

Strickland. He was back. Dressed in slacks and a plain white shirt without a jacket or a tie, looking exhausted and disheveled and like he'd lost at least twenty pounds—but he was there. His eyes locked with hers across the space from the steps to the gate, and then she felt herself being lifted up, actually being pushed across the space between the front gate and the steps, and up into his arms.

And not being pushed gently, either. She slammed into his chest and he stumbled back, their combined momentum carrying them right through the open doorway and into the front hall, where Professor Danvers landed flat on his back and she landed on top of him. No one noticed.

"I'm sorry," she said. "I'm so sorry, I didn't mean to—! I mean, I don't know—! It's like somebody pushed me!"

"Clearly, Miss Lamb. I think something wants us to be together."

All right, she wasn't completely clueless. She had felt his arms tighten around her body the second she'd touched him, and she had felt the demonstrable something that pressed against her stomach in the split-second when she'd laid on top of him. They both scrambled to their feet, and she looked down, hoping he hadn't noticed what she'd noticed (oh, come on, who was she kidding?) He mostly seemed intent on adjusting his clothes and smoothing his hands over his disordered hair, and trying to appear . . . well, older. More mature, anyway. Because she realized in that moment he looked very much like her own age.

"Miss Lamb." The professor's voice, at least, held its usual crisp sneer. "Pleasant as it is to see you again, may I suggest we continue this conversation somewhere a little more private?"

She glanced toward the open front door, where various Saturni and Skinnies were still running around outside and yelling. "You got it." She nodded as he turned and headed up the stairs, and she followed. When Professor Danvers reached his office, he flung the door open, pulled her inside, slammed it shut, and then kissed her.

It was all so sudden she didn't have time to do more than let out an incoherent yelp, which he fortunately ignored. Fortunately, because his mouth plundering hers felt so wonderful, so absolutely right, that if he'd stopped right then, she might have screamed. Luckily, stopping didn't seem to be on his radar. She couldn't even respond. She just let him do whatever he wanted, and oh, oh, yes, she wanted it too. She felt his tongue in her mouth, and his breath hot on her cheek. One hand was cupped around her jaw, and she was pretty sure tomorrow she'd have bruises. She could feel her heart racing, and finally she heard him whisper, "Don't you ever disappear from me like that again, do you hear me? Don't you dare leave me alone like that again. Don't you *dare*."

"A-all right."

For a moment, they were completely still, a tight grasp of arms and shoulders and chests and waists and hips all pressing together, and then he groaned and pulled away from her, turning sharply back toward his desk and leaving her feeling like a puppet whose strings had been cut. She clutched at the back of a chair to keep from falling.

"I'm *such* an idiot!" she heard him grind out, and then, "Sit, Miss Lamb. Or rather, get out. Get the hell out. Or . . . I don't know. I don't know what you should do. I don't know what I should do either." He slumped down in his chair. "I should probably just shoot myself and get it over with."

"I'm glad to see you too."

"Stop mocking me, Miss Lamb."

"I think we're pretty much past surnames, don't you?"

"*Stop it*!" He raked his hands through his hair. "And while we're at it, where were you for the last month, and why did you decide to come back now?"

She swallowed her anger and sat down opposite him and gave it to him with both barrels. "I was with your sister. Yes, that one. The *Lwas* have come back and mounted the children she has with her, and they're readying themselves for war. I came back yesterday, but you weren't here, so that's why you didn't know about it. I'd ask you where you've been, but Crux already told me you've been doing the grand tour of the New Orleans Skinny bars, so I suppose it's lucky you're still in one piece."

He let out a creative string of curses which included, "Jesus, Crux? Is he back too?" and finally sat back in his chair and gazed at the ceiling. "You're incredible. You know that? One month and you manage to destabilize the whole goddamn world!"

She let that go and said, "So why did you come back?"

"I work here, remember? Eventually, even I have to put on my big-boy pants. Besides, I was summoned."

He rubbed his forehead, and she had the feeling the summons might have come in mid-debauch. The sounds of the search outside seemed to be winding down, but there was still a lot of noise as people clomped up and down the stairs, and there was muffled yelling.

He glanced at her and said, "Yes. The Saturni summoned me tonight. It seems we've had some unregulated comings and goings lately."

He held up his hand and explained, "Aside from you and me. For once. this isn't all your fault. Four of our students have now gone missing, as of last count. And we've also had four visitors, whom I think you know."

Nina frowned and shook her head.

"Oh, come on, Nina, surely you remember. You released them! And by all accounts, you've been hanging out with them ever since, having voodoo sleepovers and getting all cozy with the immortals. Surely you haven't forgotten."

She finally got it, and said with amazement, "The four Great *Lwas* were here? *Why*? Why would they come near their worst enemies? It doesn't make sense!"

"It does if they were delivering an ultimatum, which I gather was their intention. All I know is, Jack Benway called me back telling me Erzuli and Grand Bois and Damballah and Oya were here, and to get my ass back to Daedalus right that second." The professor's voice held a strange mixture of anger and satisfaction, exhaustion and awe. "I came back to discover that they'd already vanished—they do that, as you know—although I suspect Erzuli may have still been sticking around to give you a little . . . push in my direction. She seemed to imply that was needed."

Nina swallowed, thinking of the powerful voodoo love goddess pushing her into Strickland's arms. She really liked that idea, but it was also a little scary. Shaking her head, she tried to concentrate on what the professor was saying.

"Their message consisted merely of the knowledge that their brethren had arrived, so, since I believe the Saturni already knew that, there may have been an element of provocation involved. 'Come out and fight,' so to speak. In addition . . ." He hesitated. "Simone Freeland and Alastaire Roget and Bella Chopin and some girl named Phoebe Passerine are now missing."

Nina tried to say, "What?" but her throat was suddenly too dry to speak. Bella? And Alastaire? They were gone too? She felt tears start in her eyes, and they were more tears of shock than anything else. Strickland looked down and said, "Yes, your two friends. I'm sorry."

"But they were just here. Tonight." Nina looked around the office, taking in the familiar clutter, the divination pendulum, the orrery of the solar system, and the open safe in which the four Great *Lwas* had once been trapped. "I—I heard Agatha and professor Seneschal talking in here just yesterday, and I found the copy of *Gabby Gator's Big Book of Fun* and I showed it to them and then Phoebe said it was about the planet Saturn and then we all laughed and—"

"Slow down. Nina. What on earth are you talking about?"

"Oh, that's right, you don't know about any of that." She hesitated and then said, "Actually, um, it's a long story," unwilling to tell him everything about the Sybil's engraving and everything she'd learned from it. She forced herself to ignore the residual sounds of turmoil coming from outside and focused on getting him the crucial information.

"The thing is, I just saw my friends two, three . . ." She glanced at the clock. "Four hours ago. Then I couldn't sleep, and I, uh, I went for a walk."

"You're an awful liar, Miss Lamb." He spoke almost absently. She watched him rub his forehead again, and asked him, "Do you have a headache?"

"Pounding. No, that's not it, though, it doesn't matter. Nina, we have to talk. Not about what happened just now. About what happened at the Fortuna Club." He shut his eyes and said, "I never should have taken you there. I can never forgive myself for putting you in that much danger."

"Yeah, well, Crux said you were kind of a world-class expert at self-punishment."

"Crux can go kiss my immortal ass."

"He'd probably love to."

That earned her a raised eyebrow and made her bite the inside of her cheeks to keep from laughing. Even in the midst of her dismay and fear, she was ridiculously glad to have him back.

"Look," she said, making a quick decision and taking the plunge, "I'm not sure if you always have my best interests at heart, but I—I'm your friend, all right? I lo—like you." She caught herself and went on. "We're in this together, and I just want you to know, I'm okay with that. I'm sure you had your reasons for taking me to that party, and you don't have to drink yourself into oblivion or, or, eat . . . people . . . or whatever . . . on my account. Okay? We're cool."

She didn't know how he'd take that, but all he did was take a deep breath and stare down at the blotter in front of him, while the seconds ticked away. In fact, he was silent for so long she finally said, "Um . . . earth to Strickland? Are you still mad at me?"

"I'm trying to decide if I deserve you. You're either a punishment for my numerous sins or a reward for something I can't remember getting right a long, long time ago. Let's call it a draw. No, Nina, I'm not mad at you. I'm just worried, that's all." He crooked a smile. "I don't have a very good track record of taking care of people. Even the little bastards here seem to slip through my fingers with alarming regularity."

Nina wasn't too thrilled to be referred to as a "little bastard," but his words brought her back to reality. Bella and Alastaire had vanished. "Where do you think they've gone?" she asked.

"I haven't a clue." He seemed to register something in her voice, because he added, "I'm guessing you do?"

"I might." She wished she could show Strickland Captain Bowman's cheat-sheet, but she didn't dare. Still, she could paraphrase. "All these mysteries go back to Guinee, right? People traveling there, and various, um, kinds of mirrors. So, I'm guessing . . ." She shrugged. "I think something may have brought them there, or . . . or something may already be there that's drawing them to it." She left him to fill in the blanks. Strickland appeared to be turning the idea over in his mind, and she wondered what he was thinking. Was he remembering Henri? Was he recalling the awful thing he and Niobe had done?

"It's certainly possible," he said at last, shutting his eyes again for an instant. Then he stood up with a gesture of impatience. "All right, Nina, I think we've both indulged in our various weaknesses enough for one night. You should get back to your room and stay there, although God knows I can never rely on you to do anything remotely sensible. Hopefully, the *miroir d'intent* will shield you. As for myself, I—I'll see you later."

He got halfway across the room before she moved to stand in front of him, her hands on her hips, barring his way. "Oh, no you don't! You're going to Guinee right now, aren't you? I know what you're up to. Well, if you're going, then I'm going with you."

"Nina, stop being Lassie. I don't need your help. The children here are my responsibility and—"

"Well, they're my friends!"

"No, they're not! You hate Simone."

"Stop splitting hairs."

"You'd just be in the way."

"Like I was at the Fortuna Club?"

"That's cold."

"Try me. If it helps to keep you all safe, I'll shit ice cubes."

A muscle twitched in his cheek, although he didn't answer. She didn't care. All her fear of going back to Guinee was eclipsed by the chance to save her two friends (or was it three friends?) and she remembered Captain Bowman saying, "You may be one of those rare people who know how to resolve impossibilities, and that's always a talent worth nurturing."

She said, "You know we work better as a team. Together we're strong. Besides, I—I was in Guinee recently with Simone. I think I know where she might have gone."

Strickland made a choked sound that might have been a laugh, and she had to admit, thinking she could find a single person in that vast, unknown netherworld was somewhere beyond thinking she could find a needle in a haystack. Still, she knew she had some hidden resources.

"All right. I wasn't going to bring this up, but I saw a lot of weird things the last time I was down there. I saw a city—"

"Ville au Camps?"

"Yes. Only it—it wasn't what I expected. Bella said it was a metaphor, like concentrated Guinee, only I saw a real place."

She paused, remembering the wall of stones thrumming with their own faint energy. She saw again the towers and parapets and domes of the glass-walled castle, and the orbs of colored light, all rising and falling under the triple sun, hanging like an eye in the blood-red sky.

*Saturn*, she thought. *The sun is Saturn.* She remembered Phoebe telling them, "Originally Saturn was a brown dwarf star lined up in a polar configuration with Earth's celestial north, and Mars and Venus were lined up with it." It seemed impossible, but now remembering it she said, "I think I saw Saturn. The planet Saturn, not the Greek myth guy. Is that . . . is that possible?"

Strickland became very still. Looking at his face, she said, "What? You're scaring me. What's wrong with what I just said? Why couldn't I have seen Saturn when it was still a sun?"

"No . . ." he said finally. "No, that's impossible. It shouldn't be. Unless . . ."

"Unless what?"

He hesitated. One finger came up to gently stroke along her forehead, just below her hairline, and then down across her cheekbone, and further to touch her chin. Oddly, she had never felt such tenderness in him before, even in his moments of passion. He looked concerned and slightly puzzled, as though she might fly apart at any moment, and it almost made her laugh.

She also wanted to reach up and soothe the harsh line that had appeared between his eyebrows, but she couldn't move, feeling like his simple gesture had rendered her as fragile as glass.

"Maybe you are," he said, speaking more to himself than her. "Maybe it's true, and there are new powers in the world beyond anything we've known before. I don't know. I've lived two-plus centuries and I barely know how to control my own temper. How can I hope to control the world? The things you saw shouldn't exist, unless the very rules that hold us together are changing, but who knows, maybe they are? I know of only one power that can do that, and if it's involved, then God help us. But one way or another, there's one other thing I do know . . ."

He sighed. "I guess we're going to Guinee."

# Chapter Twenty-Four

Nina barely had a moment to think, *Be careful what you wish for,* before they were plunging into what felt like empty space.

*Where's the mirror?* she thought. *Where's anything? Where are we?* And she glanced around her at the blue emptiness, so familiar in some ways, but so unexpected. Strickland's voice came to her in her head saying, *"I told you we could travel to Guinee by any reflective surface. In this case we're using one of the polished globes of the orrery. Saturn, to be precise."*

And when she mentally huffed at him, he added, *"Yes, I thought you might find it amusing."*

She reminded herself to murder him later, but the sensation of traveling together was so different from her recent, panicked excursions into Guinee that she could only relax and enjoy the trip, at least as long as it lasted. She felt them proceeding at a steady pace through the lovely high galleries of stone and coral, bones and shimmering reflections, and without even thinking about it, she reached out and took his hand. He returned the pressure of her fingers, and she realized he was smiling.

"What is it?" she asked.

"You. And me. Here." His voice wasn't entirely audible, but it was a bizarre combination of something she could hear inside her head and something out of it, like a harmony or an echo. "I tried so hard to keep it from you the last time we traveled here together, but in this case, we seem to have broken every rule in the book now anyway. There's another way you can go to Guinee besides death and dreaming and mirror travel."

"There is?"

"You can go there with the person you love."

The person you love. She shivered in the cool water that surrounded them. *I can't believe he's actually saying this to me now,* she thought. Of course, her rational mind reminded her, he still might be lying. She whispered, "Is that what we're doing?"

"Perhaps." He twined his fingers in hers, and they floated together, facing each other. Tiny shoals of fish surrounded them, and she could feel them swimming against her skin.

"Are we crazy?" she asked.

"Apparently. You go to Guinee when you meet your soulmate. Anyway, that's the story. It's like a flash of insight. Not all love is eternal, or even very convenient. But it seems . . . just at the moment . . . that we may have to at least consider it."

He hesitated, and then the cold, shuttered look returned to his face and he said, "Okay, let's get going," and turned away from her, his fingers slipping from hers.

*What happened?* She followed him numbly down the long bone corridor, reminding herself of why they were really there. She tried to remember whatever landmarks she could from her previous visits, but the square full of skull altars, the pool surrounded by trees, and the glassy black chasm were nowhere to be seen. Instead, they were traveling down a narrowing pathway that led down, their feet drifting over broken pieces of concrete, rotten wood, empty bottles and rusted cans. Who knew there was trash in Guinee? Looking to the left and the right, she saw the bone walls here were scarred with what looked like long slashes, deep gouges filled with ancient grime. The fretted arches overhead were hung with what looked like the rags of some kind of fluttering substance. And everything was cold.

"Where are we?" she whispered, resisting the urge to say, Wherever it is, it's certainly not a great neighborhood.

"The quarter of the suicides," Strickland said, his voice flat. "I'm not suggesting Bella or any of your other friends may have killed themselves, but this would be a good place to hide them if you wanted to. Even the dead don't go here, and travelers have no need. It doesn't lead anywhere. It's the ultimate dead end." He was turned away from her, but she could hear the reluctance in his voice as he added, "I've . . . visited it on occasion."

*I'll bet you have,* she thought. Their progress down the narrow corridor was increasingly blocked by broken debris of all sorts, cars, statues, and billboards. There were small fires burning (underwater?) and the flapping rags over their heads were making a thick, wet, squishy sound. "What . . . what are those?" she asked pointing.

"Skins," he said shortly, and then shrugged at her horror. "What did you think, suicide really was painless? All suicides shed their skins, either before or after their deaths. They long to put on the clothing of a different creature, and eventually, they do it. Their fate is all around you." He gestured. She could see even in the lurid half-light of the flames how pale he was.

"Look at the walls, Nina. Really look at them."

She looked, and it was with a physical jolt of revulsion that she saw there were actual living beings trapped in the walls. Unlike the bones of Guinee, these suicides were clearly conscious, their faces contorted with pain. They'd all been skinned, their red, raw flesh shining with living moisture. Their bodies bled against the rough stones and concrete in which they were imprisoned. The walls sweated. She shut her eyes, unable to bear the sight.

"It's what's kept me alive all these years," Strickland said finally, a note of black humor creeping in. "'The threat of something after death.' Shakespeare certainly knew what he was talking about.

So many of us . . ." He drew a breath. "Niobe . . . even Agatha . . . so many Skin Eaters dream of quitting their lives. This is why we can't."

"Can't anything be done to help them?"

"I don't know." He moved on, refusing to look at the trapped beings on either side of them, although now that she was aware of them, Nina felt like she couldn't look anywhere else.

Finally, he came to a particular spot in the wall and knelt down.

"Here." He felt around the base of the wall until he uncovered a face, flayed like all the rest. The man's eyes were shut, but they sprang open at his touch, blazing with hate.

"Ah, good, you remember me," Strickland said, patting the man's cheek. "Maybe you'll talk to me this time. I've brought a friend."

The man's eyes roved left and right in a frenzy, and settled on Nina's face. He spat.

"Now, now, don't be rude. He can't help it, you know. He was born in 1779 and was once used to deference. In life, he was one of the largest slave holders in Louisiana. Second only, I might add, to me."

Nina looked from the man's pain- and hate-maddened eyes and said, "You . . . you know him?"

"Yes. At one time he was my brother-in-law. May I present Francois Livaudais, Niobe's husband."

Nina stepped back, not knowing what to say, or even if she could trust herself to say anything. The face in the wall looked at her with scorn, but she felt her eyes filling up with tears as she said, "How—how can he bear it?"

"He has to. He made his choice." Strickland's voice was clipped.

She turned to him. "Oh yeah? And how can you bear it? He probably killed himself because he knew she loved you best!"

"Of course that's why he killed himself, but it doesn't matter.

Nina, at one point I hated this man more than anyone else on the goddamn planet. He stole my sister. He made her pregnant. He . . . he gave her what I could never give her. A child. All right, time mitigates all wounds, but he's still not my buddy, and I'm never going to be his. Now never mind. Francois. Pay attention. We need your help. There are children down here, children who've been taken away from us against their will."

He made a little *shhh*-ing gesture to Nina, and continued, laying it on thick. "They're lost, Francois. Afraid. Terrified. I know you don't like me, but this nice girl has come all the way down here of her own free will to help me find them. Surely you'll tell us if you know anything."

Nina heard Francois Livaudais blow a raspberry.

"Francois, think. Your torment here is that you can never go back and change anything. You can't take another path. Well, think about it. This time you can! You can actively change things for the better! I know it won't ease your personal pain, but what about doing something for the greater good?"

"*Merde*," Francois said. His voice was rusty, and he had to swallow convulsively before he could say anything more. "I hate you and your damn school and everything else about you. Those children can rot as far as I'm concerned."

"Francois . . ."

"Don't give me that. You turn them into monsters like you. At least I was human . . ."

"And how's that been working out?"

"Stop torturing me! Go fuck yourself and that little girl too. I don't want to have to even look at you." And he shut his eyes.

Nina had the strangest feeling as she stared at the angry, horrible face in front of her. Even though she could barely stand to look at him, she also recognized him as a fellow suffering human being. He had been Niobe Danvers's husband once, and had he despaired when she preferred to be a Skin Eater like her brother? Had he loved their little boy? Did he know what Niobe and Strickland had done? She put out her hand, despite a major feeling of yuck, and touched his wet, raw cheek.

"I'm so sorry," she said, knowing that was probably the lamest thing he'd heard in at least two centuries. His eyes snapped open, though, and he looked at her for a long moment.

"That's the first time anyone's ever said that to me," he said.

"Really? I . . . I thought it kind of sucked."

"Sucked what?"

"Never mind."

He paused and added, "Your hand is cool."

"It is kind of cold down here."

"Really? To me, it burns like fire."

"Is there anything I can do to help you?"

"Mercy." He struggled for breath. "Give me mercy. Although I don't deserve it."

"I would certainly give you mercy if I could." She figured he didn't mean the cat. "I mean . . . I certainly do give you mercy . . . at least as far as I'm concerned . . ."

He shook his head. "Only one being can give me the gift of His compassion, and He has turned his back on me. On all of us." He took a deep breath and added, "Strickland?"

The professor glanced down and said in a deliberately neutral voice, "What?"

"What do you want to know?"

"What have you heard? What do the dead say? Do they know where these children are?"

"There are . . . rumors. They say they are being held somewhere near here."

"Where?"

"Where do you think, imbecile?"

Strickland frowned. "I haven't the faintest idea, Francois. Please stop speaking in riddles. If you can't be helpful—"

"Where do they keep children down here?" Nina heard, not sharpness in the suicide's voice, but rather a far greater agony than any he'd expressed so far. He sounded as though he were gargling glass. "Sweet Jesus, don't you have any pity whatsoever?"

Strickland turned to Nina and raised his eyebrows, honestly confused. She didn't know what Francois meant either, so she said, "I'm sorry, we don't live here. You'll have to be more specific."

"You saw it! I know you saw it! I saw you with the other one! We all know what any one of us sees. The suicides never sleep, and they all talk to one another." Francois took another quavering breath, and it sounded like a sob. "We know you saw the door . . . that accursed door. The door behind which *he* remains . . . weeping . . . and weeping . . ."

Nina started back, because she suddenly knew exactly what he was talking about. The door she had found at the crossroads, at the end of a corridor of overarching ribs. The door with the cool handle, behind which she'd heard the sound of someone crying. *My God*, she thought, *if I'm right, then that's where they locked up Henri Livaudais.*

This man's son.

She shut her eyes for a moment and tried to stay calm. *Get a grip*, she told herself. *Think this through.* Strickland and Niobe brought back her son from the dead. This man's son. They'd banished him to Guinee when his resurrection hadn't worked and put him somewhere where he would be kept safe. But the Saturni had found him and moved him and put him ...

Behind the door where he was now trapped and suffering.

And from what she could see, Francois knew exactly where that door was.

She said, "You're kidding. They put Alastaire and Bella and Simone and Phoebe in there with him? Why?"

Strickland was looking back and forth between Francois and herself with mounting frustration, and she hated to leave him in suspense, but she didn't know what to reveal.

She moistened her lips and said, "It's . . . complicated. But I think I know where they are." She looked down and said, "Monsieur Livaudais, tell us. Where is the door?"

"Two turnings to the left will bring you to the place where the dogs were. You need to avoid it, and then descend, and ascend again. You'll move through the Place of the Babies and then come to the Place of the Shrines. Choose the blue corridor, and you'll come to the corridor of the bone flowers. And at the end of that, you'll find it, at the crossroads."

"Oh, for the love of God—!" Strickland began, but Nina was frowning and trying to remember all of that.

"Shut up, I think I know what he means," she said. "The place where the dogs were is the place where there was this big pool and trees, and the Nadir was there. Then . . . I fell down a chute and there were these little things like babies. The Place of the Shrines has to be the place where Simone and I sat and talked. They had Vincent Van Gogh's ear there in a glass case. And then . . . the blue corridor led to the corridor and the crossroads where the door was. Yes! I can find it!"

Strickland murmured something like, "Remind me to play Trivial Pursuit with you sometime," but she could tell he was impressed, in spite of himself. He turned back to Francois and Livaudais, and his tone was just marginally civil. "Thank you. You've done the right thing. I won't forget this."

"Bugger off. I hope you get what you deserve. And this dear girl . . ." Francois's eyes shifted to her, and she could have sworn for a moment there were tears in them. "I hope she escapes alive. But I can't promise anything. You did, after all, ask me where it was."

*Great*, Nina thought. *Let's think positive, shall we?* She leaned down and touched his flayed face one last time, smoothing his eyelids shut, and she heard him sigh. Then she stood up and said, "Okay, let's motivate."

"Eloquent as always," Strickland muttered, but he moved to join her. They floated down the narrow passageway, the walls pressing in so closely beside them they could barely get through. She didn't look to see if there were any more faces hidden in the rough stones on either side. This was creepy enough as it was.

Coming to a blank wall, she said, "Okay, I guess we turn left here," and after another left, they came out into the flat, open area where the strange silvery pool lay, surrounded by trees.

This time, the room was lit by a soft, directionless light, so the water shimmered. Nina and Strickland approached it warily. He said, "I take it this is familiar?"

"Yes, I found the *horroi* here the last time. And the, um . . . the Nadir."

She looked around, but they appeared to be alone. "Francois said we had to avoid it."

"Maybe Francois was just hoping it would be here. For my sake."

"Shh. Don't joke. If it comes, you have to kick off fast, it doesn't give you much time."

"I do have some experience with it, you know," he said, but his voice lacked its usual bite. He approached the pool, its pearly light reflecting up at him. After a moment, she came to his side.

"What do you see?" she asked.

"My face, that's all." He sighed and rubbed his jaw. "I need a shave. You're the one who could see Ville au Camps. You can beat me at mirror scrying every time. Not to mention sweet-talking the dead. I should be jealous."

"Don't be." She smiled. "I think Francois Livaudais just liked having a cute girl touch him again after all this time."

"That, Miss Lamb, is one of the coarser suggestions I've ever heard you make." He regarded her levelly. "Now, if you're quite finished, shall we proceed?"

They looked all around them, and Nina said, "I forget how I found it the last time . . . it's somewhere around here. Kind of a smooth, black-walled chute. Like a slide."

They moved all around the room, running their hands over the walls, but they didn't find anything. Nina shook her head.

"I was terrified and confused, so I don't really remember, but I know it was here. I feel like I'm staring right at it!"

Strickland had returned to the pool, and his gaze had again been captured by its eddying depths. Approaching it, her eyes caught the barest flicker of movement in the opaline depths, and she said sharply, "There's something down there."

"I know. I can see it."

"I can't quite make it out . . ."

He drew her to him and made her stand directly in front of him, his hands on her shoulders as he had when he'd first taught her divination. As before, he leaned close to her, and his whisper tickled her ear as he said, "Try, Nina. I know you can do this. Tell me what you see."

She looked and saw . . . a tiny form. Barely visible. Two small arms, a head like a large drop of mercury, minute shoulders, two tadpole legs. One, two, and then suddenly dozens of them. A shoal of almost transparent forms, their eyes glued shut, their fingers webbed, and their hearts dark pink shadows in their glassy chests . . . the babies.

"They're in there," she breathed. "They're inside the pool. That's where I went. I didn't go outside of this room. I fell in."

She felt awed, and then confused. "What are we supposed to do, just dive on in?"

"So it would appear."

"Is it . . . safe?"

Strickland raised an eyebrow. "You're asking me?"

She blew out her breath, but there really was no alternative. Taking his hand, she said, "Okay, on the count of three?"

"Nina, you really are the limit." He shut his eyes. "Okay. One. Two. *Three.*"

They jumped in, and the water claimed them, icy cold. The smooth black chasm opened up all around them, its slick sides sluicing them on like refuse down a drain. Down, down, down they went, and then up, the unborn beings rising with them, their combined momentum lifting them out of the crevasse and out over the long, flat plane of empty sand. She could see it . . . she could almost see the crystal towers and battlements of Ville au Camps in the distance . . . but she knew they couldn't go there. Not now. Not and save her friends. Taking a chance and kicking off to her left, she turned and looked back and saw in the distance the wide plaza surrounded by tall buildings and the arches of skulls where the shrines were.

"Here, this way," she said, grabbing Strickland's hand and swimming back down, working against the current now. They pushed forward, the weight of the waters of Guinee a thick barrier against them. After what felt like hours, but was in fact, probably closer to minutes, the turncoat currents reversed themselves suddenly, and she felt herself being carried forward with such speed she practically slammed into the wide skull altar that housed the heart of Heinrich von Kleist. Picking herself up, she said, "Come on, it's just down the blue corridor, and then we get to the corridor of bone flowers, and that should be it."

The blue corridor did indeed lead to the long arcade of overarching ribs, and there at the end lay the crossroads, and the door she had seen before. She stopped, feeling her hair drift up at the back of her neck with something more than the water's movement, as she heard the eerie, wrenching sound of sobbing coming from inside.

There was more than one voice crying there now. She was sure of it. She turned to Strickland and said, "We've got to get them all out. Do you think we can just open the door, or do we have to go in there and get them?"

Strickland frowned. It was clear he had never seen this particular door before, and had no idea who it might conceal, besides his students. He said, "I'll try opening it. If they don't come out at once . . . well, I'll just go in there and get them."

"I'm coming in with you."

"Nina, don't be ridiculous. You're mortal. You're eighteen. I've had two centuries to learn my way around here, and I do have a few skills. Don't be a fool."

She looked at him, and read the concern in his eyes, the veiled pleading, *"Please let me take care of you this once,"* and *All right,* she thought back. *You can be a gentleman this time.*

She swallowed and said, "It's just I . . . I really don't want you to get hurt, either."

"Neither do I," he assured her. "It's my fondest hope we can both come back from this little adventure in one piece. Now, if you'll excuse me, please step back."

She stepped back and watched him approach the door and lay his hand on the handle. It was just then that she heard the sound of movement behind her, and horribly, it was a sound she knew.

She turned, a scream sticking in her throat, as the terrible shrieking whine washed over her, part cry, part roar. She saw the black sludgy shape of the Nadir approaching her so fast she barely had time to leap out of its way, but it wasn't coming for her, she realized. It was headed straight for Strickland.

She screamed again, this time making a sound, and Strickland turned around and saw it. Moving with far greater speed than the waters of Guinee should have allowed, he practically vanished and appeared in the next moment at the far end of the corridor, far away from her. The Nadir changed course and charged after him, its floppy little hands and feet sending it skittering over the floor with a wet, sucking sound, its black eyes bulging and its teeth snapping.

Strickland yelled, "Go on! Go on, Nina! I'll draw it away!" and then he was gone back down the blue corridor to the altar room, with the Nadir following after him.

# Chapter Twenty-Five

She hesitated and tried to draw a regular breath. Don't panic, she told herself. She tried to resist the impulse to run after him and do—what? Get herself chewed up too? He was right, he had the skills to out-maneuver the Nadir in the labyrinths of Guinee, and if he didn't? What was the Nadir, after all? Mankind's concentrated fear of death? Didn't he, of all people, know death's face and form, its terrors and its finality, and hadn't he taken steps to deny it?

He'll be all right, she told herself. He's a Skin Eater. Get a grip. Right now she had to get her friends out of this terrible place, and the sooner she did, the sooner they could all go home together.

She turned and touched the smooth metal of the door's handle. As before, it turned easily under her hand. *Come on,* she thought, *just open it.* With any luck Bella and Alastaire and Phoebe and Simone will be waiting right inside.

She spared a moment to consider what she should do about Henri. *I don't want to leave him there,* she thought, but she wasn't quite sure what he was yet. Would she be risking far worse consequences by freeing him? *I freed the four Great Lwas,* her train of thought went. How much more are the Saturni going to put up with? She knew she was just stalling, and with a quick movement, she pulled the door open.

All right, so she was a little disappointed when Bella and Alastaire at least didn't barrel straight through it. Steeling herself, she looked around. The room was a shock. It was comfortable and shabby and almost . . . homey. There was a couch with a plaid slipcover, a coffee table and bookshelves, several large comfy chairs, and a window looking out at a colorful garden. A large old-fashioned TV console stood over on one side of the room, playing cartoons. She watched as Bugs Bunny and Daffy Duck and Rocky and Bullwinkle chased each other across a landscape of generic grass and trees, and she tried to figure out what the hell was going on.

Where was everybody? Were they outside? She went to the window and looked out at a Technicolor garden full of blood-red zinnias, bubblegum-pink petunias, chartreuse grass, and huge blue daisies the size of plates. It was far too colorful to be real, and she found herself getting a headache just looking at it. Glancing back into the room, she became aware of some sort of awful music playing, peppy and repetitive like the soundtrack to a video game. There was food on the coffee table, bags of Chee-Weez and boxes of Krispy Kreme doughnuts, and she thought, *oh God, maybe this is hell.*

She was just thinking that when the pain sliced into her. It began at the top of her skull but spread downward with sickening rapidity, an arrow of agony shooting right down her spine and out into her extremities, its track merciless. *No,* she thought, as it sent her to her knees. *No, I have to fight this. Giving in isn't an option.* She opened her mouth to breathe in quick, short pants, willing herself to raise her head and look around, to take in her surroundings. The comfortable room had disappeared, taking with it its fast food and banalities, and now what surrounded her was bare stone, cave rock, a cell of dark granite decorated with chains and manacles, and a drain in the floors stained with blood. And there was screaming all around her.

Forcing her eyes to focus and her brain to ignore the impossible pain radiating out to her fingertips, she looked around her. Bella was chained directly to her left, her head slumped forward against her chest. She saw the marks of whips and burns on her delicate face. Next to her, Alastaire was crying out in a single mindless yell of pain, wordless and endless, the cords on his neck standing out like wires. Phoebe Passerine was staring at her from the wall just opposite, her mild blue eyes blank with the idiocy of a mind pushed past its limits. And Simone was struggling for breath just over to her right, her beautiful face contorted as she whispered, "Help, Nina. Help us. It was a trap."

"What can I do?" Nina asked, appalled to see her former nemesis stretched out like this, her hands pulled up high above her by a taut chain. Simone breathed, "There's a key. Over on the shelf by the door. Get it. And hurry."

Nina turned and pushed against her own agony to find the shelf, and a tiny golden key there, shaped like a feather. It seemed impossibly small to open such huge handcuffs, but crossing back to Bella, she tried it on her first and found it unlocked her immediately. The Vietnamese girl slumped unconscious to the floor, and Nina immediately moved on to Alastaire, taking him by the shoulders and shaking him.

"Shut up," she told him, her voice sharp with her own pain and terror. "Shut up, it's me! Here, I'll let you go. Stop yelling, it's all right. Help me with the others."

"Nina...?" Alastaire's eyes focused on her, and then he gasped. "My God, it's actually you! I thought you were just another trick. How'd you get in here?"

"There's no time now. Here. C'mon, help me unlock Phoebe."

"What about me, bitch?" Simone yelled. "You just gonna leave me here or what?!"

"Hang on. We're all getting out of this." She unlocked the last girl's wrists, and Simone dropped and sprinted for the door. Nina helped Alastaire scoop up the unconscious Bella, and they pelted after her, Phoebe bringing up the rear. Once outside, Nina pushed the door shut and felt the pain in her own body stop as suddenly as it had begun.

"Oh. My. God," she gasped. "I'm not even going to ask what that was all about. Is everybody all right? Are you all okay to move, or do we have to wait?"

Alastaire swallowed and nodded, saying shakily, "I'm good. I think." Phoebe looked up at her, her eyes clear again, and said, "Of course, Nina. How nice to see you." Ignoring this, Nina turned to Simone and said, "Um, are you all right, you want to split?" and the black girl snapped, "'Want' isn't even remotely the right word, but yes. Let's get out of here."

Bella opened her eyes and murmured, "Nina? Is that really you?"

"Apparently." She turned and surveyed the now-empty corridor. It occurred to her for the first time that, without Strickland, she had no idea how to get out of Guinee.

"Nina . . ." Phoebe's voice sounded scared and tentative.

"What?" she asked, trying not to snap. The smaller girl said, "You're bleeding . . ."

Nina put her hand up to her face, and realized her nose was indeed gushing blood. "Gross," she muttered, wishing for the first time that the water in Guinee really was water, and would wash some of it off. She scrabbled in her pocket for a Kleenex, predictably enough not finding one. She was just turning to ask Alastaire and Bella if they had one when Strickland appeared at the junction with the blue corridor and strode toward her, his face drawn.

"Nina?" he asked, reaching out to grab her before he remembered there were other people present. He returned his hands to his sides, fisting them, and added neutrally, "What happened? Are you hurt?"

"It's . . . it's nothing. Nosebleed." She gestured. "It was horrible, but it's okay. We're out now."

"Obviously." He glanced back over his shoulder. "The Nadir was no picnic either, but it's gone, for the time being."

"How did you get rid of it?" she wanted to ask but realized they had more pressing concerns. Instead she said, "professor, do you know how to get us out of here?"

"I thought you'd never ask." His eyes met hers for an instant, and in their depths she could see concern, but also relief. Then he said, "Everybody, please take hands," and a moment later they were rising up through the air, stretching out thin and flying away from Guinee.

When they dropped back down onto the lawn at Daedalus, it was still dark. They collapsed outside the carriage house in a pile of arms and legs and bloodied limbs and half-buttoned clothing, and Strickland extricated himself and stalked off without another word. Nina figured he needed some space. She and everyone else went inside and went straight to the kitchen.

"God, I had no idea being tortured could make you so hungry," Alastaire said, rummaging around in the fridge and pulling out bread, mayonnaise, some lunch meat, and a container of tuna salad which he sniffed and pronounced, "Okay, I guess." Simone went straight for the cabinet that held the liquor and pulled out a bottle of vodka.

"I need to get hammered," she announced, taking a swig and offering it around. "Anybody else?"

Phoebe said, "Yes, please," and knocked back a couple of good stiff swallows without batting an eye. Nina did, too, feeling the alcohol burn through her, dulling a little of the residual aches in her body. Bella, who was still looking pale and sick, said, "No thanks, I don't think I can handle it."

"I think you should," Alastaire said, pouring her a shot and handing her the glass. "Here, take little sips."

Nina watched him take care of the slender girl, and a faint glimmer of warmth filled her, even better than the liquor. Then she turned to Simone and said, "So what happened?"

"Don't look at me. I got sent to Guinee by my mother. Yes, that's right. I told you, 'Love' isn't a word in the Freeland vocabulary. When I got there, I found myself in that whole 'Leave It To Beaver' room and hung around for a while until I started to realize it was all as fake as a bad hair weave. Then, just as that thought occurred to me, the whole place disappeared, and I was chained up in that cell. After that, it was pretty much your standard S & M fantasy until the rest of your crew arrived."

She indicated Phoebe, Alastaire, and Bella, and Nina turned to Phoebe and asked, "So what happened to you? Did someone tell you to go to Guinee too?"

"No." Phoebe took another belt of vodka, and said, "I'm not really sure what happened. One minute I was in my room getting ready for dinner, and the next minute I was there."

"In the phony sitting room?"

"No, in the rock cell. I never saw any sitting room."

"How about you?" Nina turned to Alastaire and Bella, and Alastaire took a bite of his sandwich and said, "Pretty much the same deal. We got back to our rooms right after dinner, and the next minute, *boom*! We're in that fake room eating Chee-Weez."

Bella murmured something, and Alastaire said, "All right, yeah, you did know better. I was in the fake room eating Chee-Weez. Bella smelled a rat. And then she said she had a splitting headache..."

"It felt all wrong," Bella said, her voice barely above a whisper. "I felt like I was in the wrong skin. Everything felt bizarre. I knew we weren't in a real place, and I said something..."

"You tried to say something," Alastaire said. He was still hovering over Bella, and put his arm around her. "All you got out was this kind of puff of air, and then you started screaming. And I was right there screaming along with you."

Nina didn't want to ask them what had happened next, but she had to know. "Who . . . who tortured you?"

"That's the worst thing," Simone said, looking angry. "We couldn't see the son of a bitch! Just these cuts and punches and kicks coming out of nowhere. It was like we were being attacked by the room itself. And it just went on and on."

"Yes, it went on and on . . ." Phoebe said quietly. She still had her usual air of strange calmness, but there was a huge bruise next to her lips, and Nina noticed she drank out of the other side of her mouth.

"I guess I passed out," Bella said, slipping away from Alastaire's protective arm and coming to the kitchen table, where she also helped herself to some more vodka. Nina thought they were going to need another bottle. "And the next thing I knew, you were there, Nina, setting us free."

The others nodded, and Nina felt a terrible weight descend as they all fell silent. They might not be in Guinee anymore, but the world had abruptly become a very dark place indeed. She remembered floating with Strickland, and it felt like that had happened to another girl, perhaps in another century.

She finally asked the obvious. "Why?"

"Why were we taken there?" Alastaire asked. "Or why did whatever it was let us go?"

They all turned to look at him, and he said, "What? They're both legitimate questions."

"I sometimes forget how smart you really are, that's all," Nina admitted. "All right, so, both questions. First of all, why were you all taken to Guinee?"

"Well, at the risk of nit-picking, I wasn't actually 'taken' anywhere," Simone pointed out. "I just did what my mother told me to do, and no, she didn't explain her reasons. But as far as the rest of you guys are concerned, it's obvious, isn't it? They wanted you to come after them." She nodded at Nina, who frowned. She'd been thinking the same thing herself, but she didn't want to admit it. It made them sound like bait.

"All right," Bella said, sitting down at the table and pressing her fingers against her temples, her mind coming back online. "So we have a theory, at least. That whoever it was—the Saturni, presumably—put us there because they wanted Nina to come after us, which she did. Does everybody buy that?" She looked around. "Okay. But Alastaire's right, why torture us and then let us go? If Nina was the real target, why not just let us sit there and eat junk? And conversely, if whatever it was really wanted to hurt us, why did he or she so conveniently disappear the minute Nina showed up?"

Nina had to admit she didn't have a clue, and none of the others seemed to have one either. She took another big swallow of vodka, spilling a little on her chin, and from habit she reached into her pocket for a tissue before remembering she didn't have one. Her hand, however, touched something else.

"That's funny," she said, removing the small object and looking at it. "I didn't know you could take things out of Guinee."

It was the little gold key she'd used to unlock the others' chains. Holding it in her hand, she felt an uncanny feeling, as though something in a dream had suddenly become very real.

Bella went on. "And how did they know Nina would even figure out to come to Guinee in the first place? It wasn't that obvious. We could have been anywhere."

Nina started to say she'd had help solving that riddle, but she paused. Really, how much did she know about Captain Bowman either? The captain had said, "You've realized now how easy it is for people to use you for their own ends," and after all, he'd been supportive and given her tea and bourbon, she had to admit he'd been kind of manipulative too. At least to the extent of making her see the truth.

"Um . . . look," she said. "I'm going to go out on a limb here and speak frankly, and maybe that's a bad idea, but I just can't deal with any more secrets." She took a deep breath and looked around at all of them. "If—if anyone wants to leave right now, that's okay. I'm not going to mince words, and, uh . . . they might hurt some people's feelings. And I may be an idiot, but well, after what we've all gone through, I just don't want to cause anyone any more pain."

Bella and Alastaire just looked confused, and Phoebe was smiling at her like she was watching a mildly interesting television program, but Simone got it. She sighed.

"You're going to talk about my parents, right? And the rest of the Saturni? Well, fine. Knock yourself out. I'm not too thrilled with any of those shitheads right now either." She looked down at her ruined manicure and worried a broken nail. "After all, they did leave me there, for whatever reason. So if you want me to sign a blood oath or touch pinkies or whatever, I'll do it. What gets said in this room stays in this room. Okay? Otherwise," she shrugged, "if you'd prefer, I'll just go outside and wait until you're finished. It doesn't matter to me. It's your call."

Nina tried to remind herself that Simone was untrustworthy, but somehow, that didn't seem to matter now. She couldn't help but remember the other girl stretched out and shackled to the wall, her body whipped and bleeding. Simone looked better now, like all the Skinnies she healed almost instantly, but there were still shadows around her eyes. Nina threw up a prayer to whatever *Lwas* might be listening and said, "Okay, look, here's the deal. I think somebody other than the Saturni may be trying to put their own plans into action here, and I'm not sure who it is, but I do have a theory."

She told them what Crux had said about there being a Greater Evil at the core of the world, and what Captain Bowman had said, finishing, "He told me I'd been played like a violin, and I think he's right. We all have. Ever since Professor Danvers first took me to see the Sybil, it's like people have been dropping all these hints and telling me to go here, go there, and all around the block. Jack Benway even told me I was one of them. The Saturni." Simone made a choking noise, and Nina said, "No shit. So here's what I think. I think there's this other entity that's been pulling strings behind the scenes, and I think that entity might be the headmaster."

The others looked at each other, and she saw their glances slide away as they each refused to meet one another's eyes. It was an obvious conclusion, but nobody wanted to admit it. Whatever the headmaster was—nice, cruel, impressive, a vicious prick—he was the missing piece in this equation, the five-hundred-pound absence that existed in every room. And Daneel's words echoed in her head. "He was strange. He seemed so powerful. And kind of tough. Like if you got on his bad side, he'd whup your ass six ways to Sunday."

But finally, the most pressing evidence came from her own fear of what Crux's words might really mean. Knowing the Saturni were all-powerful forces committed to the world's destruction was one thing. Knowing there was something even worse was a recipe for madness. She thought about the idea of an evil that existed at the core of the world . . . that had been there before anything else . . . and there was really only one answer.

The headmaster, Mr. O'Brien, was some kind of an evil God. Or something awfully close to it.

Nina looked around at the others, and they all looked scared and sick. Only Phoebe seemed remotely calm as she said, "You know, I wonder if he wants to come inside."

"W-what? *Who?*" Nina asked, thinking the headmaster might be outside right that minute.

"Janus," Phoebe said. "He's standing right by the kitchen door. See?"

Everyone turned, but there was no one visible through the glass pane in the upper half of the door. Phoebe clicked her tongue and said, "Oops. Right, you can't see him. Well, he's there, he's just too short to reach the window. You can let him in, though. He's one of the good guys."

Nina shook her head and decided Phoebe really did belong on the planet Saturn, but there was no point in not doing what she said. Maybe the dwarf could even shed some light on things.

After all, he'd known enough to try and steal her purse.

She went to the door and opened it, and Janus looked up at her and said, "Hiya, honey bunny. Long time no see. What you guys doing, having a picnic?" He spied the vodka bottle and added, "Never mind, count me in. I'll take two fingers over ice, and some cranberry juice if you've got it."

"I'm not fixing you a cocktail," Nina snapped, letting him find his own way to a stool at the counter, where he clambered up and made a grab for Bella's glass. The Vietnamese girl had recovered enough to say cooly, "Nina, do you know this person?"

"Chill, baby. I'm the Caped Crusader. Janus Passerine."

"Your brother?" Bella asked Phoebe, and Phoebe nodded. "Okay, then, I'll be the one to say it. What's he doing here?"

"I'm here to help, ladies. Gents." Janus snapped his fingers, and Phoebe got up and got him a glass and some juice and ice cubes. When he was settled, sipping, he said, "I take it you all enjoyed Guinee? No, don't bother to answer. The black and blue marks speak volumes. Guess you'll think twice about letting somebody try and do you a favor on Bourbon Street, right?"

He ogled Nina, who quickly folded her hands across her chest. She said, "You call trying to rob me a favor?"

"Natch. I knew how much shit the Sybil was signing you up for. However, you can't mess with fate. *Que sera sera.* That's why I figured you might want my sympathies now, bemoaning the big bad Saturni and all their works."

He sat there savoring his drink, and Alastaire asked, "So you're saying the Saturni really are behind all of this?"

"Who else?" He glanced down at the plate of cold cuts and snagged a piece of bologna and stuffed it into his mouth. Bella said, "Gross."

Simone murmured, "I'll have to tell my parents you think that."

"You do it, peaches. Verbatim. Get 'em all excited." He turned to his sister. "By the way, I'm glad to see you're still in one piece. Oh, and the rest of the family sends its regards."

"That's nice."

Nina said, "I'm sorry, I don't mean to be rude, but what exactly do you want here? This isn't the best time."

"Who says?"

"How did you find us?"

"Oh, I've got my ways."

She looked at him, and even though he was sitting there grinning and snacking and acting like it was no big deal, there was something essentially inhuman about him, she thought, something cool and detached and, therefore, uncanny. She noticed the crescent-shaped scar on his forehead, and then she remembered where else she'd seen scars like that.

The three strange women at the Convent all had scars like that across their foreheads, as though at some point in the past they'd been hit by various objects. She took a chance and asked, "Your family doesn't by any chance include three weird women named Rhea and Thetis and Mimas?"

"Oh, yes," Phoebe said, "they're our sisters—" but Janus glared at her and said, "Nice one, Feeb. Whyn't you tell the whole wide world while you're at it?"

"Who are Rhea and Thetis and ... ?" Alastaire turned to Bella. "And why do I always feel like I'm playing catch-up?"

"Those are the names of three women who worked at the Convent," Nina explained. "I told you all about them. They never said a word, but Rhea was like a giant, and Thetis was normal-sized, and Mimas was really tiny, even smaller than Janus, and—"

"And they're also moons," Bella said slowly, shaking her head as though she couldn't believe she hadn't seen it before. "Rhea and Thetis and Mimas and Janus and Phoebe. They're all the names of some of the moons of Saturn."

No one said anything for a moment, and then Janus slammed his glass down on the counter and shouted, "All right, goddamn it! It's getting so a guy can't catch a single fuckin' break! It's true, okay, we're all moons. God, I can't believe you didn't already guess it! Crescents on our foreheads? Strange Greek names? *Duh.* So at least now maybe you'll believe me when I say I was trying to protect you on Bourbon Street, rather than rip you off?"

"You're ... moons," Nina said. She had no idea what that might even mean. Grabbing at what she knew, she asked, "Are you saying you didn't want me to get involved in any of this, and if I hadn't seen the engraving, this might never have happened? But ... but if I hadn't seen the engraving, I wouldn't have known anything about Henri, and how would that have helped?"

Janus shut up.

"Who's Henri?" Alastaire asked, and Bella shook her head. "I don't know. Just listen."

Nina went on, "It can't be a bad thing I found out about him. It explains so much! Niobe's unhappiness, and why she distrusts Captain Bowman, and—"

And then she realized what she was actually saying.

She had left him there.

When the moment had come, she and her friends and Simone had all been so crazy with pain and fear and horror that they'd just beat feet without giving Henri another thought. All right, for the others it was understandable, they didn't know who he was, but for her part she had just left him there trapped in that room with the TV and the plaid sofa and the snack foods, which was just a mirage for a world of stone and pain.

She gasped and stood up, and Janus reacted much more quickly than anyone else. He grabbed her wrist and said, "Okay, I guess somebody's got to talk turkey here. Yes, Nina. I'm telling you exactly that. You should never have learned about Henri. You should never have gone to Guinee. You should never have seen that engraving. Capisce? I have no idea what the Sybil was playing at, but she fucked things up royally. She and whoever she's running with these days, and I'm not saying who, but the nose knows, and they have one sick sense of humor, I'll give them that much. You should have never been involved in any of this, and I'm sorry, for whatever it's worth. 'Nuff said?"

"But we've got to do something—! We've got to go get him—!"

"No. We. *Don't*! God, you people, what's with you? You got a death wish? You've already got the Saturni mad at you, you've already got a world where people like that Wolf News guy and all the Hollywood and Wall Street and Washington pundits are shoveling mile-high piles of horseshit every day just to do their bidding, and you want to make things worse? What kind of a moron are you?"

Nina felt her cheeks flush with anger, as she thought, *Everybody wants me to be their puppet, and I'm goddamn sick of it.* She looked at Simone and Bella and Alastaire and Phoebe, who were all staring at Janus, and the magnitude of her fury bubbled up and spilled over.

"Yeah? Well, you know what I wish? I wish I'd never learned about you! You . . . you *moon*! You just waltz in here and make everybody feel terrible and make Phoebe fix you a drink and make sure everybody knows how much you know . . . well, you know what you can do? Butt out! We don't need you. We just survived Guinee and the Nadir and the headmaster's torture chamber, and you know what? We did it all without you! All you're capable of doing is purse-snatching and being a little shit! I know what I know, and I know what we need to do now, and you don't get a say in it. You can just go fuck yourself! Go back to Saturn. Go play with your sister and snort milkshakes up your noses! Go to hell!"

She turned from all of them and headed out of the room, and even as she did so, she thought, *Is this really wise? Shouldn't she stay and find out everything else he knew?* She felt awful. She felt devastated, and she couldn't bear to hear any more about this. *How could I just have left him there*? The child who wept behind a locked door was still there, weeping, and she realized she'd missed the most important part of the whole trip. Hadn't she been brought there to free him? Wasn't that what all this subterfuge had been about? And when push came to shove, she hadn't even bothered to look for him. She had just freed the four people she actually knew, and run away.

And now she was running away again, although this time she had a more definite goal in mind. She felt an aching need to be held, the anguish of having gone through too much while feeling nothing but empty air and water against her skin. Goddamn it, she wasn't somebody special. She was just a girl who'd been through more than she could stand, more than she knew how to cope with, and far more than she understood. She wanted soft words of reassurance. She wanted a shoulder to cry on, and someone to tell her it was all right and she could stop being strong for a little while. Whether she was headed in the right direction to find any of those things was, of course, a perfectly good question, but it didn't matter.

She needed to see Strickland.

# Chapter Twenty-Six

When she entered the office, she wasn't sure if he'd be there. After all, he might have gone to bed, or he might have gone out. The strange connection they shared (sometimes) gave her no idea of his whereabouts, so she'd just had to follow her nose. But he was there, still working at his desk, his dark hair half-obscuring his face as he leaned over a book ... although a moment later she realized he wasn't reading.

"Miss Lamb."

Two syllables, and that didn't bode well. No "Nina." No "Hello." Just that curt acknowledgement of her presence, and she came and sat in the chair opposite him and looked at him and said after a moment (because really, sometimes falling back on old habits was the best approach), "Sir?"

He sighed. "So we're back to that again, are we?"

"Sorry?"

"So am I." He closed the book and looked at her. His eyes looked exhausted, and she remembered he'd had a horrible night too. She said, "Um, I wanted to thank you."

"For what?" He looked honestly surprised.

"For ... going with me. For ... I guess for saving my life. All our lives. You ... you risked worse than we did, as it turned out. I mean ... not being tortured ... I didn't even risk that ..."

"You're not making any sense, Nina." There was a very slight movement of his lips that faded even as she looked at him, and he added, "Would you like a drink?"

She didn't tell him she'd already chugged enough vodka to get a horse drunk. Instead, she shook her head. "No, I don't think I'd better."

"No, you probably shouldn't. Not this, at any rate." He opened his desk drawer and took out the bottle full of thick red liquid. "Well, bottoms up." He tilted the bottle, and she watched the muscles move in his throat as he swallowed. Tight as whipcords, they ran down from his jaw to disappear beneath the top of his tightly buttoned collar. He was like that all over, she thought, tightly buttoned up, a taut, coiled, lean body all held together by will. She bit her lips. "Sir?"

"Oh for God's sake, call my Strickland again. I can't bear it otherwise. Nina . . . sweet Nina . . . *la pobrecita nina* . . . Christ, I'm not even drunk yet, and I'm maudlin. What? What was it you wanted to ask me?"

*Tell me about Henri,* she thought, and saw it smack him right between the eyes as he read her mind.

"*No!*" He stood up and glared at her. She felt a push of sheer fury slap up against her own forehead, as he unleashed a spate of thoughts at her, mostly curses. But she stood her ground, even sitting down. If she was going to get mentally beaten up, at least it would be for a good cause.

She narrowed her eyes and thought, *Stop it. I'll show you my memories if you'll show me yours.* And he stopped short, staring at her.

She gathered her courage and thought about Niobe and the *Lwas,* and Crux sitting beside her on the levee. She thought about the party, about the goat's head stew and Guede coming through to mount Flyboy. She remembered Niobe sitting at the table crying, "I want him *back!*" and let him see her own guilty, embarrassed relief that she hadn't meant Strickland. Focusing her mind, she gave him unlimited access to her thoughts, and felt herself reel from the intimacy of it.

But not as much as he did. She watched him grow so pale he looked like he was about to faint, and then he broke away, turning toward the plywood-covered windows and bracing his palms against them.

"Stop it," he said. "I can't . . . I can't take seeing that. Not all at once. Sit down, shut up, and give me a minute."

He moved to his desk again, grabbed the bottle, gulped from it, and set it down with only the smallest trace of uncertainty. He then sat staring at his leather blotter as though it were about to spontaneously combust.

Finally he said, "I haven't seen them in so long. Ages. Decades."

"I'm sorry," Nina whispered. "I didn't know how else to tell you."

"I mean, I know. I know what they all look like. I can remember them. It's not like they're a surprise. But seeing them move . . . hearing them speak . . ." He shook his head.

"I didn't mean to hurt you."

"I know." His voice was, if anything, even softer than hers. He stretched out a finger and drew a careful line down the blotter, like he was amazed he could still do it. When the silence between them became uncomfortable, she said, "Strickland . . . ?"

"Yes?" He looked up at her quickly, and she wanted to look away, but somehow she couldn't. It was as if, for all the ways in which they'd delved into each other's minds, this was the first time they'd actually just looked at each other. *He has very dark blue eyes,* she thought. *I always thought they were brown. He has laugh lines at the corners. You never see them because he so rarely laughs, but they're still there.*

She felt his scrutiny as well, and she deliberately kept her mind blank, not trying to reach him. And at the same time, she wanted so much to touch him and take away all his pain, to make him forget everything and only see those eyes brightening as he smiled at her . . .

"Nina." His voice was rough, sharp, abrupt. She blinked. "Yes?"

"Henri is Niobe's son. As I think you know. And she and I . . ."

"Yes?"

"We raised him from the dead."

"Yes. Niobe told me. She said . . ." She hesitated. How much had he seen? Had he seen all of it, Niobe's revelation to Captain Bowman, and the captain's subsequent betrayal? She didn't know. Strickland took a deep breath and continued.

"He drowned. It was an accident. He was six. A careless servant left him near a pond. And Niobe was . . . distraught, as you can well imagine. We were brother and sister, and the child wasn't mine, but she thought of him as only hers, and the closest thing we could have to a child, together. And in a way, finally, that was what he became for me as well. My son. So I helped her. I really didn't have any choice."

He looked down at the blotter again, and fisted his hand, as if he could squeeze the words out. "I gave her to Jack Benway, to turn her into a Skin Eater. She needed that influx of power, the pure power only a Saturnus could give her, in order to help me to do it. Now I wonder if something else slipped in as well. She's gone so far beyond me in so many ways. At any rate, she became dead and immortal to a very high degree from her very first crossing, so she was able to assist me in bringing the child back out of the grave.

"And . . ." He opened his eyes and looked at Nina and then asked quietly, "Do you really want to see? Because I can't describe it to you. Only a lunatic would . . ." He stopped, and then his mouth quirked up. "Or you. Only a lunatic, or you, would ask to see that. But if you'd like, I can show it to you."

She hesitated, feeling at the moment like she wasn't either a lunatic or a particularly courageous sane person. Yet Strickland was confiding in her, and somehow she knew this was more important than him kissing her or anything else. She said, "Yes, please. Show me."

And so he did.

After a time, he began to think he was in a dream. The mausoleum seemed to shrink away from his blows, wincing as though it were a living thing. The wind around him sighed and moaned, and the trees that leaned their weeping boughs here by the mossy tombs stirred in half-forgotten motion as though rain were seeping through their canopy of leaves. Still, he worked to open the door. He was young and strong and as determined as if his own son lay inside the vault. In a way, he thought, it *was* his son in there. His heart expanded with the joy of that thought, and his back bent to its task with greater effort. His muscles sang. And then the marble cracked and broke down the middle, revealing the bricks behind it, and he attacked their soft surface with renewed vigor.

"Almost . . . there . . ." he breathed, tilting the lip of his shovel up under the exposed end of a brick less carefully pointed than the rest. It gave, and then another and another. Soon there was a hole in the doorway large enough to show them the darker darkness within, and a revolting stench confirmed they were near their goal. Strickland stopped and looked at Niobe.

"Are you all right?"

It was a ridiculous question on the face of it. She had been assaulted by a Saturnus, taken the first step toward her inevitable death, damned her soul (probably, Strickland wasn't sure about such matters) and watched as he desecrated her dead child's grave. But she was magnificent. Walking up to him (*and surely,* he thought, *her face has grown paler and more translucent in the last few hours; she almost seems to be glowing with a ghostly light*) she put her hand on his arm and said, "I'm fine. What should I do now?"

He licked his lips. "I'm not sure. I think you should try calling out to him."

She needed no urging. Standing at the hole in the bricked-up opening to the tomb, she called out, "Henri? Little one? Can you hear me? It's Maman. Come out now. It's time."

No answer. She raised her voice a little.

"Little one, I'm not angry with you about the pond. Truly. You just gave me such a fright. I thought I'd lost you. Now come on out and come back to me."

When this also elicited no response, she started clawing at the bricks, trying to enlarge the hole with her hands. Strickland hesitated and then reached in to help her. He wasn't sure where any of this was leading, a roiling in his stomach and a pounding in his head making him think the very earth was outraged at their actions. Suddenly, the very real possibility that this was all an ironic waste of time occurred to him.

What if he'd allowed Niobe to pollute herself only to have her son remain dead? What if he was wrong? What if the power they held was too weak to snatch a soul already gone to God? What were they doing, meddling in such matters?

"Stop," he said, grabbing her. "Look, it's impossible. I realize that now. I can't let you go on with this. I can't let you do something this terrible, even though—even though I know we both wanted to—"

She simply batted his hands away. "Be quiet. I'm going to do this."

"But we don't know how! It may be too late! It may be—"

"It's not too late." Niobe was still moving the bricks aside. Her face was set. "I'm going into the tomb and I'm going to bring him out."

"Darling, you can't! It'll be terrible in there, it's vile—"

"Of course it's vile. But Henri's in there, don't you realize that? And he needs me. Was it vile when he was born? Blood and mess and all of that, that's what life is. I know I can do it. This is just another kind of birth. I can do it, Strickland, it'll be fine—"

She was still pulling more bricks away with her hands, her hair falling down into her eyes and contrasting its darkness with her milky-white skin. She looked possessed, crazy, but also strangely calm. She reached one hand into the tomb and scrabbled around, touching what he could only assume was her son's coffin. A chortling laugh burst from her throat, and she redoubled her efforts, blood running from her hands where the bricks' sharp edges cut her skin.

And after a moment, during which he felt incapable of movement or even rational thought, he started to help her once more. After all, he couldn't just leave her to do it herself. They pulled enough bricks loose that she was able to put her head and shoulders into the aperture and pull the coffin forward. Once she had one end out, he helped her, shutting his mouth tight against the repulsive smell which threatened to make his gorge rise. They pulled the tiny coffin toward them, inch by inch, its wood splintering over the rough bricks, and worked together in silence. Whatever it was they were committed to doing, now it seemed clear they must see it all the way through to the end.

"All right, darling, on three, ready? One, two . . . *three.*"

They pulled the coffin forward enough to grab its handles and ease it down to the ground. The earth sighed, a long exhalation as it received the surprisingly heavy wooden box. Strickland was immensely grateful they hadn't broken it.

He said, "All right, do you think you're ready to open it?" but Niobe was already wrestling with the heavy lid.

"I can't . . . it's stuck . . . Strickland, help me . . ."

Something seemed to be holding the lid in place. It doesn't want us to open it, Strickland thought with superstitious dread. It knows this is wrong. He almost put his hand on his sister's arm to stop her, but instead he found himself pushing her aside and curving his own fingers under the lid.

"Here, let me . . ."

A great pull, and the lid came away with a sucking sound like a mollusk's shell being pried opened, a cracking noise like a bone being separated at the joint. Impossibly, Strickland felt stickiness coat his hands like blood, and the wood writhed under his touch. The smell intensified, and the wind whipped up, bringing with it twigs and leaves to strike against their bodies like stinging insects. He felt his own hair lift off his collar and he didn't know if it was fear or electricity that made it move.

Niobe was staring into the well of the coffin as if she were Medusa, her hair writhing around her like a cloak of living snakes, but her face was blank. Whatever lay inside the box had either struck her blind, or mute, or paralyzed her. Perhaps, if a merciful God was feeling kind, all three.

The lid still covered the upper half of the coffin's occupant. As Strickland looked into the box, his first thought was that Henri Livaudais's body appeared normal, except for his hands. His hands had assumed the greenish-purple hue of putrefaction, and as he watched, the child's small fingers appeared to move and writhe, stirring beneath the skin with the internal agitation of thousands of newly hatched maggots. There was a city of worms living inside his skin, active inside his trousers and under the sleeves of his jacket, disturbed, questing. As he watched, the restless agitation of the worms grew even more pronounced: perhaps they felt the air against their brute darkness, or else something within the two half-dead humans watching them called to their tiny minds and prompted them to flight. Strickland moved forward, helpless to stop himself—he knew he didn't want to see the dead child's face, and yet he was powerless to resist the urge to know the worst, whatever it was—and pushed the coffin lid the rest of the way off onto the ground.

There, inside the coffin, lay the tiny body of Henri Livaudais, his face a map of squirming, livid life. Worms formed a mass of animation under his downy cheeks. His forehead puckered with their spasmodic seeking—creeping, eating, digesting, liquefying the meat on which they fed—and his lips kissed the air and opened and closed with their blind movements. His eyes pulsed in their sockets, and his chest appeared to rise and fall with their collective spasms. He was a hive of swarming putrefaction, an aggregate of rot.

But he was definitely, indisputably alive.

Nina broke the contact with Strickland and pulled up and away and out of her chair and then she was standing by the plywood covering the window and she needed air. *Air*! She scrabbled at the wood, trying to pull it away where it was nailed against the sill. She couldn't get it loose! She couldn't breathe! She sobbed in frustration, and then she was locked in the strong embrace she had wanted for so long, and she heard words murmured against her hair, "Shh, my darling, shh. I'm sorry. Oh God, Nina, I'm so sorry..."

*That's all right*, she thought. *Just keep holding me like this and you can show me as many rotting little kids as you like*, although she kind of hoped she'd never have to see anything like that again. Feeling his chest rising and falling and his hands gripping her shoulders, she registered that he was shivering as much as she was. His body (cold, so cold) was pressed tightly against hers, and she could hear his harsh breath in her ear. "I didn't mean for you to see that. I didn't mean for anyone to see that . . . Nina, we did something so unforgivable, something no one should have been allowed to do . . . we brought that dear little boy back, when he should have been left to lie in peace, and then . . . I swear, I didn't know what to do . . ."

He shuddered against her, and she felt his cheek pressing against her hair. "I let Niobe take him back into the house, when I should have put a stop to it then and there. You see he was and at the same time he wasn't what he had been before. How can I tell you the horror of that? To have someone back, and be so nearly what you want . . . to have someone returned to you, when they've been lost . . . and then to know that they absolutely *must not* stay . . ."

He swallowed and went on, "I eventually convinced Niobe he had to go. Somewhere. Anywhere. We couldn't let him stay in our world, so we . . . we placed him in Guinee, on the shore below the road that leads up to the city. You said you saw it once. I saw it only fleetingly. Niobe was stronger than I was, she could not only stand there for the time it took to leave Henri behind, but she could return to our world after she had done it. She said it was like she'd left a whole piece of herself behind, tearing herself in two, right down the middle."

He fell silent, stroking her hair, and Nina wondered if this was what had made Niobe leave him, finally. She could understand it, even if she took no joy in it.

"So you didn't . . . you don't know what happened to him after that?"

"No. I assume nothing happened. I assume he's still there." He hesitated. "I also hope I haven't driven you away by telling you this."

He nuzzled her hair again, and she thought, *He doesn't know.* She tried to get her mind around that simple, impossible fact. He didn't know Henri had been dragged out of Ville au Camps and put into the hellish dungeon of the Saturni. She thought, *I have to tell him. Can I tell him? Is it safer if he doesn't know?*

And she didn't know the answers to any of those questions.

"Strickland," she whispered, "I—I don't mind your telling me what you did. And I-I'm glad I know now. And as far as the rest of it goes . . ." She paused and then took the plunge. "I don't think I could ever turn against you, even if I tried."

"Oh God!" She felt all the air compressed out of her lungs as he pulled her tight and kissed her, and she felt herself owned, possessed by him completely. She knew now he wouldn't stop suddenly and damn his own impulses. She felt a little fear (and an equal thrill) that he might not stop now at all. His hands moved from her shoulders down to her breasts, and she felt them exploring her, mapping the curves of her flesh, and she pulled back a little just to give him more access as his thumbs skimmed over her nipples.

He made a sound halfway between a moan and a growl, and then his hands descended further, to grab her ass. She was pinned against him from her shoulders to her knees, and she felt him, hard and cold and needy and urgent against her. *Oh God*, she thought, *is he that cold all over, and why do I find that so insanely hot? And also, am I ready for this?* And the answer came back to her from her own body, Apparently.

Long, hard kisses, and then he did stop and his breath was quick against her ear. "Nina, I . . . I want to . . . I can't resist what you've done to me. Now, please . . . I want to cross with you . . ."

Time came to a complete halt then. She tried to recapture the thrill of scant seconds ago, but it was gone. She bought time as she ran her hands through the soft black silk of his hair. Wasn't that what she had wanted—to become completely one with him? His voice and his breath distracted her, and *oh yes*, she thought, *I want him to put his mouth there, just there, in the soft hollow behind her ear* . . . and he did, his tongue darting forward for a languorous lick. But she couldn't forget. Crossing was how Skin Eaters made more of their kind. Crossing meant dying. Crossing meant becoming undead. Crossing meant letting him infect her with his virus and becoming a cannibal. One of the damned.

She became very quiet as she thought about that, and she knew he could feel her stillness.

*Because after all,* she thought, *sex was one thing, but this was way beyond any normal definition of going all the way.*

He ran his hand down her back, and then up again, and sighed, and said, "Yes, I know. I realize I've just put my foot in it. You don't need to expound on the concept. Clairvoyance is a useful gift sometimes, but in this case it's not necessary. A stone would be able to realize you didn't want to do it."

"I . . . I just have to think about it, that's all," she said, finally pulling back from him a little further, just a small separation, but it made her understand Niobe's feeling of being torn in half.

His eyes held hers, and she could see herself reflected in their midnight depths.

"I . . . want to," she stammered. "I really do. It's just . . ."

"It's just death." He touched one finger to the corner of her mouth, then smoothed it across, pressing against her fullness. "I understand."

"You . . . I love . . ." She couldn't say it.

His mouth twitched. "Is it so hard? I'm sorry, I didn't mean it to sound like that."

"I want . . ."

He pulled her quickly into the hollow of his throat, and held her there, so gently and yet with such desperation she could almost convince herself she could feel his pulse beat against her cheek. But of course, he had no pulse.

"No," he sighed. "I understand. I think you should go."

"I . . ." There had to be something else she could say to him, and yet she had no words for it. Instead, taking one of his hands in both of hers, she pressed her lips to each finger, to his palm, to his wrist, and then she let it go.

"I . . . I'll see you tomorrow, okay? We'll . . . we'll talk."

"Yes."

Blue eyes like night. Like a night without any stars. She felt she might die if she left him.

"I do love you." She forced out a breath. "See, there I said it."

"I told you it wasn't that hard."

But it was that hard, and she felt like she was dying anyway, a slow pulling apart of every fiber of her body as she resisted the impulse to stay with him. She had to get away, if only for a little while, and she left him and walked out of the room.

# Chapter Twenty-Seven

When she opened her own door, she saw two pairs of eyes staring at her. Alastaire's and Bella's.

"Jesus," she said. "Can't I even go to bed without you guys joining me?"

"We're glad to see you too, Nina," Alastaire drawled. "We just wanted to check in on you after you blew off Tom Thumb downstairs."

Nina flopped down on the mattress and covered her face with her hands.

"Nina?" Bella's voice was cautious. "Is anything wrong?"

"*No*! I mean, well, yes, obviously. We just escaped Guinee, and you guys were tortured, and Phoebe's creepy brother who's a fucking *moon* just told us everything we know is wrong—and where is Phoebe anyway? Did she fly back to Saturn with Sponge Bob Tiny Pants?"

"No, she went to bed." Alastaire shrugged. "And Simone went off somewhere. And we came up here. Come on, Nina, are you still going to keep secrets from us? I thought we got beyond that with the whole 'risking death and saving your best friends' business."

"I'm sorry." Nina sat up and tried to pull herself into some semblance of together. God knew what she looked like. Lips bruised with kissing, and eyes red with unshed tears, and her hair? She smoothed her hands over it. "I'm sorry. I—I've just been through kind of a lot lately."

"So it seems." Bella looked at her, and she had the uncomfortable feeling the other girl at least knew exactly what she'd just been through. She got up and went to her bureau for a hairbrush. At least this way she didn't have to look anybody in the eye.

"So?" Alastaire prompted, and Nina hesitated while working through a tangle.

"So what?"

"So, why'd you get so mad at Little Mister Muffet? All he said was you shouldn't have learned about some guy named Henri, and you tore him a new one."

Nina put the hairbrush down and gave up. Yes, there were some things she had to tell them, and the longer she put it off, the worse it would be. She sat back down on the bed and said, "Okay. You remember about that whole Lost Prince business?"

Bella nodded, and Alastaire said, "Right, he's either a savior or a destroyer, and either way, he's due to show up sometime soon, and then all hell will break loose. So is Henri *him*?"

"Well, yes and no." Nina took a moment to figure out how she should put this. "For a while I thought he might be, but now I'm not so sure. It's complicated." Could the Skin Eater Lost Prince really be a guy crawling with maggots? It didn't sound very . . . princely. She took a deep breath and plowed ahead.

"Anyway, I think he's the reason I was sent to Guinee. I mean, deep down, besides everything else. To get Henri out. But when push came to shove, I didn't do it."

Bella and Alastaire both continued to look at her, and then Bella asked, "So . . . do you want to go back with us now so you can do it?"

She was unbelievably, ridiculously touched by Bella's unthinking offer. Looking at the pale girl, with the shadow of bruises still on her face, Nina had to resist the impulse to burst into tears again.

"No! Oh God, no, you don't have to go back there! I just meant

I screwed up, that's all. I should have remembered him, but I was too busy worrying about you, and well, other things."

Stupid things. She got up and picked up the hairbrush again and fiddled with it until Alastaire said, "Okay, so who is Henri?" and Bella asked, "And *where* is he?" and Alastaire said, "And why didn't you let him out if you knew that was what you were supposed to do? Come on, Neen, start making sense," and Nina held up her hands and said, "Wait, okay, one at a time."

She took a calming breath. "Number one, I think he's Sister Aquilina's son. Shh, okay, let me finish. Sister Aquilina . . . Niobe Danvers . . . was married like two hundred years ago to a guy named Francois Livaudais. They had a son and . . . um . . . he died. The son. He drowned."

And was brought back to life as this really unpleasant zombie-thing, she added to herself, but she didn't say that out loud. Instead she continued, "Eventually he ended up in Guinee, and the Saturni got hold of him and put him in the same Marquis de Sade place as you guys were in."

"But . . ." Bella frowned. "But we were the only ones there. Just the four of us."

"Well, I don't know, maybe there's more than one room. I mean, there was that whole cheese-ball living room, right?"

"Maybe. So let me get this straight. Niobe Danvers had a son named Henri, and you think you were supposed to get him out of Guinee? Why you? Why not her?"

"Well . . ." Nina came back and sat down on the bed again and hugged her knees. "Actually, I'm not sure. Captain Bowman told me he was the one who ratted Henri out to the Saturni. He said he was hoping he could reconcile the Saturni and the Danverses, but that worked out about as well as you can imagine. The Saturni took Henri, and I'm guessing they were hoping when Niobe got wind of it, they could use him to trap her too.

"Only she never knew." Nina swallowed. "I'm the only one who knows where Henri is. And I totally messed up. I should have saved him. I could have saved him, and I probably could have gotten him out if I'd only thought to look for him, but instead I was too upset and I just—I just panicked."

She shut her eyes. "I panicked, and I left him there. I was so afraid I wouldn't be able to save you guys that I forgot about saving anyone else."

She fell silent, and Alastaire and Bella fell silent too, until Alastaire said the obvious.

"Well, I'm certainly glad you did save us."

"Me too," Bella chimed in.

"We'd still be there if it hadn't been for you."

"I'm not sure I'd still be alive," Bella said, adding, "I mean . . . at least as much as I am now . . . which is . . . well, you know . . . kind of."

"And maybe if you'd wasted time, you wouldn't have been able to save anybody," Alastaire added.

Nina sighed. She'd been trying to tell herself that too, but it wasn't working, "You didn't hear him crying. I did. I heard him one other time. It sounded like he was heartbroken."

"Yeah, well . . . we were crying too," Alastaire reminded her, touching her hand. "Crying like babies. You did a good thing, Neens. Don't beat yourself up."

Was that what she was doing? Nina wondered. Was all of this just exhaustion, and the sweet-scary stew of her emotions right now? Strickland. Niobe. Alastaire and Bella. How many people did she love? The kids at the Orphanage, so bravely giving up their bodies to the *Lwas*. What was she doing by comparison? She was back safe at home at Daedalus, with no sense of where she should go next. Niobe's anguish at her son's loss was just another tragedy enacted by the terrible beings who ruled them all. She felt, then, how futile it might be to fight the Saturni. They had millennia on their side, and they controlled everything.

*Play by the rules or go down the drain.* She sighed. *Give it up, girl. You've built every one of your hopes on sand, and the Saturni will always win.*

She felt in her pocket for a Kleenex and (of course) she didn't have one, but she did touch the little gold key she'd brought out of Guinee. Taking it out of her pocket, she pricked her finger on a sharp prong at the end and said, "Ow."

"What's wrong?" Alastaire asked.

"I just cut my finger," she said, sucking it. "I nicked it on the end of the key, the one I used to unlock you."

"Key?" Bella's gaze sharpened. "Here, let me look at it."

Nina handed it over. Her finger was hurting out of all proportion to the tiny cut, and she thought the key must have had something nasty on the end of it. *Poison? Stop scaring yourself. The worst you're going to need is a tetanus shot.*

Bella was turning the key over in her hands, a deep frown between her eyebrows, and it was such a Bella-esque pose that both Nina and Alastaire smiled.

"You gonna unlock a secret pyramid that tells us where the Mona Lisa is?" Alastaire asked, making a playful grab for it, but Bella pushed him away.

"No, don't touch it. Nina, this is very strange. You're not supposed to be able to take anything out of Guinee. It exists in another dimension, another world."

"Actually, I was kind of wondering about that myself." Nina felt her finger give a particularly painful throb, and a slight, very real chill ran down her back. *Great,* she thought. *I've broken all the rules of Skin Eater space/time.* She tried to shrug it off. "Well, I guess there's always a first time for everything."

But Bella didn't answer. Instead, she yelped and dropped the key, shaking her hands and saying, "Shit! It's hot!"

The key didn't make a *ping* when it hit the floor, but rather a *thump*, as though it were much heavier than it was. It sounded like someone had dropped a brick. Looking down, they could see it glowing, at first red, and then white-hot, a small, bright star of light. A faint, charred smell came up from the layers of old varnish on the floor, and a wisp of smoke.

"What the—" Alastaire said, and then they all jumped back as a geyser of flame shot up from the key and licked across the smooth plaster of the ceiling.

"*Holy crap!*" Alastaire grabbed both girls and pushed them out the door. Daedalus had stood for centuries, but it was still made of wood. They watched in sick fascination from the doorway as the flames spread out across the full width of the ceiling, to the crown molding that edged the walls. But for some reason, the flames didn't char the plasterwork. It burned like a magician's flash paper, harmlessly.

Coming back into the room, Nina said, "I think it's all right. I don't think it's going to hurt us."

She stood looking up at the beautiful blue and gold and yellow and white fire as it curved across the ceiling, and she thought she could see galaxies, stars, comets. There was destruction there, certainly, but it was also riveting. Something new was being born, something either terrible or wonderful, and she couldn't tell which.

"What on earth . . . ?" Bella said, coming into the room to stand with her, and Nina said, with a little frightened smile on her face, "I don't think it's from Earth. I think it's from Guinee."

The fire was still burning in a tall, shimmering column, although it was contracting, becoming narrower and more solid with every moment. It looked like molten glass, yellow and white with a dark center, viscous and thick. It twisted and spun in on itself, creating a long, ropy shape, and gradually Nina could see images below the glassy surface: arms, legs, a head. The head was flung back, drinking the flame and letting it run down its long, golden hair. The body was slight: the body of a child or a small man. Nina pushed her fist against her mouth to stifle a scream, as she realized what must be happening. He'd been in there all along. He'd been there in the room as a tiny gold key to unlock the others. It had taken her hands, her care, her blood, to bring him back, and now he was out of Guinee, and reviving. She felt a thrill of pure awe as she realized what was going on. Whatever he was, Henri was coming through.

She dragged Bella back from the gradually coalescing shape, and she realized she was babbling, "Don't hurt it . . . give it room . . . it's like it's being born . . . it's like it's being born all over again," and Bella was shaking her, saying, "Stop, stop it, and tell me. What's going on? Come on, Nina, tell me."

She looked at her friend and said simply, "It's him. I know it. It's *him*. Henri's back."

There was, she realized, nothing she could have done, even if she'd wanted to. No way on Earth could she have extinguished that flame, and even if she'd plunged her hands into its depths, all she'd have done was cook her own flesh. The fire was centering itself and pulling back, drawing down into a single, solid mass, and as Alastaire came to stand on her other side, Nina realized all they could do was just watch it. She wasn't in control of any of this, she realized, and maybe she never had been.

The fire flickered and died out as suddenly and safely as an alcohol blaze, leaving not so much as a burned mark on the floor, and the being it left behind cooled and solidified as well, gradually becoming opaque. He was still short, barely five foot five or six, but he wasn't a child.

He was a slender young man, and his eyes were like molten gold. He seemed completely fine: no putrefaction marred the perfect surface of his skin, which was as smooth as gold. He was a living youth, intact from his light-yellow hair to his narrow feet. Only his fingertips retained a faint bluish tint. Nina realized she could release the breath she'd been holding without screaming, because he wasn't a figure out of a nightmare. He was the farthest thing in the world from that.

He opened his eyes and looked at Nina and she whispered, "Perfect," and he answered, "Yes," in the voice of an adult man. A voice of knowledge and power.

And she realized something else.

He was looking right at her, and he was smiling.

# Chapter Twenty-Eight

Nina had no idea how long she stood staring at the beautiful, naked boy standing in the middle of her bedroom. It could have been minutes. It could have been days.

Alastaire finally broke the spell by saying, "Um . . . maybe I should get him some tighty-whiteys?"

Bella whispered in awe, "Don't bother on my account," and Alastaire said, "Uh, yeah I think I'll bother," and immediately left the room to get the new boy some clothes.

Nina said uncertainly, "Who are you?"

"You know me. You summoned me." Henri's voice was like thunder, muted to a low rumble. There was a little hint of a French accent, but he spoke English without hesitation. "I hoped to be released, but it took so long. So very long. I should have held onto my faith, knowing you were coming. You came to save your friends, but you also saved me."

Nina said, "I had no idea what I was doing. I just put the key in my pocket."

"It was enough."

"So it was a trick, then?"

"A trick?" His eyes narrowed slightly. "I don't understand."

"I mean, it was a way to . . . to hide from the people who wanted to hurt you and sneak out so they wouldn't catch you. It was smart, that's all I meant. Whoever it was that was holding you all there . . . I mean, they might have noticed if five people went into the room and six people came out. You tricked them, that's all I'm saying." Nina bit her lip. "Good for you."

"Yes." His golden eyes held a lovely warm light. "We tricked them together, Nina, you and I. Good for us."

"So . . ." She swallowed. She had so many questions, but she couldn't form any of them. "Are you, uh, warm?" she finally asked him. "I mean, like, my kind of warm? Alive?"

"I don't know. You tell me."

He held out his hand, and when Nina touched it, a sharp spark snapped across their fingers, sending her back with a yelp. She gulped, "Er, sorry, that freaked me out. What just happened?"

"It's still there." Henri looked at his hand with a bemused expression. "Funny, I would have thought after two hundred years it would have evaporated. You see, when my mother pulled me back from . . . wherever it was . . . she was still lapped round and round with the power she'd absorbed. She was fairly crackling with it. I would have thought it would have gone away by now, but apparently . . ." He flexed his hand. "Interesting. I'm sorry, did I hurt you? I certainly didn't mean to do that."

"No, uh, it's cool. I was just surprised."

Alastaire came back into the room carrying a full Daedalus uniform—pants, shoes, shirt, jacket, and underwear. He'd even brought a tie. Nina pulled Bella outside while Alastaire helped Henri to dress, although the Vietnamese girl sighed.

"I know, I know. I shouldn't be drooling. Still, you've got to admit . . . wow. It's not often you see somebody that perfect. But it's still very suspicious. For one thing, that power he has. It looked like he was trying to convince you he didn't know he still had it, but I'm not buying that. I think we have to watch out for him and keep an eye on him—"

"Wait a minute," Nina interrupted her. "You're not saying he's evil? Come on, he was trapped there! He was suffering even worse than the rest of you! I mean, cut him some slack, the guy suffered one thing after another, things no human being should ever have to experience. His sudden resurrection just starting it off! You've got to give him some time."

Bella nodded and said, "Okay, I get it. You brought him back. You feel responsible for him. It's like rescuing a puppy. Just don't go petting him until we know what he is, all right?"

"Fine." Nina shrugged, and then couldn't resist adding, "Besides, I'm not petting him. You're the one who was drooling."

They went back inside, where Alastaire had dressed Henri in a somewhat clownish version of Daedalus chic. Since Henri was at least six inches shorter than the other boy, Alastaire's jacket hung down past Henri's fingertips, and his trousers bagged ludicrously around his ankles. The shorter youth smiled and waved his hands and said, "Do you think a belt would help? Or maybe some suspenders?"

"You look . . . fine," Nina told him, stifling a grin. "Actually, I expected you to be smaller. A child. I saw you in a picture and you were just a little boy . . . here, I'll show you."

She got him the engraving from her desk, noticing how it only showed the three Danvers siblings again, and nothing else.

"You're not there now," she explained, handing it to him, "but you were, sometimes. It's called a 'Mezzotint conundrum' and it—"

"Yes, it communicates." Henri took the engraving from her and looked at it for a long time, his brow furrowed almost as if he were in pain. He seemed to be transfixed by the images of Niobe and Strickland and Agatha, staring at them with his mouth open as though he were drinking them in.

Finally he said very quietly, "They were so beautiful."

"Um, actually, they still are." Nina felt her cheeks grow hot, and she went on rapidly. "Agatha and Niobe are both a little bit older, and Professor Danvers tries to look older, too, although he doesn't always manage it. But they still look pretty much the same as they did 200 years ago. You'd recognize them."

"Of course I would." He didn't look up, and she didn't say anything more, because the desolate, devouring look on Henri's face made her feel a little uneasy. Finally, he said, "I'd like to see her."

"Yeah, well . . ." She was about to add, "That's too dangerous," when he bent and started rolling his pants legs up and said, "Let's go."

"No, you—you can't." She resisted the impulse to grab him, because who knew what would happen if she touched him with her whole hand? They might explode the room. She settled for glancing up at Alastaire, who bravely went and stood in front of the door.

Nina said, "You don't have any idea of what's going on. For one thing, this place is crawling with Saturni. I'm not sure you know who they are, but take my word for it, you do not want to meet them. And for another thing, there's a war going on. I mean, it's not like the Napoleonic wars or anything, but it's still real. More like . . . more like an insurrection. You see, Niobe—your mother— has brought back the *Lwas* . . ."

She trailed off, feeling a definite prickle of fear as Henri turned to her and his eyes burned into hers for a moment. She had a feeling of something large and powerful and cruel hovering just over her, like an eagle or a hawk or . . . an angel? And at the same time, she felt something mean and petty laughing at her, sniggering at her and making rude gestures, like a dirty little boy. *No,* she thought, *that's ridiculous, he's not like either of those things.* And in fact, a split-second later, he wasn't like any of those things. He was just a ridiculously handsome boy who was looking at her and blinking and asking, "The *Lwas*? You mean like the voodoo spirits?"

"Yes." She told herself to stop being silly, and explained, "Your mother has a lot of kids with her where, where she is now, and she's been training them to be possessed by the *Lwas*. The biggest ones, Erzuli and Damballa and Oya and Grand Bois, they're too big to be contained by almost anyone, I guess, but the lesser ones have taken up residence there, well, in—inside of these kids. They're like both there at the same time, if you see what I mean, and they seem to like it. And they all hate the Saturni, and they're committed to fighting them."

She wondered how much of this Henri understood, but he was nodding, so she finished up, "So maybe if things settle down, or the Saturni get bored—ha, ha, ha—then maybe we can go and see Niobe later. But in the meantime, I think maybe we better keep you out of sight—"

She jumped as there was a knock on the door, and, "Uh, who is it . . .?" she asked, trying to make her voice sound confused and sleepy, as though she'd just woke up. The garden outside her window was just starting to look gray with the approaching dawn, and the rest of the school was silent. However, all she got in response was an even louder knock, and then Agatha snapped, "I know you're awake, I know you've got company, and I know I'm going to kick this door down in about two seconds if you don't open up for me, Miss Lamb. Now hop to it."

Nina grabbed the engraving back from Henri and stuffed it in her pocket, and then she looked around to see where they could hide him. For one crazy moment, she thought he might be able to conceal himself under the bed (no luck, the covers were too short) or in a closet (there wasn't one) and she thought, *If only I could do a* miroir d'intent *now when I need one!* She said, "Um . . . yeah . . . wait a second . . . I, uh, I just have to . . . put a shirt on . . ." while she looked around wildly at Alastaire and Bella. Both of them shook their heads.

"Get in the bed," she whispered to Henri. "Quick. Come on, cover up. We'll try and get rid of her." She felt another crack of energy as she shoved Henri toward the mattress, and Agatha said, "Miss Lamb, if you're exploding fireworks in there, please stop it. It's nowhere near the Fourth of July. Now get this door open."

Nina flung the bedspread over Henri and then threw some pillows on top of that, so he made a kind of unconvincing pile. Then Alastaire and Bella went and sat on him as an, "Ooof!" escaped and Nina moved to the door. She was very glad whatever strange spell made him shoot electrical sparks whenever she touched him didn't appear to work on her two friends. She opened the door and said, "Um, yes, Miss Danvers? Was there something you wanted?"

"I can't begin to tell you my list of wants concerning you, Miss Lamb. Let's start with you not treating me like an imbecile. Now why this charade? You're fully dressed."

"Oh, well, yes . . . I mean, yes, I was just . . . I was just changing my shirt . . ."

"With an audience?" Agatha regarded Bella and Alastaire with a raised eyebrow. Bella immediately said, "Yes, she wanted to know which color we thought looked best," and Alastaire said at the same time, "You know me, Aggie, anything for chance to see Neens in her underwear," and Agatha looked at them both witheringly.

"Stand up."

"W-why?" Bella drew her legs up. "We're both quite comfortable sitting here."

"And I think I've got a cramp in my foot," Alastaire added, taking off his shoe and massaging his foot. "Ow! Yep, definitely a cramp. Guess I need to massage it."

"The best cure for a cramp, Mr. Roget, is to walk it off. And Miss Chopin, if you're so concerned with your comfort, why are you sitting on a bed that looks like it's full of rocks? Now come on, stop wasting my time and let me see what you're—"

She stopped short, as Henri pushed Bella and Alastaire up off the bed, and at the same time pushed back the covers to reveal himself. He sat up, and Agatha made a small, choking sound as if she were trying to breathe, and moved backward, groping for Nina's desk chair.

"*Mon Dieu,*" she said, her pale face going gray, "*Ce n'est pas possible.* It's not possible, you . . . you can't be here . . ."

"Aunt Agatha," Henri said, smiling. "I'm so glad you recognize me."

"I don't . . ." Agatha sat down and put her trembling hands over her face. "I won't believe . . . no. I won't believe it. I won't. I won't."

Looking from Agatha to Henri and back again, Nina felt for the first time in, well, forever, sorry for the housekeeper. Formidable, snide, rude, these were all the basic elements of Agatha. Scared and shaken was something she just didn't do. Yet here she was, looking like she was about to be sick at the sight of a single, beautiful boy.

"You know, don't you?" Nina asked quietly. "You know what they did, Niobe and your brother. That's why you're so scared now."

"Yes." Agatha breathed and then lifted her head and straightened her back and let her hands fall into her lap, although her eyes were still closed. "I knew, and I warned them. But of course, no one even listens to me. I'm just Cassandra yelling fire in a crowded theater. Still, there are powers far greater than ours, and who knows? In the end, they always do what they want." She sighed and added something else very softly under her breath, and Nina said, "What was that? What did you say?"

"I said, 'Damn them'," Agatha said, enunciating every syllable. "Damn them to hell, the beings that did this. Now. If you don't mind, let's get going. You're wanted. All of you. Downstairs. Right now."

# Chapter Twenty-Nine

"Oh, c'mon . . ." Alastaire tried to stall her. "It's the middle of the night. All right, maybe not the middle of the night anymore, but still, it's late, couldn't this wait—"

"No. No one's had very much sleep tonight." Agatha wiped her hands over her face, and Nina realized she was wiping away moisture. Tears? Or sweat? She didn't even have time to wonder, as Agatha hustled them all out the door and down the hallway, down the stairs, and across the wide center hall to the lounge.

When she opened the door, Nina's heart sank. Jack Benway and Father Ignatius and Isolde and Archer Freeland were all sitting there, surrounded by the lesser Saturni: Sabien Belu, Oswald Babb, Cecily Namath, and Toshiro Nagoichi, who was the only one among them to look grouchy and sleepy and generally pissed off at having to be there, wearing a silk kimono over what was obviously a pair of pajamas.

A quick glance confirmed that Strickland wasn't present, and Nina spared a moment to give thanks. Still, this looked bad. It looked like a trial.

Jack Benway stared at her, and after a moment a very nasty, very satisfied smile spread over his face. He said, "Miss Lamb. I'm glad you could make it."

Nina realized a split-second later what must have happened. Somehow, the *miroir d'intent* wasn't working anymore. He could recognize her, even when she was inside the school.

As if to confirm this, he added, "So nice to actually *see* you after all this time."

She stood up straight and thought, *Well, I'm not going to give this prick the satisfaction of making me cringe.* "We met just a few weeks ago, Mr. Benway, at the Thirteenth Night Ball. Surely you haven't forgotten?"

"No. I haven't forgotten anything about that night. Have you?"

She looked at her fingernails. "I seem to remember there was dancing?"

"I remember I made you an offer, Miss Lamb. And you refused it."

"Well, I guess you guys aren't the Mafia, then. Maybe you should have used a horse's head. Or a fish wrapped in newspaper."

"Miss Lamb, stop it." Isolde Freeland was looking her usual crisp self, perfectly put together in black linen pants and a cream-colored silk top that matched her white-blonde hair, but at the same time she looked distracted. Tense. She drummed her fingers on the table next to her.

"I get so bored with all the tedious histrionics of teenagers," she added, to no one in particular. "If it's not relationship drama, it's petty acts of rebellion. Don't you realize we're trying to look out for you, that we've got your best interests at heart? Miss Lamb," she continued, "Please sit down and have your little playmates join you. We need to ask you all something. In the past twenty-four hours, have you or have you not been to Guinee?"

"What's that?" Nina asked. "Is it like Papua New Guinea?"

"*Miss Lamb!*" Jack Benway slammed his fist down on the arm of his chair, making all the pictures and knick-knacks in the room shake. "Enough. You don't seem to recognize the very real danger you're in. Now, do I have to resort to harming you or your friends, or are you going to play ball?"

Nina shut up. Her mind was racing. Since the Saturni could see them all, why weren't they reacting to their having another friend present? Why weren't they paying any attention to Henri? Was it possible they didn't know who he was?

"Sir—" She sat down, trying to keep her voice calm and reasonable. "When we last met, you said I could have all kinds of worldly riches . . . power . . . love . . . influence. All of that."

"Yes." Benway was sitting forward in his chair, looking a little more interested now, all of his anger gone. "Yes, I did say that. Go on."

"Well, I was just wondering." She crossed her legs. "Um, how much power are we actually talking about? I mean, how many of you are there? As far as I understand it, you were all just the *Introim* once. The beings of light that came through from Guinee and became incarnate. So . . . let's see. There were the Grand *Lwas* . . . and the lesser *Lwas*. They're on one side." She held up one hand. "And then there's, well . . . you guys." She gestured at them. "There's eight of you here, four Grand Saturni and I mean, um, you . . ." She nodded at Cecily and Oswald Babb and Sabien Belu and Toshiro Nagoichi and thought, *No point in calling them lesser Saturni. I'm in enough trouble as it is.*

"So, I . . . I just wondered, well, I mean . . . could I join you?" She swallowed and thought, *Keep it together. Don't show him how much that whole idea disgusts you.* "If you're talking about a bribe, after all, it'd have to be a pretty good one. I'm not going to fork over my friends and everything else for a couple million dollars in chump change. So what have you got?"

She watched Benway closely to see if he revealed anything, any flicker of surprise, but there was nothing. He just frowned and shook his head.

"No. You can't join us, but you're welcome to worship us and sit at our right hand."

*Well, screw you,* she thought. Just like every other dictator, when push came to shove, he didn't want to share any of the goodies.

"We are few, and our mysteries are . . . exclusive." He smiled. "You know what they say about good things coming in small packages."

She smiled as well. They really seemed to be ignorant of what Henri's presence might mean to any and all of these equations. "So you don't think there might be, like, any stray other beings around who might be in any way like you?"

"Miss Lamb, surely you jest. There is no one else in the universe quite like us."

"Nobody you might have missed?"

"No, and we're not in the habit of losing track of each other, either!" Father Ignatius snapped. "Really, this is getting tiresome. We're not so ignorant we could be in the presence of other beings of our stature and not know it. There is, however, somebody here whom you might be interested in seeing . . ."

He gestured, and Nina turned to see Simone sitting in the window seat, looking quiet, but as beautiful and composed as ever. She looked up and met Nina's eyes for a split second, and then looked aside, and a number of things, none of them good, fell into place.

"You told them, didn't you?" Nina said, her voice louder and angrier than she intended. "You couldn't wait to run to Mommy and Daddy, could you? You couldn't even have that much respect for someone who saved your life. I should have left you there." She looked down at her hands, which were clenched together. "I shouldn't have saved you. I literally risked my life, and this is how you repay me?!"

"I didn't ask you to save me," Simone said, smoothing her hair back. "You decided to do it. I was perfectly fine where I was."

"You were what?" Nina stared at her and then let out a laugh.

"Right, I guess that's why you were screaming at me not to leave you there, because you *liked* it so much."

Simone looked down and murmured something that might have been either an apology or an insult, but Nina wasn't waiting around for either one.

"So spit it out, what did you tell them?"

"I told them about the *miroir d'intent*."

Nina nodded. "I figured that. That's why they can see me. And . . .?"

"'And' what? I told them you rescued us, okay? I told them you knew how to get into Guinee. And oh yeah, I told them you got something from the Cumaean Sybil at some point. Some kind of drawing or engraving or something. Big deal."

Simone fell silent, and Nina did too. She was suddenly, immensely aware of the conundrum in her pocket. Did the Saturni know what it was? More to the point, why hadn't the Saturni noticed Henri? Did he have some kind of a *miroir d'intent* going on now? Nina tried to reassemble her racing thoughts, but she didn't have much time before Mr. Benway stood up and approached her.

"So you see, Nina," he said, poisonously quiet. "We need that engraving. And I really don't think you have any choice but to give it to us."

"I . . . I threw it away." Nina tried to look very sorry. "It was just a crummy old picture. I had no idea anyone wanted it."

"You're lying."

"Honestly, I put it in the trash. It's probably in some landfill now."

"I never found it," Agatha commented, her voice deliberately flat. "And I should know."

Nina turned around to stare at her.

"You go through the school's garbage? You're one sick lady, you know that?"

"Actually, Agatha's been acting on my orders." Archer Freeland said, sounding smug. "I figured you can never be too careful with kids your age."

Nina thought this was probably the dumbest thing she'd ever heard, but she didn't waste time arguing. She said, "Oh, that's right, I threw it away at C.C.'s coffee shop. I spilled a Mochasippi on it, so I figured it was ruined anyway."

"Miss Lamb, you're pathetic." Isolde sighed. "I've heard better lies under ether. Now. Shall we try this with words of one syllable? *Where the hell is it?*"

"It's . . ."

"We have to tell them," Bella sighed, stammering a little. "If—if we don't, they c-could k-kill us. It's up in Nina's b-bedroom, um, under the books on her desk."

Benway cut his eyes toward Oswald Babb, who practically bounced to his feet and said, "I'll go. Last door on the right on the second floor, right? I won't be a sec."

When the door clicked shut behind him, Nina couldn't resist asking, "Does Mr. Babb know where all of the students sleep?"

"Only the pretty ones," Father Ignatius said, and when Alastaire choked, the priest allowed himself a wafer-thin smile. "You have many admirers, Miss Lamb."

Something occurred to Nina. "Um, Father?"

"Yes?"

"Why weren't you and Dr. Freeland at the Fortuna Club last January?" She pushed ahead when she saw him glance at Isolde. "I noticed your absence. Mr. Benway said you were in Rome, and Dr. Freeland was called away on a medical emergency, but somehow I didn't believe that. Where were you?"

His startled response was very slight, but it was there. The priest said, "I don't like parties."

"Even Saturni ones?"

"Especially Saturni ones."

Isolde rubbed her eyes, the first indication she'd ever shown that she might be normal enough to be tired. "You're a tedious little shit, Nina, you know that? All right, if this is all in the nature of a negotiation, I'll answer that. Some of us find our necessary actions a little . . . grotesque. We're not squeamish, in fact, we enjoy all the sensations of the body, but boredom does set in. Do you want me to be explicit? I don't like seeing human beings try and act like us, all right? People like that dreadful man, Sir Keith Wolf. So puffed up and convinced he's all-powerful. And he loves nothing so much as to wallow in what he perceives to be our divine crapulence. Call me a snob, but it's embarrassing. My objections are . . . aesthetic."

She didn't look at Jack Benway, but Nina did, and noticed his frown. So there were rifts even among the Saturni? She filed that information away for later use, but just then Babb came back into the room without the engraving.

"I looked everywhere, Chief, but it's no soap. I think the little chink bitch is lying."

Bella drew herself up and said, "That's 'gook' bitch, Mr. Babb, and I'll thank you to remember it."

A new idea was forming in Nina's mind, but it was a long shot. Still, it might be the only shot they had left.

"So, you don't like people like Sir Keith Wolf?" she asked, keeping her focus on Simone's mother, figuring she might be the weakest link. "Even though you want him to marry your daughter?"

Isolde's perfect eyebrows shot up. "My, my, you *have* been listening at keyholes. I have absolutely no intention of marrying my daughter to that old Limey fart. Perish the thought."

"You'll do what you're told," Benway said, his voice harsh. "Who's running this show anyway? So, Miss Lamb, let's try something else. Archer, Toshiro—grab her. Hold her arms. Tight. Now." He advanced toward her until he was standing almost nose to nose with her, and she could smell his rank breath. She tried to look anywhere but in his dark, lightning-bolt eyes. "Miss Lamb, I'm going to ask one more time, and after that, things are going to get very, very uncomfortable. Where's the engraving you got from the Sybil?"

Nina thought, Play them against each other, and she glanced at Isolde and Simone, and then looked aside. "It's in my pocket. But you've got to let me get it out. It's . . . dangerous."

She pulled away from Mr. Freeland and the Japanese gangster, and amazingly, they let her go. They all had truly horrible expressions on their faces. They looked like they were about to salivate. *Why do they want the engraving so much?* she wondered, but the very fact they did made her resolve not to give it to them. She stepped away from them, back toward her friends, and said, "You know . . . when I went to see that old guy again . . . you know . . . that old man . . . he told me the weirdest thing about pictures. That they're a flat surface, that reflects . . . reflects reality . . ."

Bella got it, as she'd expected her to. She stood up and pulled Alastaire and Henri out of their chairs as well, holding them next to her as though she wanted the two boys to protect her. Nina fumbled in her pocket, taking her time, pulling out the engraving as though it were made of tissue-paper.

"Okay, here you go." She glanced at Isolde again. "I thought you told me I could keep it, though. You promised."

"What the hell are you talking about?"

"Simone said . . ."

"I never said anything!"

"If I saved you. You—you told me your mother . . ."

"What are you playing at?" Isolde Freeland stood up. "Jack, I swear, the child's pathological! I never promised her anything. I certainly never once said she could keep something that important in return for freeing my daughter ...!"

That was all the opportunity Nina needed. Taking advantage of the Saturni's distraction, she held up the conundrum and then she and the other kids stared at it as though their very lives depended on it. Which she supposed they did.

Nina heard a faint whooshing in her ears, as well as the soft lapping of the waves of Guinee. She could feel the small, mouth-like touch of tentacles on her arms and legs, but there were other things as well: hot sun, humidity, and a warm wind full of scent. She could smell bougainvillea and bananas, and other smells too: grass and water, horse dung and deep jungle vegetation. There was the scent of perfume, and of fruit grown rotten ripe. She felt a world exploding around her, full of color and brightness and flowers growing bigger than the sky, and tall, tall trees—mahogany, palm, bamboo—and a garden where, on the other side of a limestone wall, a sheer cliff-face dropped 200 feet into the seething cauldron of the sea.

And the next instant they were in the engraving. They were in Haiti.

# CHAPTER THIRTY

"Well," Alastaire said, looking up from where he'd fallen onto his hands and knees on the thick Bermuda grass that covered the lawn. "You certainly know how to keep life interesting, Neens, I'll say that much. I'm going to vomit now, if you'll excuse me."

He got to his feet and tottered away in the direction of a tall stand of palmettos, and they heard him retching. The rest of them stared around at the house standing a little distance away from them, its wide gallery supported by slender pillars. The sky above was a vivid blue. There were the sounds of birds somewhere, parrots, their cries sharp. And they could smell the briny smell of the sea.

"I know this place," Henri said quietly. "I've been here before."

"Yes," Nina said. She felt an ache in her chest, almost a feeling of longing, as she realized she was actually inside the engraving she'd stared at so often. Where were the Danverses? Where was the headmaster? This was the actual garden she'd seen, with a stone bench, and bougainvillea cascading over the wall. There was the familiar thick trunk of a palm tree, although for the first time if she looked up, she could see its leafy crown.

She was there. She could see it all. And what on earth was she supposed to do now?

Could she go exploring? Go into the house and see what secrets it hid? She ached to know where Strickland and his sisters had come from, what landscape had first claimed their hearts, but it was too dangerous. The Saturni would be after them in a moment, once they figured out where they'd gone. In fact, she wondered why they hadn't come already? They had the conundrum. It had fallen to the ground the moment she and the rest of her friends had slipped into its subtle depths.

Bella clearly had the same idea, because she was looking around wildly, and then she said, "There, through there. That path, it leads away from the house. Come on. We've got to hide. Alastaire, c'mon, you can finish spewing later. We've got to hide so the Saturni can't find us."

She dragged Alastaire away from his improvised restroom, and Nina remembered not to touch Henri but simply glanced around to make sure he was following them. They raced down the path between thick stands of bamboo and huge elephant ears and gigantic tree ferns that lined the trail on either side, heading downhill, away from the house, until they got to a beach where mangroves grew, and a waterfall cascaded down into a shallow rock pool. It wasn't anything like the pool she'd dreamed of in her nightmares, Nina told herself. It had no similarity to the one she'd seen in Guinee. This one was barely a dozen feet across, and so clear you could see the sandy bottom, where pink crabs scuttled. The sound of the waterfall was loud enough that they could pause there and catch their breaths, without fear of being heard. But they realized a moment later that with the waterfall so loud, they couldn't hear anything either, or know if anyone was coming up behind them.

"We've got to hide," Bella repeated, and Nina said, "Look, there, behind the waterfall. There's room. There's a ledge. Come on, follow me."

She began picking her way across the wet stones that lined the pool, and the others carefully followed her. After a quick plunge through the falling spray, they were effectively hidden, and they looked out at the deserted beach past the cascading torrent.

"Where are they?" Alastaire whispered, as they looked around to the left and the right. They all stayed as quiet as they could, but all they could hear was the water falling. They could dimly see the waves curling on the shore in front of them across the stretch of beach, ebbing and flowing among the thick mangrove roots. But other than that, nothing else stirred.

If the Saturni had followed them, they could be creeping up on them. Or could they have gone up the other way, toward the house? In either case, they'd certainly realize their mistake soon enough and come back. Were they well-hidden here? A white-tailed bird was making its way across the shingle, dipping its long, pointed beak into the sand in search of food, and it seemed completely unaware of them, or unconcerned with their presence. She could see, far out above the waves, small clouds floating, faint smears in the otherwise unbroken blue emptiness of the sky. What would it have been like to live in this world, she thought, before gasoline and airplanes, before telephones and the Internet, when the sea was as wide as the horizon and far more mysterious? The water falling in front of her eyes was like a shadowy veil that made everything shimmery, like a mirage, and she so wanted to see things clearly. She squinted and then drew in her breath.

There was someone else on the beach now. A toothless old black woman in a bathrobe walking across the shallows, wearing strands and strands of Mardi Gras beads.

"What the holy sh—?" she whispered.

She looked around, trying to find out if anyone else was seeing this vision, or was she the only one? Henri was staring at the old woman quizzically, and Bella had her mouth open and then breathed, "Oh my God. It's Slippery Annie."

"Good," Nina said. "I was kind of figuring I'd lost it. Just to make sure, you . . . you can all see her?"

"Of course we can see her," Alastaire said, and then he gasped. "Holy crap, does that mean Slippery Annie is one of the Saturni?"

Nina didn't think that sounded likely, but then so many strange things had happened lately, who knew? The bag lady certainly didn't look very Saturnic. She was mumbling to herself and smacking her toothless gums the way she always did, occasionally looking down to check out a shell or a bright stone in the water that lapped gently around her feet. She looked vacant, but not necessarily unhappy, in spite of the fact that the robe she was wearing was now soaking wet around the hem. Nina felt a pang of sadness for her. Abandoned in this world as in any other, she was the kind of human debris no one cared about, as ephemeral as the plastic beads she wore. No one would notice if a wave carried her out to sea. The Saturni, with all their wealth and power, were probably as ignorant of this woman's existence as a man riding in a limousine would be of a paper cup that got squashed beneath his tires. They wouldn't even notice her.

"I'm going to talk to her," she said, moving over toward the end of the ledge where she could duck out from under the waterfall. "Stay here. If it's a trick, at least we won't all get caught. Shh. Stop worrying," she added, because Bella was looking at her as though she'd proposed drowning herself. "Sit tight. I know what I'm doing."

Ignoring the fact that this was a bald-faced lie, Nina crept out from under the cascade of water and walked toward the old woman across the sand. The beach was small, and once she took off her boots and waded out into the shallow water to join her, she felt that it was warm. Here on the shore, she could hear the sound of sea birds farther out over the ocean, where bigger waves crashed against some half-submerged reefs, their spume flung up high into the air. Nina said, "Um, excuse me, I think I know you," and the old woman turned around and looked at her.

The first thing Nina noticed was the woman's eyes. They were very dark and very wide, very sad, shining, ebony eyes that gazed at her with grave attention, her head tilted a little to one side. The other thing Nina noticed was that she wasn't that old. Her toothless mouth made her look like the lower half of her face had collapsed in on itself, but her forehead was smooth, and her cheeks were still plump and soft.

Like wisps of finery, her beauty still clung to her in the same way her straggled hair, which was knotted with lace and bits of ribbon and feathers, hung down around her shoulders, a filthy tangle of what once must have been lustrous black curls. She opened her mouth and said, "What . . .?" and then looked away, her attention caught by a passing seagull. She smiled a little.

"Bird. Bird. Pretty bird."

"Yeah. Pretty bird. Uh . . . they call you Slippery Annie, right? I'm . . . I'm Nina."

"Pretty bird. Come. Come here, pretty bird." She splashed out into the deeper water, and Nina went after her and reached for her elbow to steady her. "Watch out," she told the older woman, drawing her back into the shallows. "You'll get all wet. I-I wanted to talk to you."

"Wet. Wet," the older woman sang. "I was born in water. Hot mud and the delta. All down the river, long, long ago. All the way down to Shawneetown, all the way down to New Orleans, lean on the beechen oar—"

"Yes, yes, all right, but listen. I was wondering, I was just wondering . . ."

"Lean on the beechen oar, all the way down to the sea."

She was crazy, of course. There was nothing there, no landmarks to hold on to. Nina felt her own sadness welling up in her again, her irrational disappointment, because it was like talking to a shadow. Here on a lost beach that was nowhere in time, and God knew where in space, she was talking to a crazy person because she wished so much to have someone tell her what to do. Someone to help her, someone to help her find her way out of this mess.

Follow her, she heard a voice say in her head. Not Strickland's. A man's voice, though, stern and somewhat forbidding, a voice she recognized from somewhere, but she had no idea where. Follow her to where you want to go. Where Henri wants to go. Bring him home. The voice gentled and added, You've done so well. You're almost there, and then, Follow her, she also has her role to play, and as the voice faded away, Nina could hear the surf and the gulls and the wind again through the mangrove leaves, and she felt buoyed up for the first time in what felt like ages with something that could almost have been . . . hope.

She felt impossibly, ridiculously happy. All they had to do was follow Slippery Annie and she would lead them to Niobe. She would lead them *home*. She looked at the crazy woman, who was reaching her hands into the water now trying to touch a fish swimming there, and then, turning around, she called to the others, "Come on! I think I know what we're supposed to do!"

Henri and Bella and Alastaire all came out from behind the waterfall with varying expressions of wariness and doubt on their faces. They all looked around to make sure the beach was clear, and then they practically tip-toed over to Nina.

"Are . . . you . . . insane . . . ?" Bella hissed. "The Saturni could be here any minute!"

"I don't think so. Besides, we're not staying. Come on," she added, as Annie started off through the shallows, wading around the clump of mangroves that protected the beach. "Come on, don't lose her! We're supposed to follow her."

"Um . . . why?" Alastaire asked, splashing after her, and then saying, "Shit, I've got water in my shoes ... shit, shit, shit." He bent over and took them off. Bella was unlacing her boots and taking off her stockings, and Henri just kicked off his shoes and waded in. They followed the homeless woman through the warm, sun-flecked water, around the bend of the mangroves, and along the long, pebbly stretch of the shore. Bella was still arguing.

"I mean, it makes sense to keep to the water, yes, that way they can't track us, but I still don't see why we're trusting some ... some mentally challenged person to take us on a hike."

"Shh. Don't bother her. I think she can hear us."

"Of course she can hear us," Alastaire complained. "We're splashing around like a bunch of labrador retrievers! I don't think she cares, but we're not exactly being stealthy."

"Shh."

Nina was trying to keep her own dress from getting any wetter than it had to (bunching it up under her sash helped to keep it above her knees) but she had to admit the water felt wonderful, and the sunshine felt glorious on her back. Alastaire and Bella were predictably hating it, even though they'd both grabbed some thick banana leaves and were holding them over their heads as makeshift umbrellas.

"I'm going to kill you," Bella said through gritted teeth. "The minute we get back to any kind of consensual reality, you're toast."

Finally, Annie led them away from the water and up along a rising path, the way lined with tall bamboos, so the sunlight was at least dappled. Falling back a little, Nina asked Henri, "How are you doing?"

"Fine."

"Doesn't the sunshine ...?"

"No, I quite enjoy it. I've spent so much time underwater, the open air is a nice change."

Nina refrained from saying, "I'm glad somebody's normal,"

because that was too idiotic on the face of it. She increased her pace until she was walking just behind Annie. At least that way, she didn't have to walk near a reanimated corpse, or hear Bella and Alastaire bitching.

The land around them was changing as they ascended, the thick black mud of the path through the bamboo forest changing to drier soil, with palms and grasses growing lushly on either side. And at the same time, the air was becoming more humid. Alastaire slapped at his neck, murmuring, "Damn mosquitos," and there was the strangest array of smells here: jungle foliage and flowers, but also gasoline and asphalt and grass and cooking oil. And then, unmistakably, Nina smelled the pungent, spicy aroma of shrimp boil seasoning. No place else on earth smelled like that. They were approaching New Orleans! She quickened her pace, until she was moving ahead of the crazy woman who had stopped to poke her finger into the holes in a ramshackle fence, and then, coming around the end of the fence, she saw it.

The corner of Egania Street. And the orphanage. And the convent.

And there was something else.

All the Saturni were standing there waiting for them.

# Chapter Thirty-One

Nina reacted with pure instinct. She ran past them, screaming to the others to follow her, certain of nothing but that they had to get inside the Convent quickly before any of the Saturni grabbed them. Once they were in there, well, surely Niobe would know how to protect them. She had powers. And besides the *Lwas* were in there too. They could put up a fight! Racing past Cecily Namath and ducking in between Isolde and Archer Freeland, she wondered, was this what Niobe had planned all along? To lure the Saturni there to destroy them? It seemed too easy, and the passivity of the Saturni bothered her. Were they actually letting her escape?

She could see Bella running a little ahead of her up the path to the house, the Vietnamese girl's long, slender legs carrying her over Toshiro Nagoichi as the fat Yakuza made a dive to try and tackle her. Alastaire was yelling as he wrestled with Father Ignatius, and Nina saw him land a solid punch to the priest's face followed by a kick to the nuts, which doubled the Saturnus over and let the Skinny boy break away.

They ran up the steps, panting, and flung themselves against the door, which opened to their pounding. Nina caught a quick glimpse of Tish's startled face (or was it Dantor's?) as they fell in on top of her, and Bella gasped, "Shut the door, quick, they're right out there!"

Tish didn't need to be told twice. She slammed the door and shot the deadbolt and then put her head back and yelled, a fierce cry that sounded like a cross between a rebel yell and a hound baying. Feet pounded down the stairs, and Nina saw with great relief a whole knot of people she knew—Daneel and Flyboy, Sharazz and Joe Trunza, Sibelle and even the twins, all racing toward them—and then at the bend of the staircase, she saw the two people she wanted most to see in all the world: Strickland and Niobe Danvers, who were staring at her in mute shock, and then hurrying toward her.

She wanted to cry, she wanted to laugh, she wanted to launch herself at them and hug them both and beg them to tell her everything was going to be all right, but the melee of people in the front hallway prevented her. The boys were dragging furniture over to block the door, and Tish and Billie and Stephen and Santangelo were grabbing knives from the kitchen and hand weights and anything else they could think of to use as weapons, and Nina pushed her way past them and ran up the stairs and felt Strickland grab her arms in a grip like iron.

"What happened?" he asked, his face white. "What have you done?"

"We—we were caught," she gasped. "Agatha—she had to—I don't blame her—the Saturni made her bring us all down from my room and meet with them in the lounge. They knew I had the engraving, but it's all right, somebody explained to me that it's a portal into Guinee, like a, well, like a mirror, or any reflective surface. So we—we went through, and then we were in Haiti at your old house, and then we saw Slippery Annie, and a voice told me to follow her, so we did, and we ended up here. And then the Saturni were here, and they were waiting for us, but it's all right, we got through, somehow they let us get through and—"

And then even as she continued to pant out her story, she realized he wasn't gazing at her with relief or love or concern or anything remotely like that. His eyes were horrified, and he said,

"That's not what I meant. I meant, what did you bring through? What did you bring back from Guinee?"

She stopped and stared at him, as if one of them at least had to have gone mad. Hadn't he guessed by now? He wasn't stupid, and he'd been right there listening to her talk with Francois Livaudais. Had he still not realized the terrible trick the Saturni had pulled, taking Niobe's child from Ville au Camps and imprisoning him? How could he not sense his connection with the boy who was right there with them in the house, who had come home to see his mother?

And then she had a terrible thought and spun around. *Where exactly was Henri?*

She looked for him frantically in the scrum of people by the front door, but all she could see were Bella and Alastaire staring at the *Lwa* children with wary awe, and Daneel and Joe and Sharazz pushing an enormous ebony sideboard over to use as a shield, while the rest of them hunkered down behind it.

"Where's Henri?" she shouted, and then everything seemed to stop dead.

She became aware of Niobe's keening above her, sighing through her parted lips as though she had a wound in her throat, letting all the air out of her lungs. She had her eyes closed, and there were tears running down her face. "No," she whispered, and she seemed to sway where she stood above them on the staircase. "No . . . he was safe . . . he was safe . . ."

"No, he wasn't!" Nina felt a desperate need to tell her that. She had to explain, she had to make Niobe see why she'd done what she'd done. "They had him! The Saturni had him in a terrible room where people were tortured, and they were hurting him, he was crying. I heard him! They wanted to use him as bait to get to you, but I . . . I freed him! I let him out!"

Strickland rounded on her again, and if she'd thought he'd

looked horrified before, now that horror was mixed with a livid rage. "You did *what*?!"

"I-I freed him. Well, not intentionally. He was . . . there was this key. I used it to unlock the others. Then, when I realized I still had it in my pocket, I took it out, and I pricked my finger on it and then it got all hot and burst into flames and then, well, he was there. Henri." Nina shivered as Strickland continued to glare at her, and she felt her heart starting to pound strangely in her ears. "What? What is it? What have I done?"

He turned and looked up at Niobe, and Niobe looked down at him. There was a moment of wordless communication between them that Nina wished very much she could hear, but it wasn't meant for her. Strickland's face looked drawn, questioning, while Niobe's face looked coldly resistant. The tears still lay on her cheeks, but they were forgotten.

"You know what he's capable of," Strickland said quietly.

"No, I don't." Niobe's lips barely moved.

"You saw it."

"I saw nothing. He's my son. My son!"

"Torture?" Strickland's laugh was harsh, like a bark. "For Christ's sake, I saw him kill dozens, and that was when he was just a boy, just a little boy! He likes it. All your servants, everyone else who was in the house. He would have killed us, too, if we hadn't already been dead! Whatever we brought back from the grave, it isn't a child, Niobe. It's a monster. He wasn't in that room suffering. Whatever the Saturni were doing with him in there, he was *enjoying* himself."

Nina felt her skin grow as cold as ice, as she remembered the sound of muffled sobbing coming from behind the door. And then Simone's words, "We couldn't see the son of a bitch. Just these cuts and punches and kicks that came out of nowhere, like we were being attacked by the room itself. And they went on and on . . ."

*It was him,* she thought. *Henri was hidden there in the room all along, hiding in plain sight. Waiting for me to bring him out.*

*And at the same time,* she thought, *but he's beautiful! He isn't a demon.* He hid with us under the waterfall. He walked with us back out of Haiti. He said he was enjoying the sunlight. And she felt as if her head were spinning in a hundred different directions at once.

"I know." Strickland's voice was low, fast, furious, aching with tenderness as he clasped his sister's hand on the banister, trying to hold her in place. "I know how you feel, but you can't do it. You have to remember. There's too much at stake. We can't, any of us, allow ourselves to break. You, of all people, you have to stay strong, stay sane. You have other children, these children, and they need you too. For God's sake, *I* need you. You can't afford to despair now, not after we've come so far!"

But Niobe just shook her head. She started walking down the stairs, and as she did so, she said softly, "I have to see him, Strickland. I just have to see him one more time."

"You can't. Please, darling. Please. Let them have him. They deserve him. Stay here, stay with me. Can't you see it's what they want?" He turned to Nina and shouted directly into her face, "Look what you've done! You stupid, stupid girl, can't you see you've broken her heart?!"

Nina could see that all too clearly. She backed away from him with her hands over her ears, wishing in that moment that the floor could open and swallow her up. She felt as if a stone was lodged somewhere in her chest, a horrible stone of guilt and grief and shame, because she had tried, hadn't she? Hadn't she'd truly tried to do what was best? "You were being played by a maestro," the words echoed over and over again in her head, taunting and awful, along with the Sybil's prophecy: 'The lion will dress himself up as a sheep, and even the lamb will be deceived for a while." She remembered Janus snarling at her, "You should never have learned about Henri," and now she wished with all her heart she'd never seen the engraving, never gone to Guinee, and never meddled in any of this.

But now, of course, it was too late.

Niobe had reached the bottom of the stairs, and Nina thought she'd never seen anything more beautiful, more noble, and more tragic than this woman who had sacrificed everything to fight the Saturni, and who now had to sacrifice even this, her one chance of seeing her child again. *I'm so sorry*, Nina thought helplessly. *I'm so sorry.* Crux had been right. It had been too dangerous to even speak Henri's name. While he'd been just a memory, Niobe's grief had been manageable, a late-night sorrow. Now it threatened to tear her apart.

Nina watched as Strickland put his arm around his sister, and finally her own thick, snotty tears caught in her throat and spilled unnoticed down her flaming cheeks.

"You know you can't really go out there," Strickland said, holding Niobe close, his dark head bent so their foreheads were gently touching. "You can't. It's too dangerous. Please darling, stay here with me."

And Niobe simply pushed him aside and said, "I know. I'm just going to go to the front door and look out at him."

"Please, darling. Don't." His voice broke, and Nina looked away before she could see his own tears fall. *I really don't need to see that*, she thought. She watched through a blur as Niobe moved to the door and flung her hand up, sending the furniture flying apart to either side of the front hall. Then she threw the deadbolt and opened the door just the barest crack.

The shot came at once, not loud, just a single *Pop!* and Niobe crumpled to the ground like a bird caught in mid-flight. Her dark robes billowed around her, and there was the softest sound.

A startled, "Oh."

Then someone was screaming, and for a moment, Nina thought it might be her. Her mouth was stretched wide open, but she realized a second later no sound was coming out of it. The screaming was coming from Strickland, and it didn't sound human. He raced over to his sister and threw himself down on the floor next to her, saying, over and over again, "No, darling, you're not . . . it's all right, darling . . . it's all right . . . it's all right."

Nina watched as blood bloomed from a single red rose on Niobe's breast, and as she watched it pour out of her, she realized Niobe wasn't all right at all. She was bleeding to death.

"Shh . . . shh . . ." Strickland cradled his sister in his arms and pulled her up so she was sitting in his lap, so he could press his cheek to hers. "I'll heal you, you'll be fine . . . just be still . . . you'll be all right again in a moment . . ."

The blood kept pouring out of her. So much blood. Nina remembered Alastaire explaining to her once, after seven crossings, that's it, you were a full-fledged Skin Eater, and after that you were effectively indestructible. Give or take a few things.

Was this one of those things, a bullet fired by the Saturni? How had they known it was her anyway? How had they known she'd show herself?

Because you brought him here, a part of her mind told her. Because you've been doing exactly what the Saturni wanted you to do all along. Get the engraving. Learn about Henri. Bring him back from Guinee, and bring him here, to the one person who would be absolutely unable to resist the temptation to look at him again.

You baited the trap and set the spring, and then you came inside and told Niobe exactly where he was. The Saturni hadn't needed to lift a finger. She, Nina, had done it all.

For a moment, she felt as if she couldn't breathe. She wanted to run, shriek, bang her head against the wall, hit something, kill herself. Nothing could be worse than this pain, nothing could be worse than just standing there and knowing what she'd done. She watched Niobe's body spasm as blood poured from the wound in her chest, splashing onto Strickland's shirt and turning the white to red, and he didn't even seem to notice. He kept holding onto her, whispering to her in French, murmuring soft endearments and kissing her temple, while she bled her life's blood out and no one else seemed to be able to say or do anything or even move.

*"Tu es mon ame,"* he murmured, *"et tu seras toujours ma vie,"* and then he lowered his head to her breast and prepared to drink.

Nina didn't know what possessed her, she wasn't even aware of any conscious decision on her part, but suddenly she lunged forward and tried to push him away, tried to push him back from tasting his sister's blood. She heard her voice babbling like an insane person's, "Stop him, he's going to kill himself, too, if he crosses with her another time, he'll die—" and even though none of the people there fully understood what she was saying, Daneel and Tish and Sharazz and Joe Trunza all leapt forward to help her, along with Alastaire and Bella. The professor fought them fiercely, his strength at least equal to theirs, but they held on, and gradually, by agonizing inches, they forced him back. Alastaire pried his fingers from around Niobe's shoulders, and then finally they pushed him back against the wall and he released his hold on her, and Niobe's body, now lifeless, fell back onto the floor.

The look Strickland gave Nina was one of the purest expressions of hatred she'd ever seen on a human face, a malevolence so intense it made her stomach churn. She tried to say something, anything, but he turned away and shut his eyes and as soon as Niobe's body had fallen and lay still, the others released him, and he pulled away and was headed toward the door.

"Wait—" she said, knowing it was impossible, knowing it was pointless, but willing to do anything, anything at all, to stop him. *I'd crawl to him like a dog*, she thought, *if it would help. I'd let him cross with me until it killed me.* But it didn't matter. The only being he wanted was to lay in a pool of her own still-seeping blood, and she heard him say with venomous stillness, "Miss Lamb, I think you've done quite enough for one day. Your actions were perhaps well-intentioned, but you see the result. Now, if you'll permit me, I need to go back to Daedalus, where it's my fondest wish never to set eyes on you again. You may consider yourself expelled as of this moment."

He hesitated and then added, "Miss Chopin, Mr. Roget." His dark gaze nailed them, and they quivered back from him, stuffing their hands into their pockets to pretend they hadn't just been holding him down while he raved at them.

"Disciplinary action may be required for you two as well, so watch yourselves. Now, please step away from the door."

Bella said, actually raising her hand, "Um, sir, the Saturni are still out there. Maybe that's not the best idea right now?"

"Are they?" He raised his eyebrows and indicated the half-opened doorway through which no further shots had been fired. Alastaire put his hand on Bella's arm and told her to stay put, he'd look for her. "Holy hell weasel," he said after a moment. "They're all gone."

"Yes, Mr. Roget," Professor Danvers sighed. "I expected no less. Having achieved their current objective, there was no point in their lingering, and they've gone, presumably taking Henri with them. Nor is there any reason now for me to stay."

He looked around at the collection of young people who were

still standing there, stunned, in the main center hallway of the Convent, and his expression became blank, drained, dead. He looked like someone awakening from a coma, still processing the fact that his arms and legs had all been amputated while he slept. Nina locked eyes with him for a second, and she heard the word, *pathetic.*

"Pathetic," he whispered aloud a second later, his eyes darkening still further. "Your *Lwas* appear to have deserted you when the chips were down, but then I'm not surprised. That's what happens when children believe in fairy tales. You may be a little more careful next time, at least in the matter of whom you give your allegiances to, if not your hearts. You see, it always ends badly. We're not meant to believe in saviors."

And then he turned away from them, and a moment later he was gone.

# CHAPTER THIRTY-TWO

Finally, Crux explained some things to her.

He arrived about a half-hour after the professor had left, while they were still trying to wash the bloodstains off the floor. Tish and Bille had taken charge, their rivalry set aside, and Bella and Alastaire helped once introductions had been made. They got the boys to get a tarp and wrap Niobe up in a make-shift shroud, and put her in one of the bedrooms. And they got buckets and brushes from the kitchen, and they moved the furniture back. No one said much, and what was said were monosyllables like "Push," and "Here," and "On three."

Nina, abandoning any remote excuse for being useful, had gone out and sat on the back steps.

She felt numb. She was too shaken for even tears now. There was a huge hole in her heart, and the thought that occurred to her over and over was it had all been stupid, sick, wrong. They were all pawns of the Saturni, and while they were, their world, and even normal, healthy emotions like love and affection and friendship, became corrupt and twisted, like plants grown in the dark. She thought of Strickland's hatred and she thought, *I deserved that, and I deserve a lot more. I killed her. And I wouldn't even let him die and join her.*

And she thought of Niobe's grief and her stubborn words, "I'm just going to go to the front door and look out at him," and she thought, *Surely there is some way to turn back time. Surely, if you want it badly enough, you could go backward and make everything all right.But she couldn't. She had done what she'd done. And now she had no idea what to do next. She was truly lost.*

Crux came out and handed her a cold can of Barq's root beer and opened one for himself.

"I like this stuff," he said. "When I'm away from New Orleans, I always miss it."

"You missed a lot."

"Yes, I know." He swallowed a mouthful of soda and said, "Nina, I know it sounds stupid, but I'm really so very, very sorry."

She stiffened. She didn't want his pity. She didn't deserve pity, she deserved his anger and his pain, and she curled her hands into fists so her fingernails bit into her palms, enjoying at least that slight ache. She said quietly, "Shut up. I don't want to talk."

"I know." Crux hesitated. "Niobe had a blind spot where Henri was concerned. We all knew it. She asked me once to father another child with her, but I told her I couldn't . . . *Lwas* just aren't built like that. That's what I meant once by saying I tried to make something up to her, but I couldn't. And of course Strickland couldn't either. So she fixated on Henri as her only baby. She forgot all of his ambiguous characteristics and just thought of him as an innocent child."

Nina didn't want to hear any of this. It echoed too closely with her own beliefs, and how she'd been tricked. That if Niobe wanted to see him, Henri had to be good and nice and good for her and for the world. And he had been nice, hadn't he? She had spent most of a day in his company, and she hadn't sensed anything at all.

She said reluctantly, "Strickland . . . Professor Danvers said he was a monster. He said that's what I brought back. Is . . . is he?"

Crux sighed and rubbed his nose. "To be honest, I have no idea what Henri is. He's something that shouldn't exist, so you have to go with your gut on those things. For my money, I think Henri could be the Saturni's best hope or else their worst nightmare, and I'm not even sure what that means either. I told you once I'm not that sure about a lot of things. Henri's a wild card, so let's leave it at that right now. And even though you're not asking, yes, actually, I think you were always fated to bring him back."

Nina didn't say anything. She wanted so much to believe that, it was like a gnawing hunger in the pit of her stomach, but for that very reason, she couldn't do it.

"No, you're wrong," she said finally, shaking her head. "People told me not to. A whole lot of people. Phoebe and Janus. They both knew better. Even Alastaire and Belle were freaked out, and Captain Bowman, and, well, everybody." She tried to stop a sob from welling up in her throat. "If only Janus had actually stolen my purse, none of this would have ever happened!"

"Do you really believe that?"

"Yes!" She wiped her nose on her sleeve, because of course, as always, she didn't have a Kleenex. "Yes, I do. It happened because I was too stubborn, and I just wouldn't listen."

"All right, then ... let me ask you this. Why did Strickland take you to the Sybil in the first place?"

"Because ... because I don't know! Because he was hoping we'd learn something. Because he thought it was important, and she— she told him she wanted to see us both, so we went and she, well, she gave me that goddamn engraving!"

"And her prophecy. What did she actually say?"

"I don't know." Nina frowned. "Something about sacrifice and a savior. 'The seed of the pelican will return, and the mother will sacrifice herself for her child. The lion will dress himself up as a sheep, and even the lamb will be deceived. Follow the water and the mirrors. Because that's where your savior lies.' At least I think it was something like that."

"And why do you think she said that?" Crux put his hand on

hers, and Nina felt the uncanny touch of a *Lwa*, a powerful current of electricity, even though it was as soft as a breeze.

"Why did she specifically say Niobe had to sacrifice herself?"

Nina didn't know. She felt as if her head were empty, an empty gourd, maybe filled with a few grains of sand that were rattling around inside. *Too much has happened*, she thought. *How am I supposed to know the answer to that?*

She said, "I don't know. She was just standing there in the doorway. It was dumb. It was like she should have known it was coming. Strickland told her not to, but she . . ."

But she did it anyway. Nina stopped and thought about that. Niobe, who had survived for decades as Sister Aquilina, a figure of myth and menace to the Saturni, had been many things, but she hadn't been stupid. Nina remembered her teaching her, subtly, with stories and recipes and parables and little hints, how to think for herself. How not to trust the Saturni more than her own mind. She remembered Niobe hiding for the whole spring term at the Daedalus School itself, under the Saturni's very noses, pretending to be just a cook, and she'd done it flawlessly, never giving herself away.

*Niobe*, Nina thought, *had to have known the risk she was running simply by going to that door. She had to have known it. But what had she said?*

"I have to see him, Strickland. I just have to see him one more time."

Nina looked at Crux and saw his strange, archaic smile playing around his lips, the light in his eyes shining like a sunrise, if the sun could have risen over a world of chaos, worlds and stars and planets in collision. She had to look away. She couldn't breathe. It was too much.

Because there were tears in those eyes too.

She said, "I don't know. Did she know what was going to

happen? Did she know what she was doing and did it on purpose? And why would she do that?"

"I think—remember, I don't know. But I think Niobe may have known her course was close to being run. After all, there are many ways of dying, and with your child in your sight, and your other charges all around you, strong and fulfilling their destiny, surely that's not the worst way to go? I'm just guessing, mind you, but that's one explanation. And remember, there are others. Niobe sacrificed herself by becoming a Skin Eater in the first place. She may have thought she was sacrificing herself again to save Henri in a more definitive sense.

"Of course, there is also one other explanation." Crux's eyes shone. "Niobe always thought of you as her daughter. She trusted you. She believed in you. And I know for a fact she thought you were ready to take over for her, if she were ever, um . . . unexpectedly called away."

Nina sat holding onto her half-empty can of Barq's and thought about all of that. There were too many emotions colliding inside of her, too many raw feelings for her to even figure out what they all were. Relief? Yes, sure, in a way. Crux's explanation seemed very plausible. She thought, *I'd love to believe him, but then what does he know? Regret? Rage? Fear? Why had Niobe thought it was such a good idea to kill herself just so she could take over? Nina thought she was the worst candidate to lead a revolution anyone could think of. Loneliness? Loss? How was she supposed to even go on, with or without this responsibility?*

*I don't even know who I am, she thought in anguish. I'm nobody. Why do they all seem to think I planned any of this?*

She got up and walked down to the edge of the property, past the rows of vegetables which were now in extravagant bloom. Cascades of string beans and bushels of peas hung waiting to be picked. Melons, eggplants and zucchini were all swelling, and sweet potato vines ran wild. She passed the chicken coops, where the hens were clucking and settling down for the night, passed the goat-pen, where two nannies suckled their young, and everywhere around her the evening seemed full of ripeness and warmth and promise. Only her heart was as cold as a stone.

"I don't know," she said finally, stepping over the low fence that separated the property from the devastated lots all around it. "You may be right, or you may be wrong. But if Niobe sacrificed herself for my sake, all I can say is, she made one hell of a mistake."

# Chapter Thirty-Three

Bella and Alastaire found her much later, after night had fallen completely. She'd wandered over to an abandoned school that stood scarcely a block from where the Industrial Canal had crashed in and flooded the Lower Ninth Ward. Here, where the water's recession had left a slurry of mud and sewage and lumber and overturned trees, new grass had grown up almost as high as her waist, and she'd had to pick her way carefully through ruts and furrows, keeping an eye out for snakes. She was standing in the moonlight, moodily chucking rocks through the few intact windows and listening to them crash, when her two friends found her.

"Can we play?" Alastaire asked, hefting up a stone and sending it flying through a third-floor window with the accuracy of a major league pitcher. Bella clicked her tongue.

"You know, when they get around to rebuilding this place, it's only going to cost the taxpayers more money if all the windows are broken."

"Oh, come on, Bell." Alastaire laughed. "This is New Orleans. They'll probably get around to rebuilding this dump when Huey P. Long rises from the dead and walks across Lake Pontchartrain."

He looked at Nina and added, "Sorry, bad example. But still. Sometimes a little vandalism's good for the soul. At least, so they tell me."

He sent another rock flying, and then said, "By the way, we found out how Professor Danvers knew to be there at the house when we all showed up. Apparently, Agatha told him what was going on. She told him we'd escaped into the engraving, and she also told him we had Henri with us, but he didn't believe that part. He said he'd have to have the evidence of his own eyes." Alastaire sighed. "Of course, eventually he did."

Nina let her own rock drop, feeling a deeper rock plummet down into the depths of her heart. Bella came over and took her hand, seeming to understand much more of what was going on than Alastaire did. As always.

Nina said, "Gee, thanks. I was really worrying about that one loose end."

Having lost her appetite for destruction, she wandered around to the back of the building, looking up at the heavy brick structure which loomed black and massive and scary in the dark.

Nina said what they all were thinking. "I'm really going to miss Daedalus."

"Naw, it's no big deal." Alastaire made a face. "Agatha's cooking and professor Seneschal's snoring and stupid Hygiene, and professor Samson trying to get us to work out with the wolves in between putting on eyeliner? You're not going to miss a damn thing."

Nina thought with a stab of pain, *Oh, but I am. I'm going to miss all of it. I'm going to miss* him. *I'm going to miss you two. I'm going to miss everyone.* And as if on cue, Bella said, "After all, you'll still have us."

"I-I will?" Nina stopped walking and looked at her.

"Of course." Bella sat down on a broken piece of what might once have been a wall. "You think we're just going to leave you here to have all the fun, hanging out with the *Lwas* by yourself? Nuh-uh. If you're staying, then we're staying too. We'll expel ourselves and the hell with Professor Danvers. Besides, that one boy, Santangelo? He's definitely hot."

"Santangelo is also definitely gay," Nina pointed out. "He wouldn't look twice at you."

"Shows how much you know." Bella kicked at a broken piece of asphalt. "Besides, I'm thinking of switching back."

"You are?"

"Yeah. Being a girl is really difficult. I realize that now. You're so . . ." She screwed up her forehead in search of the right word. "Vulnerable. People assume you're an airhead, even if you're not, and even if they don't, they still don't trust you, because you've got female emotions. I don't mean guys are any less emotional. God no! But guys think guys' emotions are okay, while girls' emotions are a little scary.

"Now me," she added, pulling up her legs and sitting cross-legged, "I'm really more of a head-person. I realize that now. I like to figure out where I stand and then decide how I feel. I'm not . . ." She shook her head. "I'm not capable of taking the plunge and just falling in love indiscriminately. And I think that scares some guys. Although it shouldn't," she added, smiling to herself. "It should make them feel special if I do love them. But I guess most guys are just jerk offs. With a few notable exceptions."

Nina had the vaguest feeling Bella might be trying to send Alastaire a message here, and if so, she didn't hold out much hope of it being received. But there were other things on her mind. "Look, you can't stay here," she told them both. "That's final. You both have to go back to Daedalus. After all, you're . . . you're Skin Eaters too." She smiled. "You may be two of the most normal people I know, but that still doesn't mean you aren't changing. I know, a lot of what Daedalus teaches its students is junk, but one thing is true. You guys need to know how to cope with what you're becoming. How to take care of yourselves. How . . . well, how to eat. You . . ." She swallowed. "I love you both too much to risk you staying here and coming, well . . . coming to any harm. You've got to go back."

Bella looked at her mutinously, and Alastaire opened his mouth to say something, but she went on quickly. "And actually, I'm not staying here, either. I—I'm going away."

"Going away?" Alastaire sat down on the wall next to Bella as though someone had punched him in the gut. "You're kidding. Neens? Why? Go where?"

"I don't know." Nina truly had no more honest answer to give him. She looked around at the devastated ground nearby, and the lights, farther away, where the Lower Ninth was coming back, and just knew she couldn't stay at the Orphanage and the Convent, not with Niobe no longer there. She'd go mad.

"I'll probably come back. I mean, this isn't a hard and fast thing." She shrugged, trying to keep things light. "After all, there's a war to fight, right? And, well . . . lots of things. I just need to know . . . I need to figure a few things out." *Like who I am*, she thought, *and who the headmaster is. Who Henri is. And what the Saturni really want, besides world dominance and to eat up everything.*

She also wondered about Captain Bowman and the Santa Compagna, and what the moons and Saturn and the Cumaean Sybil had to do with all of it. She had so many questions she needed to answer. Somehow, they all had to be part of a larger whole.

"I just need to get away," she said finally, and hoped they'd leave it at that. "Don't worry, you can't quit my club." Bella, predictably, wanted to discuss it.

"But how are you going to survive, Nina? How are you going to eat? Do you have any money? Anywhere to stay? Are you thinking this through?"

"I'll be fine," she said, shrugging. "I'll abide. I always have. So, okay. Group hug, all right?" She embraced them a little awkwardly, and even though Alastaire looked like he didn't buy this for a minute, and Bella looked like she was about to cry (so much for the head vs. the heart business) neither of her friends tried to talk her out of it.

Alastaire asked, "What about Mercy? What are we supposed to do with him?"

"Feed him," Nina said. "He's the school cat. He doesn't belong to me. Don't worry about him, he'll be fine. I told you, I'll be back soon."

And as she walked away, Alastaire and Bella both had the strangest hallucination. It seemed for a moment that there were four ghostly presences walking along with Nina, one on either side of her, one before her, and one behind. There was the wisdom snake, Damballa, going ahead of her, and the great massive tree trunk named Grand Bois taking up the rear. There was Oya, the goddess of the winds, on her left, her breezes lifting her hair, and Erzuli, the goddess of love and life and women, on her right.

They looked perfectly visible for a few moments, their figures as tall as the dark night sky, and then in the next instant, it seemed like they had all disappeared. And there was nothing left but the grass and the mud and the small, scattered houses where people were stubbornly rebuilding, and over it all the vast, starry emptiness of the planets and their distant suns.

# About the Author

Photo Credit: Breton Littlehales, photographer

The enigmatic A.V. (Adrienne) Parks has written an exceptional four-book series, The Saturni, based in New Orleans, where there is no shortage of captivating lore. Think southern gothic, dark fantasy, magical realism . . . Adrienne has created a masterpiece quartet.

From the prestigious halls of Princeton University, where she graduated summa cum laude, to the late-night horror movie shows she hosted in Scranton, PA, she has led a life as enchanting as the stories she tells.

Born to a stockbroker and a swing musician, and the granddaughter of a Catholic priest, Adrienne's roots are as diverse as her experiences. She grew up in the bustling New York City metro area, where she and her late husband created mesmerizing music videos and documentaries. Twenty years ago, she ran away to New Orleans, where she now owns a charming (haunted?) guesthouse in the historic Garden District.